D0364080

B

ENGRAM

Also by Keith Baker

Inheritance
Reckoning

ENGRAM

Keith Baker

First published in Great Britain in 1999
by HEADLINE BOOK PUBLISHING

A HEADLINE FEATURE hardback/softback

10 9 8 7 6 5 4 3 2 1

British Library Cataloguing in Publication Data

Baker, Keith, 1945-
  Engram
  1.Suspense fiction
  I.Title
  823.9'14 [F]

  ISBN (Hardback) 0 7472 2319 X
  ISBN (Softback) 0 7472 7330 8

Typeset by Letterpart Limited, Reigate, Surrey
Printed and bound in Great Britain by
Mackays of Chatham PLC, Chatham, Kent

HEADLINE BOOK PUBLISHING
A division of the Hodder Headline Group
338 Euston Road
London NW1 3BH
www.headline.co.uk
www.hodderheadline.com

ACKNOWLEDGMENTS

For their help along the way, my thanks go to Detective Dan Jones and his colleagues in the police department at Portland, Maine; to Liam McCaughey, MD, FFARCSI, FRCA, and the staff at Craigavon Area Hospital; and to Hilary Preston, who knows everything there is to know about physiotherapy. As ever, I am also indebted to Carole Blake and Bill Massey for their editorial guidance and for encouraging me to go the extra mile.

The power of memory is most forcefully illustrated by the profound effects of emotionally traumatic events . . . Emotional trauma does not, however, always lead to vivid recall; sometimes emotionally intense experiences result in far-reaching amnesias.

– Professor Daniel L. Schachter
Searching For Memory: The Brain,
The Mind and The Past

One

They took the roundabout the wrong way at sixty miles an hour.

No one in their right mind would have done that.

But there was panic in the car and fear and in the wet blackness of the night they gambled that there was no one else on the road. Just them and the car ahead.

'Close in,' the man in the front passenger seat said, gritting his teeth and leaning into the dashboard. 'Faster, for Christ sake. Faster!'

'I'm trying.' The driver was sweating. A trickle of blood from where the woman had bitten him stained the edge of his shirt collar.

He released the pedal slightly so that the automatic transmission changed down a gear, then he slammed his foot back down. The engine roared as the big Mercedes charged forward up the hill.

'That's it, that's it. Nearly got them,' the passenger in the back grunted.

The driver felt his neck. It was very painful. She had sunk her teeth in hard. Jesus, maybe she had AIDS or something.

They were almost level. He flashed his headlights.

A little further on, the road sloped into a soft bend. He would have to pull in front and force them to stop before reaching that blind spot. It was two o'clock in the morning, they were out in the country, but what if . . .?

The lights of an oncoming car lit up the hedge.

It came round the turn towards them, into the white hot glare of two sets of headlamps on full beam, two speeding cars straddling the entire width of the narrow road. It braked with a greasy screech but in that split second the driver of the Merc found extra power in the machine and swung it in front of their quarry.

Reacting to the swift, violent movement, his wheels skidded and squealed on the wet surface, pulling the back end of the Mercedes forward in an arc. He pressed his foot down hard on the brake and waited to feel the impact of the crash but

1

suddenly they had stopped dead, almost facing back the way they had come, and there was nothing.

Just a weird silence.

The three of them looked out. There was nobody else on the road. They had missed the oncoming car. Or had it been there at all? Had they imagined it in their jangled brains?

No, ridiculous. It had been there all right, straight in front of them, coming out of the night. It must have driven on, just got the hell out of there. But where was . . .?

And then in their headlights they saw the skid marks on the muddy verge, the raw, ragged gap in the flimsy wooden fence. Beyond that there was darkness.

The driver put his hands to his face and dragged his fingers down his cheeks. 'Oh no! Oh Christ no!'

'Shut up!' the man beside him snapped. 'Pull yourself together. We'll have to get out and look. Get this thing off the road first.'

His hands shaking, the driver turned the car again. A few hundred yards further on, almost hidden from view, there was a narrower road off to the left. They parked there and scrambled out, then stood for a second.

The rain, like cold needles on their flushed faces, did nothing to subdue their agitated state. Booze and cocaine had fuelled that and the adrenalin rush of the chase had given them an extra boost. But now a new ingredient, a sense of dread, began to make its presence felt.

It was hard to see. The night was thick with drizzle, clouds blindfolding the moon, but there was some kind of light coming from below, down in the woodland into which the car had disappeared.

'A flashlight,' one of them said. 'Have you got one?'

'What?'

'A torch. Have you got a fucking torch? Jesus, wake up.'

The driver opened the boot of the Mercedes and rummaged around.

'Come on. Hurry up. Move, move!'

'I can't find it. No, here it is.'

The torch was long and heavy and encased in rubber. He turned it on and its beam lit up the face of the man beside him for a moment.

He was dark-set and bearded, his eyes on fire. Dazzled, he turned away sharply. 'Christ, you're blinding me. Here – give me that.' He snatched the torch, gabbling breathlessly. 'Right, we've got to find out what's happened to them, see if they're hurt. That other car's gone but I bet not for long. It's bound to have seen what happened, them going off the road and us skidding. But it doesn't know we're connected. They'll call the police. They might come back and try to help.'

'Maybe they've just driven on. Maybe they didn't see anything – or ignored it.'

'Not very likely. We nearly wiped them out on the road back there. Anybody see what kind of car it was?'

The others shook their heads.

'Me neither. And I don't think they'll have got our number. OK, we better get down there before anybody else does.'

'So what's the plan, then?' the driver wondered.

'Plan? There is no fucking plan. Just pray. That's your best bet.'

The bearded man led the way, hurrying back to the gap in the fence. He shone the torch into the gloom. Sloping away below them was a dank wood, its floor protected by a thick covering of fern and brambles.

They gasped when they saw what was there.

The car, a red soft top MGB about twenty years old, had crashed hard into a tall larch, the front of it crumpled like tin foil against the sturdy trunk. The light they had seen was coming from the one remaining headlamp shining into the bushes.

In its beam they could make out the shape of a figure on the ground and as they watched he pulled himself slowly and painfully to his feet.

The man with the torch began to scramble down the bank towards the wreck, the other two following suit after a second, slithering in the mud behind him. At the bottom they stood there, breathing hard, staring at the car and the man beside it. Rain pattered down on the leaves and dripped onto their heads. They could feel the heat of the engine, silent now, except for a slight hiss like escaping steam, and they could smell warm metal and the heavy odour of petrol. Christ, the thing might go up in their faces.

The man turned towards them. There was blood and dirt on his face and he stood unsteadily but he seemed miraculously uninjured. Somehow he had managed to get free of the vehicle, perhaps been thrown from it. The windscreen had disappeared and the driver's door hung from one hinge.

'Paul?' the bearded one said. 'Are you all right?'

'Where is she?' he grunted in answer.

The woman.

The bearded man moved closer to the car and shone the torch beam in through the open driver's door. The smell of petrol was stronger but it was not that that made him choke.

3

She lay against the dashboard, her face a mask of blood that left her unrecognisable. Slivers of glass and metal were embedded like shrapnel in her cheeks and head and they glinted in the torchlight.

'Jesus Christ,' he whispered.

Her bare arms were streaked with blood and her legs appeared to be trapped where part of the engine had been pushed in. There was no sound coming from her and she was almost certainly dead.

He passed the torch to one of the others. 'Keep this on her,' he said, as he began to reach into the vehicle, thinking he might try to find a pulse. But instinct stopped him suddenly. A sense of self-preservation made him realise there was a risk that he might touch something and leave fingerprints on a receptive surface. Something told him he did not want to do that. He backed away.

'You bastards,' Paul said. 'You fucking bastards. You've killed her.'

'I didn't mean . . . it was an accident,' their driver tried, his voice a whine.

Paul swung towards him, rage glaring from his bloody face. With a growl deep in his throat, he lunged forward. The two men fell in a heap, scrabbling on the ground, clawing and gouging, one out of anger, the other in wild and desperate defence.

Paul's hands reached the man's throat. 'You crazy fuck . . . I'll—'

Behind him there was a sudden movement. The torch swung in a sweeping downward arc and hit him hard on the back of the head.

He slumped forward and it hit him again. This time there was the crunch of something brittle giving way and he made a gurgling noise.

'Jesus,' the man on the ground said, scrambling out from under, struggling to his feet.

The torch swung again. The third blow sounded duller, moist, and the impact knocked the light out. Paul's limbs twitched for a scary second or two and then he was still.

There were a few moments of frozen, deathly silence until the shock waves swept over them.

'Oh Christ,' the driver said. 'Oh Christ, what have you done?' He looked from one to the other; to the bearded man and then the one with the torch.

'I had to stop him.'

'But you've killed him.'

4

'Shut the fuck up. If it hadn't been for you we wouldn't be in this mess. You don't get out of this, you of all people. We're all in this together.'

The torch was still working. After a shake or two, it came on again, its beam harsh in the driver's wet face. His lip was bleeding where the man called Paul had grasped at him. He bent over the body. 'Maybe – maybe there's something we can do.' He touched the man's head and felt something warm and sticky. 'Oh Jesus!' he said and stepped back in haste.

'Hold it!' the bearded man said. His voice was a hoarse whisper. They turned towards him. 'Listen!'

A car was coming slowly up the road. They heard it stop a little distance away. There was the sound of doors closing and then a woman's voice.

'There's some kind of light.'

A man spoke. 'Look, we've dialled 999. I think we should get out of here. You don't know what this is. It could be anything.'

The bearded man moved first. He snatched the torch back and turned it off, then he moved swiftly to the front of the wrecked car and kicked the headlamp in, thinking that he should have done that earlier. The blackness of the night enveloped them.

The sound prompted the woman's cautious voice. She called down. 'Hello – is anyone there?'

No light up on the road. They had no torch; that was good. There was just their voices, coming steadily nearer.

'I'll bring the car up a bit and get the headlights on,' they heard the woman say.

Sensible. Damn her.

'Look, do you not think we should just go?' her companion said.

There was something else now.

They began to hear the frantic whooping of emergency sirens in the distance. Vehicles were moving fast. Police. An ambulance. Sounds and rhythms colliding.

'Christ, we have to get out of here quickly,' the bearded man said, 'get back to the road further on up where we can't be seen. I don't fancy walking out into the arms of a couple of do-gooder rescuers. Let's move.' He turned.

'The girl.' The voice stopped him. 'What if she's not dead?'

'Oh, she's dead all right. But what do you want – to make sure? Finish her off, too, then stay around and get caught? After that?'

They glanced towards where the body of the man called Paul lay. In the gloom they had to strain their eyes to make out its shape.

5

The sound of the emergency vehicles was getting louder. That would mask any noise they made as they picked their way through the undergrowth but it meant they did not have a lot of time.

'Come on,' the bearded man said.

'*I can't – I can't – I can't – I can't.*'

The driver fell on his knees beside the body again, quivering in the grip of panic.

Their fear lent them strength. He was bigger and heavier than they were, but they grabbed him by the shoulders and almost plucked him from the ground, dragging him along with them until he was on his feet.

In the embracing darkness the brambles scratched at their faces and pulled at their clothes.

The man with the beard struggled forward, his mind reeling, scenes of unbelievable horror playing in fast forward across his brain.

How had it come to this?

Only a short time ago he had been looking forward to tomorrow. They had been talking about it, celebrating, drinking champagne, doing a few lines of coke, in privileged and comfortable privacy, contemplating a future of power and influence. Then, in an instant, everything had changed. One foolish, lunatic act had seen to that.

And now there was murder.

The woman. If only she had not come.

She had been brought along on a whim and her very presence had led to their doom. As simple as that.

He was not a superstitious man, not normally, not paranoid like some people, obsessed with fate and destiny. But right now, it was hard not to think like that, impossible not to focus on her as the cause of their destruction.

He looked back in the direction of the car and hoped she was dead too. *The bitch.*

That was the coke talking, agitating him. He shook his head to clear it. He had been in tough spots before. He had to think straight.

'Go carefully,' he said, out of breath. 'Try not to tear anything. We can't leave traces of clothing for them to find.'

In five minutes they made it to a solid stone wall that separated them from the road. It was not high but they had to help each other over it. There were a couple of slippery false starts but eventually they were on firm ground again.

They stood with their heads pounding from the exertion, their bodies trembling because of the awfulness of what they had done. They were soaked. their shoes were useless and their trousers were caked to their legs by soggy mud.

On the road down below them the sirens were louder. They tried to get their bearings.

'I think I'm going to be—' the driver began, and vomited the rest of the sentence.

And then they saw their car, a hulking shape in the dark only a few yards in front of them. Their route had taken them right to it.

It was hardly what you would call luck but it would do.

The driver held out the keys. His hand was shaking. 'Somebody else take these,' he said, half-falling into the back. 'I can't drive.'

'All right, I will,' the man with the beard decided. He put the torch on the floor beside him. 'We'll ditch this along the way.'

He started the engine. The big car was quiet, almost silent. He drove very slowly at first, with no lights, so that no one would see them or hear them. Within moments they were gone.

No one had spotted them. Those two people on the road would say something about hearing a noise and they would mention seeing a light but everyone would be preoccupied with the bodies and the operation to remove them and the car.

They had left footprints, three sets in the muddy ground, but no one would know to look for them. It would not be until the postmortem examination of the man's body that the truth of how he died would be revealed and by that time it would be too late. The feet of the ambulance men and the police and possibly the fire service too, if the woman's body had to be cut free, would do a thorough job of erasing all traces of their presence.

So would the rain.

The big wipers swept it from the windscreen.

'Where are we going?' A sickly odour came with the question. 'What are we—'

'Shut up,' the driver said. 'We'll talk about it back at the house.'

He thought frantically as he drove. They had got away with it. For now.

But if the girl was not dead?

It did not bear thinking about.

He shivered as the truth of it gripped him.

They had committed murder. Brutal, bloody murder. Nothing could alter that fact. They could not bring him back to life; what was done was done.

7

He fought a wave of fear for a moment, trying to shrug off the dreadful images. What happened now was what was important; how to survive this thing was what mattered.

He pressed his foot firmly on the accelerator, hastening away in the darkness to whatever lay ahead.

Two

Teresa Caffrey held the door open for the young man because he was her boss.

'Thank you,' he said in recognition of the gesture.

Raymond Porter was thirty-two, a hot shot fresh from the world of investment banking, and he was the new managing director of Grovecare Ltd, a group of nursing homes. Today he was touring his empire for the first time.

Knockvale House, on the shores of Belfast Lough, was the showpiece of the whole organisation and it was here that Grovecare had started ten years ago. Now there were twenty five such institutions, in Northern Ireland and the Republic as well as Scotland and the Isle of Man.

Teresa was Knockvale's nursing manager. There was atime when she would have been called matron, but the health care business had changed all that. Matrons belonged to the past. The word had a black and white sound to it, like an old *Carry On* film with Hattie Jacques, although most of the matrons Teresa had ever known were wiry, energetic women like herself.

Her husband had once said that there were more private nursing homes in Northern Ireland now than there were pubs. Old rectories, former schools, run-down residences once owned by minor landed gentry, they'd all been bought up and the country was littered with these places. Bloody ridiculous. But he had changed his tune when she had waved her first pay-slip in front of his nose.

She closed the door behind her.

They were on the first floor. She felt its quiet, reverential calm and wondered if Porter did. Outside there was the distant hum of traffic but, muffled by layers of insulating glass, it became nothing more than a gentle rhythm, always present, although never intruding.

'What happens here?' Porter inquired and she noticed he was almost whispering.

'We have some rather special patients on this floor. People

9

who . . .' she smiled sensitively '. . . who perhaps haven't got very long.'

He nodded. 'I understand.' His father had died of cancer when he was six.

'There's one patient – I wonder if you'd like to see her,' she said.

'I don't – I wouldn't like to intrude. I don't want to disturb anyone.'

She smiled again. 'Don't worry. You won't.'

She opened the door of a room and they stepped softly across its threshold.

In here there was a rhythm, too: the rhythm of a life. It could be heard in soft beeping sounds and observed in flickering waves on monitors attached to machines that measured its steady, never-changing progress. Even the bed itself had a rhythm, a gentle electronically controlled movement designed to keep its motionless occupant free from discomfort.

In the bed was a young woman. She lay on her side, one arm resting on top of the covers, a drip feed line attached to the back of her hand. Her long brown hair was spread out on the pillow behind her head and her face was thin and still and deathly pale because it had seen no sun or felt no wind for such a very long time.

Porter could not take his eyes off her.

'God, she looks so – so *serene*,' he said, surprised to find such a word in his vocabulary. It would sit oddly in his usual lexicon, a rare flower among expressions like 'corporate profits growth', 'industry consolidation' or 'share buy-backs'.

'This is our Meg,' Teresa said with affection.

'Meg?'

'Meg Winter. Doctor Meg Winter to be precise.'

'Meg Winter.' He struggled with the name, feeling it stir something in his memory, and then it came, helped by the image before him. 'Oh my God, of course.' He pointed a waggling finger at the bed. 'This is that woman.' He said it excitedly. 'The woman in a coma. The car crash. When that man was murdered.'

'Yes.'

'So she's here?'

'She's been here for the best part of four years.'

'Good God. Like that? All that time?'

Teresa nodded.

'But is there nothing – I mean if there's no hope – can't you just . . .'

'Let her die, you mean?'

'Well – I didn't intend—'

10

'No, it's a valid question, all right. Don't think it hasn't been discussed.' She sighed. 'Meg's a very unusual case. In the – accident – she was very badly injured, of course. Both legs broken. A hip as well. But fortunately no internal injuries. Her face was severely cut by metal and glass but there's been no lasting physical effect save for this.'

She walked towards the bed. There were birthday cards on a table beside it; a vase of pink carnations that had seen better days. Porter followed uncertainly, looking where Teresa was pointing. The young woman's right eyebrow had been broken in two by a scar which ran through it.

'She was lucky she didn't lose an eye,' she said, then shrugged. 'But of course what else has she lost?'

The question had no answer. Porter stared at the sleeping figure. She looked so peaceful. 'There's brain damage, I suppose.'

'You would think, wouldn't you? She may have suffered what's known as a diffuse axonal injury, which is very often the cause of long-standing coma after a head injury. That means there's microscopic damage to the nerve cells. They become sheared, get torn off, but no amount of neurological examination has been able to determine that for certain in Meg's case. They've also scanned the cerebral cortex but found nothing that might in any way sustain such profound coma.'

'They?' Porter asked.

'Specialists of various kinds. Consultants. Neurosurgeons.'

'Expensive.' The care here alone could cost up to a thousand pounds a week.

'Her father has money.'

'So what's the prognosis? Is that the right word?'

She smiled. 'It is and there isn't one. Basically, no one knows why she's like this. Perhaps deep inside her brain, within what are known as the medial parts of the temporal lobes, there's something which no one has been able to see. But without her being conscious, there's no way of using modern technology, like PET scanning, positron emission tomography, as it's called, which is used in order to examine the brain at work. So – here she lies. The sleeping beauty.'

'You seem to know a lot about this.'

'I've taken a bit of an interest. Books. The internet. She fascinates me. Have you any children?'

'I'm not married.'

'I have a daughter. She was very ill once. Might have died. It comes back to me sometimes.'

They did not speak for a moment. Then she closed the door

on the memory, guilty at having opened it, wondering if he would think she wasn't professional or tough enough. She felt guilty, too, because they were standing here discussing Meg as if she was some kind of specimen, a freak. She hadn't meant to do that.

'We'll leave her,' she said. 'Best get on.'

She ushered him out of the room and closed the door gently behind them. 'We're keeping her here for as long as her parents want us to. But one of these days they're going to have to decide to take her home. We give her basic nursing care because that's all she needs. To all intents and purposes, she's a healthy young woman, functioning normally. It's just that she won't wake up.'

'So she's not going to die?'

'Oh, we're all going to die, Mr Porter.'

He shot her a glance that reminded her not to treat him like an idiot so she said: 'No, not unless she develops a serious illness or there's something unforeseen.'

'Like what?' he asked.

This time it was her turn to give a look. It puzzled him for a second and then he realised what he had said.

'Sorry. Stupid of me.'

She smiled benignly. 'Now is there anything in particular that *you*'d like to see?'

She came back to the room half an hour later, after she had seen him off in his new navy blue BMW which came with the job.

Nothing had changed. There was the same stillness that you could practically touch with your fingers.

She tucked the covers in at the bottom of the bed, even though Meg had not moved since the last time she did it and would not do so between now and the next time.

Sharp January sunlight was coming through the window. She looked out at the broad sweep of the lough. The hospital gardens, privacy ensured by high hedges and mature trees, led almost to the water's edge. Far on her right she could see the shipyard cranes and the city's rapidly developing waterfront skyline. On this side of the shore, to the left, was the crusty shape of Carrickfergus Castle and somewhere out there, just a short sea journey away, was the west coast of Scotland.

The view was magnificent but the woman in the bed had never seen it, not in all the three and a half years she had been here, which was longer than Teresa's own tenure.

But then, few of the other patients were in a position to appreciate what they saw. It was, she thought in her bleaker moments, nothing more than a glorified hospice for the well-to-do. God's waiting room. That was another one of her husband's phrases.

Teresa lowered the blinds to soften the glare and wondered how she would feel if it was her own daughter lying there.

She had two children, a boy and a girl, but it was Emer to whom her mind turned now, just as it had when Porter was here. At the age of eight, the girl had developed a severe viral flu that had teetered on the edge of meningitis. She had been taken to hospital, where Teresa and her husband had spent three anxious nights watching and waiting and holding hands at her bedside.

Even now, with all that in the past and Emer safe and healthy and, at fifteen, a vigorous member of her school's swimming team, Teresa found the memory hard. Being in this room always brought it back. She had glimpsed the spectre of her daughter's death yet in the end it had not happened. The child had been spared and, please God, she had a long, full and active life ahead of her.

What would it be like to see your daughter like this every day?

She looked at the young woman. Her body was here but where was her spirit, her soul? Was it with her in this room or had it left her a long time ago?

Not for the first time, Teresa felt her faith being tested as she stood and listened and wondered what purpose was being served by all this. Was it really God's will?

Just do your job.

She walked over to the bedside table. There were fewer birthday cards this year. She picked them up and looked at them again.

There was the one from her and her colleagues. They had not wanted to send anything with 'Happy Birthday' on it. They had the same discussion every year. How could you put that? What would be happy about it?

Instead they had sent a card with doves and a heart and no message at all and on the inside they had written – 'with love from the nursing staff.'

Teresa hoped Meg's parents would see that it was a thought for them, too, an indication, if they needed one, that other people cared and that they were not alone.

The parents. That was another story.

There were just three other cards. One, from someone called Elizabeth, was a small original abstract watercolour, swirling shapes in purple and green, expensive, something to keep. It would go in a drawer somewhere, like last year's.

13

The card had caused a bit of confusion when it had been delivered, addressed to *Dr Meg Winter*. A new clerical assistant had thought it was for a member of the staff. Until somebody had put him right.

What sort of a doctor were you, Teresa wondered. Where would you be now if all this hadn't happened? Not in your job at the old Central Hospital. That closed down two years ago.

On the front of another card a Victorian painting was reproduced. In it a pale girl relaxed languidly in a flat-bottomed boat, trailing her fingers in water covered with lily pads.

Teresa looked inside. 'With love from Dad,' it said.

Beside the message, a tiny *x* signified his affection.

On the back was the name of the painting. *'Becalmed.'* Not just any old card. Thoughtfulness and a father's pain had gone into its choosing.

The third and final card was a big one with a drawing of a curly-headed child on a swing garlanded with buttercups and daisies. The words *For a dear daughter* were embossed in gold across the top. Inside there was a lilting, sugary rhyme but on the opposite page, written in ink, it said:

> *He that keepeth thee shall not sleep.*
> *– Psalm 121*

Below that came the message:

> *To my darling daughter Margaret on her 30th birthday.*

> *From Mum.*

Teresa studied the card. It was a curious mixture of soft-centred sentimentality and Biblical conviction and she wondered what that said about the woman who had sent it.

She frowned slightly. One from Mum and one from Dad.

Separate cards. Separate lives.

She put the cards back and looked at the carnations. They had stood there for a week but now the flowers were dying slowly, becoming drier and more shrivelled with each day.

Is that what will happen to you? Are you just withering away like that?

She pulled up a chair and sat down, looking into Meg's placid face. It was as if she were hibernating, hiding inside herself. Just her and the truth of what happened that night.

Somebody had murdered that poor man. He would have lived, he would have survived the accident if someone had not

14

smashed his skull in. Who in the name of God would do a thing like that?

She leaned forward and stroked Meg's hair gently. It smelled sweet because they had washed it yesterday, lifting her carefully to do so, almost as if they did not want to wake her, then using the drier with its softest setting.

Her breathing was steady and calm. Teresa opened a drawer in the bedside cabinet and took out a box. It contained a soft gel and she smeared a little of it on Meg's lips to prevent them becoming parched.

She put the box back in the drawer and stood up. An image of her own daughter once again flitted across her mind. On impulse, she stooped and kissed Meg on the cheek. Then she turned and left the room. There were other things she needed to think about, like what young Mr Porter had made of her and the way she looked after this place.

The flowers. Halfway along the corridor she remembered she had meant to take them with her and throw them out. She would remind one of the staff to take care of it.

No – she would do it herself while it was still in her head.

She turned and walked back into the room. The vase was there on the table and she lifted it.

There was something . . . something different.

It tingled on her skin. She paused and frowned, feeling an uncertainty. It was as if someone else was there with her, watching.

She looked towards the bed.

It was impossible.

Meg Winter's eyes were open.

They had been open before, fleetingly, but not – not like this. It was as if they were studying her. Teresa stared back, held by the firmness of the young woman's gaze and unable to move from the spot.

And then Meg blinked.

The vase slipped and smashed into fragments, the dead carnations skidding and scattering across the floor in a stream of water.

'She's awake!'

Teresa Caffrey, aged forty-three, mother of two, Knockvale's senior and highest-paid nurse, a woman who thought she had seen everything, ran from the room and raced headlong down the corridor, shouting loud enough to raise the dead.

Three

It was late when Peter Quinn left.

'Are you sure you'll be all right?' he said.

'I'll be fine,' Dan Cochrane told him. 'I just want to sit here for a while, do some thinking.'

It was afterwards, sitting by himself in the cold gloom of the tiny cottage he had rented for his mother before she got sick, that he started drinking heavily.

By two a.m. he had got through three quarters of a bottle of whisky. But instead of making him drowsy or dull-witted, the alcohol seemed to have sharpened his imagination, heightened his awareness of everything around him and stoked the fires of his resolve.

He knew what he had to do.

His ability to hold his drink was coupled with his preference for drinking alone, a dangerous combination, he knew, but fuck it, anyway.

He poured what he told himself would definitely be a last whisky, downed it swiftly, then wondered if he had been wise. Just one too many could tip the balance. He needed to be alert, to have his wits about him; he could not afford to be slow-brained and ham-fisted.

He took a deep breath. He was fine. In control. Nothing would stand in his way.

He took a last look around the little room, seeing the worn settee and the chipped wooden chairs, part of the collection of shabby furniture that the auctioneer in the village had agreed to take away. Cochrane had accepted a price that was less, he was aware, than the stuff might eventually fetch when it was sold on, but he just wanted rid of it. He had no one to share any of it with, no other family, and there was certainly no room in his own small rented flat in Belfast.

Everything he did want was in a tea-chest and a couple of sturdy cardboard boxes: his old school books, faded letters and papers of his father's, as well as other random bits and pieces that his mother had kept in fancy biscuit tins along with her own modest jewellery.

Mostly, though, there were the photographs, either lying loose or put into albums, none of them in any way recent. There was not even one of his own graduation of a few years ago. He had received his psychology degree from Queen's University by post. On graduation day, his mother had found herself stuck with farm chores and unable to travel to Belfast to see him get it. He had spent £12 that he could ill afford on the hire of a gown but he didn't mention that to her, didn't want to make her feel guilty. In the end he had stayed away from the ceremony himself, rather than suffer the lonely indignity of walking across the stage to the bored applause of people who did not know who he was and did not care.

Those pictures that there were told most of the story.

Once there had been the family farm and the four of them living on it: him, his mother and father and his sister Annette. And then one day fourteen years ago, when Annette was six and he was thirteen, their father, for some reason now long since forgotten, was driving her into Downpatrick in their new Ford Sierra when an IRA gang detonated a landmine underneath it.

Simple mistake, really. They thought it was the unmarked police car they had been expecting.

In a statement they had apologised in their usual ambivalent terms. It was 'regrettable' but these things happened in wartime and needless to say it was the fault of the British for creating the circumstances in which such tragedies were bound to occur.

Other people were a bit more genuinely sympathetic than that. Most of Northern Ireland, as a matter of fact. Half the country came to the funerals and it was all over the TV. But nothing anyone said made any difference. Nothing eased the grief that consumed Cochrane and his mother.

So then there were two.

And now, he thought as he got everything ready, there is one.

In truth, long before today his had been a solitary world that few people had been allowed to penetrate. He was a loner, with perhaps only one true friend, Peter Quinn, who was at home by now, sleeping, not knowing what he was up to, and that was the way Cochrane preferred it.

He looked at his watch. Twelve hours. Twelve hours since he had stood with Peter and the others by his mother's wintry graveside, watching her coffin being lowered into the ground.

He felt anger rising and he helped its ascent by pouring himself another whisky. Just a last last one. When he had finished it he went into the hall. Two suitcases sat there, filled with his mother's clothes which he had folded and packed

17

carefully as if they, like she, were going on a final journey. He didn't know what he was going to do with them.

He hated this place, now that she was no longer in it. She must have hated it too when she was here alone, which was a lot of the time. It could never have been a home to her, nor had she made much of an attempt to make it one. Dampness had seeped into the air, bringing a clinging smell of despair and defeat. But she had wanted to remain in this part of the country, here, where she was born, and this was all he could afford.

It was time to go. He had a job to do. He had what he needed.

He opened the front door and went out into the night. The moon was high and huge and it bathed the countryside in an eerie light that was almost blue. He was grateful for that; it would help him in his task.

His car, a small Fiat, stood at the door. He put the things into the boot and set off.

He did not have far to travel and he met no other car on the narrow, winding roads that were barely wide enough for two vehicles to pass. At this time of night, on this south eastern corner of the County Down coast, he would not have expected to encounter anyone. But in a couple of hours, the farmers would be rising, emerging before dawn to begin their day, as once his father had done and then, in later years, his mother.

He would be finished by that time. And afterwards – afterwards there would be a hell of a lot of people around all right but he would not be one of them.

About a mile from his destination, he pulled the car into a narrow laneway and stopped. He would walk the rest. He could not risk being heard driving up, his lights drawing attention. Surprise would be his advantage.

From the boot he lifted the things: a gallon can of petrol that was three-quarters full and two empty whisky bottles in a carrier bag. They clinked conspicuously, a sound that carried, and he worried that someone might hear it.

He looked down at himself. He was still wearing the dark suit he had worn to the funeral; still the black tie and the white shirt, too. He had no coat. It would only get in the way.

The moonlight guided him while he walked. As he passed a darkened farmhouse, a dog caged up in a pen began to bark and he hurried along in case it woke somebody. The wind had got stronger and it was brisk against his cheeks. It brought rushing sounds to his ears and it rustled the sturdy gorse and bracken that lined the roadside.

The coldness of the night collided with the false sense of warmth which the alcohol had provided and it began to occur

18

to him that he was more drunk than he realised.

Then he tripped. It was a stone or something but he lost his balance completely and fell forward hard onto the rough surface, and to his dismay he heard glass breaking in the bag.

He got up and examined the damage. One of the bottles was in pieces but the other one was all right. It would have to be enough.

Steady up, he told himself, then walked on.

When he sensed the first faint scent of the sea he knew he was almost there.

The night had become a little darker. He looked for the moon. A layer of cloud had hidden it but as he watched, it began to emerge slowly, as if an unseen hand were pulling back a heavy curtain.

And in that new revealing light there it was.

On the edge of the hillside there had once been a fine house which had been built in Victorian times. The old woman who owned it had died a few years ago and the house had now gone too.

In its place there was the vast bulk of the Emerald East Hotel.

The building had retained some of the character of the old dwelling, right enough; the hard granite, the gothic angles. But it was a bloated, excessive version of what had been there before, designed to look as if it had stood for generations, an impression for which the visitors who would eventually fill its hundred or so bedrooms would fork out extravagantly.

When guests in the front rooms threw back the curtains in the mornings they would revel in the sight of the uninterrupted open expanse of the Irish Sea, shimmering softly now in the moonlight.

But at the back of the hotel lay what they would really pay for. Spreading away as far as Cochrane could see were the curves and folds of an eighteen-hole championship-standard golf course, groomed to perfection. Much of the land on which the course had been constructed had belonged to the old woman and had come with the original house. But not all of it had been hers. Somewhere out there had stood his own family farm.

The farmhouse was gone, bulldozed into oblivion along with the few acres on which his mother's last remaining cattle had grazed. In his mind's eye he thought back to what it had looked like not so very long ago but he found it hard to sustain the image when what was before him was the grim reality of the present: the hotel building and the devastation –

that was the only way he could describe it – of the harshly beautiful land on which he had been raised, which had been carried out for no reason other than greed.

One of the consequences of that relentless greed was his mother's death. Of that he was convinced. It was why he had come tonight. To take action.

There were no lights coming from the hotel but he had not expected any because the place was not finished. The major construction work had been done but the final touches were not yet complete. The carpenters, the electricians, the plumbers still had work to do but they did not do it at night. There would be no one here except a couple of security guards.

Dogs. He wondered about dogs. But he had been around the area a few times before and had not seen any.

The grounds on the inland side were protected by a high barbed wire fence. It was an affront in this countryside where only the most rudimentary of hedges, an occasional dry-stone wall or, in most cases, nothing at all, denoted boundaries of ownership. But the big time golf enthusiasts, the rich people who would be lured from Japan, the United States and Europe, were used to high security and they would want to see it here, especially on account of Northern Ireland's traditional reputation, which was not entirely one of warmth and hospitality.

The main access to the hotel was through a huge stone gateway, the only visible remnant of the original property, and then along a short drive. The gates themselves were closed and locked for the present.

Mounted on the fence beside them was a large wooden notice which declared that the hotel would be open for business in six weeks time. Its official opening would be before that, however; just a matter of a few days away.

That was the plan, certainly. But Cochrane had other ideas.

He looked at what else the notice said. It announced that the building was:

A SEASONS CONSTRUCTION PROJECT
FOR MALONE GROUP PLC

Seasons Construction. He knew all about them.

Seasons Construction had not simply carried out the operation for Malone Group: it was wholly owned by Malone which also owned the Emerald hotel chain of which this would be the newest jewel in the crown.

But that was not the crucial issue. What he had discovered, what was important, what told him the whole story, was the fact

20

that the managing director of Seasons and the chief executive of Malone Group were both directors of the same Northern Ireland bank, the bank which had loaned his mother more money than she could ever have hoped to repay and had then refused to support her as she struggled to preserve the farm.

In the end, the bank had simply called in the debt and sold the farm out from under her to Seasons Construction. It had gone for no more than she owed them, which Cochrane knew was a lot less than the property was worth.

They had no guilt, no feelings, any of these people, and he hated them.

They did whatever they liked to get what they wanted, destroying anyone in the process. They had destroyed his mother and now they had destroyed the land she had loved so much and had fought to hold on to.

It was the shame of being ruined, he had no doubt, that had brought on the stroke which had led to her eventual death.

Now it was time for retribution. And he was here to deliver it.

He walked along beside the fence until he found a suitable spot. He would approach the building from the rear, along the edge of the golf course.

From the carrier bag he took a pair of wire cutters. He already knew the fence was not electrified. There had been a row about that in the local papers. Sheep wandered at will around here and farmers were indignant at the prospect of their animals being electrocuted. Maybe that was why there were no dogs either. Anyway Seasons had backed off. No electric fence.

It made this task a little less hazardous but it was still tough. The wire was new and unyielding and it took him a good twenty minutes, during which he worked up a heavy sweat, before he managed to cut enough of it to create a useful gap.

Carrying the petrol can and the bag with the remaining bottle, he tried to pick his way through as carefully as he could but, no longer held taut, the severed wire now curled menacingly. As he stepped forward on to the golf course, a barb snagged itself in his right trouser leg and held him back. For a second he almost dropped everything, then he pulled his leg towards him irritably and felt the material rip.

When he had broken free, he examined the tear with his fingers. There was a chunk of the cloth missing, just below his right knee.

He was wasting time. He would have to hurry. In and out quickly: that was the plan and he had better stick to it.

He looked at where he had made his entrance. Two fence posts down on the left, just below the second tee. Would he be able to locate that again? He had to; and the moonlight would help him.

Crouching to keep his shape as small as possible, he ran towards the hotel. The petrol sloshed around in the can by his side. When he reached the building, he stood against the wall, breathing hard, listening, but there was just the wind, carrying the sound of the sea lapping at the shore below.

He took his bearings, trying to peer through dark and dirty windows to see what was inside. He would stay at the back. If he went round the front there was a risk of bumping into a security guard.

He found the kitchens. He tried a door but it was locked. Not unexpected. He took the bottle out of the bag and filled it with petrol. He had a lighter and . . .

A cloth. He did not have one of those. He had not brought anything that he could use.

His tie. That would do. He wrenched it from his collar and stuffed it into the neck of the bottle.

He stood for a second, staring at the big kitchen window.

He had come this far.

Tension thumped in his temples. He needed a drink and he wished he had brought the whisky with him. His courage was beginning to dry up.

He took the wire cutters and tapped them against the glass. Not hard enough. He hit the window with more power, maybe too much, and this time the bottom section of it fell away, smashing into fragments on the floor of the empty kitchen.

Jesus, it made a hell of a noise.

He began to pour the petrol through the broken window but it was taking too long so he shoved the whole can in. It fell to the floor with a crash that was like the sounding of a gong.

He heard a voice from somewhere. He had run out of time.

He lit the end of the saturated tie and threw the blazing bottle into the kitchen.

The petrol ignited in a blast of flame that filled the room and smashed the rest of the windows, throwing him backwards. The heat and the force were sudden and shocking and he could feel his eyebrows and the front of his hair being singed.

He picked himself up and began to run blindly into the darkness. And now lights came on from somewhere, security beams mounted high on the building, shining out across the golf course. Fire bells started ringing, urgent and shrill, and a voice shouted: 'There's someone! I see him!'

He turned for a moment and saw three security guards in uniform coming after him. They were spreading out to narrow his avenue of escape. He began to run harder.

The second tee. Where the fuck was it? He was confused and dazed and partly blinded from the explosion. Yellow spots danced before his eyes. He had no time to search for it now.

One of the guards had almost reached him. He could not let himself be caught. As the man stretched out to grab him, Cochrane wheeled and struck out wildly with his fists. Not expecting this, the guard did nothing to prevent himself running into the force of a hard left hook which hit him square on the side of the jaw and knocked him to the ground.

Cochrane ran on. He got to the fence. He had to get over it. There was only one way to do that.

He began to climb desperately, ignoring the fact that he was grasping barbed twists and that they were tearing into his skin. In his panic and his drunkenness he could not feel the pain.

'Jesus, look at that guy,' someone behind him said in amazement.

And then he felt hands at his ankles, pulling him backwards. He clutched frantically at the wire and the pain was there now all right as the barbs ripped deeper into his flesh, shredding the palms of his hands.

He let go and fell backwards.

'Got you, you bastard!'

Four

She was asleep.

It was a different bed, a different place, and two weeks since she had regained consciousness. The nurse looked at their faces and read the uncertainty in them.

'She's just dozing, that's all. She gets tired. I can wake her if you want,' she offered, 'let her see you're here.'

'No, it's fine,' Sam Winter said, then glanced towards his wife. Gloria Winter nodded her head in brusque agreement but she did not meet his eyes.

'Let's go to my office,' Liam Maginnis said. 'We can have a chat over a cup of tea.'

He was a tall man with gold-rimmed spectacles and a good suit, a deep grey double breasted with a hint of silk that gave it an expensive sheen, and he led the way along the corridors of Musgrave Rehabilitation Centre with a confident swagger that said he was a man of position.

What he was was the Centre's highly paid Chief Executive and Northern Ireland's foremost consultant on rehabilitation medicine. Living at such a professional pinnacle, he did not normally descend from it in order to concern himself directly with new arrivals but he had decided to take an interest in this one. For all sorts of reasons, Meg Winter was going to be an unusual patient.

The Centre, replacing what had been an old hospital, was on the south-western tip of Belfast. The views from it were not as commanding as those over the lough at Knockvale, yet it was pleasant enough, facing out on the grassy hillsides of the Black Mountain and the trees of Musgrave Park itself, one of several green spaces dotted around the city, magnanimous gestures by municipal dignitaries of long ago.

The Centre specialised in orthopaedic care and prosthetics. Here was where people who had lost limbs learned how to live with new ones. There was a military wing, little used now but still protected by heavy security, to which army victims of terrorist attacks used to be flown, an occurrence of grim

24

regularity in past years. But the air above the medical enclave was quieter these days, the ominous clatter of hovering helicopters much less common.

One unit specialised in physiotherapy for people recovering from difficult operations or long illnesses. It was an area of expertise which Meg would need and it was why her parents and the doctors at Knockvale had approached Maginnis once they had all accepted her new, wakeful, state as permanent.

When they reached his office, Maginnis directed his guests to two soft chairs, then settled himself. Tea things were already waiting on a low table.

'When will she walk again? Even talk?' Sam Winter wanted to know almost before he had sat down.

Gloria Winter gave a snort. 'I find this eagerness touching in someone who not so long ago wanted to turn the machines off and let her die.'

Her husband looked towards Maginnis, as if appealing to his good sense. 'It wasn't like that,' he insisted. 'The chances of recovery were uncertain, unlikely even. After four years – the question had to be asked – but I didn't—'

Maginnis relieved his anguish. 'It's only a couple of weeks since she woke up. We're just going to have to be patient.'

He took his glasses off and set them on the table as he leaned forward to pour the tea. 'Milk?' They nodded. 'Sugar?' They nodded again.

It ocurred to him how they liked their tea was one of the rare subjects on which these two would agree. He poured his own, then leaned back in the chair.

'Almighty God has brought her this far,' Gloria Winter said. 'He will set her free.' Across the table from Maginnis she sat bolt upright, her face set in an expression that challenged him to argue the point.

Maginnis smiled encouragingly. 'I hope you're right.'

She reached for her cup and as she glanced away from him he studied her. She was a big-boned woman in her late fifties, white-haired and handsome. There was caution and suspicion in her eyes and she had a presence that made you careful what you said.

Sam Winter sat on a chair several feet from her but the real gulf between them was immeasurable.

Compared to his wife he seemed diminutive, yet Maginnis reckoned he was the same height, somewhere about five-nine. The difference lay in the demeanour. Sam was thin and had been handsome when younger but at sixty his face had fallen into folds, as if he had lost weight too rapidly. He sat hunched,

25

with his head bent slightly forward, looking out from under eyebrows that were like tussocks on a worn hillside.

He looked tired, Maginnis thought, past his peak, although he cautioned himself that appearances were deceptive and that Sam Winter had never been short on energy.

He was an astute businessman who had made a fortune in the building industry through his firm, Seasons Construction. Maginnis knew a lot about that because his own prosperity was due not only to his substantial salary and the fees he was able to earn in private consultancy but also to successful investment ventures. Business matters intrigued him, thus he knew that Seasons Construction had been a collaboration between Winter and a partner, Derek Sumner, who had died several years ago. When they had founded the company they had been amused at the sound of their surnames together – Winter and Sumner – and so they had hit on the name Seasons.

A few years ago, the building and property giant, Malone Group, had made a bid for Seasons, offering a sum that many now believed totally over-valued Winter's company, and Sam had been happy to sell. He had stayed on as managing director and he had also become a director of Malone Group.

The sale had topped up his already substantial wealth but it was money he had needed. Paying for his daughter's care all these years would have been an extraordinary financial drain, even to someone with his resources.

'First,' Maginnis said, 'having rejoiced in the fact of your daughter's remarkable return to the world,' he smiled politely at Gloria, 'it would be wrong of me to suggest that everything's going to be back to normal overnight. I recognise that this must be a very frustrating period for you both, in some ways almost as agonising as the past four years have been, but we can't expect miracles.' He winced inside when he said the word because he knew she could not resist the cue.

She looked at him. 'People who don't know, who don't understand – they talk about miracles. The power of prayer, Mr Maginnis – that's what we've seen. I can't speak for anyone else,' her eyes went to her husband momentarily, 'but I've prayed to the Lord night and day for Margaret's recovery, knowing . . .' she placed a fist to her bosom, '. . . that if my prayers were to be answered it would signify that He had a purpose for her, that eventually the holy fire of his love will fill her heart. I've waited a long time for this day and I can wait a little while longer. I'm content in the knowledge that she's saved from the storm, sheltered by faith.'

Maginnis nodded gently as if he understood. The woman did

26

not speak, she preached. It left little scope for a response. Other than *Amen*.

Sam Winter sighed. He sat forward with his elbows on his knees.

'Mr Maginnis,' he said, 'as you may be aware, my wife and I have lived apart for many years. I'll be straight with you – we don't see eye to eye on many things. In fact, being *together* under any circumstances is a rare thing for us. Yet we do have one thing in common and that's our daughter's welfare. My wife's a very religious woman and she believes in prayer, as you've just heard. Me . . .' he opened his arms out as if to accept suggestions, '. . . I'm just grateful to whoever or whatever has brought her back to us and like Gloria here I'll take each day as it comes. I didn't mean to sound impatient a moment ago. I have every confidence in you and your team here. I just want Meg to be well again. You can understand that.'

Maginnis smiled. 'Of course. And your attitude will make things a great deal easier both for your daughter and for those whose task it is to look after her. Because I have to tell you – there's a long way to go.'

He sipped his tea and put the cup and saucer on the table before continuing. 'At Knockvale, before she came to us, they correctly identified some of the areas of need. Basically, it means a lot of therapy. They had already started her with a speech therapist and we started her with ours yesterday. It won't be particularly demanding for the time being because she gets tired quickly. It's slow progress, as you'll appreciate. After all, here's a young woman who hasn't spoken a word for four years, whose voice box and vocal chords have been inactive. You don't just sit up in bed after that length of time and carry on a conversation where you left off. As well as that, we won't know for a while how much her current speech difficulties are the result of the long duration of her comatose condition or . . . or, well to be frank, whether they signify rather more deep-rooted problems.'

He paused to let them absorb the thought.

Sam frowned. 'But before, everyone said there was no sign of brain damage.'

'That's true, as far as could be ascertained. But there are other tests we can do now, other forms of scanning. There's just a chance that they may reveal something.'

'I see,' Sam said. He subsided into the chair.

'We don't know, for example, why she woke up when she did. We may never find that out because there might be no real reason. Coma can be unpredictable, some of the causes uncertain. Sometimes it's as if people just choose to wake up, as if they've had enough. But I have to say it's very probable that after all this time there'll be some sort of personality change. To what extent, we won't know for a while but it's unlikely that she'll be the same young woman she was four years ago. You could hardly expect otherwise.'

'She'll be fine,' Gloria said. Her eyes seemed lit from within and she smiled as if she knew something they did not. 'I know she will.'

'Physically,' Maginnis went on, 'it's slow progress, too. When she was in a coma, they would have done some mild physiotherapy with her out at Knockvale – I'm sure they explained it to you – passive movements, they're called. Someone moving her arms and legs for her several times a day to keep the muscles from atrophying altogether. There would have been some chest physio, too.'

'What's that?' Sam Winter said. 'I don't remember that.'

'Well, it's a bit unpleasant – but necessary. Your chest – well, things gather, you know. It's important to keep it clear. But she's far beyond that stage now, thank goodness. We'll go from passive movements to assisted movements: helping her a bit to bend her arms and her legs, that sort of thing, but really letting her do it for herself. A couple of weeks ago she couldn't even hold her head up on her own but now she's already getting back her sitting balance and trunk mobility, which is good. She's able to sit in a chair for periods of time and very soon we're going to try her in a wheelchair. How long she'll need it depends on how her strength develops.'

'She's very thin,' her father said. 'Almost wasted away.'

'Perhaps she looks more so now,' Maginnis agreed, 'now that you're seeing some movement from her, not just the still figure lying in a bed. Yes, she is a bit – well, slender – but she'll build up gradually. She'll have one physio assigned to her. It's better if she gets used to working with the one person and establishes a relationship. There'll be occupational therapy every day and hydrotherapy too. We've got good facilities for that here. Who's for more tea?'

They both put their hands over their cups. He poured some for himself. 'Don't mind me. I drink far too much of this stuff. With normal physiotherapy, the individual's working against gravity all the time. But in the pool, you're buoyant and it's easier to do the exercises, although the benefits to your muscles and limbs are exactly the same.'

He sipped the tea and thought. 'What else do I need to explain to you? There's ADL.'

'ADL?' Gloria asked.

'Sorry – Activities of Daily Living. All those important routine things: washing herself, going to the toilet, combing her hair. You'd be amazed how much there is. She has to be shown how to do all that, to get her co-ordination back – always provided, of course, that there's nothing more serious to worry about, nothing preventing her from regaining her normal dexterity. She seems to be eating well enough. She's on a high protein, high calorie diet but don't forget that the actual act of eating is a strain for her. She finds it hard enough to lift a spoon and manoeuvre it properly.' He smiled. 'Yesterday she got fed up and just dropped the thing on the floor but I wouldn't let that worry me. Frankly, I think it's a good sign.'

'In what way?' Gloria questioned.

'Well, it shows frustration for one thing. Her brain may want to do things which her physical condition won't allow just yet. What we're seeing may be a manifestation of that. The psychologist will soon tell us.'

He waved an index finger, remembering something. 'Glasses.'

'Sorry?' Sam Winter said.

'She needs glasses. At least for a time. There's some evidence of short-sightedness. The way her eyes reacted to the tests we did, it's evident that objects further away are less clear to her, obviously the result of the weakening of the eye muscles. It may not be a permanent state of affairs. Of course, the muscles may recover their strength, but if not, well, I guess it's not the end of the world.'

He picked his own glasses up from the table, took a silk handkerchief from his pocket and wiped them.

'Coma cases can still surprise us. That's why I have a particular psychologist in mind – Dr Paddy Sands. If you like, I can make the arrangements.'

'Go ahead,' Sam said. 'Do whatever you need to.'

'He practises in Dublin. He's very skilled in dealing with people who've suffered psychological damage through traumatic experiences. We know very little about what happened the night of your daughter's accident but what we do know is traumatic enough. It's very rare for someone to come out of a coma after all this time and, like I said, rarer still for there not to be some residual effect. Even if Meg recovers physically, we have no idea what the psychological consequences are. So she can't go out into the world until we . . .' he gestured to show that he meant all three of them, '. . . are certain that she's absolutely ready.'

29

'How long will that be?' Sam asked.

Maginnis made a face. 'How long's a piece of string? But I'd guess the best part of a year.'

'A year? That long?'

'It could be longer. Maybe shorter. It all depends on how quickly she progresses.'

'God is testing us all,' Gloria said.

Maginnis smiled thinly. He turned to Sam. 'You're aware there's a lot of media interest?'

He nodded. 'They've been pestering both of us.'

'He's testing our perseverance,' Gloria continued. 'He wants us to put our trust in Him. He wants us to believe that He'll carry us through.'

'I've seen the headlines,' Sam said, ignoring her. ' "Murder Car Girl Wakes From Coma" – that sort of thing. The tabloids are offering money for the first interview. I've told them to get stuffed.'

'Some of our staff have been approached,' Maginnis told him, 'but they won't say anything. Anyone who does will get the sack. I'll see to that. It's one of the reasons I decided to become personally involved. Look, Mr Winter—'

'Sam.'

'Sam – our job's to bring your daughter back to as normal a life as we can, slowly and sensitively. But we have to recognise that if all goes well and she recovers fully, then there'll be a lot for her to face. It's unavoidable. Although until she can talk to us, until she can respond – *if* she can respond – we can't know how her mind has been affected by everything that's happened to her and how she'll cope with everything outside these walls. And of course there's another thing. The police.'

'I know,' Sam said.

'They've already been in touch with me. It's another reason I'm keeping an eye on things. When she's well enough to talk to us they'll want her to talk to them, too.'

Sam grunted. 'We'll see about that.'

On a crisp morning ten days later, a man strolled casually through the grounds of Musgrave Park.

He was one of only a few. It was never the most populated of places, especially now, in January, in the cold. It was observed mostly, rather than visited. Stockman's Lane, one of the busiest thoroughfares into the city, ran alongside and in the morning rush every day, queues of people sat in their cars and looked wistfully at the vision of tranquillity that the park represented.

For those who were in the little park itself, the traffic beyond

30

belonged to another world and they hardly noticed it. They strolled along the paths, listening to the cheery encouragement of a blackbird, letting their dogs stretch their legs in the bright, early sunshine and sniff the hard-cropped rose beds for what creatures might have been there in the night.

The man did not have a dog.

Muffled against the cold in a waterproof jacket, scarf and cap, he carried a hold-all over one shoulder and walked with a heavier sense of purpose than the handful of people he passed, and who paid him little attention.

His route took him in the direction of the Centre. Although part of the same patch of land, its grounds were closed off to the public by high fences. Trees and shrubs had been planted all around to protect its privacy but winter had stripped away much of their covering.

When he got as close as he could, he stood for a moment, looking at the outline of the buildings, trying to spot something. There was a window he wanted, a couple of floors up, two from the end. You could not see much from this distance with the naked eye but then he was not relying on that.

He looked at his watch. Eight forty.

A quarter to nine, his contact inside had said. She was one of the auxiliary staff and he had paid good money for her to be right.

He put the hold-all down and from it he took a camera body and a bulky bag. The bag contained a massive telephoto lens, too heavy for him to support without the picture shuddering, but he had thought of that. When he had fitted it to the body, he dipped into the hold-all again and produced a metal stick which opened out into a thin but sturdy tripod which he set into the ground.

He set the camera on it and shook the structure to make certain it was secure. He looked around. There was no one about.

He tested the shot and the focus. As he pressed his left eye to the view-finder and fixed his gaze on the window, a figure appeared. It was a woman in a hospital uniform. She looked out anxiously for a moment and then disappeared from view.

In a few seconds she was back. This time she was not alone but was pushing someone in a wheelchair. When she got to the window she moved away, out of sight.

He took shot after shot. *Click – whirr, click – whirr*. All the while, the figure sat motionless in the chair. He finished a whole roll and thought about loading a new one but there was no point. He had got everything he had come for.

He struck a deal with all the major tabloids and his pictures appeared on their front pages the next morning.

The *Star* treatment was typical:

COMA GIRL – THE FIRST PICTURE

Taken from such a distance, it was not up to much. The photograph was grainy and fuzzy but nevertheless it was sufficiently clear for people who saw it to make out the thin face of a woman.

The accompanying story made up for what detail the picture lacked:

Looking gaunt and haunted, a young woman peers from a window at a world she has not seen for years.

Not since the night she was plunged into a coma.

Former doctor Meg Winter (30) is being nursed in high security conditions in a top secret wing of the Musgrave Rehabilitation Centre while police wait to talk to her.

For she is the only person who can help them solve a bizarre murder case.

Three and a half years ago she was found unconscious and critically injured in the wreckage of an MGB sports car which had plunged off the road at Shaw's Bridge, near Belfast.

A body was found nearby – that of the driver, 27-year-old Paul Everett, a high-flying executive with an American pharmaceuticals company based in Co Antrim.

But he did not die in the crash. Instead, his skull had been smashed by repeated blows which a coroner later declared as murder.

A postmortem also showed that the dead man's system was full of cocaine.

Police believe the murder was drugs-related but they have never been able to find a single clue as to who was responsible.

The case seemed destined to remain in the files, stamped: *UNSOLVED.*

Until now.

Almost a month ago Meg miraculously regained consciousness. A top psychologist said yesterday: 'It's fantastic. Her case is a medical phenomenon.'

But for the moment, she sits in a wheelchair by the window, waiting for the knock on the door . . . waiting to tell the police what she knows.

Five

Like a guilty secret, the sprawling modern prison was hidden
away deep in a part of County Down that was a mesh of tangled
country roads, damp fields and bramble hedges, hills and
sudden slopes.

Peter Quinn, red-haired and ginger-bearded, with hard,
strong, potter's hands, dry and cracked from bending the wet,
spinning clay to his will, sat across the visiting room table from
his old friend.

Bail had been out of the question.

Not that Cochrane had any money, although Quinn would
have gone surety if it had been necessary. He had a bit of cash
and he had assets, like his pottery along the harbour at Ardglass, but it was all academic anyway.

Especially when it was arson and you had damage of three or
four hundred thousand pounds, or so the insurance estimate
would claim, and there was an assault on a security guard and
maybe somebody could have been burned to death.

Not Guilty was out of the question, too, so tomorrow his old
friend would be throwing himself on the mercy of Downpatrick
Crown Court where his barrister, the one Quinn had organised
through legal aid, would try to persuade the judge to go easy,
talking about grief and stress and severe psychological problems.

Quinn looked at Cochrane and thought that there might
actually be a lot in that. His friend's face was grey with a
shadow of stubble. The dark eyes seemed deeper-set, more of a
mystery than ever.

'I don't understand you,' Quinn said.

'So you've told me. More than once.'

'It will be a jail sentence. You know that, don't you. You've
thrown everything away.'

'Don't preach, Peter, for God's sake.'

'I just wish I could have stopped you.'

'No one could have stopped me. I didn't want to be stopped.'

'Tomorrow – your barrister, Grogan, he'll spell it all out. It'll

33

get very personal. He'll talk about you as if you were – unbalanced.'

Cochrane shrugged. 'Maybe I am.'

'Have you thought what you'll do when you get out of here?'

'Leave the country, probably. Emigrate.'

'With a criminal record? Who would have you?'

'Cheer me up, Peter, why don't you?' Cochrane said.

It was worse than Quinn had predicted.

Cochrane hated Kevin Grogan, the barrister, for it. He hated the instructing solicitor, too. Hated himself for agreeing to let them do this.

Grogan had brought a psychiatrist to see him in prison so that a report could be prepared for the court. The man was a patronising old fool who treated him like an idiot and seemed totally unaware that Cochrane was a psychologist himself. Cochrane had held his tongue and his temper and had not enlightened him, just helped give the answers that he knew the man was looking for.

Now he sat in the dock listening to everything that was intensely private and painful to him being discussed by strangers who did not really care.

The courtroom was high and ancient and smelled like old breath. It was crumbling at the edges where the plasterwork was damp. The woodwork was stained with age more than varnish and in the panelling in front of him, someone had carved their initials – *J.P.T. '76*. It could have been 1876, for all he knew.

It might have been easier if Grogan had been a more effective courtroom performer but he was young and he seemed nervous and deferential in the presence of a judge who ate fresh-faced junior advocates for breakfast. Cochrane's image of courtrooms was coloured by what he saw on television or in the cinema. Grogan was not an actor in a wig. He was a mumbler, talking down at his papers, and several times an increasingly irritable Mr Justice Cunningham had been forced to ask him to speak up.

It angered and embarrassed Cochrane that the judge had to do that. He wanted to shake Grogan and tell him to get on with it, to get the whole charade finished as quickly as possible, but of course he could not do anything at all except wait it out.

He looked at the palms of his hands. When he had been hauled before a magistrates' court to be remanded, they had been in bandages like footballs. The wounds had healed well but the skin felt taut, as if it had shrunk in the process. He held his hands in front of him and clenched and unclenched his fingers rapidly several times.

The movement attracted attention. He could feel people's eyes on him, wondering what he was doing, probably thinking it was some sign of madness. He saw the court officials, the police and the young woman from the *Down Recorder*. They examined him with open fascination and without the slightest concern as to how he might feel about it.

He had forfeited all rights. He was an exhibit, a specimen, no longer a person with the kind of freedom they had. They could get up from where they sat and walk out of the courtroom if they wanted to, have a cup of coffee, a smoke at the front door. No one would stop them. He could not do any of that.

Only Peter, smiling with weak encouragement from time to time when he caught his eye, showed any feeling at all.

They had been friends since school days. After A-levels they had gone their separate ways, Cochrane to university in Belfast and Quinn to study ceramics at art college in England, but they had remained close.

In the past year or so, they had seen more of each other. Backed by an agency which encouraged local business enterprise, Quinn had been able to buy an old property on the quayside at Ardglass, just along the coast from Cochrane's family farm. He had converted it into the pottery where he worked and lived – there was a small flat above – and a shop where he sold his own and other potters' work.

He had helped with the funeral arrangements and he had been with him that night but Cochrane had never once betrayed a hint of what he planned to do.

It was in Quinn's face now, the look Cochrane had seen before. Disbelief that he could have done this thing.

The facts presented to the court left no room for doubt.

Grogan was coming to the end of his plea, trying to sum up everything he had been saying for the past fifteen minutes.

'Your honour, the defendant is a victim of a rather tragic past, the cumulative effect of which caught up with him on the night in question, and only a matter of hours after he had attended his mother's funeral. When he was very young, both his father and his sister were the victims of an IRA bomb blast in which they were unfortunately killed. That loss quite clearly, as you've heard from the psychologist's report, had a deep-seated effect. Mr Cochrane is a man who keeps his feelings very much to himself, he is not a very open or gregarious person by nature, and so bottling up all this stress and grief had damaging consequences for his psychological state.'

35

He shuffled the notes in front of him to find his place. 'Mr Cochrane is a talented young man, only twenty eight years old. He achieved a good degree in psychology at Queen's University, he went on to study for a post-graduate certificate of education, and for the past three years he has been an educational psychologist on the staff of the south-eastern education board. So here you see someone with a bright career ahead but one that has undoubtedly been curtailed by these unfortunate events.'

He had a ballpoint pen which he kept clicking. It sounded like there was a cricket in the courtroom. He looked up towards the judge. 'Your honour, the root cause of what took place, as I have said, goes back far beyond the events of that night. Here is Mr Cochrane, now an only child, with concern for his mother's well-being very much at heart. So, as you can imagine, it was a very bitter blow to him when his mother got into financial difficulties and the bank was forced to take away the family farm in order to recover the debts which she owed them. Somehow, Mr Cochrane got it into his head that there was some collusion between the bank and the construction company which built the hotel. You've heard from the prosecution that Mr Sam Winter already owned most of the land on which it was subsequently established, having inherited it from his own late mother who lived there for a great many years, and when the Cochrane farm became available be bought that too, since it would increase the size of the property and allow the construction of the golf course.'

Grogan turned to look at his client. 'By that time, Mr Cochrane had developed an unhealthy obsession with Mr Winter and his business activities and the strain of having to look after his mother and find somewhere for her to live began to tell on him. Then, when his mother became ill with a stroke that eventually led to her unfortunate death, something inside him seemed to snap. It all came to a head that night when he had far too much to drink and resolved to exact some kind of revenge on the person he saw as being responsible for what had happened.'

He put the pen down and leaned his knuckles on the bench in front of him. 'Your honour, Mr Cochrane feels great remorse for what he has done. He recognises the fact that he was indeed ill at the time – I refer you to the medical report again – and I would ask the court also to accept those findings. His behaviour was irrational and paranoid and brought on purely by grief. This episode has simply added to the chain of tragic circumstances which seem to have bedevilled him all his life. I would ask your honour to accept that this was not the behaviour of a criminal or a habitual offender but a desperate act by a distraught and lonely man who was dreadfully misguided by the consequences of a great loss.'

He drew his gown around him and sat down.

Mr Justice Cunningham had a wizened red face, like an apple which had lain too long in the fruit bowl, and the air of someone coping with some internal physical inconvenience. He tapped a pencil on the woodwork in front of him and muttered to himself as he looked at his notes. 'Yes . . . I see . . . I see . . . yes, Mr Grogan . . . thank you . . . thank you.'

He coughed, a sharp, dry bark that reverberated round the big room. It caught most people by surprise and they stiffened in their seats. He looked over his glasses and settled his eye on Cochrane, then mumbled something that only the court clerk could hear.

'Would the accused please stand?' the clerk said. The prison officer sitting beside Cochrane grasped him by the elbow as if it were a lever. Cochrane got to his feet.

'This, eh, this is a very distressing matter,' the judge said. 'Arson is a very serious offence indeed and in this case, in spite of what Mr Grogan has explained, it is difficult for me to accept any mitigating circumstances at all. We all suffer from stress, we all suffer some kind of loss at some time in our lives, yet we don't go around trying to burn hotels down, nor would we expect understanding or sensitive treatment from the courts if we did so.'

He looked at his papers for a second and scratched the side of his wig with his pencil. 'Here we have a man who got drunk on the night of his mother's funeral and deliberately set out to destroy this property. I can't accept that this was some sort of spur-of-the-moment aberration, some ill-conceived drunken escapade. It was far more premeditated than that. Indeed, Mr Grogan himself tells us that the construction company which built the hotel had been playing on the accused's mind for some time.'

He looked towards the barrister who did not attempt to meet his gaze but busied himself brushing something off his knee.

He read from the evidence again. 'He had wire cutters with him, a can of petrol and bottles with which to make petrol bombs. With this equipment, he starts a major fire in the kitchen, the fire takes hold rapidly and spreads through the ground floor, causing damage estimated at three hundred and twenty seven thousand pounds. Damage, incidentally, which will delay the opening of the hotel for several months. And, then, in trying to make his escape, he attacks a member of the security staff as they try to apprehend him. Quite a night he made of it.'

He gave Cochrane a hard stare. 'Arson is a vile and cowardly crime. Lives could have been lost as a result of your actions. Nevertheless, I'm mindful of some of the things Mr Grogan has had to say and so I sentence you to a total of twelve months on each charge, the sentences to run concurrently.'

The prison officer put his hand on Cochrane's arm again. Grogan stood quickly to lodge his intention to appeal but when he asked for bail the judge waved the thought away like a bad smell.

The eyes of the curious were on Cochrane but if they were expecting any sign of emotion they did not get it.

Peter Quinn held his head in his hands and tried to rub away a pain behind his brow.

The judge nodded towards his clerk. 'I think I'll adjourn briefly before the next case.'

'All please rise,' the clerk said and they all stood while the judge made his exit through the side door beside his bench.

The prison officer led Cochrane towards the door that would take them to the rear of the court building where the prison van was waiting.

Grogan stepped in front of them.

'Thanks for nothing,' Cochrane said before he could speak.

'Just a second. Look, it's not so bad,' Grogan said. 'You've already been in custody for a month so with remission on top of that I reckon you'll be out by the end of the summer. Do you want me to appeal? I will if you like but to be honest he went fairly leniently. An appeal judge might make it worse.'

'I'll let you know,' Cochrane said.

'Time to go,' the prison officer told them.

Six

'She's definitely lost her memory,' Dr Paddy Sands said. 'Big time.'

He put his pipe in his mouth and fumbled in the pocket of his thick tweed jacket for the tobacco.

'Damn it, Paddy,' Liam Maginnis said. 'I can't let you do that in here.'

Sands raised his eyebrows and feigned disappointment. He put the pipe away and looked at his watch. 'Then the least you could do is take me round to the pub so that we can talk about this over a drink. It's ten past five, you know.'

Maginnis looked at his own watch and drummed his fingers on his desk while he thought about it. He had been in London at a conference for a week and he had just got back. There were two in-trays, both full.

'Come on, Liam,' Sands said. 'The place doesn't own you.' He made a face and waved his hands in the air. 'Do something mad for a change.'

Maginnis went to the closet where he had hung his jacket.

The King's Head was just around the corner, right across the road from the King's Hall, the big exhibition centre and concert venue, hence the name. They pulled out of the evening traffic into a car park that was almost empty. Outside the pub there were rows of damp tables and benches. Sparrows hopped around the table legs, looking for crumbs.

Inside the bar there was the smell of old beer long soaked in, as if the place were marinaded in it. Surfaces were sticky and ashtrays sour with cigarette stubs. They found a table in an alcove which had an extinct cast-iron fireplace and shelves of old books, including a set of encyclopaedias and a complete collection of Nevil Shute in some sort of binding like linen. Sands's eyes roamed over the titles while he worked on his pipe.

Maginnis got the drinks. 'God, I haven't done this for years,' he said, delivering a pint of Caffrey's.

'You're not doing it now, either,' Sands said, nodding towards Maginnis's glass. It was sparkling mineral water with ice and lemon, all the trimmings.

'I have to go back after this. Can't smell like a brewery.'

Sands's tobacco was both robust and sweet. The smoke curled in an aromatic ribbon round the bar. He was a mousy man, ageless, with cropped hair doing its own thing, like the bristles on an old toothbrush. Maginnis had known him for years and couldn't put a figure on his age. He had to be sixty, anyway. The boyish personality was deceptive.

He had pulled a book from the shelf. 'Wait till you hear this,' he said. Maginnis looked at the cover. *A Complete System of Nursing*, by A Millicent Ashdown.

'When was that published?'

Sands checked. 'Nineteen seventeen. This edition nineteen twenty-five. Listen – "To those who are not fitted for it, many of the duties are revolting and therefore difficult to accomplish satisfactorily." ' He chuckled. 'And that's only the introduction. Maybe you'd better bring this with you in case one of your nurses comes in here, reads it and decides to give up.'

'Maybe one or two of them should,' Maginnis suggested drily. He sipped his drink and got to the point. 'So what's next? You've had – what – three sessions with her now?'

'Four,' Sands corrected. He drew on his pipe. The banter was over. 'It's psychogenic amnesia, in my view. Do you know what that is?'

Maginnis nodded. 'Often associated with war. Sometimes soldiers who witness terrible things on the battlefield simply blot their experiences out.'

'That's the one. But with her it's more than just the events of one night. She's alarmed both by what she now knows and by what she doesn't know and doesn't understand. There's the murder. She's horrified by that, of course – but she has no earthly idea who this American guy was, this Paul Everett, or what she was doing with him. Not a clue.'

'You believe her? It's not just a convenient act?'

'Oh, I believe her absolutely. I'm convinced she's not faking anything. And this business about cocaine . . .' he shook his head, '. . . she knows nothing about that either. Then to cap it all, not only has her memory of anything relating to the accident gone but a huge tract of previous experience, stretching back goodness knows how long, has disappeared with it.'

'So what does she remember – anything?'

'Oh yes, lots. She can give you a run-down on most of her life: childhood, parents, growing up, university. She knows she was a doctor, too, that she worked in the accident and emergency department at the old Central Hospital. The trouble is, she knows that bit only because people have told her. She hasn't any recollection of it herself, of her work there, any of the staff. Nothing.'

He blew a mouthful of smoke into the air. It was like a little cloud.

'I've told her what we know about that night: that she rang this friend of hers, Elizabeth what's-her-name, and arranged to meet her at some place called the Clarendon Dock where they have rock concerts and so forth. But she has no memory of that. Says she's never been there. Knows nothing about it.'

'And her friend didn't go anyway, of course. We know that.'

'True. Or so she told the police four years ago.'

'What else?'

'Interesting – Miss Winter – sorry, *Doctor* Winter – doesn't seem to have forgotten her medical training. She tells me she's been talking to the staff about cases and treatments in a way that's taken everyone by surprise, herself included.'

'Nobody told me that.'

'You've been away.'

'So explain to me how that works.'

'There are different kinds of memory. What I've just described is her semantic memory. That's a kind of general knowledge base, the foundation of what we know of the world around us. She knows how to treat a gunshot wound, for example, and what the capital of France is, all that stuff. So her semantic memory seems unimpaired. Then there's what's called the procedural memory, which is simply a matter of knowing how to do things. Like using a knife and fork. Playing the piano, maybe, which takes in both the procedural and the semantic. All the physio she's been getting has established that that part of her memory's in good shape too.'

He took a drink and wiped the froth from his lip.

'So now we come to her episodic memory, which is where the problems lie. It's as if a chasm has opened and swallowed part of her life. That's the way she describes it to me. She says she feels like she's drowning sometimes. That she's reaching out for something to hold on to but it keeps drifting away from her. Poor woman. She's trying very hard. She's desperate to get her memory back.'

'And is she likely to?'

'Maybe. In time. There's no doubt in my mind that this is her response to some deep psychological trauma. There's the crash and the murder, of course. But what happened before that? Why

41

is so much of her more immediate past a blank page? Something else may have happened that was profoundly scarring – maybe even a whole combination of things – an overload, and her mind simply couldn't cope. The crash dropped her into a well and she's been falling down it for four years. Now she's hit the bottom and she doesn't know how to climb back up.'

He tapped the contents of his pipe into an ashtray and sat back. They were silent for a few moments, thinking. Behind them the pub was beginning to fill up with regulars. There was laughter and the clink of glasses.

'How will her parents respond when they hear all this?' Sands asked.

'The mother'll think it's a sign from God.'

'Good sign or a bad sign?'

Maginnis shrugged. 'Whichever she wants it to be.'

Seven

Meg Winter stood naked and still in front of the long bathroom mirror.

Its glass reflected the white enamel fittings, the sickly mint green walls and her own changed shape.

She took her new glasses off and put them on a shelf.

It was May, five months since she had been admitted to Musgrave Rehabilitation Centre.

Her memory was not returning but her strength was beginning to. She was learning to do things unaided, a little more each day. By now she could bathe and shower by herself and she was using the wheelchair less. But she got tired easily.

She looked at her reflection. It was not that she did not recognise herself exactly but every now and then it threw her when she saw how much she had changed. There were soft curves at her cheek bones where once she might have worried about looking a little chubby and the thinness of her face made her mouth seem ridiculously wide.

She stepped closer to the mirror and looked into her eyes, almost as if she expected them to be different, too, but they were the same soft grey. Yet she felt uncertain of what lay behind them. Somewhere in there, in her mind, things were hidden away. Things that she could not even guess at.

She had been very drunk. That had come as a bit of a shock.

The rest was worse. She had been in a car crash with a man she'd never heard of before, a man called Everett, who had then been murdered. By whom, she did not know, or why.

She was in the midst of a nightmare. Instead of waking to a new dawn she had emerged into something frightening and incomprehensible.

She stared. Her hair, long and straight, made her face seem narrower. She pulled it back and tied it up behind her head, seeing the faint scars at the edge of her scalp where glass fragments had been embedded. She felt the spot with her fingertips, then she moved the hand to her torn eyebrow, touching it gently, as if it would break off.

43

She tried to picture what she must have looked like when they found her that night, her skin slashed and bleeding, her body broken. But like everything else it was impossible to imagine.

She looked at her body. In the past months, she had graduated from being painfully thin to being slim and sinewy although her shape would never again be as full as it used to be. But that was the least of her worries.

As a matter of fact, it was not a worry at all.

Back in her room there were photographs which she had asked her father to bring. She looked at them frequently, thinking about the past, wondering about the future. There were two that highlighted the physical change. They showed a full-bodied young woman in a low-cut evening dress, then in jeans and a t-shirt that accentuated her curves.

She stepped into the shower and turned the water on. She closed her eyes and lifted her face to it, letting the warm spray beat against her skin.

Tomorrow the police were coming to see her.

They had been patient but they knew she was not going anywhere. Liam Maginnis and her father had held them at bay for as long as they could but her progress to recovery, at first ponderous, had picked up pace which meant that it was unreasonable to keep them away any longer.

Several times she had insisted that she did not mind.

'Really,' she had told her father and Maginnis, 'it's all right. I don't know what you're so afraid of. Do you think they want to charge me with something? I can't imagine what.'

'Nevertheless,' Sam Winter had said, 'I think I'd like to sit in on this. I'll ask my solicitor to come along too. You never know.'

'And I'd better be there as well,' Maginnis had said. 'We can use my office.'

'Honestly,' Meg had told them, 'you're being ridiculous. I just want to get this thing out of the way. The fact is that I can't help them because I can't remember anything. Nothing they say to me or ask me is going to change that. And that's the truth.'

It was not the truth.

The truth was that she was afraid. Afraid of the unknown.

They had left it that Maginnis alone would sit in on the discussion and she had said she was happy enough with that.

The warm water brought a glow to her body.

She was alive but she was incomplete. A part of her was missing. It was not a physical loss, although perhaps in a symbolic way it did manifest itself in her less substantial form.

Paul Everett.

44

The first time she had heard the name was when her parents and Maginnis decided she was well enough to be told what had happened. Then her father had shown her cuttings from newspapers. Some of them were four years old, others were recent and dealt with Meg's recovery and the re-opening of the case.

She lathered her body, then stood and let the water flow over her. She bent her head and as she watched the suds course down her legs and drain away across the floor of the shower she had the feeling once more that she did not know exactly who *she* was, never mind this Paul Everett.

It was later, during one of her sessions with Dr Sands, the psychologist, that she had learned about being drunk. Her parents must have known but they had not mentioned it. Embarrassment, perhaps. Insult added to injury.

She turned the water off, stepped out of the shower and began to dry herself.

Some things had not left her.

A couple of weeks ago she had asked her father to bring her some of her old medical textbooks and she had been pleased to discover that she could remember titles specifically. She had been equally happy when she found their contents familiar, even the very smell and feel of the books, like a reassuring old friend.

But the hospital where she had worked was a blank page. She could remember nothing about it: what she did, the staff – nothing. She wouldn't even be able to try to jog her memory by visiting it when she got out of here. Two years ago it had been closed down and amalgamated with two other hospitals on a fresh site, becoming New Central Hospital.

The staff from the old days were all over the place, many of them out of the country. She had been shown photographs and she thought she knew some of the faces but she wasn't sure. She wanted to remember, that was the problem, so she told herself that she did.

But it wasn't the truth.

She slipped into pyjamas and a dressing gown as a ward auxiliary rapped on the door.

'All finished yet, dear?'

'All finished.'

The wheelchair stood outside and she folded herself into it gratefully, yet annoyed that she was so tired. The slightest exertion took a lot out of her but she wondered if the fatigue also stemmed from the anxiety that often kept her awake at nights.

She could doze on and off during the day but at night it was different.

Crazy, that.

She had been asleep for four years and now she sometimes couldn't sleep at all. They had offered her pills to help but she had turned them down flat. No way. She would just put up with it.

The auxiliary reached over to the shelf. 'Glasses, love. Don't forget your glasses.'

'Thanks. I'm always doing that, aren't I?'

They headed down the corridor. Her bed was in a private room just outside a main ward and there she could be on her own. Some of the other patients were all right, others were just nosy. They knew all about her. The Musgrave grapevine was a healthy plant and the stuff that had been in the papers helped it flourish.

The episodic memory. That's what Dr Sands had told her it was.

An entire part of her life was a mystery and she found herself no nearer to recovering it. It was as if every time she turned a corner she ran into a brick wall.

She felt awkward and uncertain, ill at ease with her own personality.

For an attractive, young single woman with a good job, her past seemed curiously empty. There were no traces of a recent social life of any kind. Her photographs were all at least five years old. Any letters her parents had been able to dig out were just bank and credit card statements and a few bills which her father had long since settled. There was no correspondence of a more personal nature and even her old diary contained nothing except her hospital rota pattern.

The diary.

When she had got her hands on that she had gone straight to the day it happened, turning the flimsy little pages hurriedly.

June 5. There it was. An early shift, finishing at three.

She looked at June 6.

A day off. She gave herself a bitter smile. Well over a thousand days off after that.

The sight of her own writing on the page, the italic scrawl in blue ballpoint, did nothing at all. It could have been a stranger's diary, a stranger's hand.

She tried her address book; her father had brought that, too.

It did not yield anything. No Paul Everett, no cryptic initials, or even any kind of a code that might have been him.

46

What names it did contain were either family – her mother, her father, an aunt who lived in New Zealand – or else long-standing friends and acquaintances. People from way back. From the part that she remembered.

She settled herself in the bed and lifted a magazine.

People were not exactly beating a path to the door of the Musgrave Centre to see her, were they?

Her parents sometimes brought messages of good wishes from whoever they met but no one wanted to become involved. There was something kind of seedy about all this, that was the thing.

She thought of some of the bizarre headlines she had read. She reckoned 'Drug Murder Coma Girl' said it all. Although she had liked the 'girl' part.

Girl, indeed. She was thirty now. Good God.

They all wanted to get the first interview. Her father got letters and faxes all the time. Some had arrived here, too. Newspapers, television programmes – they wanted to feed on her story for their circulations and their ratings.

She could not blame them. Northern Ireland had changed; she was finding that out. There was a kind of peace now with the result that a media which had been accustomed to a constant diet of stories about terrorism was grasping at anything new and different. And hers was one hell of a mystery.

But she passed all this over to her father to deal with. The answer, every time, was no. No interview.

The only one of the old faces who had kept in contact was Elizabeth.

She really wanted to see her again. Was it possible she could help in some way, fill in any of the gaps?

They had been friends almost all their lives, first at school, then sharing a flat while they were both at university. But those weeks before it happened, months maybe – where had Elizabeth been then? She closed her eyes and tried to see but there was nothing.

She yawned and put the magazine down, then lay back in the bed. She had made the mistake of mentioning this tiredness to her mother.

Gloria had nodded knowingly, with that smug smile.

'The Bible teaches us that we must have a very positive attitude to suffering,' she had said.

'Well, that's nice to know,' Meg had responded and then they had lapsed into a tense, fidgety silence.

Thinking of her parents did not bring her any comfort.

Why couldn't I have forgotten all that?

47

But even if she had, their hostility to each other would have been an instant reminder.

Her father had changed. He seemed weary, older than he should be. She could only guess at the extent of his suffering, as well as the enormous financial expense involved in keeping her in comfortable care in a private hospital. It had all taken its toll.

She found it hard to picture him as the man her mother still treated with such bitterness: the philanderer who had ruined their marriage with his reckless affairs.

A knock on the door interrupted the thought.

'It's OK,' she said, sitting up. 'Come in.'

It was Liam Maginnis. 'I'm not disturbing you, I hope?'

'No,' she said, 'I was just lying here thinking.'

'About tomorrow?'

'No, not really. About the past.' She gave him a wry smile. 'What there is of it.'

He pulled out a chair. 'May I?'

'Of course. Make yourself at home.'

Before he sat, he moved to close the door.

'Leave it open a little,' she said. 'Would you mind?'

'Sure. Too warm in here?'

'No, it's just – I feel a bit enclosed sometimes.'

He nodded as if he understood.

There was something. It wasn't him, it was her, she was certain of that, but for some reason she felt uneasy about being in a closed room with him.

As he sat down, she got a whiff of his aftershave, always a little over the top. He was a good-looking man and she could detect that some of the nurses had an eye for him but she found him just a bit too conscious of his own appeal.

'Everything will be all right tomorrow,' he said. 'They just want to have a talk. I'll explain all about the amnesia. I'm sure they'll leave you alone afterwards.'

'I hope you're right,' she said, although she doubted it.

He changed the subject. 'Have you thought about what will happen, what you'll do when you leave here?'

The idea surprised her. 'Well, no, not really. When's that likely to be?'

'Sooner rather than later, I would say, the way things are progressing. You've done remarkably well so I think we might aim for August. How do you feel about that?'

'Not sure,' she said, a bit vaguely, then shook her head. 'No, that's not true. To be honest, now that you mention it, it frightens the life out of me.'

48

Maginnis smiled. 'Only to be expected.' He looked round the room. 'This place, it's like a nest. You feel safe here, well looked-after – at least I hope you do?'

'Very,' she acknowledged. It was true. She felt secure and protected. Outside would be different.

'But there'll come a time when you'll have to be on your own again,' Maginnis said.

'I know that. I just didn't think it would be so soon.'

'Don't worry. We won't throw you out on the street. When you first came here I said that to your mother and father. Your recovery is all that matters, I told them. I said you wouldn't leave here until we all agreed you were ready. I include you in that decision now.'

She smiled at him and he returned it. He had lovely skin, perfectly pink and smooth. She thought of her father's drained features.

'What do you make of my parents?' she said.

The question took Maginnis unawares.

'What do I make of them? I think they're both very – *nice* – people. Very honourable. They both adore you.' He stopped and looked at her. 'That wasn't exactly what you meant, was it?'

She shook her head.

'OK. Well then, I guess – it's not fair of me to be critical – but to be honest I guess I've found it a bit difficult dealing with them. They – they don't like each other very much. That can happen – relationships. Sometimes they go bad. But the thing that does unite them is their concern for you.'

She could see he was awkward with this and did not want to say any more.

She said: 'My mother seems to be even more steeped in religion than I remembered.'

'They've reacted to the crisis in different ways. Your father's carried the emotional and financial burden for both of them. Your mother's had her faith, an unshakeable belief that everything would turn out all right. Now, you may not consider that a very practical way of handling things but it has certainly lightened her load.'

'My father's got old. But she seems to look just the same.'

'She's a very striking woman,' he said. 'Very strong.'

'She wants me to move in with her for a while when I leave here. She's worried about me being on my own. But I've got my own house. I want to see it. Do you know, I can hardly remember living there.'

'We should take you for a drive soon. A day out. Go there perhaps.'

49

She pointed to the window. 'It's just along the Lisburn Road. You could walk from here. Truesdale Street. I only bought it about six months before this happened. My father tells me it's now worth £30,000 more than I paid for it. Incredible.'

'Your father's taken good care of everything.'

'My mother doesn't give him much credit for that. But you're right, he has. He didn't get rid of the house. I'm glad of that.'

'You'd have been upset if he had.'

'Probably. I'd have felt disposed of. He did sell my old car, though, but that's all right. I don't mind that.'

'If you think the price of property has gone up, wait until you go looking for a new one.'

She had not thought of that. 'Yes, of course, I suppose so. It's going to be a bit expensive out there. It'll be quite a shock to the system. Thank God I'm not broke. My dad took over my mortgage payments for me and the house is rented out at the moment. He's investing the income in an account in my name.'

'Well then, that's a demonstration of his belief, isn't it? His faith. Perhaps not the same as your mother's but pretty impressive nevertheless.'

Meg nodded. 'He also invested my salary. Did you know that?'

'He mentioned something, yes.'

'The old Central kept me on the books for the first six months but then they stopped. No choice, really.' She considered. 'I suppose there'll be tax on the income from my investments.'

'I'm sure your father and his accountants will sort something out. And if they come up with any useful new financial wheezes, maybe you'd let me know.'

She smiled. 'I'm sure you don't need much assistance.' She looked at the soft grey suit and how well it sat on him. How much did he earn in today's money – £150,000? £200,000? More, maybe, with all his consultancy work.

'You know,' Maginnis said, 'it's not up to me to decide but maybe it's not a bad idea for you to move in with your mother for a while, just until you get on your feet a bit more and get used to the outside world. My plan is that before you actually leave here, you should sort of go home on a day release basis once a week or so, coming back here in the evening. It's better to do it gradually. That way we'll all know how ready you are. But you can't go home to a house on your own. That's not on.'

'Especially since some other people are still living in it,' she told him. 'Their lease isn't up for a couple of months.'

'Well, then, there you are. Your mother'd be happy to look after you.'

She frowned. 'I don't know. My childhood with her wasn't a very carefree one. Maybe there'd be too many memories.' She gave a little laugh when she realised what she had said. 'Now, that would be something, wouldn't it?'

'Do you remember living with both your parents?'

'Not really. They split up when I was very young.'

Dr Sands had asked her about this, too. When talking to him, she had had the strangest feeling that she was opening up more than was normal for her. The second time round it was even easier.

'My father left home. My mother turned to religion. For me that meant lots of Sunday School and Bible classes. I hated it. It was all God this, God that and colouring in pictures of bearded men with sheep. You were taught to believe that enjoying yourself was sinful. I went elsewhere for my fun – and my friends – but my mother didn't like any of them. And some of them were even Catholic as well. My, my. Outrageous. Big black mark there. We bickered a lot, especially when I hit adolescence. Boys – you know. She didn't approve of anyone who wasn't from our church.'

'And you didn't approve of anyone who was?'

She smiled. 'That's about the size of it. I knew my own mind – just like she knew hers. She was certain her way was the only one. I fought against her all the time. I even changed my name to get back at her. She christened me Margaret after her mother, my granny. I hated it. So I started calling myself Meg when I was about fourteen.' She shook her head. 'It all seems a bit silly, doesn't it?'

'That was a long time ago.' There were grapes in a bowl and he plucked a couple. 'Strange that they never got divorced.'

'My mother – I asked her once. She said she didn't believe in it. She'd made her marriage vows and she was sticking to them. Not that that meant much, if you ask me. They were divorced in everything but name. My father, well, he kind of played the field, you know. That was why they broke up. She'd had enough of it. But neither of them ever wanted to remarry, definitely not my mother, and if my father did he certainly didn't push it. No, they've simply lived apart for all these years with my father providing for my mother's financial needs. And mine. He supported me through university, helped me get a flat. That was another row. My mother thought he was trying to drive a wedge between us.'

She reached into a drawer in her bedside table. 'My friend Elizabeth Maguire,' she said, taking out a letter. 'Have I mentioned her before?'

'Yes,' Maginnis said. 'I think you might have.'

'She's coming to see me sometime. I don't know when. We shared the flat when we were students together. We had some good times then, that much I do remember. She's an accountant, worked for Price Waterhouse. Only she's not Maguire any more – I must remember that. She's Elizabeth O'Malley now. While I've been in a coma, she's been getting married. A guy who works for a merchant bank. *And* she's got a two-year-old daughter. *And* she's been living in Malaysia for the past eighteen months. But she's coming home.' She shuffled the pages in the letter. 'She doesn't say for how long. I wonder why.'

She folded it into its envelope and put it in the drawer again.

'I'm sure she'll tell you,' he said.

She looked towards the window. 'Why was I with him that night?' she asked, almost in a whisper, a question directed to herself more than to Maginnis.

He gave her a sad smile. 'I'm afraid we just don't know.'

Outside there was the blue sky of early summer. Little puffs of cloud like smoke signals cast blotchy shadows on the slope of the Black Mountain.

Her eyes misted over.

'I feel as if we've both been away for a long time, Elizabeth and I. Except that I haven't been away anywhere. Nowhere at all.'

He stood and patted her on the arm. 'You're tired,' he said. 'I'll let you get some rest.'

She closed her eyes when he had gone but she felt hot in the cotton pyjamas. The central heating seemed to take no account of the seasons. She got out of bed and stripped. There was a nightdress on a shelf in the wardrobe. Naked, she leaned in and got it.

As she pulled the thin garment over her head, she thought she saw a shape reflected in the mirror behind her wash basin.

She started and tugged the nightdress down quickly.

Her door was not quite closed. Was there someone in the corridor, watching?

She grabbed her glasses and her robe and stepped outside the room.

The corridor was empty.

But she thought she scented the faint, lingering presence of Liam Maginnis's aftershave.

Eight

At eleven a.m. the following day Meg said no to the offer of a wheelchair and walked beside a nurse to Maginnis's office.

The police were already there. Maginnis got to his feet and went towards her. 'Ah, Meg, you're here.'

'I'm always here,' she joked, her smile tense.

She felt uneasy. It was not just the presence of the two police officers, it was Maginnis now, too, and the worrying thought that he might have been watching her, seeing her naked. Yet he seemed just the same, open and welcoming. Was it all in her mind? Her imagination?

She could see he had spotted that she was wearing make-up. It was nothing much, just a dab of lipstick and a little foundation to take some of the pallor out of her cheeks, but she saw the quick appraisal and the smile of approval that went with it. She had plucked her eyebrows, too, but she doubted whether he would notice that.

She had wondered what to wear for this, not that she had a lot of choice. None of her old clothes were much of a fit so she had put on the lightweight sweat suit and moccasin slippers she wore a lot and in which she felt comfortable. It hadn't mattered before but now, facing the people in this room, she felt under-dressed and somehow exposed.

Maginnis turned to the others with an apologetic smile. 'This is terrible. I'm so sorry. I'm afraid I've forgotten your names already so maybe I should just let you introduce yourselves, if that's all right.'

'Detective Sergeant Hugh Nixon.'

A hefty man of forty plus in a grim worsted suit, he gave a little involuntary grunt as he pushed himself out of his seat and stood to shake her hand. His felt like a baseball glove.

'Meg Winter,' she said unnecessarily.

'And this is my colleague, Detective Inspector Florence Gilmour.'

'Pleased to meet you,' the woman said. She had blonde hair, very short, and forty was still a few years off. Her hand was cool and firm. She was the senior of the two and Meg chided herself for assuming it was the other way round.

They smelled of the outside world, an odour of fast food and smokiness, lives led in a hurry, which the undercurrent of Gilmour's perfume could not erase. Meg felt herself receiving a swift, practised once-over delivered by two experienced professionals. It was like an x-ray and she wondered what they saw.

They sat. The others had coffee but she declined Maginnis's offer.

'So,' he said, clapping his hands together, 'here we are at last. As I was saying before Meg arrived, when I was filling you in on what's been happening. I'm going to sit in on this conversation, if you don't mind.'

'We don't mind at all,' Nixon told him.

'Meg has made great progress since she regained consciousness but there's some little way to go. I know she's more than happy to talk to you but I've got to be careful she doesn't suffer any undue stress. I'm sure you'll bear that in mind.'

'Of course. If she gets tired or anything, she's only got to say,' Nixon assured him.

She felt a flash of irritation. They were talking about her as if she could not understand them or answer for herself.

She glared at Nixon. 'I—' she began.

'Years ago, I was in uniform down in Armagh,' Florence Gilmour said abruptly, leaning forward.

Meg stopped in surprise. She saw something in the woman's eyes that asked her to let the thing pass.

'There was this kid, ten years old, and he and his mates decided to play chicken with the traffic one night, except that this one time he didn't get out of the way fast enough and a car hit him. Drove on, too, and we never did get the driver. Anyway, the boy suffered a fractured skull and he went into a coma which lasted for three months. One of the doctors told me this story later. When he came round, his parents were at his bedside. A couple of right hard cases, as I recall. The doctor sat and told the kid what had happened and broke the news to him that he wasn't ten any more – he was eleven. His birthday had come and gone while he was unconscious. Do you know what the wee fella said?'

Meg shook her head.

' "Fuck me," – that's what he said. At which point the parents looked at each other and the mother said, "Isn't that great? He can still talk." '

The swear-word shocked for a second. Maginnis's face was a picture. Then they all laughed. Gilmour sat back, having broken

54

the ice. 'I'm afraid that's my only experience of someone coming out of a coma.'

'My contribution might be just as brief,' Meg said, 'but maybe not as colourful.' She began to relax.

'It must be an extraordinary feeling for you,' the other woman said, getting serious again. 'I can't possibly imagine what it would be like.'

'No, indeed,' Nixon agreed. 'Listen . . .' He looked into Meg's eyes and lowered his voice in a way that suggested he was speaking in absolute confidence. 'I've been talking to Mr Maginnis here and I understand the – the problems – everything you've gone through.'

He paused and considered what he had just said.

'Well, that's overstating it a bit. No one knows what this is like except you. But we don't want to make things any more difficult than they already are. To be perfectly honest, this is a case we don't know much about. We've been catching up through the files. It was one neither of us worked on the first time round . . .' he looked at Gilmour and she shook her head by way of confirmation, '. . . but it's been handed to us now and we've got to deal with it as best we can.'

'I can appreciate that,' Meg told him.

'So,' Nixon went on, 'I kind of thought that maybe the best thing to do was go through what we know of what happened and take it from there.' He raised his heavy eyebrows questioningly.

'That's OK by me,' Meg said.

There was a folder on the table in front of him and he took out a photograph which he handed to her.

'That's Paul Everett.'

She accepted it delicately. There had been pictures in the papers but this glossy colour print seemed to make him more real.

As she studied the face, Nixon gave her a commentary. 'Aged 27 when he was found murdered. US citizen, came from Portland in the state of Maine. Graduated from university with a science degree – chemistry his speciality – then head-hunted by Vectra, the big American pharmaceuticals company, and went to Harvard Business School. He had been in Northern Ireland for about six months before he was killed. Chief Executive of Vectra (NI) Ltd, established just outside Antrim. Seen very much as one of Vectra's high fliers. He was sent here to set up the Northern Ireland operation and he would eventually have gone back to headquarters in New Hampshire with a big promotion.'

The face in the photograph was boyish. A lop-sided smile.

Dark hair brushed to one side. Meg thought it looked like a snap from one of those American high school yearbooks.

Nothing registered. 'It's better than the picture in the papers,' she said.

'That's the best we have of him,' Gilmour told her. 'It was the most recent, taken for his company ID card. That's about the way he would have looked that night.'

Meg stared at it for longer than she needed to, then she looked up. 'If you're expecting some sudden dazzling revelation from me, then you're in for a disappointment. I've never . . .' She paused. 'I was about to say that I've never seen him before in my life but' – she handed the picture back – 'the facts would kind of indicate otherwise, wouldn't they?'

She could feel their eyes search her face, looking for anything that might be hidden in it, then Nixon nodded, as if satisfied, and took a sheet of paper from the file. He began to read, starting with the date.

'Almost four years exactly,' he noted. 'At approximately 2.06 that morning, an emergency call was made from a public telephone.'

'Do you mind if I write some of this down?' Meg said.

'Not at all,' Gilmour answered.

'Here, take this.' Maginnis put his hand in his pocket and gave her his Mont Blanc ballpoint. Then he handed her a notepad from the desk. It bore the logo of a company that made ulcer medication.

Nixon went on. His accent was thick, rural. She found herself listening to his voice as well as hearing what he had to say.

'The caller was a Mrs Fiona Jackson of 43, Willoughby Park off the Saintfield Road who said she believed there'd been a serious accident out on the road at Hydebank, Shaw's Bridge direction. She said she and her husband had been driving in towards the city along the back roads from Lisburn and when they came round a bend they were confronted by two cars coming towards them, one trying to pass the other. She said it all happened very quickly and they managed to get past without hitting anybody but she believed one of the cars might have gone off the road. She asked for the police and an ambulance and said they were going back to have a look. So emergency services were tasked to the scene.'

He took another photograph from the folder but waited before passing it to her. 'This is a picture of the wreckage of the car. Are you happy enough to look at it?'

She nodded and he handed it over.

'It's a red MGB soft-top, 1968 vintage, which the police at the

56

time established was owned by Paul Everett. Beautiful machine. Not like that, of course.'

The picture had been taken in a police yard somewhere after the car had been removed from the scene. The rear of the vehicle seemed intact but the front was an incomprehensible twisted mess of metal. The red paint looked like blood.

Meg stared in disbelief.

'I – I survived that?'

'Yes,' Gilmour said. 'It's amazing.'

'I, I recognise the car. I mean – the type. But I never knew anyone with a car like that. At least not that I can remember.'

Remember. How often she used that word. How useless it was.

Nixon continued the narrative. 'When the emergency people got there they found you in the vehicle and a young man lying beside it. It was very quickly established that he was dead but that you were still alive, although very seriously injured. They couldn't free you on their own because your legs were trapped so a fire tender was sent for and they used cutting gear to get you out.'

He stopped to drink some of his coffee. 'Now, when the medical examiner got a look at Paul Everett—'

'By the way, who identified him?' Maginnis butted in. The two officers gave him a sharp glance. 'Sorry,' he said. 'Didn't mean to interrupt.'

Nixon answered anyway, taking a second to check the file. 'Well, they found ID on him, driving licence and so on, and established that he was the owner of the car, then they notified Vectra and the head of personnel came down to the morgue. Miss Winter here was identified by documents, too. Her hospital identity card, her licence as well. They were found in her handbag.'

Meg listened to them, detached. She couldn't associate herself with any of it. It was as if they were talking about somebody else.

Nixon said: 'Everett had some minor injuries from the actual accident. He seems to have been lucky up to a point, if you know what I mean, in that the crash itself didn't kill him. But the medical examiner very quickly discovered that he had sustained severe trauma to the head, inconsistent with the accident but totally consistent with being beaten with a heavy object. In short, the back of his skull was smashed.'

Meg felt a shiver at the back of her neck.

'With what, we don't know,' Nixon added. 'No weapon was ever found.'

Gilmour came in. 'It had been raining heavily that night. By the time the police realised they had a murder on their hands instead of a fatal road traffic accident, the emergency services – the ambulance team, the firemen, not to mention the police themselves – all of them had been tramping over the scene, destroying any kind of evidence there might have been, like footprints and so on. Not very good.'

'The postmortem examination of Everett revealed that he'd been drinking,' Nixon said, 'but it also revealed strong traces of cocaine in his system. Our drugs squad got interested. They'd been hearing rumours about an American doing a bit of business on the local scene. They searched his home and the dogs sniffed out more. Not a huge quantity, mind. Looked like it was for personal use.'

'I don't know anything about any of this,' Meg said. 'I know nothing about cocaine. I've never used it in my life. I don't know anyone who has.'

She felt a bit agitated. She twisted Maginnis's pen in her fingers.

Gilmour spoke, her voice soft, calming. 'It's all right, Meg. We're not trying to put you on the spot. We don't think this had anything to do with you directly. There was certainly no cocaine as far as you're concerned, that's not in question. But both you and the dead man had had a lot to drink. Are you aware of that?'

She nodded.

'That was a bit of a problem which the doctors had to navigate when they were trying to operate on you. When the accident happened you'd have been at least twice the legal limit for driving.'

Meg's palms were moist. 'I don't remember,' she said in a whisper.

'You're sure?' Nixon said. It was a reflex response.

'Of course she's sure,' Maginnis snapped. 'What sort of a question is that?'

'I didn't intend—' Nixon began.

Maginnis did not let him finish. 'You're already aware that Dr Winter's suffering from a loss of memory. I've given you a summary of the psychologist's report. What Dr Winter – Meg – has is a form of what is known as psychogenic amnesia, which has most likely been brought on by extremely traumatic events which have quite simply been obliterated from her mind. If she says she can't remember, then you're just going to have to take her word for it because she's telling you the truth.'

Nixon said nothing. Gilmour gave Meg an understanding smile. 'I'm sorry. We're not trying to put any undue pressure on you but we do have to ask these questions. This is a murder case; a young man brutally beaten to death. We have to find out what we can.'

'Believe me, I'd like to find out more, too,' Meg said. 'I'm just as much in the dark as you are.' She looked at Maginnis, grateful for his sudden forthright defence of her, but surprised by it as well. She had never heard him raise his voice like that.

'Then are you happy to go on?' Gilmour asked.

She nodded.

Nixon started again. 'When the police talked to the Jacksons, they said that when they went back to the scene after they'd made their phone call, they thought they saw a light for a time, coming from where the wrecked car was lying. But then it disappeared. Mrs Jackson said she thought she heard a noise but in the darkness she couldn't see. She called out but no one answered and then the emergency services arrived shortly after that.'

'What about the other car?' Meg wondered. 'The one that drove . . . *us* . . . off the road.'

'Still a mystery,' Nixon said. 'The Jacksons didn't get a number and they didn't see the make, except they both thought it was a biggish car. But no one's ever had any luck tracing it.'

Meg thought of something. 'What were those people doing on the road so late?'

'Mrs Jackson owned a shop in Lisburn,' Nixon explained. 'The burglar alarm had gone off and the police had called her. Her husband didn't want her going out on her own so he had driven her over there to get the thing switched off and they were heading home again to the Saintfield Road where they lived. This would have been the most direct route, along the back roads.'

He stopped and closed the file, then put it down on the table with what seemed to Meg like an air of finality.

Gilmour took over. 'There are several ways of looking at this. One is that the car drove the MGB off the road by accident and then fled the scene. Not very probable, given what subsequently happened to the unfortunate Mr Everett, unless you think that someone just happened to be waiting in the bushes at the time, knowing that's where he was going to crash, or happened to be passing and decided on the spur of the moment to kill him. Hardly likely, wouldn't you say? The second possibility is that the presence of this other car wasn't a coincidence, that the killer was in it, that he ran you off the road, whether by accident or design, then went back and, well, you know the rest.'

She didn't really. That was the trouble.

'So now we come to your movements and those of Paul

Everett that night,' Nixon said. 'We have some idea of what your intentions were: where you planned to be. Your friend Elizabeth Maguire helped.'

Elizabeth.

Elizabeth had told the police what she knew about that night. Dr Sands had mentioned that fact to her and at the time Meg had felt a sudden sense of betrayal which she knew was totally irrational. But now she felt it again.

Gilmour explained. 'She contacted us after it happened. One of the officers on the case interviewed her. It's all in the file. You called her that night, round about seven, wondered if she fancied going somewhere for a drink. You told her you'd had a hell of a day and you needed to go somewhere where you could let your hair down. You said you'd been looking in the paper and there was some kind of music thing down at the Clarendon Dock.'

Meg gave her a blank look.

'It's along near the ferry terminals. There's a couple of bars there, very popular, the Rotterdam at one end and Pat's Bar at the other. There's an open space in front. Barrow Square, they call it. They have open air concerts.'

'And did I go?' Meg asked. It felt weird posing a question to which she, more than anyone else, should have the answer.

'We don't know for certain,' Gilmour said.

'If I did, it was the first time. I'm sure of that.'

Gilmour nodded. 'Well, that's more or less what Miss Maguire said, too. Neither of you had ever been, which is why you suggested giving it a go. You arranged to meet there at nine thirty. What happened after that, we don't know. Your friend Elizabeth didn't go, as it turns out, and so we don't know whether you did or not.'

'Elizabeth said some boyfriend or other came by,' Nixon added. 'She said she called you at home but you'd already gone. She also tried both of the bars to see if you were there but it was hopeless. All she could hear was the music drowning everything out. Nobody would take a message or try to look for somebody they'd never heard of. So, as far as Miss Maguire's end of the story's concerned, that's it – oh except that when she was asked about Paul Everett she said she'd never heard of him.'

'O'Malley,' Meg corrected. 'She's Mrs O'Malley now.'

'When did you last see her?' Gilmour asked.

'I can't recall.' She gave a little smile. 'Now isn't that a surprise?'

'So you see,' Nixon said, 'we've no idea whether you went to the Clarendon Dock or not. As soon as your friend told the police, they went down there and talked to the bar staff but nobody remembered you. There would have been a couple of hundred people milling about that night. It was needle-in-a-haystack stuff.'

'And Paul Everett,' Maginnis wondered. 'Was he there?'

'Possible,' Gilmour said, 'although nobody could say for certain about him either. What's definitely known is that he was at a dinner in the Europa Hotel, a business thing for a visiting United States Senator. A lot of American executives working over here were invited. It broke up around eleven thirty and everybody went home. Nobody knows what happened to Everett after that. But according to those who were there he seemed fine when he left. No one seems to know a whole lot about his personal life, who he mixed with. He lived on his own. He had a nice apartment in a converted old farmhouse near Ballinderry in County Antrim, not too far from the factory and handy for the airport, too. He did a lot of travelling back and forth between here and the States. And of course his company shipped a lot of stuff to and fro. It would have been a convenient cover for his cocaine supplies.'

'He could have gone down to the Clarendon Dock after he left the Europa,' Nixon said. 'We just don't know.'

'Although we've no hard evidence,' Gilmour said, 'we tend to go along with the gut instinct of the officers who investigated at the time. Our theory is that somehow you met Everett, probably at the Clarendon Dock, and unfortunately you got caught up in something that was nothing to do with you.' She shrugged. 'Someone was after Everett, maybe, some drugs-related dispute most likely, outstanding debts, whatever, and he was trying to get away from them when he was run off the road. So, even though you're alive and well, we're no further on than we were four years ago and we won't be unless or until you regain your memory.'

Meg looked at them. In their faces she could see no real concern as to whether they solved this case or not. She thought about what Gilmour had just said.

'But nobody knows that. Outside this room, nobody knows that. The person who killed Paul Everett doesn't know that. You saw the photograph in the paper, what it said. He'll think I'm telling you everything that happened. What if he comes after me to shut me up?'

Nixon tried to reassure her. 'I don't think that's likely to happen.'

'How can you say that? How can you say that for certain?'

'We'll keep an eye on you,' Gilmour said and smiled.

'Oh really? When I'm in here maybe. But what happens when I get out? You can't possibly watch over me then. Don't pretend that you can.'

They said nothing for a few moments, sitting awkwardly with her indignation. She looked at the three of them, thinking that she was in the hands of two police officers half-heartedly working an old case that wasn't theirs and a physician who for all his apparent concern saw her merely as an object, some kind of medical phenomenon, a trophy.

And how else did he view her, she wondered.

Ultimately these people were just doing a job. They didn't care, not really, about what happened to her.

She felt alone and vulnerable. 'There has to be a way,' she said to no one in particular.

'Of what?' Maginnis asked.

She pointed towards the window. 'Of telling whoever's out there that I'm no threat to him.'

Nine

Brenda Brennan, 'BB' to the senior people in the company, 'Miss Brennan' to all the rest, was at her desk at seven a.m. as usual.

She had been coming to work at that early hour for the past thirty years, first as the young secretary to Brian Malone, when he was an up-and-coming property developer and estate agent, now as the personal assistant to his son, Christopher, the chief executive of Malone Group.

There was something about being in the building when no one else was there. It felt like a private domain of which she was in control. In the quietness she could order her thoughts and her papers, prepare for the day. Or, as was becoming more frequently the case, steel herself for it.

She did not mind being alone; much of her life was solitary. She had been married once, a long time ago and briefly, but that had been a mistake. Her job was what mattered most to her and it was a job which would not tolerate conflicting demands on her life and her loyalty. So she had made her decision. Here was where her affections lay.

But of late she had begun to have doubts.

She made coffee for herself. It was the only time during the day when she did so. The girls in the outer office would take over that task but they would not be here until eight fifteen.

She stood cradling the warm mug, breathing its aroma, as she looked out of the window. The Malone Group headquarters was in Belfast city centre in what had once been a sooty old corner building erected by an austere Victorian insurance company. But in an extensive restoration operation some years ago the grime of a century had been power-washed away to reveal the warmth of the russet sandstone underneath. Now it stood proud and revitalised, an ancient hero among the upstarts of glass and steel.

The chief executive's suite of offices took the whole top floor. From the windows on one side, Brenda could look out on to the dome of the City Hall, green and streaked by time and weather, and from another she could look down the thoroughfares that led to the waterfront. She saw the traffic building from a trickle to a metallic stream, watched red double-decker buses decanting Lowry figures onto the pavements.

The softness of the early morning light was beginning to sharpen but Brenda did not feel herself brightening with it.

Maybe she should finally admit to herself that at fifty three she was getting too old for this game. She did not need the salary. She was comfortably off, she had a good portfolio of investments, a house which would make a substantial profit if she chose to sell it and move somewhere smaller, and there was her Malone Group pension to come. She could take early retirement any time she liked and she did not believe that Christopher would stand in her way. In fact, he might be glad to see her go; it was getting hard to tell with him.

But then, she reflected, maybe she was not the problem at all.

When he had taken over as chief executive several years ago, she had felt certain that he would be a youthful version of what had gone before, not that Brian had for one second ever lost the spring in his step. Hardly. He was a player on a world stage now. He was *Sir* Brian Malone, the tycoon.

He had stayed as chairman, keeping close to his roots, even though Malone Group was a tiny grain of sand in a business empire that now included banking, newspapers and television stations in the United States and Canada where he spent most of his life.

Christopher had persuaded her to stay in the job she had done so long and so well, even though she had volunteered to step aside so that he could appoint his own PA if he wished. He would not hear of it. He had insisted on maintaining her as that vital link between his father's stewardship and his own. But no matter how affectionately he put it, it was not a decision based on sentiment or loyalty; she was under no illusions about that. He needed her because she was bloody good at her job. No one could do it better.

At first it had been fine. He had a bright business brain, an instinct for profitable development and he had attracted a handful of new and youthful executives made from the same mould as himself. But very soon he had begun to change. Most of that fresh team had gone now, exhausted, either sacked or else driven out by the ferocious style of a boss who could not tolerate seeing any of his managers with both feet on the ground at the same time.

Brenda had watched the confident veneer crack and peel and even she herself had felt the sharp end of his rage once or twice.

But she had not allowed it to wound her. She had been employed by a tougher man than this.

Christopher's father could get angry, too. Yet in all the years of working with him she had always known that it would be only temporary, soon forgotten. It was never personal, there was never any spite in it, nor was she ever in any doubt about Brian Malone's ability to overcome whatever crisis had sparked it and to move on to new and greater achievements.

The son was different. Stress drove him and it clung like a wet shirt to everyone around him.

All of which had created an unstable environment, made worse by a couple of dubious acquisitions which had not entirely worked but which had been off-loaded quickly before becoming a profit drain.

Then he had recovered his poise with an audacious proposal to take over an ailing leisure group. It had required all his powers of persuasion to swing the board behind him but he had done it with the aid of a very thorough business plan.

It had worked, too. The leisure division seemed to be thriving and the market appeared to smile on it. But here, on this lofty plateau above the city, Brenda was sensing the first cool breath of a wind that was beginning to change direction.

She heard what was being said. She wondered, as she knew the market and then the directors and the shareholders would soon wonder, if too much of the powerful energies of Malone Group and its chief executive were being channelled in one direction. Confidential assessments passed across her desk, documents that he seemed to ignore, and they hinted that the rest of the group's activities were not flowing as vigorously as they should. Stagnation was a real risk.

She turned from the window. Christopher was obsessed with this leisure business. She picked up a folder. Here was another example of it, the papers for a meeting at nine o'clock at which he would talk about his idea of buying a chain of cinemas. She would sit in on the session and take the notes, watching the new clutch of wan-faced young executives squirm under his bullying interrogation if any part of their preparation did not come up to scratch.

Sometimes she wished one of them would stand up to him, just get to their feet and tell him not to talk to them like that, but no one ever did. They got paid a lot of money to put up with this abuse and some of the men had wives and families to support.

If anyone ever did tell him where to get off, it would be a woman, Brenda reckoned. Only a woman would have the balls.

Then why didn't she do it herself? She gave a little smile. Life was too short. This, too, will pass.

Occasionally she wondered if Christopher would have been any different if his marriage had not broken up. There had been a son. His wife had remarried and she lived in London now. He hardly ever saw the boy. But then he had not seen much of him before the divorce, either.

It had been his own fault. As well as working hard, he threw himself into his chosen recreational activities with exactly the same enthusiasm. The list had included squash, tennis, sailing, drink and women.

Only the last two had survived and now they were getting the better of him. His heavy looks were over-ripe. When he had turned forty a while ago, a lot of people had been surprised to find that he had not passed that milestone already.

She looked at her watch. Seven thirty. He would be on his way from his home in County Antrim, sitting in the back of the car buried in the newspapers which his driver had brought. Lately, he got the lot, not just the heavyweights like the *Financial Times* or the *Daily Telegraph* but the red-top tabloids, too, and he scoured them every day before getting to work.

When he had finished, her phone would ring and she would take down instructions about the day and details of calls for her to make straight away. Sometimes the car was pulling into the parking bay at the rear of the building and he had not reached the end of the list.

She turned on the radio. Terry Wogan was playing the Bee Gees on Radio 2. She poured another coffee.

She had finished it and he still had not phoned.

She checked her watch again. Seven forty-five. He would be here at any minute.

But no call. That was odd.

The phone rang.

'Miss Brennan?' It was not him. Instead, she recognised the voice of Damian, his driver.

'Damian?'

'Yes, miss.'

She was puzzled. 'Where are you? Everything all right?'

'I'm not sure.' He was speaking very quietly on the car phone and she could hardly hear him against the engine noise. 'I'm just pulling into the back of the building. Look – could you come down?'

She did not say anything. She hung up and headed for the lift. So far she had been the only one to use it today and it had stayed at her floor. When she got to the ground, she turned left and out through the rear door that led to the private car park.

Damian was bringing the big BMW in. The shutter was rattling down behind him at an unruffled electronic pace. Other people would be arriving soon but at the moment the only other car here was her own, an Alfa Romeo saloon.

As Damian pulled into the chief executive's space, she hurried towards him. He got out. He was a man of about thirty five, athletic and fit enough to be a bodyguard, which was one of the reasons he had this job. He looked anxious.

'What's wrong?' she asked him.

'I don't know. It's the boss. He . . .'

She pulled the rear door open, noticing for a moment that the pile of newspapers was untouched on the seat. Christopher Malone sat beside them, his briefcase open on his lap. Documents from it were strewn on the floor. His head lay back against the seat. His face was red, blotchy. Round the bridge of his nose the broken veins seemed lit up.

For a second she thought that he was dead. Then she saw that his eyes were wide open and that tears were pouring down his cheeks.

'Christopher?' she said. She never called him that. Usually, she did not call him anything.

He lifted his head and turned to her. She saw desolation in his face, raw fear in his glistening eyes.

'BB,' he sobbed. 'Help me. I can't handle this any more.'

Ten

Two weeks after the visit from the police, another newspaper story appeared. It was in the *Belfast Telegraph* and this time it did not alarm her.

Not when it was her own doing.

She had discussed the idea with her father and Maginnis. Together. She tried to avoid situations where she might be alone with the Chief Executive. Just in case.

Maginnis had put his people's public relations office to work negotiating with the paper for what they were now describing as an 'exclusive'. Meg had said no to an interview or a picture so they had used an old shot of her that had been supplied to the police by her parents at the time of the accident.

But there was a photograph, a brand new one, of Maginnis, who had made himself available to a *Telegraph* photographer. In it he affected a look that he hoped would show him to be wise and authoritative.

It was the sort of story which journalists loved and assumed that their eager readers also did. Since the *Telegraph* had it to themselves they had splashed it across the front page with two big banner headlines:

COMA GIRL IN MEMORY BLACK-OUT

The woman who is a living link to a bizarre unsolved murder is suffering from amnesia, the *Belfast Telegraph* has learned.

Former doctor Meg Winter (30) who miraculously came out of a four-year coma six months ago remembers nothing about the murder of 27 year-old US business executive Paul Everett whose battered body was found lying beside the wreckage of his sports car.

Miss Winter was discovered in the passenger seat with very serious injuries.

The *Telegraph* has also learned that the police have been to interview her at Musgrave Rehabilitation Centre where she is undergoing an extensive course of treatment.

Musgrave Chief Executive Liam Maginnis said today: 'Miss Winter is making good progress. Physically she is getting stronger and she does not have any brain damage. But she is suffering from what is known as psychogenic amnesia as a result of a great trauma.

'It is similar to what happens to soldiers who have been exposed to horrific events on the battlefield and can no longer remember these experiences.'

He said it was possible that Dr Winter's memory of what happened that night might never return.

A police spokesman confirmed that two officers had visited her but would not comment further.

The rest of it consisted of some more quotes from Maginnis and a rehash of everything that had gone before.

Nowhere did it say that she didn't even know who Paul Everett was. Maybe that should have gone in, too. Still, the article made her breathe more easily. For the first time in weeks she did not feel as if someone was looking over her shoulder.

But there were other feelings now.

Guilt. That was one of them. She was alive; Everett was dead. Someone somewhere would have mourned him. His parents. A girlfriend, perhaps.

She agonised over everything Gilmour and Nixon had told her about the events of that night, although she kept her thoughts to herself and did not discuss them with anyone. The police were stuck on this drugs-related theory because that was all they had. Like them, she had thought of herself as someone caught up inexplicably in events that had nothing to do with her. But as the days passed she had begun to wonder, more and more, what if that was wrong? What if all this *did* have something to do with her?

She felt hungry to know and at the same time afraid of finding out.

Nothing they had told her had made the slightest bit of difference to her memory, yet she knew instinctively that everything they had said was important. Somewhere in it there were answers.

A door was ajar in a dark place. She could not see it but she could feel its draught. What had she been doing that night? Hanging around some dockland place, drunk? She saw Everett's photograph in her mind. The youthful smile seemed to tease her. He was the key.

Just below her window there was a secluded grassy patch

with a garden seat and a bed of peonies.

Elizabeth came to visit her the day the story appeared. She brought her daughter, two-year-old Catriona, a pretty little thing with auburn curls. Since it was a fine June afternoon the ward sister suggested they might like to sit outside.

Meg had changed but she hadn't expected Elizabeth to look so different.

She had always been attractive but now she was decidedly glamorous. Her hair was blacker than Meg remembered, and cut expensively. She wore a sleeveless shift dress in blue silk, open-toed Chanel shoes and sunglasses with Gucci frames. Rings glittered and a gold rope at her neck caught the sun.

Meg thought she looked like something from the pages of *Hello*, a magazine with which hospital life was making her increasingly familiar. But the image was slightly marred by the large canvas shoulder-bag she carried.

They hugged eagerly and grinned at each other, then began to talk at once.

'I can't believe it's really—'

'You look so different—'

They laughed and hugged some more. Elizabeth reached into the bag and got a small carton of orange juice which she handed to Catriona.

'Look at all the stuff you have to carry around.' She held the bag open for Meg to see. It held all the support materials for a two-year-old: a box of tissues, wipes, creams, a plastic, non-spill drinking cup, spare pants, a cherished teddy, goodness knows what else. 'That's my handbag these days.'

'Prada?' Meg asked with a grin.

'Hardly.' She turned to help Catriona stick a straw into the carton. Meg couldn't help staring. She seemed, well, heavier or something, more voluptuous.

Elizabeth saw the look. She smiled and stood up, then she faced Meg and cupped her hands under the curve of her breasts.

'So what do you think?'

'Of what?'

'My new tits. I had them done. Marvellous, aren't they?'

Meg stared, wide-eyed, and struggled for words. 'Well . . . yes . . . they're . . . they're amazing. I'd been wondering.'

'You always had an advantage on that score,' Elizabeth laughed. 'Not any more, I see, you poor thing. Let me have a look at you.'

Meg spread her arms like thin, featherless wings. She was wearing baggy tracksuit bottoms and a t-shirt with a shuttlecock and 'Musgrave Badminton Club' printed on it. They had found a baseball cap from somewhere to shield her from the sun.

Elizabeth's face changed. 'Oh Meg,' she said. 'I'm so sorry.' She bent forward and hugged her friend again. Meg felt a kind of desperation in the embrace. 'Everything you've been through.'

She sat and they talked for a bit, small talk at first, while Catriona roamed among the flowers. As they chatted, Meg could sense herself being assessed and she knew that her friend was trying to figure out whether any mental as well as physical change had taken place.

They talked at last of the crash and Meg's four lost years.

'I just can't believe it,' Elizabeth said, 'that you can't remember anything about that night. Nothing at all?'

'Nothing.'

Elizabeth glanced round to see what Catriona was doing.

'No, not the big flowers, darling, the little ones, the daisies. That's it. Good girl.'

She turned back. 'You need eyes in the back of your head.'

'She's lovely,' Meg said.

Elizabeth seemed to consider the notion. 'You think so?'

'Of course. She's a beautiful child.'

Elizabeth said, 'When I heard about the accident, the next morning, I didn't know what to do. I was in a state of shock. And then I pulled myself together and realised I had to go to the police.'

All at once she looked upset.

'I know,' Meg said. 'You did the right thing.'

She took Elizabeth's hand. It was hot, the palm damp.

'I went to see you in the hospital. It was awful just watching you lying like that. I used to go when your parents weren't there. I didn't want to intrude. Then they moved you to that Knockvale place. I went there once, after the wedding, just before I went away. I found it very upsetting, the thought that you might be that way – you know, forever. Or that they might decide . . .'

Meg put her arm round her. Elizabeth shook her head to clear whatever image was in it. 'When you called me that night it was such a surprise. I hadn't heard from you for months. And there you were on the phone, asking me to come out to play, talking about this Clarendon Dock place which neither of us had ever been to. You said you'd had a bad day and you felt like going out somewhere, having some fun. You also said you'd something to tell me but when I asked what it was, you said it would wait until you saw me.' She looked at Meg. 'I suppose I'll never know now, will I?'

71

'Maybe not.'

For a moment Meg pictured Paul Everett's face in the photograph, the smile that would last forever. Was he what she had wanted to talk about?

'I'd been wondering what you were up to,' Elizabeth said, her mood brightening. 'I'd called you a couple of times but you were always busy, always otherwise occupied.' She looked at Catriona then turned back and whispered. 'I thought he might be married.'

'Who?'

'Whoever you were seeing. Well, you had to be seeing someone, hadn't you? That's usually the reason for somebody dropping off the scene like that. Meeting in secret. Can't be seen together.'

Everett had not been married.

'Had I ever mentioned anyone?' Meg asked.

'No but like I said, we hadn't seen each other for a while.'

'When was the last time?'

'Let me see . . . Easter maybe. No, before that. March. Maybe even February, come to think of it. A lot could have happened in that time.'

'We hadn't fallen out?'

'Of course not. Don't be silly. We don't fall out. We go our separate ways sometimes, do our own thing, but we don't fall out. You know that.'

Meg smiled as if she understood.

'Anyway,' Elizabeth said, 'I thought it would be good to see you so I agreed to meet you at about nine thirty.'

'But you didn't go.'

'No, I got a better offer.'

She stuck her arm into the bag like it was a bran tub and rummaged around until she found a folder of photographs. Meg waited as she sifted through them, finally selecting one particular picture. It was a shot of a pleasant-looking man in his early thirties with sandy hair and glasses. He wore morning dress and a satisfied smile on his big day.

'Vincent O'Malley. The better offer.'

But Meg thought she said it without much conviction.

'Your husband. So this is him?'

'Yes.'

She selected some more photographs and passed them across. Meg thought Elizabeth looked beautiful in them. Dark-eyed. A great smile. More at ease with herself than she was now, despite all the expensive plumage.

There was one in particular, of Elizabeth on her own under a

72

tree. Meg held it up so that she could see. 'You look fantastic there.'

Elizabeth stared at it, then began to cry.

Meg put the pictures down and put her arm round Elizabeth's shoulder again. 'It'll be all right,' she said.

Whatever it was.

Elizabeth took a crumpled tissue from the bag. There was a smear of chocolate on it. She blew her nose.

Catriona looked at them with a child's curiosity, squinting her eyes against the sun.

'She'll get too hot,' Elizabeth said. 'There's a hat.' She began to search the bag again.

'It's OK,' Meg said. 'Let me.' She found it quickly, a little cotton thing with a thin brim and sailboats round it. She lifted Catriona onto her knee and put it on. 'There we go.' She gave her a kiss on the cheek, set her down again and saw that Elizabeth had been studying them.

'How did you meet him in the first place?' Meg asked.

'I was attending to some client investments. I had to go to Dublin for meetings and he was at a couple of them. One thing led to another.'

She stood abruptly, as if the seat had become uncomfortable, and began to pace up and down on the grass.

'Oh, you know the way we used to be with men. Just a bit of fun, no long-term attachments. A trail of conquests in our wake.' She waved her arm in an extravagant gesture.

Meg tried to remember but didn't succeed.

'Vincent was different. He pursued me – *wooed* me, really. I became very fond of him.' It struck Meg that she did not use the word *love*. 'I'd have told you about him that night. But then, some time before nine, just as I was getting ready to go, he turned up unexpectedly. Champagne and flowers. Sometimes it works, you know. I couldn't send him away. Didn't want to. So I told myself that since you hadn't bothered about me for ages, then too bad.'

'Probably what I deserved,' Meg said. 'But you tried to phone me, just the same.'

Elizabeth sighed and sat down again. 'Conscience. I wouldn't just leave you in the lurch. The trouble was you'd already gone. I tried those bars but that was hopeless. And eventually, as the night wore on, I really didn't care.' She gave a coy smile.

The *Belfast Telegraph* was on the grass. Meg had been reading it before Elizabeth arrived. She lifted it and showed her the headline. 'Did I ever talk about him: Paul Everett?'

Elizabeth shook her head. 'No. The police asked me the same

thing. It wasn't a name I knew.' She thought for a second. 'Of course, you mightn't have known him before that night. Maybe he was there and you picked him up.'

Picked him up.

'It's just an expression,' she said, noticing Meg's look. 'The men like to think *they* pick *you* up, don't they. It flatters their little egos.' She paused. 'Oh, come on, Meg.' There was a rasp of irritation in her voice. 'This is me you're talking to. You were no shrinking violet, darling. You were the girl who always had the condoms in the handbag in case you got lucky. Remember?'

Her eyes flashed. Meg fell silent. She was ill at ease with Elizabeth's lurching changes of mood and a little startled by what she had just said.

Condoms in the handbag in case she got lucky.

Her handbag.

The police had said her identity had been established from documents found in it. She had forgotten about the bag. Her mother had all her things. She would have the bag, too, whatever bag it was, and she would undoubtedly have looked inside. What would she have found?

'Did you tell the police this – this theory about Everett and me? That we might have been ships passing in the night?'

'I think maybe they saw the possibility themselves.'

'What did they ask you?'

Elizabeth looked evasive. 'All sorts of stuff. I don't really remember. It was a long time ago.' She thought. 'They asked me what you were like.'

'What I was like?'

'Yes. What sort of a person you were.'

'And what did you tell them?'

'That you were nice, a good friend.' She gave a weak smile that could not mask the guilt.

Meg stared at her. 'What else?'

Elizabeth sighed. 'I told them you enjoyed going out and having a good time. They asked me if it was possible you might have gone off with someone you liked at the end of the evening, someone you didn't know before, and I said it was, although you wouldn't go off with just anybody.'

She avoided Meg's eyes.

'It sounds terrible now, when you ask me. I didn't mean it like that. I just meant that you enjoyed a bit of fun, meeting new people.'

Meg felt humiliated. Undermined by her best friend. But there was no point in getting angry about it, was there? The damage was done and Elizabeth would know from this awkward silence exactly how she felt.

This reunion was not what Meg had thought it would be. But she had wanted to find out more. Like it or not, that was exactly what was happening.

A handful of daisies and buttercups landed without ceremony in Elizabeth's silken lap.

'Oh darling they're lovely, thank you. Mummy'll put them in water when we get home.'

A thought. 'Where are you staying?' Meg asked.

'That's another thing,' Elizabeth said, sounding relieved by the shift in direction. 'I'd just decided to buy a new flat and I'd put the old one on the market. People had been ringing, making appointments to see round it. When the phone rang that night I thought it was another viewer. But it was you.'

'I don't understand—'

'I kept the new flat in the end, didn't sell it. It's down by the river at Stranmillis. Vincent and I, we thought it would appreciate in value and it would be somewhere to have when we came home to visit. He has a house in Dublin. We kept that, too. I've had tenants at Stranmillis, on and off. My brother keeps an eye on the place for me.' Carefully she brushed away little grains of soil which had fallen from the flowers onto her dress. 'What about you? Are you going back to Truesdale Street when they let you out?'

'Let me out? You make it sound like a prison. They're very nice here, as a matter of fact, but no, I won't go home straight away. They don't want me to be on my own just yet. I've agreed to move in with my mother for a short while.'

'You're doing what?' Elizabeth looked amazed. 'Did I hear you right? Your mother?'

'What's so odd?'

'I thought you hated your mother.'

Meg raised her eyebrows. 'No – I don't hate her.' She paused. 'Granted, she can be difficult to love sometimes but I don't hate her.'

'I'd have thought hers was the last place in the world you'd want to go to. You used to talk about her with such venom. I can't imagine the real Meg moving in with her.'

They stared at each other.

The words hung in the air. There was a silence all around them.

Elizabeth spoke first. 'God, I'm sorry, Meg. I didn't mean to put it like that. That was dreadful.' Then she thought. 'But I suppose, I suppose that's it, that's what's so strange. You don't –

75

you don't seem like Meg – my Meg. The old Meg. You're different.'

'I look different, I know that.'

Elizabeth shook her head. 'It's not just your appearance. It's your attitude. This thing has changed you. You used to be brash, a bit too loud sometimes. You were always so driven, so impatient. For example, you wouldn't have been content to sit here, in this hospital, saying polite things about the people. You'd want to get out of this place. And children: you wouldn't take them under your notice, not like the way you've been with Catriona. And now this business with your mother. It's not like you.'

Meg frowned. 'But it is me,' she insisted. 'I don't know what I was like before. Some of the things you've told me – I feel like you're talking about a different person. All I know is . . .' she prodded herself with a forefinger, '. . . this is me. This is the way I am.'

She felt tense. There was a tightness in her chest.

A nurse appeared and interrupted the moment, much to their mutual relief.

'I think maybe you should come in soon,' she said. 'It's quite hot out here. We don't want you getting too much sun. I'll give you five more minutes.' She went again.

'You look done in,' Elizabeth said.

'Yes.' Meg found that her voice was trembling slightly. 'I'm going to have to go in and rest for a while. I'm sorry.'

'It's my fault, getting you all wound up like that.'

Meg smiled a tired smile. 'Will you come again? How long are you planning to stay?'

Elizabeth's face changed. 'I'm not sure.' She muttered it.

'You're not sure?'

Elizabeth took her sunglasses off and stared at her hands in her lap. Catriona skipped up and leaned on Meg's knee. The hat had come off and she had decided that this was her job. Meg put it back on for her.

'It was fine at first,' Elizabeth said quietly. 'A new country, exciting, a lovely house which Vincent's company was paying for. Lots of money for nice things. I got pregnant practically straight away. And then the problems started. It was a difficult pregnancy, as they say.' She mimed quotation marks in the air with her fingers. 'My blood pressure shot up and so did my weight. I was retaining fluid, all the usual things that can happen. Vincent goes out to work at seven in the morning and isn't home much before eight at night. There were other Brit wives around, of course, but they didn't want to be bothered with a fat lump with swollen ankles who had to keep her feet up all day.'

She took Catriona's limp flowers and began idly entwining them into a chain.

'The birth was unbelievable. Eight hours in labour. Vincent was in Hong Kong at the time, too. I'll never say another word about the British health service again, believe me. Afterwards I got post-natal depression pretty bad. It took me ages to lose the weight. Vincent hired a nurse to come in, more to keep an eye on me than Catriona, I think.'

She looked at Meg. The sun was in her eyes. She put her hand over them like a visor. 'I just regretted the whole thing. Vincent, marriage, Malaysia, everything.' She glanced towards the child. 'Even her, sometimes, God forgive me. I'm not the world's most natural mother. And I was angry with you.'

'With me?'

'Yes. You'd left me. I couldn't talk to you, tell you how I felt. I had no one. I even thought that maybe if I'd told you about Vincent, you might have talked me out of it. I wished you had. Now he's talking about having more children. But there's no way.' She shook her head. 'Not after what I went through with her. He says she'll get lonely. Lonely? He doesn't know what it means. Living out there. I hate that damned place.'

Her voice trailed off. Meg waited.

Elizabeth took a deep breath. 'So,' she said, exhaling, 'I've . . . I've left him.'

'God, I'm sorry,' Meg said. 'I'm really very sorry.'

Elizabeth shrugged.

'How did he take it?'

Elizabeth said nothing. She looked uncomfortable. Meg frowned, then realised.

'Oh God, don't tell me he doesn't know?'

Eleven

'Peter, I was wondering,' Dan Cochrane began, 'when I get out of here—'

Quinn interrupted him. 'I know. Don't worry. I've got a proposition for you. That's why I've come today.'

Cochrane looked at him and waited.

His appeal had failed and he had done six months of his sentence. His release might be only weeks away.

They were on the same plastic chairs in the same visiting room at the prison where he had been on remand. Now he was a longer-term fixture but not as long as some. Other prisoners sat near them with wives, brothers, girlfriends. They talked morosely, dead-eyed. Nothing left to say.

'We're all ODCs,' Cochrane had told Quinn on a previous visit. 'Ordinary Decent Criminals. That's what they call us. No terrorists in here.'

Quinn peered at him. He seemed to have lost a bit of weight. The rough regulation cotton shirt hung loose on his frame.

Quinn had been a regular visitor, not just because he knew there was no one else who would bother. He was Cochrane's friend. He had helped him board up the shutters on his derelict life, sorting out financial matters, like his pay-off from the Education Board. The lease on his flat in Belfast had come to an end, too, and the landlord had wanted the place cleared. Quinn had dealt with everything.

'Something's come up,' he said. A broad grin gleamed through his beard. 'A wonderful opportunity for me. I've been awarded a grant by the Arts Council to go to Japan for eight months and study with one of the great potters. It's the thing I've always dreamed of. The grant isn't huge but it's something and with what savings I have of my own I can manage it. The problem is, I'll need someone to look after the business while I'm gone. Will you do it for me?'

Cochrane's eyes widened. 'Me? Peter, I don't know anything about running a shop.'

78

Quinn waved a hand, dismissing any suggestion that there might be a problem. 'It's not difficult. Jesus, if I can do it ... Now, I know they haven't given you a firm date yet but you'll be out of here at the end of July, the beginning of August at the latest. You need somewhere to stay. I've got the flat above the pottery and all your stuff from your old place is sitting in boxes in a corner of my storeroom anyway. As for running the shop, I'll show you everything before I go – there'll be plenty of time. All the extra stock for Christmas is in hand so you don't need to worry about that. I'll take you through the accounts, who the suppliers are, get you organised at the bank so that you can act legally, signing cheques and so on. There's the van, too. And your own car's sitting down in Ardglass. I taxed it for you. Oh and I'll pay you, of course. We'll agree a sum and you can draw on it when you need it. It won't be a fortune, mind, just some handy cash. I haven't got a lot to throw around. What do you say?'

Cochrane looked bewildered. He opened his arms wide. 'I don't know *what* to say. I'd been about to ask you if you'd put me up in your spare bedroom for a few weeks until I found my feet. This – this is totally unexpected. Why are you doing it?'

'It suits us both. You need a bit of help – I need somebody reliable.'

'Reliable? But Peter, look at me. I'm in jail, for God's sake. When I come out, I'll be an ex-prisoner. People see me behind the counter in the shop, they'll be aware of who I am. Ardglass is a small place, you know that. They'll run a mile. Are you sure this is a good idea? Wouldn't it be better to get a girl in or something?'

Quinn shook his head. 'With you living in the flat above the premises I'll feel a lot happier about being thousands of miles away in Japan. As for you being bad for business, well, very few of my customers are local anyway. They come from Belfast, Bangor, Downpatrick, as well as from across the border. They won't know who the hell you are. Anyway, I think some of my ladies might quite like you. The fact that you're young and not bad-looking won't do any harm.'

Cochrane smiled. 'And maybe I'll grow a beard.'

'There's one thing.' Quinn's glance hardened. 'I need to know that you've come to your senses, that you've dropped all this nonsense about that construction company, about Sam Winter.'

Cochrane fiddled with his fingernails. 'Yeah, well, six months in here has kind of sobered me up.' He looked up at Quinn. There was contrition in his face.

'So it's over and done with?'

79

'Dead and buried. I won't be setting fire to any more hotels.'

'Or anything else belonging to Seasons Construction, I hope.'

'I want to put it behind me, Peter. I can't say that being in here has changed the way I feel about those people but it's made me realise how stupid it is to think I can do anything about it.'

'I'm relieved,' Quinn said. 'Whatever happened to your mother's farm, it's done now. What's past is past. There's nothing to be gained by storing up hate. You only hurt yourself.'

Cochrane agreed. 'I lost my freedom. My sense of being an individual. All that was taken from me. I don't want to lose it again.'

Quinn sat back, rocking slowly on the spindly hind legs of the chair. He nodded his satisfaction. 'Then my friend,' he said with a smile, 'I reckon we have a deal.'

A nurse held Meg's arm as she walked through the main door of the Musgrave and into the late June sunshine.

It was her first trip out.

It would only be for a few hours but she was nervous.

If all went well today, she would start going out a couple of days a week, coming back in the evening, before leaving altogether sometime next month. The nurse had joked that this was her first day of parole.

There was so much space. Distance. She felt light-headed.

Her father was beside his Range Rover, standing almost to attention. She thought of the letter that was tucked in her pocket, that had been sent to her here, the letter that she would show him later. He marched forward to help but she gathered herself, straightening, holding her head up.

'It's all right,' she said, 'I can manage.'

'Are you sure?' the nurse said. Meg nodded.

Sam opened the passenger door and held her arm as she climbed in. The door closed behind her with a confident clunk. The Range Rover smelled warm and sweet. It mingled the odours of metal and leather, polish and rubber.

The picture of the wrecked, blood-coloured MGB flashed through her mind.

It was the first time she had been in a car since that night. She felt suddenly enclosed, trapped in this high, steel cocoon.

Her father got in. 'Ready?'

She swallowed her panic. 'Ready,' she said, then drew the safety belt across and clicked it into place.

He drove at breathtaking speed. 'Dad, don't go so fast,' she said and put her hand on his arm, gripping the sleeve of his jacket.

He glanced at her, puzzled. 'I'm only doing twenty miles an hour.'

She looked at the dial. It was true. 'Sorry,' she said. 'It just seemed—'

'Don't worry,' he told her. 'I'll take it easy. Everything's all right.'

But it was not all right.

They stopped at a red light at the end of Musgrave Park where it joined the hurly burly of Stockman's Lane. In front of her, kamikaze traffic hurtled by in both directions. Cars, container lorries, buses – it was overwhelming. The speed of it, the dreadful noise. She held her breath, waiting for them to crash.

A jabberwocky roared and rumbled past, earth-shaking. Its vertebrae were two rows of 4 x 4 Toyotas. She flinched and gripped the edges of her seat and her knuckles were white.

Her father looked anxiously at her. 'Are you OK?'

They had told her that at first she might suffer a mild form of agoraphobia but that it would pass. She tried to reassure herself with that but what she really wanted to do was fling open the door and run back as fast as she could to the safety of her little room.

She nodded. 'I'll be fine.'

The lights changed and he drove on, turning right up the hill towards the junction with the Lisburn Road.

'Where are we going?' she asked.

'Your house. Truesdale Street. I want you to see what I've done with it.'

'What do you mean?'

He gave her a conspiratorial smile and then winked. 'You'll see.'

They were in the traffic, in the middle of utter confusion. There were buses, cyclists with masks and satchels, motorbikes, delivery vans. Now that she looked at them, many of the cars were strange. There were models and shapes she had never seen before.

A few were trying to nose their way out of side streets. A small Ford was so far into the road that she was convinced they would clip it. Her right foot remembered what to do. It hit the floor, pressing hard on a phantom brake pedal.

'Driving,' she said.

'What?'

'Driving. I don't think I ever want to do it again.'

'Just give yourself time,' he said.

Time. Everyone wanted her to give herself time. Had they forgotten how much of it she had lost?

81

He slowed down as another set of lights went red. People crossed quickly in front of them, intent, all with their own sense of purpose. Why was everyone in such a hurry? Where were they all going? And who were they?

Had one of them killed Paul Everett? She stared, trying to see if she could read murder in the faces of strangers.

Her father moved off.

Along one side of the road, men were digging in a trench with the machine-gun rattle of a pneumatic drill. A sign explained that they were putting in gas pipes.

Further on, the doors of a big van were wide open and she could see sides of meat hanging in racks. Two men in white cotton caps were carrying a huge haunch of beef into a butcher's shop. Outside it an effigy of a jolly Edwardian victualler in moustache and striped apron gave them his fixed avuncular smile as they passed.

The shops. They were different. On this stretch alone there was a patisserie, a couple of smart, discreetly fronted clothes shops that were more like art galleries, their windows almost bare, and a florist of exotic appearance selling voracious-looking plants of bizarre shape. The new kids on the block. They rubbed shoulders with older residents: the hardware shop, the bicycle repair man, the antique dealer, the corner store that sold everything from crisps to coal.

'Tesco?' she queried, noticing a sign.

'All the big British chains are here now,' her father said. 'Tesco, Sainsbury, Safeway – they're all over the place. It's what the politicians are calling the peace dividend. I can't complain. The construction business is doing very nicely, I have to say.'

'No soldiers,' she noticed suddenly. 'I haven't seen an Army patrol.'

'Withdrawn to barracks. Twiddling their thumbs just in case this is only temporary and wholesale warfare breaks out again. There's the occasional eruption, of course, the annual atrocity, but mostly we're all managing to live together in what I suppose you could call an atmosphere of quiet mistrust.'

As they drove, there were restaurants she had not seen before either, with an array of ethnic choices, and there seemed to be a coffee shop every hundred yards or so, tables and chairs set outside under sun umbrellas.

'I can't believe all this,' she said. 'It's like another world.'

'It's not. It's the same old one with one or two changes. But you'll like it. You've come back at the right time.'

He made it sound like she had been out of the country, away somewhere on a long trip. She looked at him and smiled. She was beginning to feel calmer.

Something just ahead caught his eye. 'Hey, do you think you'd be up to a cup of coffee?' He glanced at her, then backtracked. 'Still, maybe that's a bit too much at this early—'

'No,' she said. 'I'd like that. A cup of coffee would be nice.'

They parked outside a delicatessen. He opened the door for her and she walked in, taking a mental deep breath. The place had metal-topped tables and chairs, like light alloy garden furniture. Tony Bennett was on the speakers and a coffee machine gasped loudly in a corner. There were shelves of olive oil and sauces, with salami, prosciutto, cheese and fresh salads cool in a display case.

They sat down. 'This isn't new,' she said. 'I think I remember this place.' She could smell the warm sweetness of fresh baking.

'No, it's been here a while.'

A waitress came. 'What can I get you?'

'Just coffee, I think,' Winter said.

'Me, too.'

'Any particular kind?' the waitress asked. 'Straight filter, cappuccino, espresso, latte, mocha—'

'Just the regular kind,' Winter said. 'One of those little jug things.'

'A cafetière?'

'That's it. For two.'

'What was all that?' Meg asked when the girl had gone.

'Oh, the coffee fad has taken off in the past couple of years. You ask for an ordinary cup of coffee now and you have to explain what you mean. I'm too old for all this nonsense, too set in my ways.'

'Surely not,' she smiled, teasing him. He was looking a lot better these days, perhaps even putting on a little weight. The weariness seemed to have lifted and there was colour in his cheeks. But even on a day off, he found it hard to relax. He sat across the table from her, in suit and sober tie, looking as if he should really be at an important meeting somewhere else.

She took in her surroundings.

Over at the window, three women with glossy lips and smart handbags were in an animated huddle about something very confidential indeed. One had bought new shoes. They were in a bag labelled 'Charles Jourdan'. An elderly couple, moneyed, clothes very county, ignored each other behind separate sections of *The Times*. Two young men were eating scones and jam and reading faxes. One of them was talking into the smallest mobile phone she had ever seen.

Tony Bennett sang over the top of it all:

I wanna be around to pick up the pieces . . .

Life was going on, as it had been doing for the past four years without her. People were wrapped in their own worlds. It was mundane, everyday, and part of her was thrilled by the ordinariness of it.

Another part of her thought of a crashed car and an unknown killer in the woods.

The coffee came and her father poured.

'You're sure you're OK about staying with your mother for a while?'

It was a question she hadn't been expecting; she had thought this was all settled.

'I think so. It'll just be for a couple of weeks, until I get my bearings. We did discuss it, remember. You said you wanted to spruce the house up a little, now that the tenants were out of it.'

He nodded but she thought his agreement was a bit reluctant.

'Is there anything wrong with that?'

'No,' he said, 'nothing. Your house is more or less ready now but I know it's a good thing for you to be with someone for a while. It's just that – I shouldn't say it – well, I'm suspicious of your mother's motives, that's all. She and I feel differently about the fact that you're back with us. She thinks it's all some sort of divine plan, that you've been spared for a purpose.'

'She's mentioned it.' She raised her eyes to heaven.

'I just worry that she'll want something from you, that she'll expect you to change.'

'I think maybe I *have* changed a bit.' She thought of Elizabeth's visit.

'You probably have,' he said.

'In what way? You've never said – but you must have come to some conclusion.'

He looked at her, thinking. 'It's lots of little things, I suppose. You're certainly a lot more – what's the word – *reflective*, I suppose you could say. Less impetuous.'

She gave a little laugh. 'Well, I've hardly had much of an opportunity to be that, have I?'

'Your mother ...' He was struggling, picking his words. 'When I talk about her expecting you to change, I mean – I think she's waiting for you to – you know, *choose the way of the Lord.*' He gave her a forlorn look. 'I just hope she doesn't try to put too much pressure on you to do anything you don't want to.'

'I'll be fine, Dad. I know what Mum's like. It's just for two weeks, to keep her happy. I think I can handle it.'

'You didn't always, you know. You're much more tolerant of her now than you used to be. That's another thing I've noticed. But that's good, of course. For both of you.' She had her hand on the table and he patted the back of it. 'I worry that she sees this as an opening. I don't want anything to distress you.'

'Well, let's wait and see what happens.'

She sipped her coffee. It was so much better than anything the Musgrave provided and with a touch of guilt she realised she felt a kind of liberation. She was outside, unconfined.

Dr Sands had been frank with her. He had told her there was a risk that people who had been in hospital for a long time could become institutionalised. Like long-sentence prisoners being released, they sometimes found it difficult to cope with a world where there were no walls, no barriers. She did not think that would apply to her. True, this afternoon she had experienced mild distress at first but she had recovered herself. Whatever problems, even dangers, lay ahead, this was preferable to what had gone before.

But now she had something to tell her father. She steeled herself for it, taking her glasses off and setting them on the table.

'Dad,' she said, 'I need to let you know about a couple of things. I've been doing an awful lot of thinking.'

'Let's hear it.'

'First of all, I want you to know I really appreciate everything you've done for me for all these years.'

He waved the sentiment away.

'No, listen,' she said, 'please. The cost of all of it – it must have been astronomical.'

'It wasn't a problem,' he insisted, shifting in his chair. 'Selling out to Malone Group left me very comfortable. The money was there. I'm your father. End of story.'

'Look, I don't want to embarrass you – I'm not going to make a speech.'

'Thank heavens for that,' he smiled.

'I just want you to know I'm conscious of the sacrifices you've made. You've been very good to me in other ways, too, looking after my financial affairs and everything. I know that for the time being I've no worries on that score but I've got to think further ahead. Like – what am I going to do with the rest of my life?'

She paused to sip her coffee, letting him work on the thought. 'It seems to me that there's one thing I've got to try – indeed that I *want* to try, very badly. I'm a properly qualified physician with several years experience. I've got to find out if I can pick it up again.'

'It won't be easy,' he said. 'With your background—'

'I know what you're going to say. I couldn't just walk into my old job, even if it was still there for me. Of course not. People will need a lot of convincing. All the stuff in the papers – they probably think I'm some sort of mental case. But I'm prepared to do whatever it takes.'

'So what have you in mind?'

'I've decided that when I get out and get settled, I'm going to make an appointment to go and see the head of emergency medicine at the New Central. I'll simply ask for advice about re-training and so on and we'll go from there. It'll be a start. What do you think?'

He was unsure. 'What if they say it's impossible, that there's no way you can practise again? I can't see the medical profession exactly welcoming you back with open arms, can you? You've got amnesia. What if you were to forget something else, at a crucial time, have a black-out during an operation or whatever?'

'Dad?' She raised her eyebrows. 'Come on, you know my amnesia's not like that. I've got to give this a chance. Don't write me off before I've even made the effort.'

He held up a hand. 'I'm not. I'm just putting myself in their shoes, seeing it from their point of view.'

'Well don't. Why can't you just see it from mine?'

They stared at each other.

'I'm sorry,' she said. 'I didn't mean to snap.'

'It's OK. I just want what's best for you, you know that.'

'There's something else.' She put her hand into her pocket and took out the letter she had brought. 'This was sent to me at the Musgrave.'

He opened it. It had Granada Television's letter heading.

'It's from a producer on a morning show,' she explained. 'They want to interview me. They want to take me to London and put me in the studio, talk to me about my experiences, what it's like to come back from the dead. You get the picture.'

'Oh, I certainly do. Bloody vultures,' he said, reading. 'We'll put it in the bin with all the others.'

'No, I think I'm going to do it.'

He looked up. 'What? You're not serious.' He saw that she was. 'God, Meg, I don't think that's a terribly good idea.'

She smiled. 'It's all right. I want to do it.'

'But why, for heaven's sake?'

'Well, for a start, if I do this one thing it might just get all the others off my back. The story we got into the *Telegraph* was all right as far as it went but I didn't feel up to doing an interview then and anyway print's different. They can twist things, re-write what you say. On a live TV show I can be myself and tell my story in my own words without anybody editing it. I need to talk about this, to get it all out in the open.'

'But why?' he tried again.

'All sorts of reasons. To let people see how normal I am, that I'm not a freak. It might even help me get a job.'

'Meg, this isn't wise. I don't want you to do it. I have to insist. God, just now I was saying you weren't impetuous any more. Have you any idea how stressful appearing on television is at the best of times? But for you, just coming out of hospital, it could be disastrous. Does Liam Maginnis know about any of this?'

'No,' she said firmly, 'and it's none of his business either. He doesn't own me, the hospital doesn't own me. Nobody does.' She looked at him and meant *neither do you*. 'Dad, I'm afraid I'm the one who's going to have to insist.'

It was difficult but she had to stand her ground. Over the past few months she had noticed how they were behaving but she had said nothing. In both his mind and her mother's she had become a little girl again, someone to be guided and advised, to be looked after. Just like a child.

She could not let it go any longer. She had to remind both of them that she was a grown woman.

'It's time I tried to stand on my own two feet,' she said, 'and started making my own decisions. If they're not good ones, then that's my problem. I have to live with it.'

He looked towards the window, silent for a moment, his face turned away from her.

'The real reason . . .' she said.

He turned back.

She sighed. When she spoke there was a tremor in her voice. 'It's Paul Everett. God, even saying his name makes me feel . . . weird. I can't get him out of my mind. I see his face all the time, that damned photograph. I just know that if I'm ever to recover properly from this . . . this thing, I've got to find out more about him, to somehow discover how I came to be with him that night. And I thought: maybe if I do this television show, then someone out there will remember something and be able to help.'

She did not ask him what he thought. She could see it in his face.

He told her anyway.

'Meg, it could be damned dangerous. Somewhere out there is the person who killed Everett. Don't forget that.'

'I don't. I can't. I think about it every single day. For God's sake, all the way down the Lisburn Road just now I was looking for him. But I can't go through the rest of my life without knowing.'

'What if this person comes after you?'

'It's a risk I have to take. Then again, maybe there is no person any more – maybe he's dead or something, left the country. But wherever he is, I can't let the fear of him stop me doing what I feel I have to do.' She tapped the table with her forefinger to make the point. 'I need to reclaim my memory, to find out what happened and why I was with Everett. Nothing's more important than that.'

'Even your life?'

'What sort of a life is it going to be without a memory? With all this emptiness? I can't just leave it like that, no matter whether it's dangerous or not. Until I find out more about Everett, about why he was murdered, I won't know for certain whether I'm at any kind of risk. Dad, I've got to give it a try. This TV show might be a start. It's the best shot I've got.'

She looked around, aware that she might have raised her voice, but if she had, no one had noticed. The elderly couple had gone, leaving *The Times* crumpled and discarded. The women were still in a huddle and the young business types were scribbling notes on their papers. Tony Bennett kept on singing. It seemed strange to be thinking about danger.

'Meg,' her father said, 'don't rush into anything. Promise me you'll think about it.'

'I have,' she said at once. But she saw his concern and knew she couldn't just dismiss it. 'All right, I will. I promise.'

She pushed her cup and saucer away in a gesture that said the subject was closed. Then she sat back and gave him a smile. 'Well now, I thought you were going to show me this house of mine.'

Truesdale Street was familiar straight away and the sudden sense of recognition excited her, making her wonder if being here would open any locked doors.

It had been built in the thirties, bathrooms added later. The thin terraced houses with their little bow windows faced each other across the narrow street in which, she remembered, she always had trouble parking. There were the same tiny front gardens with their low front gates and paths you could cover in a single stride. A couple of 'for sale' signs leaned drunkenly.

Her father found a space at the bottom of the street, parking half up on the footpath so that other drivers could get past his bulky vehicle. The Range Rover was like a green cuckoo in a nest of Clios and petite Peugeots.

They walked back to number thirty. The front door was open and a man in white overalls was painting it red. He stopped when he saw them.

'Don't mind us, George,' Winter said. 'Just you carry on. We'll try not to get in your way.'

George gave an unintelligible mutter as they walked into the house. Meg saw the look he tried not to give her. He knew who she was.

Just inside the front door, they stopped and her father turned.

'Well?' he asked with a big smile.

It was a different house.

The whole downstairs, which had consisted of a front living room, a kitchen and a tiny hall, was now one open room. Even the stairs had gone, how and where, she could not understand. The floor was bare polished wood with a couple of big middle-eastern rugs. The walls were magnolia, the woodwork white and shining in its freshness. There was a small dining table and four chairs at the window, two small leather settees and big plants in terracotta pots.

'Come and see the kitchen section,' he said.

Not a kitchen any more: a *kitchen section*.

It was lined with cupboards made of dark wood over work surfaces with a grey marble effect. There was a small Aga, black and gleaming.

'And there's more.'

She found where the stairs had gone. They had been re-sited at the back of the kitchen and just beyond that was the downstairs bathroom, ripped out and replaced. There had been stripped pine before but now there were speckled Italian tiles everywhere, a new bath and wash basin and a proper shower instead of the flimsy curtain that had always made her think of *Psycho*. She was glad that had gone.

'Up here.'

He led her up the stairs and she discovered that instead of two bedrooms there were now three.

'But how—' she began.

'I had a whole new extension done a year ago,' he said proudly. 'I knocked down the old bathroom and rebuilt it and then I put all this on. And have a look out here.'

He directed her to the window in a back bedroom that had not been there before.

She looked out on to what had been an empty, plain patio made of square stone slabs. Now it was floored in weathered brick and it sat on two levels. A small garden seat with wrought iron legs faced the sun. Petunias, fuchsia and geraniums bloomed in pots and wisteria had claimed ownership of the wooden fence that formed the border with next door.

They went back downstairs.

'Well, what do you think?'

'I don't know what to think,' she said with an honesty she knew he would not want. It was a lot to take in. She felt bombarded by change, the curious fusion of styles, none of them hers.

'Don't you like it?'

'Oh, I do,' she tried to assure him, 'it's fabulous. It's just . . . I thought maybe that when I came in here I'd find something.'

'Like what?'

'I don't know – something in my mind, perhaps. But this . . .'

She gazed around the unfamiliar room. Nothing here seemed right. The place had no spirit, no resonance for her at all.

'It doesn't feel like it's my house,' she said. 'It's as if I've never even been here before.'

Twelve

Travelling rarely tired Sir Brian Malone, which was just as well since he flew more miles in a month than many people did in a lifetime.

He was a tall, broad-faced man with small bright eyes but there was a heaviness beneath them this Saturday morning as he sat in his usual seat on the Concorde from New York and waited for it to touch down at Heathrow.

He wore no coat and carried no luggage, not even a cabin bag. Wherever he happened to be in the world, everything he needed was already there waiting for him, along with someone from Malone Global, the huge corporation he controlled.

One such executive was on duty now as he was shepherded through a special immigration channel and into the VIP lounge. Gerry Bruce, hair as sleek as an otter, was the head of corporate communication in the London office, paid a generous six-figure salary out of which he could well afford to buy the expensive tailoring he wore, but Malone did not seem conscious of his seniority and barely acknowledged his greeting.

'Some papers for you, Sir Brian.' He handed over a black leather folder of faxes and messages. It was embossed in a corner with the letters BM. 'Flight OK for you, sir? You seem to have made a little extra time.'

He hurried alongside, trying to get in step with Malone who kept on walking and did not respond. Instead he glanced quickly at the contents of the file then shut it with a snap.

Silence was one of his most effective weapons; he used it to instil fear and to keep control. It was at its most potent during the phone calls he made regularly to the editors of his newspapers. It was his practice to ask an awkward question and when it had been answered he would say nothing at all, leaving an eerie emptiness on the line which the quietly quivering editor felt intimidated into filling. In the end, inevitably, the man would let slip something he had not intended to, digging a hole for himself in which Malone would proceed to bury him.

Malone used another form of silence, too, sometimes not

ringing his top people at all for days, even weeks, so that the victim was left to agonise over whatever misdemeanour might have been committed. There was always one. When the call of punishment did come, it was often a relief.

In his nervousness, Bruce kept up a running commentary of small talk, even though he knew it made him look like a gibbering idiot.

Malone tired of it at last. He fixed Bruce with a murderous stare. 'Don't speak to me. Just get me out of here.'

'Of course, sir. Of course.'

Bruce felt his silk Armani shirt begin to stick to his armpits. His task was to see Malone through Heathrow as quickly and as unobtrusively as possible without the great man being spotted by one of the freelance photographers who patrolled the airport seeking out the rich and famous.

Malone always avoided personal publicity where possible, not to the obsessive extent of locking himself away like a Howard Hughes, but he shunned high profile events and places where he was likely to find himself in the spotlight. He hated seeing his picture in the papers, even in his own.

They went out of the VIP area through a side door and climbed into a dark Mercedes which had its engine running. An airport police car led the way on a short journey that ended at the steps leading to a small black Learjet.

Bruce stood at the bottom as Malone took the steps two at a time. 'I'll be here when you return, sir,' he said and wondered if he would. Christ, it was like working for Stalin.

Malone settled into his seat as the aircraft was cleared for take-off. It taxied towards its runway slowly, to Malone interminably, then picked up speed suddenly and took off like an arrow, climbing sharply, then banking left, heading north west towards Northern Ireland.

He opened the folder. There were progress reports on various projects, proposals which would need his approval, but he found it impossible to concentrate. He closed it again and put his head back with a sigh.

He had made some tough decisions in his time and carried them out without a flicker of uncertainty because he knew they were right for the future of the company.

Over the years he had sacked a lot of people personally – always quick and to the point, getting it over with and ensuring they were off the premises straight away. He had closed whole businesses so that he could strip away their assets and in the process he had put hundreds of people out of work. It had never cost him a thought.

But this morning was different. This morning he was on his way to Belfast to fire his son.

He looked out of the cabin window at a searing blue sky and clouds like fields of fluff.

Had he been foolish putting Christopher into that job? It had been a little rocky at first, although soon things had started to come good. The boy had shown flair and imagination but Malone had begun to wonder if he had enough judgement. Now his doubts had turned to a gloomy certainty.

Drive and enterprise were one thing but sometimes caution was needed. Christopher mistook caution and judgement for weakness and indecision.

He blamed himself for all this. His son saw the way he did business, like buying into a sleepy group of Canadian newspapers all those years ago, a move that many thought was simply throwing money away.

In eighteen months he had changed both the image of the papers and their fortunes and had started his own swift rise into the super league. He had gone from there to the ownership of a group of papers on the US east coast, including a tabloid New York daily. Now there were magazines, television stations and banking interests as well, both across the Atlantic and in the UK where he was a major operator in the new digital field.

In the US he was an outsider, resented by the old-money establishment who loathed the idea of him buying into their publishing heritage. He had rubbed their noses in it even further by the generous funding of a chair in European business studies at Harvard.

Newspapers and magazines, not those he controlled, liked to portray him as a lucky gambler and an adventurer who took huge risks which always seemed to pay off. The trouble was, Christopher believed it, too, and wanted desperately to emulate his father's achievements.

He knew Christopher drove himself and everyone else in Malone Group hard but there was nothing wrong with that. It was a management style they shared and it got results. You pay people well enough, you deserve to get every last drop of sweat out of them.

He had never interfered. The only thing he had ever insisted on was that BB remain as personal assistant because there was no one who could do it better.

And, of course, there was the additional motive: he could rely on her, rather than his son, to be his eyes and ears in case of trouble.

93

And now trouble had arrived. In spades.

BB had called him the morning it happened. He had flown straight to Belfast. When he saw the problem he had snapped at her for not warning him earlier but the truth was that he should have seen the signs himself a long time ago.

It was all there: the extremes in Christopher's personality, elation that could turn to despair, the drinking and the women, a messy marriage break-up with his wife alleging that he had been violent to her on occasion.

The Lear changed direction. The engine altered pitch and he could feel the aircraft begin to descend.

He sat up straight. This self-recrimination would get him nowhere. The simple fact was that Christopher had not fulfilled the trust he had placed in him. He had not been able to cope and he had had a breakdown.

Malone and BB and a couple of reliable cronies on the board had taken over. They had whisked Christopher off to a sanatorium on the Isle of Man for a month and told everybody he was on holiday. Malone had made sure to keep well back in the shadows since any hint of his unexpected presence in Belfast could cause a wobble in Malone Group's share price and perhaps even start the market, ever paranoid, to wonder about Malone Global.

While the boy was in the hospital, Malone had got some of his best people to carry out a very confidential analysis of the Group. The news they had brought him, nervously, was not good. Malone Group was nodding off to sleep. Its results for the moment were healthy but they were too static; there was no evidence of real development.

Alone at his home in Toronto one night, he had read the report and raged in his seclusion.

'Christopher. You stupid fucking idiot.'

He had said it aloud, his voice echoing in his empty, high-ceilinged study.

All the frantic activity involving the leisure division had obscured dwindling performance in other areas. Christopher's monthly reports to the board had been a carefully constructed illusion of smoke and mirrors.

He had felt shame, an emotion which seldom troubled him, mixed with anger. But then he had calmed himself and got on with the job.

He had contacted the board members individually to inform them of the findings. There was no question about what had to be done, he told them all. Christopher would leave and move to an unspecified position with Malone Global. This way it would look like a promotion rather than a sacking and shareholder confidence in Malone Group would not weaken. One of the Group's most experienced senior executives would take over until a permanent replacement was found.

The Lear slipped into the clouds which were thick at first, billowing, then they began to thin, drifting past in wisps. He saw Northern Ireland below him, a deep, damp green.

He had the house in Toronto, an apartment in New York and a villa in Spain but he had a special affection for the place he had built among the trees on an island on Lough Erne in County Fermanagh. He could be there in less than half an hour by helicopter.

It was in the ancient stillness of the lakeland, gazing out on its timeless waters, that he felt most private. But he would not go there today. He would be in Northern Ireland for only a few hours. He would do the thing he had come for and tonight he would be back in New York.

The plane touched down and taxied towards a squat building which joined the main terminal. A sign above it said it was the Business Centre.

He descended from the aircraft, strode into the building and almost immediately he was out again through a side door. His life was a succession of private rooms, discreet entrances and exits.

Outside, dressed in blue trousers and a chunky sweater, BB stood beside her silver Alfa Romeo. She looked tense but when she saw him a smile warmed her face.

'Good to see you,' he said. They embraced fleetingly and he felt the tight grip of her hands on his upper arms.

She opened the passenger door for him. They had agreed that in order to talk freely on the way to Christopher's home, there would be no company driver this time.

'How is he?' Malone asked as he belted himself in and she headed for the gate that led to the main road. They would be at the house in twenty minutes. It always amazed the people he occasionally brought here to realise how near everything was to everything else.

'Calm. Thoughtful. He called in yesterday briefly.'

'Depressed?'

'No, not at all. He was on his way to Royal Belfast for a game of golf. He looked well. He had some stuff he wanted to leave in his office. He didn't hang around.'

'Do you think he knows what's coming?'

'Of course he does. When you ring him from New York and tell him you're flying in today and flying out again straight away he knows it's not a social call.' She glanced at him. 'He's your son, Brian. He knows.'

No one had the strength of BB. No one else talked to him like this.

He looked out of the window. They were passing a country hotel.

Once, many years ago, there had been a conference there. They had been working late in his room, him and BB, going over a presentation he would give in the morning . . .

They had never spoken about it afterwards and they had never repeated the experience. They were both alone now, married and divorced: once in her case, three times in his. He glanced at her but she was looking straight ahead and there was no hint of anything in her face.

'Do you think he's well enough to take it?' he asked her.

'I think so. The report about his treatment on the Isle of Man was good. He seems to have hit a kind of an emotional brick wall but the damage isn't permanent; there's nothing that can't be remedied. As you know, the doctors recommend a change of lifestyle. He might feel relieved, rather than resentful.'

'Resentful? He has no right to feel resentful.'

She said nothing, letting him brood. And unlike any other Malone employee, the silence did not unnerve her.

Ten minutes later she swung the car abruptly in through an old stone gateway almost hidden from view. Christopher's house was not visible from the road. Set among rambling gardens and behind high hedges, it had been built in the late forties, a large place with a tiered roof and big windows, what Malone in his early days as an estate agent would have described in the brochure as a 'gentleman's residence'.

The drive curved past slim beech trees and a sloping lawn. BB pulled up at the front. There were broad steps up to the house, begonias and azaleas wet and drooping in big pots.

'I'll just wait for you here,' she said.

Malone went up the steps and rang the doorbell. He heard it sound somewhere far away. There was no reply. After a few moments he rang it again. Still no answer.

He looked at his watch. Twelve thirty, the time they had agreed.

His temper was like an itch. *Damn fool. Where was he?*

He thumped the heavy door hard with his fist. 'Christopher!' he called, then bent down and pushed open the letter-box. He shouted into it. 'Christopher!'

There was no response.

He came back down the steps, giving BB an exasperated look

as he passed, and went round the side of the house towards the kitchen.

He tried the door. It was unlocked so he walked in.

The television was on, mounted in a little alcove above the breakfast table. There was a grunt and the thump of a tennis ball being hit very hard. He saw the intense face of Pete Sampras.

He looked around. The kitchen was big and airy and very tidy. The work surfaces were bare and spotless and above them gleaming saucepans hung neatly from their hooks in perfect order of size.

A small coffee pot stood on the table. Beside it there was a single cup. He touched the pot and felt a faint warmth lingering in it.

'Christopher?' he called again.

'Game and first set to Sampras,' a voice from the television said. He found the remote control and turned it off.

He went through the ground floor rooms. The dining room was cold and felt little used. There was a big sitting room that looked equally untouched, everything in place like a stage set, then a smaller living room with a television that was much too large for it and newspapers strewn on the floor.

He went upstairs. Christopher's room was the one that had been slept in. The bed was unmade. There were clothes on a chair and on the floor, a John Grisham novel open face down on the bedside table.

'Christopher?' He stepped onto the landing and listened. There was nothing. He tried the bathroom: nothing. Then he hurried downstairs again, opened the front door and went outside to BB in the car. She lowered her window.

'He's bloody well not here,' he said. 'What the hell's he playing at?'

She got out. 'Is there no sign of him at all?'

'The kitchen door wasn't locked. He's left the TV on.'

'Then he must be somewhere. Is his car here?'

They went round to the garage. Malone twisted the handle and the door opened upwards. A grey Daimler was parked with its rear to them.

'Well, wherever he's gone, he's not using this. He hasn't another car, has he?'

'Brian,' BB said softly.

He turned towards her. She was standing absolutely still, looking down the long slope of the back garden towards a cluster of trees at the bottom. For a second he thought she must have spotted an animal, a fox or a squirrel or something, and did not want to disturb it.

But then he saw what she was staring at.

There was a chestnut tree, branches outstretched and welcoming.

A dark shape was hanging from one of them.

He began to run towards it.

Thirteen

To his relief, Gerry Bruce saw that he would keep his job, at least for the time being. Malone needed him.

Personal publicity could not be avoided on this occasion and even Malone did not think it was a good idea to try.

Bruce flew to Belfast with some of his people, took over the top floor of the city centre building, and got down to work. By the time the markets opened on Monday morning, Malone had been made available for a whole series of interviews and photo-opportunities. No one got very long: just enough time for him to portray himself as both the grieving father and the dedicated business tycoon.

For the moment, he said, to provide stability, he would assume personal responsibility for the overall management of Malone Group as well as Malone Global.

'The death of my only son is a great loss and a great shock,' he told television viewers, who believed they were seeing for the first time the private face of this enigmatic man. 'But I have responsibilities which cannot be neglected.'

His voice was low and even, his emotions in check.

Bruce looked on. 'Great stuff,' he whispered to himself. 'Great fucking stuff.'

The market was reassured and Malone shares rose by several points.

And as they did, Malone's sorrow began to turn to anger.

A week to the day, he buried his son in great privacy.

There had once been a church on Malone's Island, which is what the people living along that stretch of the Fermanagh lough shore had come to call it. All that was left of the church itself were a few stones where once the walls had been and a stone floor covered with lichen and briars. But there was a tiny graveyard alongside. In it there were a dozen headstones, their faces worn almost smooth, the names of the dead erased by the passing of the centuries. All around, sweet honeysuckle threaded its way through a sturdy hawthorn hedge and foxgloves, bowed by the wind, stood like frail holy men in purple hoods.

Nearby, sheltered by pine trees, stood Malone's house, wood-framed, triangular under a huge roof that sloped down either side, with a balcony and big windows that faced out towards the lough.

Christopher's mother, Malone's first wife, would have objected to the remoteness and inaccessibility of such a grave site, but she had died ten years ago and so there was no one to argue with his decision. Certainly not BB, who was the only other mourner.

As for Christopher's ex-wife – or was she some kind of a widow now? – living on her lucrative divorce settlement in the Cayman Islands, with their son in a private school in England, to no one's surprise, there had been no communication from her at all.

At least, BB thought, she had the decency not to pretend to care. Although the boy should have been here. That wasn't right.

In spite of the fact that it was July, the day was cold and bleak. Rain was not far off. It was in the fullness of the clouds and the grey light.

The rector of a mainland parish had agreed to carry out the burial ceremony. Looking bewildered and frozen, he sat with Malone, the coffin and BB as they made the mile-long journey in the powerful motor launch which Malone kept in a boat-house on the island.

Billy Lowry, the caretaker who travelled across three times a week, took the wheel. A granite-faced man who wore a cap permanently, today he had found a suit from somewhere. The boat was capable of speed but in deference to their mission and the weather Billy kept the throttle low. Even so, the rector felt his stomach rebel against every movement of the choppy waters.

When they reached the island, they were met by Billy's cousin, a forestry worker who sometimes gave a hand with the more physical chores. He was a short man, chest strong beneath a jacket which would not button across it. Billy threw him the line and in silence he tied the boat up and helped its passengers off.

They had already dug the grave. Now they were on hand for the rest.

They went to the house first to gather themselves and then, under darkening skies, the little group stood silent and still as the rector intoned the funeral rites, trying to make his voice heard above the insistent wind. It whipped the thin strands of his hair into his eyes and caught his surplice like a sail.

100

Malone stood at the edge of the grave, BB a few feet behind him.

In the house, on a table in the study, she had left a pile of letters of condolence, faxes, telemessages, that he had yet to read. There was one from the Chancellor of the Exchequer, another from the Irish Prime Minister and one from the deputy Canadian Premier. Several American senators and congressmen had also written and there were messages from the heads of corporations all over the world.

They would wait. For now, Malone was alone with his anguish, staring at the damp earth in which his son would rest.

The clergyman finished, closed his prayer book and gave the benediction.

'In the name of the Father and of the Son . . .'

Malone felt the words stabbing at him.

Afterwards, he did not invite anyone to remain behind for a drink, not even BB. He wanted to be by himself. He would stay on the island tonight. He had arranged for a helicopter to come tomorrow and take him back to Belfast where he would spend a couple of days sorting out Malone Group.

And then there would be an inquest and he would have to give evidence and talk about his son's disturbed state.

They walked back towards the boat as the rain began. Thin rain, like mist. It fell with a kind of hiss. On the mainland shore, Damian, the driver, waited for BB and turned the big BMW's wipers on.

'People have been asking me if there's going to be a memorial service,' she said.

Malone thought for a second, then decided. 'No. I'm having none of that. It wouldn't be about Christopher at all. They're only talking about a service because they want an opportunity to fawn over me with their phony condolences.'

'Whatever you think,' BB said. She opened her handbag. 'Listen, Brian, there's one thing.' She took out a small padded envelope and handed it to him. 'I didn't find it until yesterday and I decided not to give it to you until all this was over.'

The little package was thickly sealed with tape. It contained something that was thin, flat and hard.

'It was in his safe. That day, when he was going to play golf, he came in. Remember I told you? He must have left it then. He knew that if anyone found it, it would be me.'

Malone looked at the envelope. On the front, in Christopher's handwriting, it said: *For Sir Brian Malone ONLY.*

There was a date in the top left hand corner. It was not the date of the day the package had been left – it was the date of the day his son had died.

Fourteen

'Have you got everything?' Liam Maginnis asked.

'I think so,' Meg said, giving a last look round. She saw nothing that was hers. The little room was anonymous again.

Her mother lifted a soft suitcase containing her belongings, of which there were more than when she had arrived seven months ago: tapes and a player, make-up and washing things, books which had accumulated, including a couple of exercise guides which the physiotherapist had given her. And basic clothes.

A couple of the nurses had helped with that over the last couple of months, popping into Marks and Spencer in their spare time to find things that were her new size and were the sort she might choose for herself if she had the chance.

Gloria herself had volunteered to go shopping for her but Meg had declined the suggestion, relieved to be able to say that the nurses had already offered. She wouldn't trust her mother's taste but she didn't want to offend her either. She had been caring in other ways, looking after all her washing, bringing freshly laundered things a couple of times a week, and now she was taking her home.

'Let me help you with that,' Maginnis volunteered, and took the suitcase.

'Kind of you,' Gloria said.

Meg watched him and wondered if she was wrong, wondered if the reflection in the mirror had been all in the mind. As time passed she found it difficult to see him as anything other than what he appeared to be. She took a deep breath. 'Right. Better get this over with.'

She went out of the room and stood at the entrance to the main ward. A nurse was checking someone's chart. There were five patients currently, two of them dozing while the others stared at the TV without much real interest.

Meg glanced towards the screen. It was that Granada programme, the one which had written to her. She had replied to them and said yes, she would do it, and they had written back

103

with a couple of suggested dates. The final decision would be hers.

Seeing it now up there on the screen, all superficial smiles and flower arrangements, she had a sudden feeling of doubt.

'Och, are you away?'

The nurse had spotted her.

'Yes,' she smiled, 'you're getting rid of me at last.' She waved down the ward. The patients were all alert now, looking in her direction. 'Cheerio, everybody,' she called. 'I hope everything will be all right for you.'

They called back to her.

'They're letting you out?'

'Watch you don't hurt yourself going over the wall.'

She laughed and waved again, then turned away and walked the few steps to the nurses' room. Freda Doran was the senior nurse, the ward manager. She sat at her desk where a huge box of chocolates lay open. Meg had asked her mother to bring it and she saw that the staff had been dipping into it already.

'I'm off now,' she said.

'So you're going?' Freda got up and hurried over to her. Two other nurses and a couple of the auxiliary staff appeared in the corridor where Maginnis and Gloria were standing with the case. Word was spreading.

Freda was a small woman who did everything at speed. She grasped Meg's hand to shake it, then changed her mind, reached up and hugged her. When she stepped back, she said: 'Now you look after yourself, do you hear me?' She glanced towards Meg's mother. 'You make sure you keep an eye on her, won't you, Mrs Winter?'

'Don't worry about that,' Gloria said.

Meg had not wanted this; she had been dreading giving in to an emotional scene. There were people all around her now, shaking her hand, hugging her as she made her way into the corridor again. She felt tears in her eyes but two of the younger nurses were way ahead of her, sobbing into handkerchiefs. Even Freda Doran was trying hard to stay composed.

'I wish I could take you all home with me,' Meg said. She took her glasses off and rubbed her eyes with the heel of her hand.

Maginnis stepped in. 'Right, I think we'd better get you out of here while we can.' He raised his voice with mock authority. 'I can't see much work being done around here if we don't. What do you think, Ms Doran?'

She caught his pitch. 'Quite so, Mr Maginnis. Right, everybody, get on with whatever you were doing. And don't worry, she'll come back to see us, won't you, dear?'

Meg nodded and blew her nose in a tissue her mother gave her. 'Of course I will,' she said. 'Just you try to stop me.'

They went on down the corridor, past the day room to which the most mobile patients had access, where they sat and read or watched television. Two from an adjacent ward were there, in front of a brand new wide screen digital set that had been installed two days ago. It was Sam Winter's way of saying thanks.

She had recovered well enough by the time her mother swung the Golf into the driveway of her bungalow on a hill at Carryduff.

A Yorkshire terrier trembled eagerly at the living-room window when it recognised the car. The house was in a development which was a manifestation of the way Greater Belfast was steadily annexing the countryside around it, open fields and farming land giving way to new estates with names like Pines and Meadows. Some of the houses were red brick, others were white and pebble-dashed. They fought for individuality and superiority through the exaggerated splendour of their front gardens and the quality of their owners' cars, posed outside garages that were used as storerooms and DIY dens.

Meg had seen the house for the first time a couple of months ago, on one of her days out. It was not the house where she had grown up; Gloria had sold that two years ago. It had been a bungalow, too, built by Seasons Construction in a prosperous corner of North Down, and Sam had let her have it as part of the separation arrangements. But when she sold it and pocketed enough to allow her to buy this house and have a lot left over he had not exactly been ecstatic. He had moaned about it to Meg.

In fairness, the change of address had not been motivated by financial gain. The real reason for the move could be seen if you walked to the top end of the avenue and looked back down the tiered rows of low roofs and across the main road.

Up a long drive, surrounded by green lawns, stood a white building that seemed to shine like a mirage. Above its door, in black gothic letters, were the words *Pentecostal Baptist Church*.

'Nearer my God to thee,' her father had said cynically. 'This church your mother belongs to, they've got this big new place so she decided she'd like to live close to it. The pastor is supposed to be a kind of charismatic figure, draws the crowds. Your mother's become devoted, whether it's to him or the church I don't know. I don't suppose she knows herself.'

105

Meg stepped into her mother's hallway and sniffed. Something was cooking.

'Mmm, smells good,' she said.

The little dog had mastered the vertical lift-off, springing up and down in an ecstatic greeting. Meg patted him and told him he was a good boy. 'Bet you'd like some of whatever it is, wouldn't you?'

'Chicken casserole,' Gloria told her. 'It's in the oven. I thought it would be nice for lunch. Something a bit special.'

'Lovely,' Meg said, walking on into the house. 'Is there anything I can do to help?'

Her mother was already in the kitchen. 'No,' she shouted back, 'I'll take care of everything. You just relax and make yourself at home.'

It would not be easy.

Apart from the cooking smells and the dog's happy greeting, there was little she found welcoming. It had disappointed her, the first time she was here, to discover that her mother had managed to transfer to this house the same lack of warmth which had always characterised the old one.

Familiar ornaments were placed here and there, things she had known all her life. In a glass cabinet and on delicate tables that smelled of lavender polish, there were Hummel figures and porcelain animals, small dogs mostly. Although they were evidence of a sugary streak, not the frosty exterior most people saw, she had always disliked them. In her early childhood, the regular addition of new pieces, their loving handling and careful positioning, coupled with dire warnings that she should not go near, had always made her feel that they were more precious to her mother than she was.

On days when she was unhappy or lonely, and there had been too many of those, she had felt as if she were being mocked by their poses of constant bliss. Once, frustrated and angry for some reason impossible to recall, she had swept a willowy shepherdess from the mantelpiece, breaking the thing's arm off in the fall to the hearth. There had been war over that, followed by long days of silence.

As with the other house, this one was kept in a permanent state of perfection. Every surface shone. On the armchairs and settees, there were cushions puffed up as if no one ever sat and disturbed them.

On a coffee table in the living room, reminding Meg of a doctor's waiting room, there was a handful of Christian magazines, their covers showing happy, healthy faces glowing with an inner spirituality.

106

Yet her mother demonstrated none of this open-hearted joy.

Seeking comfort in religion, changing her way of life when her marriage broke up, had not been a totally unexpected step. Gloria had been brought up in the Presbyterian church, and she had always been a regular attender. Her mother, Meg's grandmother, had been *good living*, to use the time-honoured Ulster expression. Even the name, Gloria, had a hymnbook ring. When things went bad she had simply sought comfort where she hoped it would be found and her search had led to the open doors of the Pentecostal Baptist Church.

Meg looked around. Whatever fulfilment the church gave her, this was the home of a lonely person, someone without much in her life.

Not to mention a daughter who did not really want to be here.

She took her bag down the hall to the bedroom that would be hers for a while.

'Can you manage all right?' Gloria asked, coming out of the kitchen.

'Yes,' she said, 'I'll just leave this and unpack it later.'

There was a wardrobe and chest of drawers, a dressing table with a mirror. A pink duvet, smooth and straight, without even a hint of a crease, covered a single bed. On a table beside it stood a small vase containing a couple of pink roses. A shelf above that held a solitary book: a Bible with a soft black cover and gold-edged pages.

It felt like a hotel room.

She opened the wardrobe and was startled to find it full of her own clothes, all in plastic dry-cleaning covers. She stopped and stared for a moment, not quite knowing what to do, then she took some of them – skirts, jackets – out, and held them against herself. They felt as if they belonged to someone who no longer existed.

'Most of these clothes of mine are too big – absolutely no use to me,' she called. 'Does your church take things for charity?'

The Yorkie heard her voice and ran into the room. It jumped on the bed and began bouncing on it like a trampoline.

'God, you're wrecking the place,' Meg chuckled. 'You'll not be popular.'

Her mother came in to answer her question and saw the dog. 'Oh, look at that stupid thing. Look what he's done.'

'It's all right, Mum. He's just a bit excited.'

'He usually has a walk about now.'

Meg lifted the animal off the bed and held it under her arm. 'Well, then, why don't I take him while you're doing things in the kitchen?'

'There's no need to do that,' her mother said hurriedly. 'You've just arrived. You don't want to get yourself too tired.'

Meg gave her an exasperated look. 'Mum, I'm fine. I'm not suggesting an overland expedition. I won't take him far and I won't get lost. I'll be back in half an hour at the most. Now, does he have a lead or anything?'

As if it had somewhere to go and was late, the dog kept her hurrying along. It pulled against its harness, like a husky dragging a heavy sled, pausing only to irrigate selected garden walls and lamp posts.

Two doors down, a woman came out of her front door. There were flowering cherry trees along her driveway, a three-series BMW estate at the door.

'Good morning,' she said, then stood and watched Meg pass.

Meg nodded. 'Hi.'

Outside another house, a tall, elderly man in a body-warmer and a cap was washing a Volvo. He paused and straightened as she approached, watching her with crinkled eyes.

'Good morning,' he said, touching the brim of the cap.

'Morning,' Meg said.

It was not an Ulster characteristic to greet strangers in the street but these people did and she knew why. In their faces she saw the same look of curiosity the painter in Truesdale Street had given her. They knew who she was. As she and the dog moved on she wondered who else was watching them, peeping from behind their curtains.

Her mother had been uneasy about her going out and now Meg understood the reason. Gloria Winter was the mother of the *Coma Woman*. The whole neighbourhood would know that and now they would know she was home. Here she was, large as life and walking down the street, just what her mother did not want them to see.

She felt their eyes on her back.

The dog seemed to have a route. It led her along places called 'Park' and 'Close' and 'Rise' and eventually she found herself down at the main road. There was a petrol station and a fast food place and a taxi firm beside that.

On the other side of the road was the Pentecostal Baptist Church.

Viewed closer, it was a peculiar building, with turrets and peephole windows. Rough-cast, painted brilliant white, it was like a desert fort made out of icing sugar. The gateway was a huge arch that reminded her of the entrance to the Southfork ranch in *Dallas*, all those years ago.

On a big hoarding a poster proclaimed: *Special Free Offer This Week – God's Love.*

With this was a picture of a man with an exaggerated grin and hair like folds of whipped ice cream.

She turned, letting the dog lead her home. The little animal's energy had made this a much more brisk walk than she had expected and when she got back she felt a bit breathless.

She opened the kitchen door. 'Boy, he knows how to take you for a walk, doesn't he?'

Her mother was draining saucepans in a cloud of steam. 'You need to keep the lead short. That'll hold him back.'

Meg bent to liberate the beast. 'We met some of your neighbours,' she said.

'Met?' Gloria stiffened slightly but did not turn from the sink.

'Well, said hello.'

'Who were they?'

'I wouldn't know. A woman a couple of houses down. A man at the house next to that. Looked like he might have been a policeman.'

'Oh, him. He was a chief superintendent. Retired now. Did they wonder who you were?'

'I don't think so, Mum. I think they know perfectly well, don't you?'

Gloria said nothing for a moment, then she announced in a subdued voice: 'Lunch will be just a couple of minutes.'

'I'll go and wash my hands.'

When she went into the bathroom she found her washbag on a shelf and her toothbrush in a rack. She turned quickly and went into the bedroom. Her case sagged empty in a corner and her books were stacked beside the Bible.

She opened drawers. Her underclothes had all been put away, so had her tapes and the little player. In the wardrobe she found her new things hanging beside the old.

She sat on the bed and sighed. Damn it, this would have to stop. Right here. She felt invaded, as if everyone was spying on her, even her mother.

Take it calmly. Explain quietly but firmly why this is not acceptable, how intrusive it is.

But she could already hear the response – 'I'm only trying to help.'

As she stood up to close the wardrobe door she saw something at the bottom, in among her old shoes. It was a shoulder-bag and she remembered it. It was small, with a long strap. Nothing too bulky.

Just the sort of bag she would have taken to the Clarendon Dock.

She paused for a second before lifting it out. There were faded brownish stains across the front where something had been spilled and her heart tied itself in a knot because she knew at once that it was her own blood.

It was a couple of minutes before she could bring herself to open it, fingers trembling as she twisted the little golden clasp.

From inside came the waning scent of a perfume she could not quite name. There were two unused tissues still neatly folded inside a little Kleenex wrapper. There was a comb, two mints twisted into the tail end of a packet, an emery board and a lipstick. She opened it. The shade was a deep red. Like blood.

There was nothing else.

Her purse had been there, and in it the things they had found to identify her, but she had that herself now. Her mother had given it back to her.

You were the girl who always had the condoms in the handbag in case you got lucky. Remember?

Had there been any? Had her mother found them?

'This is on the table,' Gloria called. 'Are you ready?'

The voice startled her and she put the bag away quickly.

'Coming,' she said and went back to the bathroom. She washed her hands vigorously, as if trying to get rid of something.

Her mother had set the table in the dining room. There was a perfect white embroidered linen tablecloth, linen napkins in silver rings and laminated place mats showing Victorian rural scenes. Apart from the casserole she had cooked new potatoes and broccoli.

She was pouring elderflower cordial into crystal glasses. Meg sat down opposite. Her mat was a group of men in collarless shirts and heavy moustaches working at a dangerous-looking machine in a field of flax.

But all she saw was the bag.

Finding it had knocked her sideways. And now, in the stuffy formality of this room, she felt awkward and uncomfortable, like a new lodger, afraid to lift the wrong knife or fork or leave a speck on the spotless cloth.

She forced a smile. 'This looks terrific,' she said and opened the napkin carefully across her knees.

Gloria closed her eyes and clasped her hands in front of her.

'We thank you, Lord, for your generous bounty.' Her voice

110

was unsettlingly loud in the small, square room. 'We thank you for the gift of your grace, we thank you for the gift of health which you have provided so that we may be sound in mind and body as we proclaim your glorious works. *They will celebrate your abundant goodness and joyfully sing of your righteousness.* We thank you for Margaret's recovery, for her safe return from the emptiness of the wilderness into which she was cast and we pray that the peace of Christ will rule in her heart.' She paused. 'Amen.'

Meg held her breath and stared at the men in the flax field. They seemed to be waiting. She looked up and saw her mother's eyes fixed on her.

'Amen,' she whispered in response.

'Now, then,' Gloria said and passed her a plate. 'Help yourself.'

The stress of the morning, as well as the walk with the dog and a much heavier lunch than she was used to – apple crumble and custard had followed and been eaten with her mother's insistence; 'you need building up' – all of it had exhausted her and so she said she was going to lie down for a little while.

She slipped under the duvet in bra and pants but in spite of her tiredness, she did not drop off to sleep straight away. She was too tense.

She got up and opened the window slightly. It was stifling in this house. She needed space of her own and freedom to be able to think clearly but she would have it soon, she consoled herself; this was just for a few weeks.

Could she stand it that long?

She got back into bed and told herself that she would let it all wash over her and not feel intimidated by it. The prayers, the good china – it was just her mother's way.

She turned on her side, facing the wardrobe. The bag was in there, back in the place where she had found it, behind that closed door. She closed her eyes but she could still see it in her mind, a bloody souvenir. She tried to blot it from her thoughts.

No. That was wrong.

She was planning to go on TV and she couldn't even handle this?

She leaped out of bed, opened the wardrobe door and grabbed the thing. She put it on the bedside table where she could see it and then she got into bed again.

The long thin shoulder strap hung down towards the floor.

Facing things. That was the only way.

★ ★ ★

111

At first, when she woke again, she did not know where she was.

Then she saw the bag.

There were voices somewhere. That must have been what disturbed her. She could hear her mother and there was the deeper rumble of a man's voice. She looked at her watch. Half past five. She had slept for several hours.

She got up, slipped into her clothes and brushed her hair, wondering idly for a second what it would look like short.

She walked down the hall and into the living room. Her mother was sitting on the settee. A man was in an armchair by the fireplace with his back to the door.

'Margaret,' Gloria said, getting to her feet. 'Did you have a good sleep? I didn't want to wake you.' She smiled broadly. It felt like an act.

The man stood and turned. He was somewhere just past fifty, tall in a dark suit and a white shirt that showed off a tan. The even, gleaming teeth, the waves of hair, were brighter than in the poster outside the church.

He stepped forward and lifted Meg's right hand, enveloping it in both of his. 'The Lord bless you,' he said.

'This is Pastor Alan Drew,' Gloria explained.

'So wonderful,' Drew said, still holding Meg's hand. The heat of his grasp was like a current. His bright eyes examined her face, the smile unyielding. 'So wonderful to see what can come from the great healing power of the Lord and the strength of a mother's prayers.'

His voice was a baritone blend of Belfast and Bible belt.

'Let us give thanks.'

He stepped back slightly, raised his right hand high and placed his left on Meg's shoulder. The grip was hard and firm and it took her by surprise, leaving her unable to move.

She looked towards her mother. Gloria was standing with head bowed.

Drew closed his eyes and raised his face towards heaven, which was somewhere above and beyond the light fitting with the frilly shade that hung over the centre of the room. The walls seemed to vibrate with his voice.

'We thank thee, O Lord, for the safe return of this beloved child.'

'Amen,' Gloria agreed.

'We know that she has been restored for a purpose and we pray that she may take you to her heart as her own personal saviour. Like you, Lord, she is risen.'

Meg felt his hand grip her tighter.

'See – the risen Jesus has entered the tomb!'

112

His voice became more urgent, excited, as if behind his flickering eyelids he was watching something happening.

'He takes hold of you and the life enters your body. You feel it growing, spreading within you. It is not the old life, not the life of the flesh and sinful desires, but it is the new life – His life.'

'Praise the Lord,' Gloria said, a quiver in her voice.

'He lifts you to your feet and you follow where he leads. He brings you out of the tomb, out into brilliant sunlight. It is the same world that you left, sin and all manner of evil still abounds within it, but you will be different now, a new person, your soul and spirit restored by his grace. By the power of his blood.'

Blood.

The word was like a click of the fingers.

Meg saw the bag on the bedside table. She saw Paul Everett's face.

She blinked, then looked at Drew. His voice, his hands, his *presence*, that was the only word for it, were almost irresistible.

Almost.

She dropped her shoulder and moved back out of his grasp. Drew's eyes flicked open and in that second she saw in them something that was less than an unbounded generosity of spirit.

And he knew that she had seen.

Got you, she thought.

'Sorry,' she said. 'This is very difficult. I . . . I don't want to appear ungrateful but I'm not quite ready for any of this yet. I'm not sure it's what I want just now. It's all a bit overwhelming.'

Her mother looked shocked. 'What are you—'

Drew interrupted. 'Then let us pray in our hearts that the barriers may be removed.' He smiled, understanding and compassion miraculously restored. 'Fear, suspicion, doubt – these are barriers. But to walk in the light means that there are no barriers separating you from others. To walk in the light is to live in love.' He nodded, as if agreeing with himself. 'I know you will come to live in that gracious state. I know that is the will of the Lord Jesus Christ.'

'Amen,' Gloria said automatically. Her face was flushed with embarrassment. Then she said: 'Pastor Drew, I'm sorry you've—'

He shook his head in a way that said he had come up against this sort of problem before and nothing was insurmountable.

'Don't reproach yourself,' he told her. He took a card from his pocket and handed it to Meg. 'Jesus stands and knocks at the door and waits for a response, a response of faith, an invitation to take up residence. When he gets that response, the door is opened and he enters the hallway and it is full of light. But there

113

may still be many rooms in that mansion where the light has not yet penetrated.' He smiled. 'Jesus understands.'

He shook Meg's hand. 'Your heart is troubled and uncertain but you have no need to feel alone. There is love here. Should you feel the need for a voice to talk to at any time, then all you have to do is call me. And now, my dear Gloria, I must go.'

Her mother showed him to the door, still murmuring apologies which he kept on dismissing.

Meg felt able to breathe again. The man seemed to have soaked up all the oxygen in the room. She heard a car engine start and she turned to the window in time to see him depart in a sky blue seven-series BMW.

The Lord moves in mysterious ways.

Her mother came back, her face spelling trouble.

'You humiliated me,' she said.

'Then I'm sure I'll be forgiven.' She had had enough. 'That's the Christian way, isn't it?'

Just as quickly she softened. 'Mum, I'm sorry, but look at everything that's happened today. Look at the way you reacted when I went out. You didn't want the neighbours to see me, did you? No, too much of an embarrassment. Then, going through my things as soon as my back was turned, putting them all away. How do you think that made me feel? And then this . . . this pastor, bringing him here without discussing it with me. Mum, I had to call a halt.'

'Call a halt? Call a halt? God himself called a halt to your . . . your . . . the way you lived your life, the sin and shame of it.' Her voice seethed with emotion. 'I prayed. Night after night, day after day, I prayed. I blamed myself. I confessed my own inadequacy to the Lord for not having done more to guide you on to the true path. But God knew. The drugs, the drinking, people murdered – he punished me, punished me and shamed me in the eyes of the world for what I failed to do. And then he brought you back, restored you. There can be only one reason for that – can't you see? It's so that we can both be united in Christ.'

It was all there, all feeding away in her mind.

'Take this opportunity,' Gloria said, holding out her arms. 'Seize it. Repent of your sins. Think of the things you did. All the lust. The, the . . . sex.' She forced herself to say the word.

Meg thought of the bag.

'Find the true path,' Gloria said.

'I think I will,' Meg said. 'The path out of here.' She walked past her mother out of the room. 'I think that would be best.'

Gloria followed her. 'What do you mean?'

114

'I mean I'm leaving.'

She went into the bedroom and lifted her case. She turned to her mother, realising she was behaving a bit petulantly, thinking she should try to explain, to be reasonable. 'Look, this isn't going to work, is it? It's best if I pack up now and go. There's a taxi company beside the filling station at the bottom of the hill. I saw it earlier when I was out with the dog. I'll get a cab there.'

'And go where?'

'Home. My own place. Truesdale Street. Dad gave me the keys.' She paused. 'He was right.'

'Right about what?'

'You. Your church. He warned me. I didn't expect anything quite so – so oppressive. Or quite so soon.' She gave her mother a look. 'That's some car your friend the pastor has. How much do you contribute to his church funds?'

'That isn't any of your business.'

'No, I don't suppose it is.' She began to open drawers and put things back into the case.

'Why?' Gloria said, pain in her voice. 'Why is God punishing me like this?'

She looked suddenly helpless and Meg began to wonder if she was doing the right thing. But then she told herself she was. She put her hands on her mother's shoulders. Gloria flinched as if stung then moved away.

'It isn't like that, Mum. No one's punishing you for anything. It's you and me, that's all. We see things a different way. It's – it's torture for you having me here. So it's best if we cut our losses.'

'I kept you alive,' Gloria said. Tears were close at hand.

'You prayed for me,' Meg said. 'I appreciate that.'

Gloria gave her a look, then smiled a secret smile. 'No, I kept you alive. Your father would have let you die when you were at Knockvale. I kept you alive.'

'What do you mean? What are you talking about?'

'Ask him.' She turned and left the room.

She had enough cash to pay for the cab.

There were two locks on the front door and the phone had been ringing for a while by the time she got inside and managed to find it. It was a cordless thing set into a charging mechanism in the kitchen, or rather, the kitchen section.

It was her father. She knew it would be him.

'What's going on?' he asked her.

'Hello, Dad.'

'I rang your mother's to talk to you and she said you'd gone. She sounded upset. Are you all right?'

115

'She says you would have let me die.'

'What?'

'She says that when I was in that nursing home you would have let me die. Is it true?'

'Look, this isn't the time—'

'Is it true?'

'Meg, it wasn't like that. Watching you lying there, day after day, all I did was wonder—'

She hung up.

The phone rang again almost immediately but she didn't answer it. Eventually it stopped.

In the descending dusk of the summer night, she sat alone in the strangeness of the big open room, watching lights coming on in windows opposite and curtains being drawn.

Fifteen

The woman at the podium in the Grand Ballroom on the third floor of the Waldorf Astoria Hotel was winding up her short, nervous speech.

The wife of the chairman of one of New York's great museums, Nadia Hibbert was in her late thirties, dressed in blue silk, and with every movement she made her diamond choker spark like a fusillade of flashbulbs.

She was a regular and familiar figure in the glossies and on the magazine pages, portrayed as a wealthy socialite with time on her hands and money to burn, an image she resented but the one which the media preferred. They did not give her any real credit for the constructive, philanthropic things in her life, did they? Like all the hours and energy she devoted to the charitable institution of which she was president and which provided much-needed food and care for the city's homeless.

Not glamorous enough, perhaps. Only when there was glitter and superficiality did they take an interest; like this, the annual charity dinner, to which they came not in deference to the cause but in order to spot the rich and famous, to analyse what they were wearing and see who they were with.

But it was a bit more heavyweight than that tonight. There were political writers scattered around, as well as the usual society page people, and the television crowd were out in force, which made Nadia edgy as she stood in front of the fifteen hundred guests.

Cameras were trained on her, their hooded stare impersonal and cold in spite of the heat of the lights. She could see NBC, CBS, ABC and CNN, as well as the locals, but she was well aware that it was not her face which would make the news bulletins.

But aren't you lucky, my dear, she told herself, that he agreed to come? Some of the publicity was bound to rub off on the charity itself and that would be all to the good.

She came to the end of her introduction. With an exuberance

born partly out of relief that her ordeal was over she announced: 'And so, ladies and gentlemen, will you please welcome... Senator Aiden Ross!'

She stood back and began to clap with polite enthusiasm, the fingertips of her right hand beating on the heel of her left.

Others were not so restrained. As the cameras and lights swung to the big table at the front of the room where a tall sandy-haired man was pushing back his chair, people rose to their feet and applauded with vigour.

Aiden Ross smiled in acknowledgement and began the short walk to the podium, the spotlight and the audience with him all the way. He did not hurry, nor did he idle; his pace was measured and confident.

When he reached Nadia, he took her hands in both of his and thanked her warmly and generously and just long enough for the cameras to see how genuine and gracious he was. Then he turned to face the room, his hands raised in what he hoped would be a futile attempt to still the applause.

And it was. At that moment, as he looked at the room full of smiling, expectant faces and listened to their approbation swirling all around him, he knew that in a year's time, if he played every single card right from here on in, he would be the next President of the United States.

He glanced quickly down towards his wife, seated at the table he had just left. Her eyes danced with excitement. She mouthed a kiss at him and he blew one back.

Then he looked in the direction of a table over on his left, seeking out three other familiar figures. They were applauding, too, but their smiles were different, more knowing. They felt what was in the air the same way he did.

This was the nucleus of Ross's election machine, the best and the brightest, his most trusted. There were other people involved, of course, the hidden engine room that would drive the campaign, but he did not like to parade around with a vast entourage. There would be plenty of that, unavoidably, once he was President.

'The people,' he was in the habit of saying, 'the people of the United States of America – they're my campaign team.'

Phyllis Halpin was in her mid forties, a dark-set woman with flecks of grey in her hair that she did not bother to cover up. A Texan, she had inherited from her father a huge General Motors dealership with hundreds of outlets and she had been its CEO for the past ten years. Now a change of life was galloping rapidly across the ridge towards her. Ross, whom she had known for a long time, had asked her to become his White

House Chief of Staff when – he never said if – he became elected.

Recently divorced, very rich and just a touch bored, she had said yes. Listening to what was going on around her, she could not wait to get started.

'Paydirt,' she said, smiling triumphantly up at Ross, although she knew he could not hear her.

In Ross's experience, people who loved the work but had their own wealth did the job better than someone who needed the money. They were tougher, their personal security meant their decisions were clear-cut and unemotional, and how they themselves would be affected entered less into the equation. That was certainly the case with Phyllis who never hesitated to tell him what she thought, often in a tangy Texan turn of phrase which could shock those not used to it.

Stan Rybeck, Ross's speech writer and designated Director of Communications, was not one of them. And anyway, once he got his head into drafting a speech, he rarely heard anything being said around him. Rybeck was thirty five, a former Pulitzer Prize-winning reporter from Wisconsin who had become *Newsweek*'s chief White House correspondent. He was not doing the job for the money either. It was the action, the juice, that he craved.

At the moment, he also craved a cigarette from the packet of Marlboros in the inside pocket of his tuxedo. They bulged there against his heart, forbidden.

He loved writing the speeches but he hated the nerve-wracking business of having to listen to them, even though he knew Ross would more than do justice to this one.

They had been over and over it together, ever nuance, every pause, getting the pitch absolutely perfect. It was not the most important address which Ross would make; there would be many more to follow it. But it was a milestone, his first major speech since announcing his candidacy. From this moment on, he would have to swing popular opinion firmly behind him, to carry him through the Primaries, on to the nomination at the party convention and up to the door of the White House itself.

The people in this room had money. Old or new, it didn't matter, it was money. They had a feeling that Ross was a guy who wasn't going to monkey around with their profits, pissing on them with new taxes like that bastard currently in the White House had been doing.

Tonight's speech was designed to reassure them further but Ross and Rybeck were aware it would be tricky. Here he was, talking to the rich, at an event for the poor. He had to stroke the wealthy and at the same time not alienate those who weren't, which was the vast bulk of the American public. He had to hold out the hand of friendship and hope to everyone.

Rybeck had crafted a speech which would be all things to all people, which would be long on heart but short on specifics. It would be about Ross, his hopes, his dreams, his mistakes. It would be the speech of an honest American.

The contrast between that image and the growing public view of the man at present in the White House would be striking. But the speech itself would not attack the President, Todd Vernon. That was something Ross hoped people would note: the positive approach, always looking forward. The negative stuff was taking care of itself and for that he had to thank the third member of his team: his younger brother.

As the applause faded at last, Matt Ross sat down. He was a stocky, muscular man, sombrely handsome, with looks that came from their mother's side of the family, whereas Aiden strongly resembled their late father.

He took a sip from the glass of Chardonnay at his hand and turned his chair at an angle away from the table so that he could get a better view. Even he, who had heard it all before, who saw the way his brother rehearsed, pacing the room, watching himself in a full-length mirror, never failed to be caught up in the mood. Somehow, on the night, there was always that extra, exhilarating edge.

The President did not have it; that was for sure. Todd Vernon sounded weary and slow and he was looking older than his fifty-seven years whereas Aiden Ross, roughly ten years his junior, seemed full of an inviting blend of youthful vigour and wise counsel.

But then it was unlikely that President Vernon was sleeping much these nights since he was trying to fight his way out of a sleazy swamp that just kept on pulling him back in again.

For a start there were the girls from the old days who kept popping up with embarrassing inconvenience, drowning out any campaign message he wanted to give. No one gave a damn about what he had to say on the subject of welfare reform or the crisis in the Middle East when there was some blonde with a make-over prepared to talk about what he liked to do in bed.

Whether the allegations were true or false, they were all from a long time ago, not relevant to the present, which is what Vernon supporters clutched at, but what the public saw on their television screens was Todd Vernon's lined and prematurely old face, verging on the haggard, not the virile handsome man he used to be, and the thought of him in action between the sheets turned their stomachs.

Then there was the other matter which had begun to surface recently: a complex story about an engineering company which had been awarded Government contracts shortly after Vernon was elected and whose chief executive had just been charged with filing false income tax returns. Off-shore bank accounts were involved, too, apparently, and, lo and behold, he was being represented by a law firm with which Vernon had been associated in former times.

It was a simple matter of fact. Admittedly, the connection to Vernon was tenuous, no actual impropriety was being alleged in any of the reporting, but his name was always right up front, either in the headline or in the first couple of paragraphs.

There was a smell in the air and people knew it had to be coming from somewhere.

Matt Ross had not made any of this stuff up; it had all been out there waiting to be discovered. What he did, through a network of clandestine contacts and a communication system of Chinese whispers, was to give it a gentle tug and help it on its way to the surface. As his brother's special adviser, that was his job.

There was just about nothing he would not do for him.

What he felt was much more than brotherly love; it was close to adoration. All his life he had looked up to him, even physically. At law school, which they had attended a year apart, he had watched proudly as Aiden had begun to gather a clique of admirers who appreciated his charm and his nimble mind. Aiden was a young man with ideas, with the imagination that could start the endless late-night conversations, fire the campus debates.

They had had some high times together, both then and later, but Aiden had never allowed pleasure to get in the way of his progress.

Eventually, they had both joined the same legal firm in Boston, Aiden first, and Matt was conscious that his own employment there had been assisted by his brother's obvious talent. Aiden found promotion within the firm easily but his eyes had always been on politics. He had worked hard at cultivating those who could help him, who would be useful patrons, and in Boston his Irish roots had not exactly been a hindrance.

By the time he was thirty-five he was a Senator and until recently he had been chairman of the Senate Judiciary Committee, from which he had now resigned in order to compete for the greatest prize of all.

121

At the convention before the last election, it had been he who had sponsored his party's candidate, introducing him with a speech far more thrilling than anything the man himself had had to say. In the election, the candidate had sunk without trace but everyone remembered Aiden Ross's words, seeing it as a speech which undoubtedly marked the beginning of his own campaign for office.

It was a long, hard road but the end was in sight.

Matt looked around the room. They were listening intently. Aiden was in full flow.

'We are all Americans, whether we are on Wall Street or on welfare. That is our unique bond, our greatest resource. Together we must find ways to harness our ideas, our energy, our strengths . . .'

When Aiden had begun to gather his closest cohorts around him, Matt was one of the people he had come to first.

Since Boston, their career paths had diverged. Matt had not stayed long with the law firm. Instead, through some of his brother's political contacts, he had found himself being recruited by the CIA, eventually working for them in Central America, the Middle East and in Europe, his speciality being political analysis and the creation of strategies designed to undermine organisations and individuals whom 'the company' believed were not helpful to American interests.

But then the Director of the Agency had fallen foul of a couple of old adversaries on the National Security Council and as a result there had been one of those tedious stable-cleansing operations.

Matt had jumped ship, again thanks to his brother's influence and assistance, finding friends and a home in the State Department. His intimate knowledge of difficult corners of the world was an asset which the diplomatic service found attractive and so he had landed himself a new career as a US Consul.

That was where he was in his life when Aiden came to him. He would never forget the day he accepted the offer, the day his world changed.

He took another sip of wine.

Aiden was on the subject of money now, which was dear to the hearts of his listeners.

'American business corporations make a huge contribution to national economies all over the world, providing literally millions of jobs. But sometimes I think we forget just how much they are the heartbeat of our own country, how much they do for our economy and our well-being here at home.'

He spread his arms wide. 'This great land of ours was

122

founded on the spirit of enterprise. We've got to make sure that that spirit continues to thrive. Whether it's the corner drugstore-owner or the Fortune 500 corporation, we've got to provide incentive for people in business, not bleed them dry.'

He waited for the hearty agreement that he knew would come.

'I know,' he said, as it began to trickle away again, 'I know you're all wondering out there: *what kind of a President would this guy be*? We've seen it all before, right? How people change when they go behind those great doors, how election promises just evaporate into thin air.' He held up his right forefinger and waved it from side to side, smiling. 'Uh-huh. Not this time. This boy's not going to make promises he can't keep, he's not going to say anything he'll regret. You can read my lips all you want.'

There was laughter. He paused, serious again. 'What I will promise you is smaller government. Smaller government – and bigger people. I want to see families and individuals who feel secure in their own country. I want to get the wheels back on the wagon of child care, of better education. We've got to make this a greater nation than we've ever known, a nation we can be proud of again, a nation leading the way in the global economy, the information age, in new technology that can enhance how we live, how we work, in unimagined ways.'

Something seemed to occur to him. 'Knowledge is in every country the surest basis of public happiness.' He pondered on the words and let the audience do so with him. 'George Washington said that. The first State of the Union address. 8 January, 1790. And he was right.' He thumped the lectern. 'Let's get working on it. Not tomorrow. Today.'

He stood back. The acclaim rose. People were on their feet, Matt and the others among them, applauding with just as much vigour.

'That's our boy,' Phyllis said.

It was several minutes before Ross could leave the podium and go back to the table to take his place beside his wife and a delighted Nadia Hibbert. People began queuing up to come and speak to him, shaking his hand and slapping him on the back.

'Fine speech, Stan,' Matt said. 'Well done.'

Rybeck was never satisfied. He shrugged and nibbled a fingernail. 'Yeah, well, there's a couple of things I think I could have changed for the better.'

'Never mind,' Matt told him. 'Nobody's perfect.'

'Washington say that, too?' Phyllis cracked.

'No – Joe E. Brown, *Some Like It Hot*,' Rybeck informed her.

Their glasses were empty. 'Hey,' Matt said, 'what do you

think – we could order a bottle of champagne on the strength of this?'

'We could, honey,' Phyllis said drily, 'but we won't. Let these other folks do that, if they want. Better not look too *uppity*, you know, even if you are his brother. We're just the workers, don't forget, down in the dirt, brows furrowed from sweat and honest toil.'

She tickled him under the chin, then stood and lifted her handbag. 'But I could sure use another glass of that very fine domestic Chardonnay we've been drinking. Why don't you find a flunkey and get us a bottle while I go and locate the ladies' room?'

'I'm going somewhere for a smoke,' Rybeck said and scurried off in her wake.

A waiter came and took the order. Matt watched the continuing parade to Aiden's table.

A tall, broad-faced man rose from his seat and began to make his way across the room. A couple of nervous acolytes got up from the same table and tried to come with him but he turned momentarily and waved them back. They fluttered uncertainly for a second or two, then sat again.

The face was familiar. Matt could see others recognising him as he passed and then suddenly, with a start, he knew who it was. Of course.

The man did not attempt to attach himself to the group around Aiden. Instead, he seemed to be heading in Matt's general direction.

Their eyes met. Matt got to his feet as he drew near.

The man held out his hand. 'You're Matt Ross,' he said, 'the Senator's brother.'

'That's right.' They shook hands.

'A wonderful occasion,' the man said. 'Congratulations. You've got a good man there.'

'Thank you.'

'My name is Brian Malone.'

'Yes,' Matt Ross said. 'I know.'

Sixteen

Waking in the house after that first night, lying under a cover-less duvet on a bed without sheets, she felt like a squatter, an unwanted guest.

Unwanted.

Her father had tried to explain but she had refused to hear it. She felt betrayed by him.

She was also hungry.

There was nothing to eat. The fridge and the cupboards were empty. She dressed, then went up the street to the corner shop for milk and tea and cereal. But when she had it all out on the counter and it was being added up on the till she discovered she didn't have enough money. Flustered, she said she would be back, then made an embarrassed exit.

It was eight thirty and the traffic down the Lisburn Road, heading into the heart of the city, was clogged and irritable. She glanced at people she passed to see if they were looking at her but no one was. She was anonymous, just another person hurrying by, yet she felt certain that if they didn't know *who* she was, they would see *what* she was: a fraud, an imposter pretending to be as normal as they were. They had a purpose, places to go, people to meet. She had nothing, not even a past.

She didn't like it on the street. She hadn't been out like this, alone, before.

She needed to find a bank with an ATM. She had to get money; the taxi ride last night had used up nearly all her cash. She had her cash card. She had credit cards, too, the old bills long settled by her father, the cards renewed automatically because she was such a reliable customer. It was difficult to use your plastic when you were in a coma.

She spotted a Northern Bank on a corner. A man was huddled over the cashpoint so she waited a discreet distance until he had moved away. She put her card into the slit and the screen asked for her number.

She froze, her finger poised. Damn, she couldn't remember.

Wait, it was 4851, wasn't it? She tried that but the screen did

125

not agree with her and told her so.

A man and a woman moved up behind, waiting their turn.

OK, 4581, then. No, the screen did not know that one either, but it began with a four; she was certain of that. She had another stab at it and then to her horror the card disappeared into the wall with a sharp sucking noise. The screen said something about her card being retained.

The couple behind whispered to each other and stared at her suspiciously. She turned from them, trying to hide her reddening face, and hurried home, wondering what she was going to do now.

She found her father in the kitchen.

There was darkness around his eyes. It was the face of a man who had not slept much.

Two bulging bags of groceries were standing on the work surface. It was hopeless. How on earth could she complain about people doing things for her when she had just demonstrated that she was incapable of doing anything for herself?

'I let myself in,' he said. His voice sounded strained. 'I was worried when you weren't here.' He gestured towards the shopping bags. 'I brought you some things. It occurred to me that there wouldn't be anything in the house.'

'No,' she agreed, 'there wasn't.' She was finding it hard to stay mad at him. Then she told him what had happened at the bank. All of a sudden she thought it was funny and she could not help laughing.

He did not join in. Instead, he asked: 'Last night – what happened at your mother's?'

Her smile went. 'Oh, it doesn't matter now,' she said.

'It does. Please. I want to know.'

She sighed. 'All right, then.'

He listened, his brow knotted, as she told him about the visit from the pastor and the subsequent spat with her mother. Then he said: 'The things she told you about me – I had to come this morning, to try to explain.'

This time she let him do so, waiting as he sat down wearily on a kitchen chair, which was black metal and not very comfortable. She did not like them much.

'Meg, it's not true that I wanted you to die,' he said. 'I wanted you to live. But I wanted you to be alive the way ... the way you are now. After almost four years, there was no sign that you were ever going to recover. Somebody had to start thinking of the future, to ask what the options were.'

He looked at her for some response but she did not know what to say.

126

'You know that birthday card I sent, the one with the girl in the boat?'

She nodded, remembering that her mother had all her cards in a box somewhere.

'That's the way I saw you,' he said, 'going nowhere, neither backwards nor forward, frozen in time. You were showing no sign of recovery at all. I discussed it with the doctors but it was a difficult topic. In circumstances like that, well, there wasn't a lot to discuss. It wasn't as if you were brain dead, you see. You weren't being kept alive by a whole lot of machines doing everything for you. You would have stayed the way you were until you went one way or another. Either you would have become ill or you would have recovered. I'm just so happy you got better.'

He shrugged his shoulders. 'It was just a conversation, that was all, but your mother found out about it and went into one of her holy rages, accusing me of going behind her back and planning to murder you.'

He stared at the floor and shook his head. 'But I wasn't, Meg. I need you to believe me. I was . . .'

His voice cracked. All of a sudden he put his head in his hands and began to cry. As if floodgates had been opened, it burst out of him, great racking sobs of pain and remorse that seemed to reverberate in the openness of the room.

It took Meg unawares. She crouched beside him and put her arms round his shoulders. She scented the faint whisper of his shaving cream, the tweedy sweetness of his skin and his clothes.

'Oh Meg,' he said, 'I'm so sorry.'

'It's all right, Dad,' she whispered. 'I'm here. I'm here now.'

Later she sat alone and in silence, the stress of the morning and the evening before like a heavy weight pressing into her chest.

He had desperately wanted her to understand so she had assured him she did and when he left he had felt better. He had been holding all this inside for a long time. Such anguish. She felt guilty that she had ever doubted him.

Guilt. She thought of her mother.

The hurried departure from Carryduff gnawed at her. She couldn't leave things like that.

She invited her to the house two days later.

Gloria hated the place as soon as she saw it – it was written all over her – although she did not say as much. Meg wouldn't have minded if she had.

127

She plunged straight in. 'Look, Mum, I'm sorry about what happened the other night. I didn't intend to upset you or embarrass you in front of your pastor. I guess we both said things we didn't mean but now I want us to make a fresh start. To be friends. What do you say?'

Gloria did not answer. She stood in the middle of the big room and looked around. 'Of course, you know he's bought several houses round here?'

'I'm sorry?'

'Your father. Another of his little sidelines. He fixes them up cheaply, he can get the labour and the materials, you see, and sells them at a big profit. He'd probably have done that with this if you . . .' She stopped and they stared at each other.

Later, they had lunch in the delicatessen along the road. Chicken in a lemon sauce with whole grain rice. They did not mention the subject again but it hung over Meg like a cloud. She watched her mother. Gloria ate heartily, believing, clearly, that fresh concerns about Sam Winter's motives had been planted firmly in her daughter's mind.

You are being used.

That's what this was. Her mother was trying to drive a wedge between her and her father. There was so much anger, so much poison. She did not want to be a part of it.

She called Elizabeth and they arranged a shopping expedition so that Meg could get some new clothes.

When the day arrived it was wet and miserable. Elizabeth had left Catriona with her sister-in-law. Over coffee, Meg brought her up to date and gave her the details of her short-lived stay with her mother.

'I hate to say it,' Elizabeth said, 'but I told you so.'

By lunchtime the wind was blowing the rain in waves that billowed down Belfast's long streets. People ran out of its path and huddled under dripping awnings. Gutters flowed like rivers and cars had their headlights on, the wipers set to frantic. Elizabeth had booked a table for lunch at Deane's in Howard Street. They tumbled in, laughing, clasping carrier bags from Gap and Monsoon and shaking streams of water from an umbrella.

A waiter with black hair like a shiny shell took their things, and when they had collected themselves in the ladies' room, he glided ahead to their table, pulling their chairs out for them.

'I'll have a gin and tonic,' Elizabeth said before she was firmly on the seat. She wore a suit and gleaming knee length boots in expensive leather. She opened her jacket. Her breasts pressed against a white silk blouse.

The waiter gave her an approving look then raised his eyebrows to Meg who was in chinos and a jumper and felt dowdy beside her richly upholstered friend.

'Just a mineral water, thanks.'

He nodded and headed for the bar.

'Not having a proper drink?' Elizabeth wondered. 'You're back in the big wide world again. It's time to celebrate.'

'No, I'm fine. Somehow, rediscovering alcohol isn't high on my list of priorities.'

'Oh, don't be silly. A little drink now and again can take the edge off. When was the last time you had one?'

Meg shot her a look.

'Ah, stupid me,' Elizabeth said. 'The night of the accident. Sorry, I forgot. You know, maybe if you had a drink your memory would come back. Sometimes that works. You get into the same frame of mind or something.'

'Thanks, I'll not bother, if it's all the same.'

Another waiter brought the drinks. He was small, in a waistcoat too big for him. He took their food order. 'Oh and I'll have a glass of the house white as well,' Elizabeth said.

When he had gone, Meg lifted her glass. 'Cheers,' she said.

They clinked, then Elizabeth took a belt of her gin and tonic and looked around the restaurant. At a table nearby four men in suits were glancing their way. She smiled over at them and raised her glass slightly. Meg noticed.

'What are you doing?' she muttered.

'Just being friendly,' Elizabeth said through her smile. 'The thin one with the dark hair's not bad. What do you think?'

'I'm not looking,' Meg said. 'Behave yourself.'

'Oh, I'm not doing any harm,' Elizabeth insisted, still eyeing the other table. 'Lighten up, darling, for goodness sake. There's nothing wrong with having a look, seeing what's on offer, a bit of window shopping. And you'll be wanting to get yourself laid again one of these days, don't you think?'

'Elizabeth – do you mind?'

'Well, you will.'

'But not here. Not over the first course.' She glanced at the other table at last. 'And certainly not with any of them.'

'Spoilsport.'

Meg looked at her. 'So what's the news on Vincent? You've been avoiding the subject all morning.'

Elizabeth's face seemed to darken. She took another drink. 'He's coming over next week.'

'Where?'

'Here. He's coming next week.'

'Really? You were keeping that quiet. How did all this come about?'

Elizabeth shrugged. 'We've been talking on the phone. He calls all the time. Damn it, if he'd threaten me with a court order or a lawyer or something it'd be easier to handle. But he doesn't. He just says he understands: says he's not going to talk about having any more children if I don't want to, says it'll be good for me to have a break for a while, to have some space.'

'And is it?'

She frowned. 'I don't know. I'm confused. I don't know what to think.'

'Do you love him?' Meg asked.

It was a straightforward enough question but it seemed to sting.

'Love him? What sort of a thing is that to ask? Love. What does it mean anyway? Well? Can you tell me that?'

She gave Meg a harsh stare.

The moment was relieved by the waiter who arrived with their starters, seared scallops piled high on a bed of something green.

Elizabeth finished her gin and lifted her glass of wine as Meg began to eat. It tasted great but her appetite had waned.

'Well, then,' Meg said eventually, trying again, 'I'll put it another way – do you miss him?'

'Catriona does,' Elizabeth offered.

'But you – do *you* miss him?'

Her friend gave an abrupt nod that was a bit reluctant. 'Sometimes, yes, I suppose I do.'

'So you should sort it out. Face to face. It's good that he's coming here and that he's being reasonable about this. Running away like that, it could have been part of the whole post-natal stuff, you know. That can take a long time.'

'And you would know?' Her wine was finished and she signalled for another one.

'That's right,' Meg said and gave her a sharp look. 'I would. Apparently I'm a doctor.'

When Elizabeth and a taxi dropped her and the shopping off at Truesdale Street later she was glad to be on her own again.

She was running out of sympathy. For her father, for Elizabeth. Everyone.

She unwrapped her new clothes and put them away. Then she made a cup of tea and stood with it, looking out her front

130

window. Like some sort of tropical storm, the rain had stopped as suddenly as it had begun. The clouds were drifting away towards a new target and the sun was casting a blanket of light across the sturdy flanks of the Black Mountain.

They were draining her, Elizabeth with her moods, her parents with their emotional hang-ups and their problems, pulling her one way, then another.

No one was thinking of her needs at all. It was like, *great, she's back. Let's dump as much baggage on her as we can.*

She had to free herself of this. She had more important things to think about. She had to get her life back on track and it was time she made a start.

Seventeen

She did so at lunchtime the next day as the sun toasted the pavements and beat on the roof of the taxi that took her through the city streets.

It was ridiculous, she conceded. She would have to learn to drive again.

Her father had a car which he said she could use.

'It's a Saab. I never bother with it, I'm always in the Range Rover. It's yours whenever you want it. Just let me know and I'll sort the insurance out.'

Lessons – that might be the answer. She had not forgotten how to drive and her licence was still valid. A couple of refresher sessions would get her into shape.

In any case, Belfast had changed a lot. There were new buildings, new road systems. She would have to get familiar with them before letting herself loose on the unsuspecting travelling public. But so much for independence. Here she was, contemplating borrowing her father's car.

It would be just for a little while, not forever, and surely that was all right?

They were in the docks area now, amid multi-lane confusion. She looked out on new office blocks and huge grain silos that were sheer sheets of corrugated cladding. She saw the old dark stone of the Sinclair Seamen's Presbyterian Church with its Italianate tower. The cab stopped in somewhere called Pilot Street, which didn't sound right.

'It's the Clarendon Dock I'm looking for,' she said.

The driver put his arm across the back of the passenger seat and twisted round to look at her. He had dark jowls and would never be clean-shaven. A picture of two little blonde girls was stuck to the dashboard and she assumed they looked like their mother.

'This is it, love,' he said. 'In front of you.'

She peered out. There was a gap straight ahead and a small wrought iron archway with the words 'Clarendon Dock' worked into it.

'Where exactly is it you're trying to get to?' he asked.

'There's a pub,' she began.

'There's a whole lot of them,' he said. 'You've got the Rotterdam Bar just there,' he pointed, 'and round the corner there's Pat's Bar.' He winked at her. 'Or you could try the Dockers' Club. We just passed it.'

'No thanks,' she said. 'This will do.'

She paid him, got out and asked if he would come back for her in half an hour.

As he reversed up the narrow street again she walked through the arch and found herself in a stone square. There were tiered steps curving around, like rows of seats, creating a little amphitheatre. Against a wall stood an empty, black-painted stage with the words Guinness Gig Rig across the top. A string of Guinness pennants flapped in a breeze that carried a mealy smell from the silos.

She stood, looking at it all. She could have been here before; she just wasn't certain. She didn't recognise any of it but the place was such a part of her mystery that she felt some kind of familiarity, as if she were visiting an historic site.

New buildings stood all around, mellow brick and stone and smoky blue glass that threw the sun back on itself with dazzling flashes of light. Over to one side, behind a high wire fence, a building was just being started, only a framework of girders so far. She could see construction workers in hard hats and hear the ringing echo of their hammers on the metal skeleton.

A sign on the fence announced that it would be a block of new luxury apartments, ready at the end of the year. There was an artist's impression of the finished product but it was partly obscured by a proud banner that said 'All Sold'.

She walked left towards the sign for Pat's Bar. Outside the pub, office workers, men in neat suits, the women in cotton dresses, sat at picnic tables. She passed two young men and three girls crowded together, plates and glasses in an untidy jumble. The girls laughed at something suddenly and the sound echoed off the old stone walls.

Meg glanced around. At another table were a couple of men in dusty jeans, pints of lager golden in their fists, racing pages open. Near them, two women sat soaking up the sun on the warm steps.

They were like performers in a drama or figures in some kind of tableau that had been arranged just for her. No one bothered with her, yet she could not shake the feeling of being watched.

Had he been here that night, the man who killed Paul Everett? Was he here now?

Pat's Bar was crowded. Cigarette smoke danced in shafts of sunlight. It was dark, a place for the drinkers mostly, the men from the building sites and from the flour mills. Trying to avoid their stares, telling herself that they were men and she was a woman, that was all, she went up to the bar where she ordered a cup of coffee and a chicken sandwich.

'Is that stage always there?' she asked the barman when he set her order in front of her.

'Only in the summer months when there's gigs on. They take it away in the winter.'

She went back outside with a tray and found a seat along the wall just at the door. From there she could survey the whole of the little square and as she did she knew that if she sat there all day, or for a million years for that matter, it would make no difference to her memory.

When she had finished eating she got up and began to explore further. There was a cobbled pathway in new stone, lined with young trees. It took her round the corner of a building which housed an education department of some kind, and suddenly she was at the edge of the old dock.

The oily water shone in rainbow streaks and the smell from the silos was stronger. Straight across from her were the yellow shapes of Samson and Goliath, the giant cranes, standing astride the shipyard, but further along towards the city, the landmarks were not so familiar. The Waterfront concert hall was like a huge glass hat box. Behind it the Hilton hotel and the new BT headquarters were two stiff-shouldered sentries in honeyed brick.

The city had changed; it was reborn. All around her were examples of regeneration against the odds.

She wanted to be a part of that but it was going to be hard.

She turned away. There was nothing here for her, nothing that evoked a memory of that night.

But it had started her thinking. There was a name. She had it on a piece of paper somewhere at home.

It was on the page of notes she had jotted down the day the police came to talk to her.

Mrs Fiona Jackson and her husband. She didn't know his first name.

She looked them up in the phone book. Jackson, 43 Willoughby Park. There it was. At about six that evening she rang to see if anyone was in.

A man answered. 'Hello?'

She hung up straight away. She had withheld her own

number so she knew he could not dial 1471 and call her back. She did not want to talk on the phone and if she said who she was they might not agree to see her. The best thing was to turn up on the doorstep.

She rang for a taxi, then changed out of her jeans into a skirt and blouse and a light linen jacket. The cab reached her in fifteen minutes. 'Coming,' she called when she heard the doorbell, stuffing her purse and a few things into a canvas shoulderbag. She would get a bus back.

They headed across to the Malone Road and over the Stranmillis embankment. Elizabeth's flat was somewhere near here. She had yet to visit it but right now she was in no rush to do so.

They joined the Ormeau Road near its top end where the Forestside shopping centre sprawled, vast, ugly slabs of windowless brown and grey like some sort of a prison built on the site of what had been the city's first supermarket thirty years ago.

They reached the Saintfield Road and in a couple of minutes the driver started indicating to turn right.

Willoughby Park curved downhill, a sloping dormitory of bungalows behind red brick garden walls and bushy hedges.

'What number did you say?'

'Forty-three.'

They drove slowly, exploring unfamiliar territory, peering out at the numbers on the gate posts. Even numbers were on the left, odd on the right.

He pulled over on the other side of the street and stopped. 'Forty-three. Here you are.'

She got out and looked at the house. The grass in the front garden needed cutting and dandelions had laid siege to the flower beds round the edges. Across the front window, a partly closed venetian blind obscured any glimpse of what might be inside.

She paid the driver and wondered for a second if she should ask him to wait but in the end she didn't. He drove off, leaving her standing alone and apprehensive on the pavement.

She rang the bell. The door was opened almost instantly by a small man in his early fifties, strands of hair across his head like thin leather straps. He wore white trousers and a blue sports shirt, opened deep to reveal a gold chain at his neck.

'Haven't seen you before,' he said. He looked past her furtively.

'No, I—'

'Come in,' he said and pulled her by the arm, glancing out to make sure no one was looking.

'Mr Jackson,' she began again, caught by surprise. 'I—'

'In here,' he said, closing the front door and leading her a few

135

swift steps into the hall. He opened a door. 'Make yourself at home. I'll be with you in a minute.'

'Look, I—'

He disappeared, closing the door behind him.

She was in a bedroom of kind. The curtains were pulled shut and light came from lamps with rose-tinted bulbs. Candles cast flickering shapes on the walls and there were a couple of oil burners scenting the air with jasmine.

She looked around. What sort of place was this?

In the centre of the room was the bed. It was wide and uncovered, apart from a sheet that appeared to be made of rubber.

And as she began to get used to the light, she saw that there were objects mounted on one wall.

Whips. One of them was a cat o'nine tails.

Oh Christ.

She started to move towards the door but just as she did it opened. Jackson stood there. He was a little breathless. 'Now then,' he said and smiled strangely.

He was wearing a short white towelling robe that was almost purple in the unearthly light. His legs were bare and she felt something nauseous in her throat because she knew he would be naked underneath.

She stared at him. His smile vanished and he looked puzzled. 'You've still got your clothes on. And where's all your stuff?'

'Stuff? Listen, Mr Jackson—'

'Your oils and stuff. For the massage. The taxi – I thought—'

'Mr Jackson,' she said as firmly as she could to cover the tremble in her voice. 'I think there's been a mistake here. I'm not who you think I am. I—'

He stepped back, trying to wrap the robe tighter round himself. 'Are you the police?'

'No, I'm not the police. My name is Meg Winter. I called on the off-chance that I might be able to have a word with you and your wife.'

'My wife's dead,' he said.

She was shaken. 'Oh . . . I . . . I'm sorry. I didn't know. I didn't mean—'

'Car accident. A year ago.'

'I'm terribly sorry.'

He was getting angry, trying to recover his dignity, but he wasn't dressed for it. 'Just who the hell are you, barging into my house like this?'

'I didn't barge in. You more or less dragged me in.'

He closed the door and stared at her, his eyes narrowing.

She felt her mouth dry as if something had sucked all the

moisture out of it, then she glanced around hurriedly for some way to defend herself. There was nothing except the whips and she doubted if they'd be much use in a crisis.

She was taller than he was but he was strong. She had felt his grip on her arms.

A kick. If he came nearer that's what she would do. Somewhere just below where he had tied the belt of his robe. Then she'd be through the door and away.

But he didn't move towards her. 'What do you want?' he said. He looked at her bag. 'Are you trying to sell something?'

'No, I just want to explain. Four years ago, you and your wife witnessed an accident. A sports car was run off the road. A man was murdered and a woman was injured, left in a coma. I – that was me.'

He looked hard at her. 'Who did you say you were again?'

'Winter. Meg Winter.'

His eyes widened as he remembered. 'You? I read that you'd recovered. So you just turn up at my door, do you? Out of the blue? You're all right now but my wife's dead. That's just great, isn't it? What the hell do you want with me?'

'I wanted to talk to you . . . both. I wanted to hear from you what you saw that night, to see if there was anything you might have forgotten to tell the police at the time. You see, I've lost my memory.'

'Well, that's your problem. Nothing to do with me. So why don't you just get the hell out of my house?'

He opened the door wide and she felt herself breathe again.

She walked quickly past him into the hall, then she made straight for the front door in case he changed his mind. But he didn't. He stayed where he was and watched her go.

She had opened the door and turned. 'Mr Jackson, I'm really sorry. If I'd known—'

He waved angrily. 'Just go on. Get out. And keep away from me in future.'

She closed the door firmly behind her and hurried away, feeling as if the smell of the room was still on her clothes.

As she walked up the park towards the main road, a taxi passed her, slowing down. There was a young woman in the back with bright blonde hair and a wary glance.

Meg walked on. She heard a car door slam but she did not turn to see. She knew where it had stopped.

Eighteen

It knocked her off course for a day or two. She hardly went out, except to the corner shop for essentials, worried that she would see Mr Jackson, unable to get the image of the disgusting man and his awful room out of her mind.

But he had been just as frightened as she was. He had been caught in the midst of his sordid little pursuit and now she knew about it. It did not help her peace of mind to know that he was out there somewhere thinking about that.

She agonised over the possibilities, even wondering whether Jackson had been involved in Paul Everett's murder. What if the Jacksons had been lying and there had been no other car? But that was impossible. She was torturing herself with crazy thoughts.

Her father and Elizabeth rang but she did not want to see either of them. Instead she sat on her own in a house that she was gradually warming to and watched television aimlessly. Game shows, soaps – the more mindless the better.

A telephone call snapped her out of it.

It was from Granada, a producer called Giles something.

'I hope you don't mind me calling you like this,' he said, 'but you said you'd get back to us and we've got some programmes coming up next week that you'd be perfect for.'

Next week? She almost said no. Instead she said: 'Well, yes, that would be fine. You're still interested in interviewing me, then?'

'Of course we are. We've got a couple of days dealing with strange things that happen to people, things that can't be explained. You know – miracle recoveries such as your own, people who've had out-of-body experiences. We thought you'd be great for it. You'll fit perfectly. Fantastic.'

She took a mental step back. 'I don't want to be treated like some freak. There was a murder, remember. I'm doing this because it's important for me to find out what happened that night. The programme might jog someone's memory.'

Maybe even her own.

Then she thought of Jackson watching, sitting there in his robe, and she shuddered.

'Of course,' he said. 'Anything we can do to help.'

She thought for a few seconds. 'Then if I have your assurance, I'll say yes.'

'Fantastic,' he told her.

A week later she flew to London on an afternoon flight for a programme the following morning. In the days following the producer's call, they had rung again and brought the trip forward by twenty four hours. Something about having to alter their schedule for the week.

She was in row twenty, sandwiched in a middle seat. On either side of her two men sat poring over incomprehensible paperwork. The one on her right was reading spreadsheets, and he underlined every few lines with a red marker pen.

The man on the left was more interested in her legs. She could feel his sideways glance as she tried to concentrate on the magazine in her lap.

She felt trapped and hardly able to breathe. The two men smelled warm, male, suffocating. Their bulk seemed to pinion her, forcing her elbows down by her sides.

She squeezed an arm out and reached up to twist the air blower open. A stewardess came past and it must have been written all over her face.

'Excuse me, madam, is everything all right? Is there anything I can get you?'

'I . . . I'm just finding it a bit claustrophobic,' Meg said. 'I haven't flown for a long time.'

'Just a moment,' the stewardess said and walked back towards the front of the plane. She returned in a few seconds.

'There's a seat in row three. An aisle seat. Perhaps you'd prefer that?'

Meg smiled. 'That would be great.'

'I'm sure this gentleman won't mind,' the stewardess said.

'Sorry,' the man on the right grunted, then he moved to let Meg out.

She had a bag in the overhead locker. The stewardess got it for her, then led her to her new seat. Tea and a scone with Devon cream in a tiny carton arrived and she began to feel better.

She had thought Belfast was crowded but it was tranquillity itself compared to Terminal One at Heathrow on a sticky summer afternoon.

She walked down corridors that seemed endless, being passed by streams of people in a rush. Others stood confused, peering at unfamiliar signs, muttering anxiously to each other.

She could hear, French, Spanish. A man scurrying by with a briefcase and a suit bag almost knocked her down, then shouted in German over his shoulder as he ran on.

'—schuldigen sie, bitte.'

She felt hot and bothered but she told herself not to panic. This was the way the world was. Yet it was a world that seemed to her more hostile and unyielding now than it had ever been before.

At the top of the stairs in the arrivals hall a bunch of men with expressionless faces stood behind a barrier and held up white pieces of card with names scrawled on them. She had been told that a driver would meet her there. She could not see her name but then she saw *Winder*.

'Winter?' she suggested.

The bearer of the card was heavy-set with a moustache. He looked Greek.

'Win-der,' he insisted.

'Winter,' she tried again. 'Meg Winter.'

He looked puzzled.

'Granada TV?' she said.

His face lit up. 'Yes. Winder.' He smiled and reached for her bag.

His car was a Mercedes with pine fresheners hanging from the mirror and air conditioning all the way to freezing. When they got out of the car park, she asked him if he could turn it down a little.

He looked at her in the mirror and shrugged. 'I have Japanese people in my car this morning. They like it this way. Too cold?'

'Too cold,' she said, rubbing her arms to make the point.

She gave him the name of the hotel they had booked for her but he already knew. They headed towards west London and she settled into the soft leather upholstery, feeling the air becoming warmer. But as they drove and she looked out of the window at the traffic, doubt began to uncoil in the pit of her stomach. What was she doing here?

Yesterday she had written a letter. She had sent it to the Chief Executive of Vectra Pharmaceuticals at Antrim, explaining who she was and asking if it would be possible to speak to someone about Paul Everett.

It was another shot in the dark. She did not know how they would respond; probably not very favourably. The chances were that they would want to steer clear of the whole business and leave it buried in the past.

The car slowed to a crawl. Hammersmith in the rush hour.

She sighed. She couldn't very well back out now. She was here and she would go through with it. And if it turned up any answers, well, that would be all to the good.

The hotel was over at the South Bank, not far from the television studios. Like a child on a day out, she found herself peering at the sights on the way there: Big Ben, St Paul's, all the lovely bridges over the Thames. It was a long while since she had been in London. She could not remember the last time.

She checked in and went up to a room that was comfortable but dull with hunting prints on the walls and a view of a flat roof with sooty air vents. There was a note from the manager on the writing table at the window. It apologised to guests for any problems with the air conditioning system, which was in the process of being replaced.

On the floor just inside the door, she found an envelope containing a fax from the producer telling her that they were taking care of dinner, bed and breakfast and that he would ring her at about seven to discuss tomorrow's arrangements.

She had time to have a bath and wash her hair. She had finished and was in a towelling robe, watching the news on Channel 4, when he rang. After she had spoken to him and told him she was fine, all settled in, and he had said how great the show was going to be, she went down to dinner, wearing a light blouse and a skirt that had survived the journey without too many creases.

It was warm in the hotel and open windows made no difference. The air outside was still and clammy. There was a little bar next to the dining room so she lifted a menu and went in there first. She had forgotten to bring her glasses down, although it did not really matter: she did not need them for reading.

Two men were at the bar, laughing loudly at something. No one else was around except a barman in a mauve tuxedo. She slid along a banquette, in behind a table where somebody had left an *Evening Standard*. She began to glance through it. The barman came over and she ordered a mineral water. The two men had stopped talking and she knew they were looking at her but after a couple of minutes she had forgotten about them.

'My friend bet me I wouldn't come over and tell you you look just like Julia Roberts.'

She hadn't noticed him approach.

He was in a double-breasted suit, too heavy for the weather, and his accent was from the north of England somewhere. He

141

leaned over the table, eyes and face glistening, and she could smell his boozy breath.

'So now you've won,' she said. 'What was the bet?'

'He has to buy you a drink.' He pointed vaguely over his shoulder.

'No, thanks,' she smiled as politely as she could, turning back to the paper, 'I'm fine.'

He seemed to notice something. 'Hey – what's this? Are you Irish, Julia? Well, then you'll definitely have a drink, begorrah. What'll it be?'

'Nothing, thanks.' She wanted him to go away.

'Come on, what're you havin' there?' He made a stab at a Belfast accent.

She glared up at him. Enough was enough. 'I'd like you to leave me alone,' she said firmly.

'Come off it,' he said. He narrowed his eyes. 'Who are you kidding, sweetheart? You don't fool me. I know what you—'

'Geoff,' his friend said abruptly. 'Eh – I think this might be a mistake.'

She could see the barman looking on anxiously, muttering something. The other man came over and pulled his friend by the arm. 'Come on, Geoff. Come away and leave the lady alone.' He smiled at her. 'Sorry, miss. Some confusion, that's all.'

They went back to the bar, mumbling to each other.

There was a mirror along the wall beside her and as she watched them walk away she caught a glimpse of herself.

Washing her hair had left it fluffed out a lot. The blouse she was wearing was a bit revealing, nothing too outrageous, just slightly see-through. She looked down at her long legs crossed under the little skirt.

They thought she was a hooker.

A woman alone in the bar of a business hotel. Yorkshiremen, or whatever they were, down in London for the night.

Julia Roberts. That film. *Pretty Woman*.

Christ.

Even though she knew it was the drink that had prompted him, she had found herself flattered when he said it. Now she felt foolish and cheap.

A picture of the Clarendon Dock flashed through her mind.

If this man had thought she was available, then maybe Paul Everett had, too. If so, then she had responded very differently that night.

You were the one with the condoms in the handbag in case you got lucky. Remember?

She did not want to be here with these two leering at her. She got up and hurried back to the lift, all thoughts of dinner abandoned.

She did not sleep at all well, tossing and turning and pummelling the pillows as if they were a punch bag.

She breakfasted early and heartily, bacon, eggs – the works, and she felt the better for it. She had packed up and was going out through the lobby to the car that had been sent when she saw them again. They were having a disagreement with the receptionist about their bill and they did not notice her. They looked sickly, especially the one who had tried to pick her up, and she could hear the hangover catarrh in their voices. They would feel like death, that was for sure, and the thought gave her a vengeful satisfaction.

At the studio, a girl in jeans was waiting at reception and ticked her name on a clipboard. 'I'm Sally the production assistant,' she said. Her voice was plummy. 'Hi. I'll take you straight up to make-up and then on to the green room.'

'What's that?'

'The green room?' She said it with the incredulity of someone who thought that hers was the only world. 'It's a kind of waiting room. There's coffee and things. You'll meet one or two of the other guests. And the presenters of course.'

Someone else was in make-up when she was ushered in, a handsome man in his late twenties with perfect hair and teeth. She recognised him from bored mornings watching television in hospital.

'Dr Peter Jenner,' Sally said, 'and this is Meg Winter, one of our guests.'

He shook her hand and gave her a smooth smile but the effect was spoiled by the bib under his chin to keep the make-up off his shirt.

'I'm the resident psychologist on the show.'

'I know,' she said. 'I used to watch it from time to time.'

'You're a doctor, I see from the cuttings. What area?'

'General medicine. I was in A and E for a while.'

'Your case – it's fascinating. I've been reading about you.' He stood close to her and looked deeply into her eyes. 'A coma for so long.'

'What's your role today?' she asked quickly, feeling crowded by him and stepping back towards comfort.

'Well, you'll do your interview, of course, and then they'll talk to me about what can cause something like that.'

'But you don't know anything about me,' Meg said. 'We've never spoken before.'

He smiled knowingly and waved away her objections. 'Don't worry about it. If you were a patient of mine that would be important. But this is television. Anyway, like I said, I've read what's in the file.' He laughed and headed for the door. 'Don't expect any great depth this morning. It's just a bit of entertainment.'

Her heart sank. Sally handed her something to sign and the clipboard to lean on.

'What's this?'

'It's your contract, so that you get paid. And there's a lot of general stuff about waiving rights and all that kind of thing. It's pretty much standard.'

Meg signed.

'We had actually booked the American Ambassador for today,' Sally told her, 'but he cried off. Afraid he'd get asked about the President's latest problems, obviously.'

Meg hardly heard her. After make-up, Sally took her to the green room. Someone got her a coffee. It was very strong and hit her bloodstream with a jolt.

A tousled-haired man in heavy-rimmed glasses and a shirt like sackcloth burst into the room and thrust his hand out. 'Meg, hi, I'm Giles. We spoke last night. Great that you could come. You look terrific. It'll be fantastic.'

She was about to tell him about the areas she hoped they would cover when the door flew open again and the two presenters came in.

It was a royal entrance.

In their train came a clutch of assistants, a couple of them speaking on mobile phones. Giles introduced her to them. The woman was a plump blonde in a cream suit and she seemed as nervous as Meg felt. The man was skinny, with a cosmetic tan and an attention span as lasting as a blink.

'You're the coma woman,' he said. 'Great. Fantastic.'

He moved off to talk to someone else.

'Looking forward to chatting to you,' the woman said and as abruptly as they had arrived, they all disappeared again.

'Stay here and relax,' Sally said, 'I'll come and get you when the band's on.'

It was all going very badly indeed. 'Which one's doing the interview?' Meg asked.

'She is,' Sally said, 'but he likes to join in with some stuff of his own.' She looked apologetic.

When she had gone, Meg sat and watched the monitor with a sense of dread.

The opening titles began. There was applause from the audience and then a shot of the two presenters on their chairs, extravagant vases of flowers on each side and behind them a huge window out over the Thames. A barge that looked half a mile long took an eternity to drift past.

They went to a close-up of the woman looking earnest. 'Imagine what it would be like to wake up after being in a coma for four years. Four whole years. Imagine, too, what it would be like when you discovered that what led to the coma was a car crash in which someone was killed. Not killed in the accident – but actually murdered afterwards. Bizarre? And now – imagine what it would be like not to be able to recall anything about the night all this took place – to experience total amnesia. Horrifying, isn't it? But that's exactly what happened to our first guest this morning.'

She turned to her partner. 'But before all that,' he said, picking up his cue, 'a hot new band from Manchester has been storming up the charts with a cover version of an old song by the Osmonds . . .'

Sally came back. 'OK, I'll take you now.'

She led the way into the studio, making sure Meg did not trip on cables entwined across the back of the set, then directed her to a settee beside the presenters. They barely seemed to notice her. They were looking at notes and listening to the voice of the director on their earpieces. In the dusk behind the studio lights, the audience waited.

Meg could hear music but she could not see anyone playing it. 'Where's the band?' she whispered.

'Oh, they're on VT,' Sally explained. 'We recorded them yesterday.'

The woman turned and smiled as Meg sat down. 'There's an ad break coming up and then we're with you. OK?'

Meg nodded. Someone came and flicked a brush over her make-up to stop it shining. A sound technician appeared with a clip microphone on a thin lead and asked Meg if she would mind threading it underneath her blouse.

'Dr Winter, would you mind looking this way?' a man's voice said.

She glanced towards the sound and a camera flashed.

It startled her. 'What was that?'

'Studio stills,' Sally said. 'Publicity stuff for the papers. It's in the contract you signed.'

'What was it like when you first woke up?' the anchorwoman asked all of a sudden.

Meg swallowed. 'Well, I suppose it was a bit confusing. I didn't realise—'

145

'Great,' the woman said. 'Just keep it at that kind of level. That'll be fine.'

'Ten seconds,' the floor manager called. The woman straightened herself and stared at the camera.

'Five, four, three, two.' Then he pointed at her.

She gave a big smile. The audience applauded on cue. 'Welcome back. As I was saying at the beginning of the programme, our first guest has gone through some extraordinary experiences. In fact, it's a miracle she's alive but it's wonderful that she's with us here in the studio. Meg Winter, good morning.'

'Good morning,' Meg said, then cleared her throat.

'What's it like to come back from the dead?'

Meg's brain felt like a loose bundle of string. 'I . . . it's . . . well, it's kind of strange. There's a lot to get used to. A lot of things to learn all over again, like walking.'

She didn't know why she had said that.

'Walking?'

'Yes. Walking, talking, learning to do things for yourself. Your muscles aren't up to much after all that time. I lost a lot of weight.'

'What was the first thing you saw when you woke up?'

'A nurse. She had some flowers in her hand. She dropped them on the floor.'

'You gave her a bit of a fright, then.' She laughed.

'She looked like she'd seen a ghost. In a way I suppose she had.'

'Now, you were seriously injured in that accident four years ago but I'm right in saying that you didn't suffer any brain damage.'

How delicate. 'Not that anyone's aware of, no. I don't suppose I'd be here talking to you if there was anything wrong with my brain.'

She looked towards the audience. Some of them got the joke and laughed.

The woman ignored it. 'Yet you were in a coma for all that time and you don't remember anything about what happened. Why do you think that is?'

'I can't say.' She smiled. 'I was about to say that I'm not a doctor but actually I am. I am a doctor. Just not that kind of doctor. No, I don't have any answers. But there are a lot of things I'd like to find out.'

The man stormed in. 'Somebody murdered the bloke you were with. That's weird, isn't it? You must have been cut up about that?'

'I was shocked, yes,' Meg said. He had the sensitivity of

146

someone kicking a door down. 'Confused, too. I should explain. You see, I don't know anything about him. I don't remember him and I don't know why I was with him that night.'

She could see that she had thrown them. This was not in any script or in any of the cuttings either. It had not been said before.

The woman recovered hurriedly. 'You don't – didn't – know him?'

'I know his name because I've been told. The police interviewed me but I wasn't much help to them. His name was Paul Everett, he was 27, he was an American who came from Portland in Maine and he was running a pharmaceuticals factory in Northern Ireland. That much is in the public domain, of course, you'll have seen all of it in your clippings, but what you don't know is that I've no memory of ever meeting him and no idea what I was doing with him that night.'

'So this is all part of the amnesia, you reckon?' the man said.

'Of course.' She felt better. 'One of the reasons I agreed to appear here this morning was the hope that it might somehow shed some light on what happened. Perhaps seeing me may spark someone's memory. I don't know Paul Everett, or anything about him, but his death is part of my life now. I have to know more about him and find out why I was with him. Then there's the question: why was he murdered? Somebody beat him to death. Who would do something like that and why didn't they kill me too?'

'Amazing,' the woman said.

'They found drugs in his system, didn't they?' the man chipped in. 'Do you think it might have had something to do with that? A drugs-related killing?'

'It's possible,' Meg said. 'That's what the police believe. They think I was just unfortunate to get caught up in it.'

'So where had you been that night?' he wondered.

'I'm not sure. There's some suggestion that I was at a concert at a place called the Clarendon Dock in Belfast but I don't really know for certain. I went there a little while ago to have a look at it but to be honest it was like going there for the first time. The place rang no bells. None at all. But,' she shrugged, 'who can tell? Maybe I met him there.'

The woman was about to say something but Meg kept on going. 'What I do have to say is that I feel a tremendous sense of, well . . . guilt is the only word for it. I'm alive and this poor man is dead. Somehow I feel responsible for that. He has relatives somewhere, I suppose, back in the United States. They'd have been told about me when it happened, that I was with him. I guess I've been as much of a mystery to them as he is to me. They've lost a loved one. In some way I've been a part of that and I feel bad about it.'

There was a little pause while they all let the thought linger. 'But your own parents,' the woman said, 'they must be delighted.'

'Of course. They've both had a lot of pain to contend with. I'm glad for them that it's over.' She smiled. 'Their prayers must have worked.'

'Are you religious yourself?' the woman wondered. 'Is faith important to you?'

'Actually, no. I'm afraid I'm not much of a believer. Since I'm Irish you might find that a bit odd but I don't think it's got us very far, do you? There's too much religion, if you ask me, too much dangerous rubbish talked about God and Christianity. But that's another topic.'

'And what does the future hold in store for you now?' the man asked. 'You're not married but is there a boyfriend?'

Meg shook her head. 'No.'

'No old flames?'

'None that I can remember.' She gave a wry grin.

'I wouldn't worry,' he said with a leer. 'After this they'll be queuing at the door.'

'So what next?' the woman said. 'You've got the rest of your life ahead of you.'

'It's difficult,' Meg said, 'with so much of my memory *unavailable* to me. I know I'm a doctor and that I worked at Belfast Central Hospital but my work there's a blank page, too. The good news is that my medical knowledge, everything I learned in the past, seems to be intact. I know it's going to be hard to make a new start but that's what I want to do. I'm determined.'

'To return to medicine?'

'Yes. But first I need my memory back.'

'And just what is the last thing you remember?' she asked.

'It doesn't work like that,' Meg said. 'It's not like there's . . . like there's a moment I can recall and then just nothing. I can remember a great deal about my past, of course. Most of my past, in fact, but there are huge gaps involving periods of time and involving people. Every now and then I run into a kind of glass wall that I can't get through and all I can see is me staring back at myself, like it's a mirror. I know there's something behind it, something locked in there in my head. I don't know what it is or how to get to it and the only link I have is this murdered man.'

The woman nodded. It looked to Meg as if she was responding to something being said into her ear. 'Well, in a few

148

moments we'll be talking to Dr Peter Jenner about the prospects of your memory returning but let me ask you: what has surprised you about the world you've come back to?'

'Everything,' Meg said. 'Of course, it seemed terribly hectic at first. The pace seemed faster, everyone in such a hurry, but maybe that's just me trying to come to terms with it. I tried to read through old magazines and so on to catch up with what had been happening in the world but there was too much to take in. My doctors reckoned I shouldn't try to bombard myself with information but to take each new thing as it came along.'

'Have you managed to catch up with *Coronation Street*?' the man asked all of a sudden.

She looked at his happy, empty grin. They had got the thing back on the rails. The cosy superficiality was returning but it didn't matter; she had said what she wanted to.

'I never really watched *Coronation Street* that much,' she said. 'Although I noticed that some of the actors who've been in it a long time, they seem to have got older all of a sudden. That took me by surprise.'

She thought of something. 'Diana, of course. That was a blow.'

'Diana?' the woman queried.

She nodded. 'One of the nurses was chatting to me one day and made a reference to something that had happened: "after Diana and Dodi died," was how she put it. I didn't know what she was talking about. I'd never heard of anyone called Dodi. She had to explain it all to me. I was terribly shocked.' She gave a weak smile. 'I was probably the last person in the world to find out. They got me a video of the funeral and I cried my eyes out. I couldn't believe it.'

'Of course,' the woman said. 'You wouldn't have known. How extraordinary. There must be lots of things like that.'

'OK,' her partner cut in before Meg could respond, 'we're going to take a short break but we'll be back to this in a moment with Dr Peter Jenner and we'll be hearing from a woman who claims to have twice had an out-of-body experience while on the operating table and says that on the second occasion she met her deceased husband. After that, we'll be taking your calls. So don't go away.'

There was more applause. He turned to Meg. 'That was great. Marvellous. Brilliant stuff about not knowing the guy. Fantastic.'

'You did very well,' the woman agreed.

'It wasn't a performance. I was telling the truth.'

'Of course,' the woman said, missing the point, patting her on the knee. 'I'd have just *loved* a bit more about Diana. Wish we'd been aware of that. We could have got to it earlier.'

Sally came and led her away. They passed the psychologist coming in. 'Great show,' he said.

In the green room, she had a glass of water. She felt thirsty, flushed from the experience and the coffee before it.

Sally had a handful of letters secured by a rubber band. 'I take it you get a lot of mail?' Meg asked.

'Oh absolutely loads. We get a huge post bag every day.'

'If there are any for me, will you forward them? You've got my home address.'

'Do you want all of them?' She looked doubtful. 'Sometimes they're a bit unpleasant. Cranks, you know.'

'It doesn't matter. Send them on. I'll deal with them.'

'If you're sure.'

She sat and listened to what Dr Jenner had to say and she had to confess he wasn't bad. He talked about the different branches of memory: episodic, semantic, procedural, and he did it in a way that the audience would understand easily.

'So why do you think she's lost her memory?' the woman was saying.

'Obviously, the cause is traumatic. Her brain has responded to something it can't handle by shutting her memory off, even closing down altogether for the past four years.'

'Is this rare?'

'In psychology we come across new phenomena all the time. There's so much about how the mind and the brain work that's unfathomable. Every coma case is unusual and distinctive. Most involve brain damage, however slight, and it's possible that that's the case here, too, that a kind of a connection of some kind has been jogged loose. But if I had to put a bet on it, I would say that what Meg suffered for four years was the result of something dreadful that happened that night. There's a murdered man to prove it. But we don't know the events that led up to it.'

'And will we ever?'

'Perhaps, if her memory returns.'

'And what's the likelihood of that?'

'It's possible. I won't give you odds. Don't forget – Meg's in a very peculiar position. It's as if she's locked in a kind of struggle with herself. She says she wants her memory back and that's true. The problem is, her brain doesn't agree with her. Her mind's holding tight to whatever's in there.'

His words stayed with her for the rest of the day.

On the way home on the plane, she thought about it. Maybe it would be best not to know. But she dismissed that notion almost as quickly as it had formed. She could not live her life like that. Anyway it was too late. She had started something now and she had no control over where it might lead.

The cabin staff were dishing out copies of the *Evening Standard*. On an inside page, she was shocked to find a picture of herself. She folded the paper tightly so that no one else could see.

It was the picture that had been taken in the studio and there was a short news item to go with it. The programme publicity department was obviously good at its job.

But when she looked at the headline she threw the paper down in disgust:

MY SADNESS OVER DI – BY DRUG MURDER
COMA WOMAN

Although she did not know it, another journalist was looking at the story but taking a different angle.

At the London headquarters of Reuters, Louise Purdy, an American reporter working for the agency, had been watching the show, waiting for the American Ambassador to appear. The TV magazines and the programme press releases had said he would be on and that was the only reason she had got an engineer to record it.

There was no Ambassador but there was something else instead.

Louise was from Massachusetts and here was an intriguing item for the folks back home. It was not a big network piece but she could package it with old library material – the Belfast office would have that – as well as extracts from the interview, and turn it into a nice little story about the unsolved murder of a guy from Maine and the woman who was the last person to see him alive – apart from whoever killed him, of course.

With all the amnesia and everything, it was a strange tale indeed and she was sure they could offer it to the local stations around the dead man's home town.

It ran the next morning.

WGME13 in Portland took it on their breakfast show and were grateful because it was a slow news day. In fact, although nationally there was always the President's latest predicament, on the local scene it was a light news week. People were on vacation and there was just a load of summer stuff to contend with: drownings, forest fire warnings and the like. Which was why some of the other stations a bit further afield took it on their morning programmes, too.

In a little town in New Hampshire, an elderly man saw it as he drank a cup of coffee and smoked a cigarette at the kitchen table in the apartment where he lived alone.

When the story came round again an hour later, like he hoped it would, he had his video recorder ready.

Nineteen

The physiotherapist at the Musgrave had advised her about exercise.

'You've got to keep it up but don't overdo it. Nothing too strenuous. No running on hard surfaces because it might jar your spine. Something steady. Power-walking, that's the thing. You see women out doing it all the time.'

And, to her surprise, she had.

At first she had thought they looked ridiculous. They were in twos or threes, mostly, all shapes and sizes, striding red-faced up and down the Lisburn and Malone Roads, those well-trodden middle-class fitness paths. But then she got used to the sight and she saw that nobody else thought it was in any way unusual.

So, kitted out in leggings and sturdy trainers, a sweatshirt tied round her slim waist, Meg joined the parade, just once or twice a week to begin with, walking during the day at busy times when she would not be on an empty street alone.

She did not stray far, nor did she walk for long, an hour at the most. She was still in the habit of resting when possible in the afternoons and she always went to bed early at night. Every now and then her body reminded her of how short a time it was since she had been a hospital patient.

A couple of days after her London trip, she went out for some exercise and when she came back, perspiring and looking forward to a shower, the phone was ringing.

It was Detective Inspector Florence Gilmour, wondering if Meg remembered her and asking if she could drop by.

She called the following morning. Meg made tea.

'So how are you getting on?' Gilmour said, looking round the living room, admiring it. 'Your house is nice. Did you always have it like this?'

Meg handed her a mug and noticed that her hair was even shorter than the first time. 'No, my father did all this while I was . . .' she thought of a word, '. . . *absent.*'

153

'It's very nice,' she said again.

Meg sat and cradled her own mug. 'I'm getting used to it. It's not quite as cosy as I remember it.'

'Remember?' Gilmour queried.

'It's just a word.'

Gilmour smiled. 'I just wondered.' She sipped her tea. 'Are you living here on your own?'

'Yes.'

'And you're not lonely?'

'A bit, at first,' Meg confided. 'I missed the nurses and the other hospital staff, the routine. But I've got used to it now. It's not a lonely place to live. The Lisburn Road's so lively. And I've got my parents. Then there's my friend Elizabeth. I see something of her.'

As she heard herself say it, it did not sound like much of a life.

'You should get a cat,' Gilmour said. 'I've got a cat. I like cats.'

'Do you live by yourself?' Meg asked, surprised.

'Oh good gracious, no such luck. I've got a husband and two boys. One's eleven and the other's nine. Believe me, there are times when the thought of living alone is very attractive indeed.'

'How's your tea?' Meg asked.

'I'm fine,' she said then changed the subject. 'Why I'm here – we saw you on television. I – well – our boss, the Chief Superintendent, wasn't too pleased. I volunteered to come and see you. He doesn't like unwelcome publicity about ongoing cases, especially when the case isn't actually going anywhere. The local papers have been back on to our press office as a result of the interview. The TV people have apparently let them have an up-to-date picture of you and they've been looking for your address. They didn't know you were out of hospital. They might try to find you, you know.'

Meg felt something sink inside her.

Gilmour said: 'We told them the case is still under investigation and that there's nothing to add to what's already been said. Frankly, the whole thing's a bit of an embarrassment because it's been lying unsolved for so long.'

'You mean I'm a bit of an embarrassment because I've brought it back to life,' Meg said. 'If I hadn't recovered, it might have been forgotten about.'

Gilmour laughed. 'I suppose that's the height of it, yes.'

Meg looked at her. She had an easy manner, a personality that drew you in. Meg found herself liking her. 'So, are you here to tick me off for going on TV?'

'If you like,' the other woman reflected. 'Mostly though, I'm here to tick you off for going to see Mr Jackson.'

Meg stared. 'How did you know about that?'

'We went to see him ourselves, just to go over his statement of four years ago, to see if there was the slightest chance of his remembering anything else about that night. He said you'd turned up at his door and tricked your way in under false pretences.'

'Did he, indeed? Not quite the way I remember it.' Then she told her what had happened.

Gilmour arched her eyebrows. 'Well, now, massages, eh? Girls in taxis? I think our vice team would be just a bit interested in that. You didn't notice the name of the taxi company? Was there a sign on its roof?'

'I think there was, yes, but I don't remember what it said. I was only interested in trying to get away from there as quickly as possible.'

Gilmour nodded. 'Look, Meg, this is an active case.' She pointed to herself. 'Let us do the investigating. Don't muddy the waters.'

'I'm not trying to get in your way. But you've no idea how desperate I feel about all of this. I'm just trying anything I can to see if it will help my memory.'

'I know,' Gilmour said. 'It must be very frustrating for you. The interview that you did, who knows? Maybe it will yield something.' She leaned forward and looked into Meg's eyes. 'But have you thought that it might put you in danger?'

'So you think I'm at risk? If I remember rightly you didn't seem to think so before.'

'Of course there's the possibility of risk. We can't rule anything out. But we've had no reason to think of you as being in immediate danger. Until . . .' She stopped.

'Until I went on television. Is that what you mean?'

Gilmour shrugged. 'There are a lot of funny people about. Your friend Jackson, for example. You must be careful, look after yourself. We can't be with you all the time. But if anything unusual does happen, a letter, a phone call, someone in the street, will you let me know?'

Meg felt cold. She nodded. 'Yes,' she said. 'I will.'

The detective took a card from an inside pocket and handed it to her. 'This is my direct line and my mobile number. You can call me any time you like.'

Meg looked at the card. It had the crest and the red, black and green stripes of the Royal Ulster Constabulary proudly emblazoned down one side. When Gilmour had gone, she stuck it on

155

the fridge door under the magnet where she kept notes and phone numbers.

Someone in the street.

If someone wanted to harm her, there was nothing the police could do about it. They could not watch her night and day. Gilmour had said as much.

Someone in the street.

She did not want people recognising her.

There was a hairdresser's that she passed regularly on her exercise route. She liked its stylish look and the appearance of the women she saw going in and out.

Seeing Florence Gilmour – that and what had happened in the bar of the hotel – made her mind up.

Twenty

A week later the long hair had gone.

In its place, not quite as short as Gilmour's, was a carelessly tossed bob, cut tight into her neck and above her ears, with blonde streaks like honey.

With that and the glasses she now wore so much, she looked and felt like a different person. Not, at any rate, like the Meg Winter in the photographs. Nor, she hoped, like a hooker.

She met Elizabeth for lunch at the local deli. Elizabeth thought the hair looked terrific. She herself looked well, too. Her husband had been in Belfast for a couple of days and she seemed much the better for the visit.

She didn't waste any time telling Meg exactly why.

'Five minutes after we started talking we were in bed. It was fantastic.'

'I'm glad to hear it,' Meg said. 'So you're back together again?'

'Do you know,' Elizabeth said, 'before he met me he'd never gone down on anyone? I had to teach him what to do. He took to it like a duck to water, I'm happy to say.'

'Jesus, Elizabeth, do you mind? I'm eating.'

'Exactly.' She laughed, then choked with a kind of snort that made people look round. Meg wondered if any of them had heard. The place was tiny.

'Keep your voice down,' Meg said. 'So what now?'

Elizabeth chuckled at her discomfort. 'He says he realises how much I hate Malaysia. He's applied for a transfer back to the UK, a job in London.'

Meg put her knife and fork down. 'Well, that sounds good.'

'But we've agreed that Catriona and I will stay here in Northern Ireland until that's definite, which won't be before the end of the year, and in the meantime I can nip over now and then to look at houses. You can come with me if you like.'

'Maybe,' Meg said. She had had enough of London for the moment. Apart from that she had to keep an eye on her finances. The money which had been untouched for so long would not last forever.

★ ★ ★

She went to see her mother, a visit she had been putting off. She hadn't told her she was going to be on TV. Then there was what she had said about religion. She hadn't intended that. It had just come out. Nerves.

Her mother didn't mention the subject. That was bad. She did not like her new look either.

'Your beautiful hair. You've destroyed it.'

'It's just a bit of a change, Mum,' Meg said, trying to be cheery. 'I've had that other style for rather a long time.'

They were in the kitchen. Meg sat at the table. The little dog made a fuss of her and she stroked its head as it stood on its hind legs with its front paws resting on her knee.

Her mother was in the process of making a pot of tea but she seemed confused about something.

Meg got up and went over to her. 'Can I help? What have you lost?'

'The sugar,' she muttered. 'I can't find the sugar.'

The door of the cupboard above her head was open. Meg could see the sugar bowl on the bottom shelf.

'Here it is,' she said, reaching for it.

Her mother tried to get the bowl at the same time. Neither of them grasped it successfully. It came crashing down, bouncing and spilling its contents onto the work surface before smashing in fragments on the floor.

'Oh dear God, what a mess,' Meg said, crouching and beginning to pick up the pieces. 'I'm sorry, Mum. I'll clear it up.'

Gloria stood ramrod straight. 'How dare you take the Lord's name in vain in my house.' Her voice was quivering.

'I'm sorry. It just slipped out. I didn't mean—'

Her mother stared down at her. 'Why? Why did you do it?'

'It was an accident. I was trying—'

'Shaming yourself before millions of people like that. Shaming me. Attacking those of us who do the Lord's work.'

Meg straightened. The sugar crunched under her feet.

'You didn't tell me you were going to go on television,' Gloria said. 'And then – the things you said.' Her eyes blazed and Meg saw pain as well as anger in them.

'No,' Meg sighed, 'I didn't tell you because I knew it would mean a row. I suppose I should have known it was inevitable either way. And what I said – it wasn't aimed at you. I just responded to a question, that's all.'

'Did your father know about it?'

'Yes. I told him some weeks ago what I was planning to do. I didn't tell him when it was happening.'

158

'No doubt he encouraged you.'

'If you must know, he didn't approve at all.'

Her mother opened a drawer. 'I got these,' she said. She dropped two envelopes on the table and then rubbed her fingers as if trying to wipe something away.

'What's this?'

'Read,' she said. 'See for yourself.'

Meg opened one of the letters. There was no address at the top. She looked to the bottom of the page. There was no signature either. Just the words, *True Christian*.

Your daughter sups with the devil, the letter said in tiny green capitals. *She is a heathen and flaunts herself like a harlot before the world. The Son of Man will send out his angels and they shall gather out of his kingdom all things that offend and them which do iniquity. And shall cast them into a furnace of fire.*

Nice. Truly Christian indeed. 'Is this some sort of quotation?'

'Matthew, thirteen.'

She was not surprised to see that the second letter was also anonymous. It was less imaginative and did not draw on fearsome Biblical firepower. Its message was curt, in a spidery hand.

'You are not welcome among us. Keep away. You will be struck down.'

By whom it was not clear.

Meg was disgusted and angry.

'This is awful,' she said. 'What are you going to do about it – apart from throwing them in the bin?'

'I showed them to Pastor Drew. He said he would pray for me and for you and that he would pray for the poor misguided people responsible.'

'Well, that's very helpful of him,' Meg said with a sarcasm she could not be bothered to hide.

'But why did you do it?' Gloria asked.

She was tired apologising. 'OK, maybe what I said will have offended some people but that's just an excuse.' She lifted the letters. 'In fact, this kind of proves the point. These are from members of the congregation of that church down there. They've made that pretty obvious. But what sort of people write things like this? What sort of Christian sentiments are these?'

'It doesn't have to be anyone from our church,' Gloria said, not even convincing herself.

Meg did not bother to argue. 'Mum, this isn't really about me – it's about you. There are clearly some bitter people, jealous for some reason, perhaps, and they've taken a dislike to you. I'm their way of getting at you. Maybe they think you and the

159

pastor are too friendly. I don't know.'

Gloria's eyes widened. 'What are you suggesting?'

Meg raised her hands in protest. 'I'm not suggesting anything. You don't know what goes through people's minds, that's
all.'

She thought of her mother's own dexterity at spreading
poison. There was something of an irony here but she got no
satisfaction out of observing it. Hate mail was cowardly and
sick. It was easy to suggest dismissing it as the work of a couple
of cranks but a lot harder to do so.

Faith, what she believed was her Christianity, was important
to her mother but through it, and more important still, was
prestige, position, the admiration of her peers. That was being
eroded. Meg felt like telling her what she thought of the
Pentecostal Baptist Church, that Drew was a charlatan, using
people and taking their money, but she did not want to undermine her more than her nameless correspondents had.

'I'm going away for a couple of days,' her mother said, more
subdued. 'I have a friend who has a cottage on the North
Antrim coast. She's always asking me to come and visit her. I
thought perhaps I would.'

'Good idea,' Meg said. 'It sounds great. Nice walks, fresh air.
Just the thing you need.'

She looked at the letters on the table. It was ridiculous. The
damned things were driving her mother out of her own home.

Her gaze returned to the floor. 'Is there a dustpan and brush?'
she asked. 'Better clean this mess up.'

The following morning, she got some letters of her own. There
were two of them in a brown envelope with a compliments slip
from Sally at Granada.

'Haven't looked at them. All yours,' she had scribbled.

After what had happened to her mother, Meg opened the first
with some trepidation. But it was innocuous: a letter from a
woman in Doncaster who ran a group for the families of people
who had suffered brain injury. She wondered if Meg was on the
Internet and would like to contribute to their activities.

The second was from a woman whose husband had had a
stroke and had been in a coma for several weeks. She wanted to
know if Meg thought he would recover, the way she had.

She could feel the desperation in the thin notepaper and
wished there was something she could do to help. What the
letters reminded her more than anything was that she should
consider herself lucky. Preoccupied with Paul Everett and his
killer, caught up with her parents and their problems, not to

160

mention Elizabeth, it obscured the fact that she had survived. With or without a memory, she had a life of sorts to lead.

A couple of minutes later, she was dialling a telephone number.

A woman answered; a real person, not an automated system. That was rare, as she was discovering.

'New Central Hospital, Betty speaking, how may I help you?'

'Oh, hi, yes,' Meg said, 'I wonder if you could give me the name of the doctor who's in charge of emergency medicine.'

Twenty-one

Dr Clare Gilleece,
Accident and Emergency,
New Central Hospital,
BELFAST

August 27

Dear Dr Gilleece

Until approximately four years ago, I was a doctor on the staff of the old Central Hospital, working latterly in A and E. Unfortunately, my medical career was interrupted by a serious accident. I am sure you may be aware of it from reading about it in the press.

However, I am pleased to say that I am now fully recovered and am keen to discover if it will be possible for me to resume my career in some way. I realise how difficult that is likely to be but I would like to talk to as many people as I can in order to find out what hurdles I have to overcome.

As a first step, I wondered if you would have time to talk to me. I realise how busy your job is but it would be a great favour and it would help me collect my thoughts before I decide to approach anyone else. I would also love to see inside an A and E unit again. I am sure an awful lot has changed in the past four years, new technology, equipment, and so on, but talking to you would be a tremendous start.

Hoping to hear from you soon,

Yours sincerely

Meg Winter

Dr Meg Winter,
30, Truesdale Street,
Lisburn Road,
BELFAST
September 3

Dear Dr Winter

Thank you for your letter of August 27. I would be
delighted to talk to you, as you suggest, and if I can be of
any help and guidance for the future I will be only too
pleased.

Perhaps you would telephone my secretary and arrange
a suitable appointment.

Yours sincerely

Clare Gilleece,
Manager,
A and E Unit

She arranged some driving lessons. Three were enough to
reassure her that she could manage. The instructor agreed and
said she didn't need any more. She also liked driving her
father's Saab and although it made her feel like a spoiled child it
gave her a freedom of movement that had been missing.

On the morning of her appointment with Clare Gilleece, there
was a veil of thin cloud and hazy, milky sunlight. She dressed in
a pale blue silk and linen mix suit she had bought in Marks and
Spencer and she took the car. She left it in the hospital car park
and locked up, then walked to the main reception area where
she had been told someone would look after her.

The hospital was a tower of glass and pink brick. Outside the
entrance, two fat women stood smoking. They wore housecoats
that said they were employed by an office cleaning company. A
layer of cigarette butts littered the ground all around them
where there were yellow lines and the words 'No Parking.
Emergency Only'.

Glass doors parted to let her into a big open waiting area. On
one wall was a mural which had been painted by the pupils of a
nearby primary school. It showed the various activities of the
hospital but the children's perspective made it look as if everything was stacked in layers. Surgeons in gowns and masks
stood around an operating table which floated above a large
white blob with wheels and the word 'ambulance' painted in

163

bright red letters. Below that there was a row of beds in which all the patients were bandaged like mummies.

On another wall a plaque told her that the hospital had been officially opened a year and a half ago by the Health Minister. Beside it was a framed notice which had been put there by the Trust which ran the place. It was the New Central's mission statement. There was a lot in it about customer care but Meg did not see the word 'patient' anywhere.

On rows of seats anchored back to back like in an airport lounge people were waiting, leafing absently through rumpled glossy magazines while their minds remained fixed on whatever problem had brought them. She wondered whose customers they were.

There was a smell of warm plastic and rubber floors and distant disinfectant. It kindled something in her but she didn't know whether it was an old memory or just a reminder of her months in Musgrave Park. All hospitals smelled the same.

She crossed to the reception desk.

Two women sat behind it in identical dresses with a small floral pattern, clearly the administrative staff uniform. One of them looked up from a computer screen. She had glasses with bright red frames and a badge that said her name was Janice Drayne. She smiled. Her lipstick went with the glasses.

'May I help you?'

'Yes. I have an appointment with Dr Gilleece. My name is Winter.'

The woman peered at the screen again and began clicking the mouse.

'Doc-tor Gill-eece.' She intoned each syllable as she searched. 'Ah yes, here we are.'

The screen told her something she did not know. She looked up at Meg with added interest. '*Doctor* Winter, is it?'

'That's right.'

'According to this, Dr Winter, I think you're seeing someone else, actually. There's been a change.'

She picked up the phone just as Meg was about to ask her what she meant.

'Oh, hello, it's Janice at main entrance reception here. I have a Dr Winter with me at the moment. She had an appointment to see Dr Gilleece.' She listened. 'Right. Thank you.'

She rang off and turned to Meg again. 'Take a seat for a moment, Dr Winter. The Medical Director's secretary will be down in a moment.'

'The Medical Director? Why isn't Dr Gilleece seeing me?'

But Janice's attention had moved elsewhere. The phone had

rung, she was answering it and two men in white nursing tunics were standing at the desk now, waiting for her to finish.

Puzzled, Meg sat. A few feet away a couple of toddlers with dirty faces crawled noisily around the chair legs. Their mother paid no attention to them. She was pale and hollow-eyed and looked no more than nineteen.

Meg lifted a copy of the *Ulster Tatler* that was a year old and began to look through it. Ruddy-faced men in tuxedos posed with their dressed-up wives at old-school reunion dinner dances. There were full-page advertisements for perfect kitchens and diamond rings.

Halfway through she turned a page and saw her father.

The picture had been taken outdoors in front of a marquee. He was wearing a blue blazer with silver buttons and he was one of a group of four men holding glasses of champagne. The headline said they were the sponsors of the Malone Group PLC annual charity golf tournament.

She looked for the caption to see who the others were.

'Dr Winter?'

A woman was smiling down at her. She had neat shiny hair pulled back tight behind her head and thin black eyebrows plucked to painful perfection.

'I'm Rose Hurst, the Medical Director's secretary,' she said. 'Sorry if you've been kept waiting. Would you like to come with me?'

Meg threw the magazine down on a seat and stood up.

'The lift's just over here,' the woman said and set off briskly.

'I don't understand,' Meg said, catching up with her. 'Why am I not meeting Dr Gilleece?'

'I'm afraid I can't help you there. All I know is that the Medical Director said he would see you when you arrived. You may be seeing Dr Gilleece as well, of course,' she said as that thought occurred to her. She flashed another smile.

They got into the lift and she pressed the button for the eighth floor. 'Excuse my ignorance,' Meg said, 'but who is the Medical Director?'

'Dr Kennedy,' the woman said casually, studying the lights on the panel as they passed each floor.

Kennedy. Kennedy. Meg tossed the name around in her brain.

The lift opened. 'Here we are. I'll lead the way.'

They walked along a gloomy corridor of closed doors, like a tunnel. She was shown into an office and caught the name on the outside:

Noel Kennedy
Medical Director

'This is us,' Rose said. 'I'll just ask you to wait a moment.'

She was in an outer office that was cramped but less claustrophobic than the narrow corridor which had led to it. There were windows which would have given an airy view out on to the city if that had not been blocked by angled blinds keeping the glare off computer screens.

The room had two desks. On one sat a tray of correspondence and a big open diary with a lot of appointments scribbled into it. Some had been scored out, then replaced. In a propped-up frame she saw a photograph of a family: Rose Hurst, her husband and a clutch of children. At the other desk, a younger woman sat typing something from a dictaphone. She had earphones in and she glanced round from her private world with a faraway smile.

Rose gestured to a small settee. There were papers and magazines on it, including a couple of British Medical Journals, and she cleared them away.

'Take a pew,' she said. 'I'll just let him know.'

At the end of the room was another door, open a little. She leaned in through it, rapping her knuckles lightly on the frame. 'Dr Winter's here to see you,' she said quietly. Then she turned. 'OK?' She smiled.

Meg entered a long thin office. It had a table for meetings, round, the wrong shape for the room. A settee and a couple of armchairs took up too much space.

At the far end was a desk. Noel Kennedy had posed himself leaning back against it, his hands clasping its edges and his legs crossed at the ankles. He was in his early forties, trim, with dark hair going grey unevenly.

Meg felt something reverberate within her.

It was not the sound of Rose closing the door firmly as she left the room. It was something else.

She felt it as a surge of power where her heart was and it sent out waves of both familiarity and alarm. She stood in the centre of the room trying to anchor her feelings, unable to stop herself staring at this man.

Kennedy's pale blue eyes examined her openly, his head inclined slightly. He did not speak. Instead, his face carried a smile of undisguised affection.

He stepped away from the desk and came nearer.

'Meg,' he said.

His voice was light, youthful, and she felt it reaching her in deep, hidden places.

'I can't believe it's you,' he said. 'You look so – so different. But I'd have known you.' He reached out a hand and put the

166

tips of his fingers to her torn eyebrow. 'That lovely face.'

It was only a fleeting touch but she felt as if she had been burned. She stepped away from him.

'Look, what's going on?' she said, although in her heart she thought she already knew.

His brows arched in puzzlement. They stood apart from each other, frozen into position.

'Meg?' he asked, unsure.

She kept staring at him. There were no words she could find. What she was thinking; the way he was speaking to her; his touch . . .

She felt weak. Trembling, she sat down on the settee.

He frowned. 'Are you all right?'

'I . . . I'm . . . I don't know.'

'Meg, darling, what is it?'

Darling. The word frightened her and made her draw breath suddenly. Her eyes were wide, startled.

And with that his face changed. Concern gave way to shock.

'Oh my God,' he said.

He sat down gently at the other end of the settee. 'God,' he said again, like a gasp, as he looked into her face, searching and not finding. 'You don't remember, do you?' His voice quavered.

She looked at him, helpless, then shook her head.

'It's not just that night,' he went on, as if explaining it to himself, 'it's everything else, isn't it?'

She said nothing.

'You don't know me,' he said.

She grasped her confusion and held it still for a moment. 'I know I should,' she said. 'There's something I can . . . feel.'

'Jesus Christ,' he said in despair. He looked down at the floor. His body seemed to slump as if something had gone out of it.

They sat for what seemed like minutes without speaking, each of them trying to regain their emotional balance. She could hear the rumble of traffic going past in the streets down below. The frantic wail of an ambulance siren rose into the air.

He said: 'Dr Gilleece – you wrote to her. We had a meeting last week and she mentioned it to me, asked me if I remembered you from the old Central.' He gave a wry smile. 'Remember you? What a question. She didn't mean anything by it, of course, she didn't know. I told her that I did remember you and she showed me the letter and said you'd arranged an appointment. I volunteered to see you instead.'

A window was open, causing a draught and disturbing the papers on his desk. He got up and closed it firmly. The street noise stopped.

167

'I thought all sorts of things,' he said. 'Like – were you avoiding me? Why had you contacted her instead of me? Did you resent the fact that *I* hadn't tried to contact *you*?' He shook his head in disbelief. 'Well, now I know, don't I.'

He stood gazing at her as if he could not accept any of this, then he opened a drawer in the desk, took out a slim white envelope, and handed it to her. 'I've waited four years to give this back to you.'

The envelope had his name on it. In her writing.

She looked at him, questioning silently. He nodded. 'Go ahead. Open it.'

Inside was a slim sheet of the old hospital's notepaper. The writing looked stronger and more determined than it was these days, but it was undoubtedly the same hand.

Dear Dr Kennedy

I wish to tender my resignation from the staff of Belfast Central Hospital, effective from today's date. I understand that a month's notice is required. However, as I have four weeks' leave still outstanding, I intend to leave immediately in lieu of notice.

Yours
Meg Winter

She checked the date and her heart leaped. In the early hours of the following morning, her four lost years had begun.

'I don't understand this,' she said. She looked at him apologetically. 'Any of this.'

'Then I'd better explain,' he said, 'from the start.'

He came and sat on the settee with her, then gave a little smile and shook his head. 'The final slap in the teeth.' He said it more to himself than to her. 'Haunted by you for so long and you don't even remember.'

He gazed round the room, as if looking for a clue. 'Damn it, where to begin?' He faced her again. 'All right. Look . . . we'd been having an affair.' He blurted out the words and held his arms out as if handing the concept over to her. 'God, it seems ridiculous to have to spell it out. I can't believe I'm doing this.'

She sat there, an icy fist clenching and unclenching in her stomach, wanting to know, not wanting to know, telling herself she *had* to know; that what she was about to hear would be the first real step forward towards the past.

'I was married at the time. You were in general training; I was

168

the medical director. I was appointed to the same post here when this hospital opened.' He shrugged. 'We got to know each other. One thing led to another. We both wanted it to happen and neither of us did anything to stop it.' He paused and looked at her softly. 'It was good, Meg. You should know that. While it lasted, it was the most wonderful time of my life.'

His eyes had become moist. She did not know how to respond. He blinked hurriedly and cleared his throat. 'I was married. Did I say that already?'

'Yes,' she said. She looked at his left hand. There was no wedding ring.

He read her glance. 'I'm not married any longer. That's a part of the story you couldn't have known. You and me, we lasted five months. Until I started to get too serious for your liking. My wife and I, we weren't getting along well, even before you and I happened.'

'Children?' She felt strong enough to ask the question.

'Two. Gillian and Sinead.'

She saw the thought of them cast sad shadows on his face.

'They're eleven and thirteen now. They live with their mother. She has the house. I've got a flat. I have them every other weekend. They don't enjoy being with me very much. Patricia, my wife – *ex*-wife – has turned them against me, I think. They've become very greedy, very demanding, and I think she encourages it. She wants to drain me. Money, emotions – everything.' He changed course. 'Anyway, you and I had a big bust-up one night in Truesdale Street.'

It caught her unawares.

Truesdale Street. He would have been in her bed. They would have made love there. How often, she wondered, and when? At night? On snatched afternoons?

Both of them naked. Her and this stranger who wasn't.

She felt her heart pounding.

'I told you I was going to leave my wife, that I wanted to get divorced and marry you. You said you didn't want that, you didn't want a long-term commitment. You thought we should end it. There and then. I'd admitted the affair to Patricia although I didn't say who you were. She'd given me an ulti-matum: her or you. I chose you.'

'Why?' Meg asked. It seemed to her like the wrong decision.

'Why? Why?' He looked as if he could not believe she had asked such a thing. His voice shook with intensity. 'Because I loved you, Meg. I loved you with every part of me. I loved being where you were, I loved a room if you had been in it. I used to go down to A and E when you weren't on duty so that I

169

could feel your presence in it, touch things, desks, chairs, anything that I knew you would have touched. I would have given up anything for you. I . . .'

He stopped to take a breath and then he became calmer. 'That night at your house – I was desperate. Distraught. I couldn't bear the thought of not being with you, my life without you in it. We both got angry. There was a lot of shouting. Later on I left. I was never in your house again. That was the last time.'

He gave a sigh and allowed himself a few moments with the shreds of his memories. Meg looked at him, wondering what her feelings for him had been, wondering what they were now. She certainly did not feel remote from him. She could feel herself being drawn to his sadness and for a second she almost reached forward and put her hand on his shoulder, disturbed by the thought that she had been the cause of such desolation.

She drew back. Damn it – what was she doing? How did she know any of this was true?

But the resignation letter . . .

'Patricia and I,' he said, 'we decided we would try to pick up the pieces, for the sake of the girls really, but there were rows, recrimination, and it just prolonged the inevitable. We got divorced three years ago.'

She looked at the page of notepaper in her hand. 'This letter,' she said. 'The date. It was that night—'

He nodded. 'It was a couple of weeks after we split up. There was an opening for a specialist registrar in A and E and you were a strong candidate for it. We interviewed you along with a couple of other people but we decided to give the opportunity to someone else. When the result was posted you marched in and accused me of acting out of some kind of revenge for what had happened between us. I told you at the time that you were wrong and I'll tell you that now, too. The decision was a fair one, Meg. You were young, your chance would have come again. Anyway, we had words. You slapped down your resignation on the desk and stormed out again.'

'What time did all this happen? Can you remember?'

'Middle of the afternoon some time. About four o'clock, I think.'

It was bringing her a little bit closer. At last she knew something of the hours before the accident. But the police had mentioned none of this to her.

'The police,' she said. 'Did you tell them anything about this?'

He looked uncomfortable, then shook his head.

'After you left, I sat here looking at the letter. I knew you well enough to know how you could blow up and do something impulsively. It was one of the things that made you a good doctor and held you back at the same time. You could act quickly and decisively when an emergency demanded it but sometimes you didn't show maturity of judgement. It was why you didn't get the specialist registrar position. We thought you needed to grow a bit. So I decided not to do anything about the letter, just leave it until the next day and try to persuade you to take it back when your anger had cooled. Of course, there was no next day.'

He had not answered her question. 'But the police – did they contact you?'

'Yes. I was in bed at home when they rang that night to inform me what had happened. I got up and went down to the hospital. You were in surgery. It was terrible, knowing there was nothing I could do. I spoke to the police the next day.' He paused. 'I didn't tell them.'

'You didn't?'

'No. It had nothing to do with what happened to you – the accident. Nothing I could say would have helped them with that.'

Meg looked at him and knew what had gone through his mind. She saw weakness in his face and she understood instinctively why their relationship had not lasted. 'You wanted to keep yourself out of it, isn't that it?'

He gestured awkwardly. 'I . . . well . . . I didn't want to tell them about us, no. It wasn't public knowledge. At least I didn't think it was, although I know what hospital gossip's like. I didn't want any of it to get out in the open. For your sake, your reputation, I thought that would be best.'

'*My* reputation?'

'Yes. Of course. Apart from that, I would have had to mention your resignation. It would have had to become official then. You see, at that early stage, you were injured, seriously of course and unconscious, but it wasn't fatal. Everyone thought you'd be all right.'

He shook his head slowly. 'Day after day I waited. There was nothing I could do, watching from afar, no one I could really talk to. I went to see your parents, offered them the hospital's condolences, wearing my official hat. And then of course later – the decision to stop your salary. You can imagine what that did to me. It was like I was cutting off your lifeline, declaring you officially dead or something. But you're not, Meg.' He smiled suddenly. 'You're here.'

She did not smile back. She felt uncomfortable sitting here now, almost repelled by his affection, but she wanted more of

171

what he knew. 'What did I do when I left here? Have you any idea?'

'None. If I'd had any information like that, then I *would* have told the police. I did consider calling you that evening, after you'd left, but I decided to leave it. Meg, I've missed you. You've no idea how much.'

He moved nearer and reached for her hands. She pulled away.

'I'm sorry,' he said. 'You're right. I don't know how I can expect you to take all this in. It will need time. We need to talk some more. There are things I need to know. Maybe we could meet somewhere, have dinner, perhaps?'

She had to get away from here, try to think. She stood up and his eyes followed her like a sad animal's.

'I have to go,' she told him, fumbling for words. 'Everything you've said – you've shaken me. I didn't know. I'm sorry for what's happened – the past.'

'Then we should talk about it,' he begged her. 'Please.'

'No,' she said. 'I need to think, to come to terms with this.'

And all of a sudden it struck her that she had left him twice before: once when she had ended their relationship and then when the accident had taken her. Now she was with him in this room and she was going to leave him again.

'What will you do?' he said. 'Will you tell anyone about this?' He looked nervous.

'I don't know.'

'We have to talk about it. I can help you with your job, you see. Help you get a new start. That's what you want, isn't it?'

He gave a broad grin but fear was in his eyes and she saw what it was, that it was his life that he was worried about, not hers. Oh, he would find something for her, to shut her up, maybe try to start a cosy little affair again, but he was a fool if he thought she would go along with any of that. She stooped to lift the letter from the settee and as she did, he grabbed her arm.

'Meg,' he said. 'I can't let you go like this.'

His grip was strong. 'Don't,' she said. 'Don't do this.'

'But Meg—'

'Let me go,' she said with more force.

His hold softened and she pulled her arm away.

'I'm sorry,' he said. 'I shouldn't . . .'

But before anything else happened, she had opened the door.

In the outer office, Rose Hurst stood. 'All finished?' she said pleasantly. 'Do you need to be shown down again?'

'No, I'll be all right. I can find my own way.'

She hurried along to the lift and pressed the button. As its door opened she turned and looked back. He was standing outside the door of his office, a shadow in the gloomy corridor.

She was out of the building and hastening along towards the main road, putting as much distance as possible between them, when she remembered her car. She cursed herself for her forgetfulness then turned and walked back.

She sat in the car for a few minutes. He had not chased after her. She rubbed her wrist, feeling the ghost of his grip still on it. Would he have hurt her? There was no way of knowing. His feelings for her felt more like obsession than love. She had not sensed anger in him but he was weak and frightened and who knew what he might do if he was cornered.

One thing was certain: she understood why she had ended the relationship. But what puzzled her was why she had allowed it to get so far in the first place. Had she been using him, trying to advance her own career? That thought troubled her.

And in their encounter she had glimpsed something else. It was in his explanation about why she hadn't got the job.

You could blow up and act impulsively.

It all fitted neatly over the outline which Elizabeth had already drawn for her.

She started the engine and then began to navigate her way round the one-way system that led out of the car park, wondering if she should tell Florence Gilmour about any of this.

173

Twenty-two

September was golden, as if it had decided to leave something worth remembering before handing over to the harder months to come.

'This used to be the view from my grandmother's drawing room,' Meg said. 'I'd forgotten how beautiful it could be on a good day.'

She sat at a window in the Emerald East Hotel and gazed out to the open expanse of the Irish Sea, green and blue and silver at the spot where the midday sun touched it. The waves of a gentle tide unfurled onto the tiny beach below, polishing layers of speckled granite stones.

'Well, it solves one mystery,' Elizabeth said.

'Which is?'

'At least I know now what you wanted to talk to me about that night and that you *were* involved with someone all that time. *And . . .*' she whispered, leaning across the dining table and pointing a fork at her friend, 'I was right. He was married.'

It was the subject which had occupied them all the way down in the car. Just for a second, looking at the sea, Meg had managed to take her mind somewhere else.

Elizabeth turned from her and resumed cutting up the plate of fish fingers in front of Catriona. They were at a table in the hotel dining room, with the toddler strapped into a high chair beside them. The grown-ups were having open prawn sandwiches on wheaten bread but Meg eyed the fish fingers enviously.

It had been her idea, in this run of good weather, to get out of the city and she had suggested going for a drive along the coast to see what her father had done with the old house. It had been beyond repair, he had explained when she had expressed shock and dismay that it was gone, full of dry rot and damp because it had not been lived in for so long. In its place now was some sort of nouveau stately home, comfortable but overpowering, and apparently people spent the earth to stay in it.

She looked around the room with its light oak panelling and

174

gold-plated fittings, watching waiters moving among the few other early diners, most of whom were in bright golf sweaters. She felt as if they were all intruders, invading the privacy of her childhood memories.

'Somebody tried to burn this place down,' she said, not overly disturbed by the notion.

'Really? Who?'

'Oh, I don't know. Some nutter. My father told me about it. He got sent to prison.'

'*There you go, darling. Now you eat those up like a good girl.* You should go to the police, you know,' Elizabeth said, refusing to be diverted.

Meg made a face. 'Elizabeth, we had all this out in the car.'

'And we're having it out again. You know I'm right.'

'I'm not sure,' Meg said. 'What would it achieve? He had nothing to do with what happened that night. I just want to forget about him.'

Elizabeth was unmoved. 'What makes you so sure he's completely innocent in all of this? Look – here's a theory. What if he followed you and saw you with Everett? There was a car that ran you off the road, wasn't there? Well then, what if it was Noel Kennedy's car? Maybe he thinks you're dead and he kills Everett in a fit of jealous rage.'

'That's impossible. The police called him at home that night. He got up and drove down to the hospital.'

'Ah – but was he at home all night? Maybe he'd just got in.'

'Rubbish. They would have checked.'

'No, they wouldn't. They'd no reason to think Kennedy was in any way connected, other than that he was your employer. They could check now, though – if you told them,' she said with emphasis.

Meg frowned.

The gaps in her memory – she appeared to have blocked out not just the events of the day but anyone she had come across during it. Had Noel Kennedy played a bigger part? Had something else happened that day that he was not revealing, something she had forgotten? Could there be anything in Elizabeth's suspicions?

'Well?' Elizabeth said.

'I don't know. I'll have to think about it.'

Later, with the sun-roof open, they drove along twisting roads, heading for Ardglass.

Near the shore, wild violets were a purple mist amid oceans of green fern. They crossed a little stone bridge and watched

175

cows grazing among the bulrushes at the water's edge. They spotted a heron and pointed it out to Catriona. It moved with stiff, slow strides, then its long neck dipped swiftly and suddenly there was a fish wriggling in its bill.

All of it took Meg worlds away from everything that was on her mind and led her back to the County Down coast of childhood summers.

'You know, I don't think I've been along this way in my life,' Elizabeth remarked.

'It's that Van Morrison song, you know,' Meg said.

'What is?'

'*Coney Island*. We pass it just along here. You know, that one where he kind of narrates. This is the area he's talking about. Buying potted herrings in Ardglass and stuff. On and on over the hill in the jam jar. You know the thing.'

'Potted herrings in a jam jar?'

'No, *they're* in the jam jar – the people in the song. It's rhyming slang, I think. This is a jam jar.' She slapped the steering wheel.

'I don't like Van Morrison,' Elizabeth said.

'I like jam,' Catriona announced and they laughed.

When they reached Ardglass, they parked at the side of a new marina. Gleaming racing yachts and smaller boats bobbed in the sheltered water, ropes clinking against their masts in the breeze.

Meg looked around. 'I don't remember this.'

'You do surprise me,' Elizabeth said, lifting Catriona out of the car.

Much further along the quayside, there were vessels for work, not play. They counted half a dozen muscular trawlers tied up, watched over by tough-looking herring gulls standing like guards on the harbour wall.

'How about an ice cream?' Meg suggested to Catriona.

The little girl smiled and nodded furiously.

'We'll all have one,' Elizabeth said.

She and Meg each took a hand and swung Catriona in the air between them as they walked along the harbour towards the nearest shop. They bought three cones with chocolate flakes and sat on a bench to eat them. Sunlight sparkled on the water and an oily, fishy smell from the trawlers, not at all unpleasant, drifted in the wind.

'Apart from the marina, I would say this place hasn't changed much since I used to come here when I was a kid,' Meg said.

'What's that over there?' Elizabeth asked.

Meg looked to where she was pointing. Just beyond the marina there was an old stone building, like a warehouse of some kind, that seemed to have been renovated. There was a colourful sign above its doorway: *Harbour Pottery*.

'That looks new as well,' Meg said. 'Want to go and have a peek?'

'Why not?' Catriona's ice cream had turned to mush. Elizabeth took it from her and dumped it in a litter bin. Then she wiped the child's sticky face and hands with a tissue.

A bell jangled as they opened the door of the pottery and they smelled the instant heady odour of scented candles and baskets of pot pourri. Soft jazz was playing from speakers hidden somewhere. The place was dark, a welcomingly cool retreat from the heat of the afternoon.

When their eyes had adjusted to the dim light they began to take in what was around them. Hand-painted glass and dishes in rich glazes were in carefully lit display cases. Everyday ware, bowls and mugs in earthier hues, was lined along shelves or hanging from hooks, and there were silvery trinkets with Celtic designs as well as the inevitable array of tiny aromatherapy bottles.

Elizabeth looked down at the bare flagstones. 'Just don't touch a thing, Catriona,' she warned. 'This floor won't take any prisoners.'

'Can I help you with anything?' a man's voice said.

He was sitting on a little stool behind the counter with a paperback open on his knee and they had not seen him. He stood up.

'Oh, hello,' Meg said, laughing. 'We didn't notice you hiding there.'

He wore jeans and a checkered shirt that looked a bit heavy on such a day. But then it would get cold stuck away in here out of the sun. She looked at him. He was dark-haired, with shy brown eyes, and she felt as if they had disturbed him in his lair.

'No,' she told him, 'we're just having a look around. Haven't been here before. Have you been open long?'

'About eighteen months, I suppose. I'm not the actual proprietor, as a matter of fact. He's away in Japan. I'm just looking after the place for a while. That's why we don't have a lot of his own pieces on display at the moment.'

'His own pieces?'

'Yes, he's the potter.'

He picked up a sturdy side plate and turned it upside down, pointing to the stamp on the bottom. 'Harbour Pottery – you see?'

'Oh, right,' Meg said. 'They're made on the premises?'

He pointed over his shoulder. 'Thrown and fired in the workshop back there. But there's lots of other stuff, of course.

177

Give me a shout if there's anything you need to know.'

'Thanks,' Meg said.

'You're welcome,' he replied with a little smile and sat down with his book again. It was a Milan Kundera. She had read a couple of his in hospital and found them demanding but absorbing.

'*Laughable Loves*,' she said. 'I've not read that one. Are you enjoying it?'

'I might be if I knew what he was on about,' he said, giving her a confused look. They both laughed.

'Have you seen these?' Elizabeth said from behind. She was holding a bulbous beaker with an intricate design which looked as if it had been sponged on. 'Flash, aren't they?'

'Yes,' Meg said, walking over. Something occurred to her. 'It's my mother's birthday soon, you know. I really ought to get her something nice to cheer her up. I feel so sorry for what's happened to her.' She had told Elizabeth about the letters.

'You think she'd like something like this?'

Meg made a face. 'Not sure. Maybe a bit gaudy. Something a little more subdued, perhaps.'

They wandered through the shop, idly lifting things and putting them down again. Elizabeth kept a firm grip on little Catriona who wanted to touch everything.

'Look, Mummy, look.'

'Yes, dear, very nice.'

'Something like this might do,' Meg said. It was a small coffee cup in a deep brown with a blueish purple coming through the glaze. She checked the price sticker, then looked on the bottom and saw something squiggled into it. 'These aren't yours, I take it?' she called to the shopkeeper.

He stepped out from behind the counter and came over to her. He moved softly and she thought he looked agile.

'No,' he said. 'These are made in Staffordshire. Believe it or not, this is the last one but we're getting more in.'

'That's what people in shops always say, isn't it?' she teased.

He smiled. 'Except in this case it happens to be true. I was talking to the suppliers yesterday. There's an order due any time now. Part of the Christmas stock.'

'Christmas?' Elizabeth said. 'Oh my God, how can you think about Christmas on a day like this?'

He looked at her and shrugged. 'We have to. It's just around the corner. Nice afternoons like this make you forget.'

He turned back to Meg and caught her studying him. Their eyes met.

178

'My mother's birthday's on the twenty-fourth,' she said hurriedly, embarrassed. 'They'd make a nice present. Do you think you could guarantee to have more by then?'

'No problem at all. How many would you like?'

'Half a dozen, I suppose. Do they do jugs, sugar bowls?' For a moment in her mind she saw the mess on her mother's kitchen floor.

'Yes.'

'Well then, I'll have a jug and sugar bowl as well, please. How much are they?'

He had to go back behind the desk to look it up and then he told her.

'That's fine,' she said.

'Well then, if I could take your name and address and maybe your telephone number, I could call you or drop you a note when they arrive. It shouldn't be very long. And, eh,' he sounded a bit apologetic, 'would it be possible for you to leave a small deposit?'

For a second she thought ludicrously of a little pile of salt or something. A small deposit. She almost laughed.

'Look, why don't I just pay for the whole lot while I'm here.' She put her bag on the counter and took her credit card out of her purse.

'Well, if you're sure?'

'Yes – why not?'

'I'll just take a note of your name first,' he said, grasping a pen and a pad.

'It's Winter,' she said. 'Meg Winter.'

He had his head down and she could not see his face. 'I'm sorry. Winter, did you say?'

'Yes, Meg Winter,' she told him again and gave him her address and telephone number. He wrote it all down.

'That's great, Miss Winter,' he said. 'Or is it Mrs?'

'Mizz,' Elizabeth said in the background.

'Doctor, actually,' Meg corrected.

He smiled, then moved to the till to tot up the bill. He took her card and ran it through the machine. While they waited, Meg glanced round. Elizabeth was at the other end of the shop looking at something. She had let go of Catriona for a moment. The credit card slip clattered out and Meg turned again to sign it. He gave her back the card and her copy.

'That's great,' he said.

'Look, me a witch.'

Catriona was in a corner where there were wicker baskets and brooms. She had straddled one and she was starting to

179

bounce through the shop on it.

'A *witch*,' she said again, giggling.

The handle swung violently towards a rack of tumblers.

'Catriona!' Elizabeth shouted but Meg was ahead of her. She reached the child first and grabbed the broom, just inches before it brought the whole lot down.

'Very good, sweetie,' she said calmly. 'But I think we should put that back.'

'And I think it's time we got out of here,' Elizabeth said, taking her daughter's hand, 'before we do any more damage.'

'It's OK,' the shopkeeper said. 'You haven't actually done any yet.'

Meg looked at him and they shared a smile of relief. She lifted her bag. 'So I'll leave you to get in touch with me?'

He nodded. 'Thank you very much,' he said.

They went out into a warmth they had forgotten about. The sharpness of the sunlight made them blink.

'God, the car'll be like an oven,' Meg said as they walked to it. 'I'll have to leave the doors and windows open for a while.'

'Well, you liked *him*,' Elizabeth said.

'What do you mean?' Meg said with a little too much surprise in her voice.

Elizabeth laughed at her. 'Don't give me that.'

That night she lay in bed with a magazine, wondering about what Elizabeth had said.

Had she been that obvious?

She had liked him, right enough. She thought they had made some kind of a connection, too, and she hadn't felt crowded by him.

She threw the magazine aside, thumped the pillow and turned out the light. He was only a guy in a shop, that was all. She lay down and closed her eyes. In the end, it would be nothing. She didn't even know his name.

In her dreams she heard a telephone.

It was on the counter in the Harbour Pottery and Catriona ran to answer it, although when she picked it up it kept on ringing.

She woke with a start, realising that it was not a dream but her own phone, beside the bed.

She looked at the luminous dial on her clock. One fifteen. Who would call this late? Something had happened to somebody. Her father, maybe. She always worried about that.

She lifted the receiver. 'Hello?'

There was no answer, just a couple of seconds of silence and then the dialling tone.

She put on the light and dialled 1471. The computer voice spoke to her. 'You were called – today – at one fourteen. The caller withheld their number.'

She sat there blinking, tiredness and anxiety fighting for control of her.

And then the phone went again.

She grabbed it on the second ring. 'Hello?' There was silence once more but it lasted longer this time.

'Hello? Who is this?' she said. There was a tingle on her skin. She felt certain someone was there and for a moment she could swear she heard breathing.

'I'm going to ring the police,' she said and then the line went dead.

She tried 1471 again but she knew what the result would be.

Anxiety won. Tiredness retreated.

She got out of bed and put on a robe, then turned the bedside light off. She went to the window and pulled back the side of the curtains. The street was empty and quiet, the houses opposite dark and wrapped up for the night, pavements cooling down after the heat of the day.

She went downstairs and checked that the windows were shut and that both the front and back doors were locked securely, then she sat in darkness and silence, listening, trying to convince herself that she was getting alarmed over nothing, thinking of Florence Gilmour asking her if she was happy about being alone.

Twenty-three

A glorious brightness filled her bedroom when she pulled the curtains the next morning, but it did not entirely clear away the shadows of the night.

She debated telling the police about the calls. But then again, she was not in the phone book; there might be nothing more to it than just some weirdo dialling a number at random. She felt torn: concerned for her safety yet anxious not to appear to be over-reacting to something that might be nothing at all.

Kennedy, too. What was there to achieve by telling them about him? They would go to see him, probably make a lot of trouble because of what he had kept from them four years ago, and she would gain nothing from it except to make him think she had been vindictive.

It was nine thirty and she had slept late. She had sat for an hour last night before going to bed again. She hurried downstairs. The postman had been and there was a slim white envelope on the floor inside the door. She lifted it and saw a company logo in the bottom left hand corner. With it were the words *Vectra Pharmaceuticals*.

She had almost forgotten.

She tore the letter open:

Dear Dr Winter

Thank you for your letter. I am sorry it has taken me so long to respond but I have been away on leave.

I am grateful to you for explaining your situation. Like many people, I was aware of your circumstances and the tragic death of Paul Everett, as well as its connection to this company.

I am not sure how much assistance we at Vectra can be but I would be happy to meet you to see what is possible. Perhaps you would telephone my secretary to arrange a suitable appointment.

Yours sincerely

Alice Harte,
Chief Executive

She was standing there reading it for the second or third time when the doorbell rang loudly right beside her, making her jump out of her skin.

She opened the door and for a moment she could not quite take in who it was. She stood staring at him with a blank look.

'Dr Winter?' he said when she did not speak to him. 'Dan Cochrane. From the Harbour Pottery? You called in yesterday?'

'Of course,' she said, collecting herself, noticing he was wearing the same shirt and jeans. 'You caught me by surprise for a moment. But what on earth brings you here?'

'Sorry if I alarmed you. I had to be in Belfast early today to collect some things. I was passing this way and I thought I'd pop this in.'

He handed her a little envelope.

'I found this on the floor this morning. You must have dropped it. I didn't want to post it in case anything happened to it so I was going to put it through the letter-box if you weren't here.'

She looked at the envelope. It had her name on it and he had sealed it with sticky tape. On the back, he had scribbled:

From Dan Cochrane, Harbour Pottery, Ardglass. You left this behind.

She opened it up and found her Visa card inside.

'It can't be,' she said. Then, leaving him standing at the door, she went into the house and came back with her handbag, searching through it as if she expected the card to be there as well.

'What am I doing?' she said. 'This is stupid of me.' She looked at him. 'How in heaven's name did I lose it?'

'I think it must have been when the wicked witch appeared,' Cochrane said and smiled. 'You ran to do your bit of damage limitation and you probably knocked it off the counter somehow. I almost didn't see it at all.'

She shook her head at her carelessness. 'Look, this is really very good of you and I haven't said thanks.' She stood back from the door. 'You've come all this way. I was just about to make some coffee. Would you like some?'

He looked beyond her into the house, as if considering, then said: 'That would be nice but I can't. I've got to be somewhere before ten. Some other time maybe?'

183

She smiled at him. 'Thanks again. I'm very grateful.' She wondered what she should do – shake his hand or something – but she did nothing at all.

He backed away down the path. 'I'll give you a shout when those things come in,' he said, opening the little gate and closing it carefully behind him.

'Of course. Look forward to that.'

He got into a dusty Citroën van parked further down the street and as she shut her front door she heard its throaty diesel engine start up.

She looked at the Visa card and the letter from Vectra Pharmaceuticals and smiled to herself. In the kitchen, as she spooned coffee into a pot, she was humming.

Just before eleven a.m. two days later she drove into an industrial park on the outskirts of Antrim.

At the entrance, a big sign displayed a map of the complex and the names of the companies which operated from there. Vectra was the last on the list.

She did not know what she had expected to see; grimy, unpleasant-looking factories with chimneys and warehouses, perhaps. Instead, she found a meandering road lined with trees and high hedges, behind which were, in the main, computer software firms with small premises, few staff and high technology.

She found Vectra easily enough. It was right at the end of the park, down a dip, a low-roofed structure that seemed to be all glass. A little beyond it, hidden so that it did not spoil the environment, she could glimpse another, bigger building that she assumed was the manufacturing plant.

As she pulled in towards the main gate, a small blue car passed her. A security guard directed her to a series of neat little parking bays surrounded by fuchsia bushes and flower-beds. She got out and locked up then set off along the winding path, feeling the autumn breeze on her skin. A row of silver birch trees rustled like paper and water flowed gently through a rockery. The setting had the elemental peacefulness of a Japanese garden but it did not relax her. She was nervous about the meeting to come.

The reception area had an air-conditioned stillness, cool tiling on the floor and squat leather furniture where no one waited. The receptionist noted her name in a book and gave her a *visitor* sticker for her lapel, then pointed to a long corridor and told her to walk down to the end of it until she reached the Chief Executive's office where she was expected.

A secretary met her and showed her in.

Alice Harte was a few years older than Meg with short ash blonde hair swept straight back from her face. Her earrings were little silver ingots that danced as she walked across the room to greet her. She was wearing a grey silk blouse and soft-flowing black trousers that were probably Armani. Meg was in the blue suit again; it was her only one.

'Dr Winter,' Alice said, extending a cool hand. 'Please.'

She gestured to a thin, high-backed armchair. Meg could smell fresh coffee. The office was unfussy and uncluttered, with furniture that was muted without being dull and subdued lighting built into the ceiling. A serious-looking computer was set up at a workstation and Meg could see that the screen saver was the company logo.

'Coffee?' Alice said, walking to where it was spluttering in a pot on a corner unit.

'Please,' Meg said. 'Milk. No sugar.'

Alice poured for both of them and took milk from a fridge disguised as a cabinet. She handed Meg a cup and sat opposite her, a long low table between them.

'You're not American,' Meg remarked.

'No,' she conceded, 'I'm not. Very few of us here are now.'

'I'm sorry,' Meg said. 'That just came out. It's none of my business. Look, it's good of you to see me and I don't want to take up too much of your time.'

'Don't worry,' Alice said, 'I won't let you. There's a meeting in here in twenty minutes. That's all the time you've got. But before we start, there's something I've got to say to you.'

She fixed Meg with a firm look.

'I've agreed to see you out of courtesy but I've got to make it clear from the outset that what Paul Everett did in his own time was his own business and not the responsibility of Vectra. I say that just in case you might be harbouring any ideas about taking a civil action against this company. Frankly, you wouldn't get very far.'

Meg felt startled. She had not expected this – such a forceful shot across the bows. It had been delivered with civility and a smile but it was a shock nevertheless.

'I . . . no, it's nothing like that,' was all she could think to say.

Alice smiled again and her tone softened. 'Then let's see what we can do.'

'All right,' Meg said, gathering herself. She set her cup down on the table. 'You obviously know all about me, about Paul Everett's death.'

'Yes, it was a horrible business. But you – it's a miracle you're alive and in one piece.'

185

'I know,' Meg said.

She looked at this striking, successful woman and wondered fleetingly where she herself would be now if none of this had happened.

'I should feel more grateful than I am. But with the amnesia – you see, I'm desperately trying to get on my feet again but I must get my memory back. The only way I can think of doing that is to find out everything I can about that night. So I need to know more about Paul Everett – what sort of a person he was, how I came to be with him.'

'How far have you got?' Alice asked, then listened as Meg told her about the Clarendon Dock possibility, that the police had accounted for Everett's movements up to a point, but that they had no idea where he was between the last time he was seen and the time the accident and the murder took place.

'There was a man who reported the accident,' Meg said. 'He and his wife told the police they were nearly in a head-on collision with two cars racing abreast up the hill just before it happened. I went to see him.'

'Was he any help?'

She shook her head. 'It was a wasted journey.'

'Mmm,' Alice said, sipping her coffee, disagreeing, 'it might not have been. That was enterprising of you, to seek him out. What do the police think about you doing all this private detective work?'

'They don't like it much. They've sort of warned me off. But I can't just sit on my backside and do nothing.'

'So what do you know about Paul so far?'

'Only what the police said: that he was the Chief Executive here, the first one when the company was starting, that he came from Maine, I think it was, that he was a high-flier and would have had a great career with Vectra if . . .'

She paused.

'If he hadn't been killed?' Alice finished for her.

'Every now and then it hits me that this man is dead – murdered, a man who's a complete stranger to me – and that somehow I've played a part in what happened to him. The thought tortures me.'

'I think you're probably punishing yourself a bit unduly, don't you?' Alice said. 'It wasn't you who killed him.'

She swung round to her desk and lifted a buff folder from it. Meg could see that it was Paul Everett's personal file. She stared as the other woman began to flick through it, the turn of each page tantalising.

'There's not a lot more that I can add to what you already know, I'm afraid,' Alice said. 'It's a question of company confidentiality. I'm sure you appreciate that.'

'I understand,' Meg answered without enthusiasm.

Alice glanced up at her, closed the file and sighed, as if making a decision. 'All right.' She thought. 'What can I tell you: Paul was everything you've described. He was a talented young man with an awful lot going for him. It's thanks to him that I'm here myself. I went to Warwick University and then I did an MBA. I was a personnel manager with one of the rail companies in England when he headhunted me. I got the position as head of human resources here with a seat on the management board.'

'You must have been very young.'

'Under thirty, let's say,' she smiled.

'And now you're Chief Executive. Did they appoint you after he was killed?' The words were out before she could stop herself. 'I'm sorry. That was thoughtless of me. I didn't mean to suggest that you'd capitalised on—'

Alice waved away her apology. 'No, it's all right. I feel it myself sometimes. I did benefit from what happened to Paul although I reassure myself with the fact that it wasn't entirely an easy job to step into. There was, shall we say, a degree of controversy attached to his death. It wasn't just the fact that he was murdered, it was the question of the cocaine. The markets, considering the risks they take every day, they're surprisingly conservative about some things. The drugs issue affected business confidence for a while. But I'm happy to say that we've recovered rather well from that now.'

She said it with a feeling of achievement and Meg saw that she credited herself with the turnaround. It was probably true. She would be a good executive; tough, decisive. Meg had got a taste of some of that.

'I wondered,' Meg asked. 'Where was he buried?'

'Home. Portland, Maine. The company flew his body back, packed all the things that were in his apartment and shipped them to his parents. He was an only child. Very sad business for them.'

'The police told me he had a place out near the airport somewhere – Ballinderry direction, wasn't it?'

'That's right.'

'Look, you'll probably say no, but do you think you could give me the actual address? If I went there, I don't know, maybe I might remember something. Maybe I was there before. Who knows? It's just a chance.'

Alice pondered. 'I suppose it won't matter. The apartment isn't anything to do with Vectra any more.' She opened the file and found the address, then wrote it down on a pad. She tore the sheet off and handed it over.

'That's great,' Meg said. She paused, considering an idea, then decided to share it. 'There's – there's something else on my mind. It's Paul Everett's parents. I think about them a lot, the pain and the grief they must still be suffering. I feel bad about that and I've decided that I'd like to write to them. So I wondered if you would have their address.'

Alice gave her a look. 'Did you ever hear of quitting while you were ahead?'

'I suppose you're right,' Meg said. 'It's too much for me to ask.' She stood up to go. 'I'm keeping you back.'

'Hold on a minute,' Alice said. 'I didn't say no, did I?'

She looked quietly through the file for a few moments.

'Here we are. Ah yes, I remember now. The parents moved house not very long after he died. The new address isn't here, though. There's just a post office box number in Portland which they gave us so that any correspondence for him could be forwarded.' She thought. 'That box wouldn't be active now but our people in New Hampshire would have sent someone to visit them when the insurance problems were being sorted out. They would know. They'd have the address.'

'Insurance problems?'

'It's a pension thing. Death in service, it's called. With the circumstances of Paul's murder, the cocaine and so on, it got a bit awkward for a while but the company were keen to do the best for them.'

'The drugs,' Meg ventured. 'Was there any talk—'

'Whoa,' Alice said and stood up. 'Your meter just ran out. I'm afraid I'm not going to get into any of this.'

'Sorry. That's OK,' Meg said. 'I shouldn't have brought it up.' She lifted her handbag.

'What are you going to do now?'

'I don't know. It's not easy and I don't have a lot of choice. But I'm confident that my memory's going to come back. I feel certain it will.'

Even to her own ears she did not sound confident or certain at all; the words seemed hollow and unconvincing.

'Look,' Alice said, 'I can't leave it like this. I'll level with you. You feel bad about what happened to Paul, I feel bad about you. Whatever took place that night, you were with the chief executive of this company when you were injured.' She put her hand to her chest. 'That's me speaking as a person, you

188

understand. It's not the company talking. But why don't I try and get someone to track down the Everetts' address for you? We'll write to you or call you if we get it. I've got your address and phone number. But after that you're on your own. The company can be of no more assistance.'

'That would be great,' Meg said, shaking her hand. 'I would really appreciate it.'

After they had said goodbye, she walked back to the car park, feeling as if a weight had been lifted. Talking to Alice Harte had not been an ordeal. The woman had been engaging and frank. Meg had not got a great deal of actual information out of the encounter but as she got into her car she thought that if Alice had given her anything at all, she had given her a raising of the spirits and an encouragement to go forward.

She looked at the piece of paper with Everett's old address.

There was no time like the present.

As she turned right out of the industrial park, a small blue car was a little way behind her.

She reached Ballinderry in under half an hour, turning past an ancient whitewashed building that housed an antique shop, passing farms and fields and comfortable homes poised proudly at the head of enormous gardens.

There was a farmhouse with corrugated iron barns. A herd of black and white cattle were gathered in a corner of a field as if they were holding a meeting. Just beside the farm, a laneway led to a long two-storey building in stone and brick.

Its unfamiliarity did not inspire her but she turned towards it nevertheless.

The area in front was covered with loose gravel and the wheels of the Saab ground into it noisily. She had hoped to drive up discreetly, have a peek and then go away again but that wasn't working. She was on private land and if someone came she would have trouble explaining herself.

She sat for a few seconds and then got out. The place was at least a hundred years old and had probably once been a grain store but now it had been very well restored and converted into two roomy-looking apartments.

She walked towards the building, almost going over on her ankle a couple of times as the thin heels of her good black shoes slipped in the gravel. There was a door at the front, broad and painted white, with a Georgian fanlight above. An identical door, this time in red, was at the side, leading, she supposed, to the first-floor apartment.

It all looked very elegant but she had absolutely no recollection of ever seeing any of it before. She should not be here, staring at some stranger's property. She turned back towards the car.

'Can I help you at all?'

A woman had appeared at the side of the building. She was about sixty, stocky, with tight white curls and eyebrows raised in curiosity. She wore a grubby apron and heavy gardening gloves.

'No, it's OK,' Meg said, smiling and walking a little way towards her. 'I used to know someone who lived here. I was just passing. I haven't been in this neck of the woods for quite some time and I thought I'd have a look at the building again. It's very beautiful.'

She turned towards the car.

The woman was not convinced. 'Oh? Who did you know?' She had a gentrified accent. 'I've lived here . . .' she gestured towards the ground floor apartment, '. . . for the past twelve years. Since it was restored. My husband used to own this property, you see.'

Meg's mouth went dry. She was locked into a lie and she could not release herself from it.

'It was a young man. He died, I'm afraid.'

The woman thought for a second. 'That chap Everett? Paul Everett? Is that who you mean?'

Perhaps there was an opening here.

'Eh – yes. Did you know him?'

'Not well, no. What did you say your name was?'

'It was terrible – what happened to him,' Meg said.

'Yes.' The suspicious stare grew more intense. 'You're not a reporter, are you? We had a lot of them sniffing around at the time. Damned pests.'

'No, I'm not. Did you see much of Paul when he lived here?'

'Not a great deal. He used to go out early in the morning and come back late at night. I would hear the car, you see. I heard you. I was in the garden at the back. The sweet pea. Have I seen you before somewhere?'

'I shouldn't think so,' Meg said.

'They found drugs, you know. What did you say your name was?'

She did not want to tell her and she did not want to lie. She had done so already, saying she knew Everett. That had been stupid.

'I didn't. My name doesn't matter. I was just a friend.'

She opened the door of the car.

The woman walked forward, peering at her. 'I know who you are now,' she said. 'You're that woman. The one who was in a

190

coma. I saw you on the television. You've cut your hair.'

'I'm sorry to have disturbed you.'

The woman paused. 'But I remember – you said you didn't know him. When you were on television. That's what you said.'

Meg could not answer her. She smiled thinly, shut the door and started the engine. She turned the car in one movement, churning up the gravel fiercely, and drove off down the lane. In her mirror she could see the woman watching her.

Shit, she thought. *What have I done?* Her heart was pounding. She felt like a criminal escaping from the scene of the crime.

She had made a mistake. She had told this woman, someone who would have followed the case in detail, that she was a friend of Paul Everett's. What if she called the police?

More important, she told herself later as she turned into Truesdale Street, was the truth, or what she felt to be the truth.

She had never been at that place before.

She felt calmer. She had blundered, fair enough, but she should not let that put her off her search.

There was something else she had to do, somewhere else she needed to go, somewhere she *had* been before. Of that there was no doubt whatsoever. The thought of it chilled her.

She parked and went into the house. Upstairs, she changed out of the suit into jeans, trainers and a loose denim shirt, then went back to the car.

She had been putting this moment off. But no longer.

Her route took her south along the Lisburn Road, then into Balmoral Avenue and onto the Upper Malone Road. Where that came to a fork, she took the left-hand option, heading past Barnett's Park and the Queen's University playing fields where she could see rugby training in progress on one of the pitches.

All around, there were rolling meadows and country walks alongside the curve of the River Lagan. A mile or so further on, the landscape became more unkempt, with abandoned building sites, weedy and crumbling, and huge hoardings offering land for sale with planning permission for hotels or road-houses.

She felt tense.

As she circled a roundabout and drove on up a hill, road signs warned of bad bends. Another bore a big 'H' to denote a hospital nearby and below it . . . No A and E.

She wondered if it would have made any difference that night if there had been.

The hospital itself, Belvoir Park, was on her right, doing its best to look pleasant, with trimmed flower-beds and freshly

191

painted railings, but it was the cancer hospital; everyone knew that. In spite of the care and expertise it offered, it was a place to which you never wanted to be admitted.

She reached the steep junction with Purdysburn Hill and took a left towards Purdysburn village which consisted of a handful of houses of picture postcard perfection with latticed windows and latched doors. Old, distinguished roses climbed trellises on the red brick walls. It was just around the corner from a busy road but there was an instant peacefulness and no through traffic at all. Belfast was like that. In minutes you could be out in the country amongst the winding lanes and hawthorn hedges.

She could see a field of maize stubble almost orange. Ragged-feathered crows were scattered over it like pieces of charred paper. She pulled her car into a cul-de-sac that led to the back of some of the houses and got out. There was an old stone wall, the boundary with what would once have been a grand estate but was now a wilderness of towering trees. Sycamore, larch, elm and beech encased in rampant ivy all creaked and jostled together in a breeze which had developed force. The blue sky of the morning had gone, replaced by clouds at first white but now a gradually deepening grey.

She looked over the wall. The forest floor was dense with bracken and a thickly interlocked network of bramble. There were no paths that she could discern, no sign that human presence ever tried to carve a way through.

She walked back to the main road. There was no footpath where she was but there was one on the other side – and a constant flow of cars to be negotiated in order to get to it. When the road was clear for a few seconds, she dashed across.

Looking back to where she had been, she saw a curved metal barrier running along the roadside. There had been a wooden fence before, hadn't someone said, but this protective strip was obviously a consequence of the accident, erected to prevent anyone crashing down into the woods as Everett and she had. It was going to make it harder to find the place where they had gone in.

But there was the hill and the bend. That spot was still there, naturally enough, and it would give her some indication of where the Jacksons said they had met the two cars. She walked along towards it, waited for another break in the traffic, then ran back across.

There was nowhere for her to stand and look in. She was much too near the road, too much at risk from a speeding vehicle coming over the crest of the hill and not seeing her until it was too late. She hopped up on to the barrier and jumped down the far side.

Too late she learned that what she thought would be solid ground was a platform of ferns concealing a sloping clay bank. Unable to stop herself, she fell on her backside and slipped down it. Hanging loose, her shirt rode up behind her and she gave a cry of pain as she felt something dig into her back. She slid hard into a web of thick brambles at the bottom of the slope, put her arms up to cover her face and knocked her glasses off in doing so.

She swore. 'Christ!'

Her ears rang with shock. She was on her back, staring straight up at the trees rocking above her. In here, their sound was a roar, like a storm tide breaking on a beach.

She struggled to her feet, trying futilely not to catch herself on the thorns. There were scratches on the backs of her hands, raised pink weals with pinpricks of blood. She put her hand to the small of her back and winced. There was blood on her fingertips. Something sharper, a stone, a torn branch maybe, had cut her.

She found her glasses, put them on, and when she looked around she saw that she was going to have trouble getting back up the bank. But then she remembered that at the wall, where she had left her car, she had seen that the drop was much more shallow. Getting there, though, beating her way through the undergrowth, that would not be easy.

All she had meant to do was find the spot where the accident happened and have a look at it. It was not as if she expected to find any clues lying about or for it to trigger any memories, although that was always a hope. It was just that this was where her life had stopped for four years and she thought she ought to see it. It was a place of significance, like a grave or a monument.

Several years of changing seasons and unchecked growth had obliterated any sign of the awful thing that had happened here. Yet she could sense it in the dank, earthy smells, the whiff of death and decay. And she could hear it in the violence of the wind in the trees.

In addition there were other noises now, she realised, not just in those high steeples but down here on the ground. She heard sounds in the bracken. Snapping sounds, like twigs breaking. All sorts of animals shared this safe habitat. Rabbits, badgers, foxes.

But what else might lurk?

Someone had come here and bashed Paul Everett's brains in. Where had it happened? Down there, where that sycamore was and where the floor was freer of brambles? Or here, near this beech tree? She peered around her, noticing that the light was deteriorating as the afternoon and the weather drew in.

What if there was someone in here now, watching? Stalking her?

She felt her chest tighten and she tried to tell herself that there was no reason to feel frightened. It was just her imagination running away with her.

A trickle of sweat ran down her spine and the palms of her hands dampened.

She heard something rustle in the bushes to her left. She swung round in that direction but she could see nothing.

Standing here, alone like this, was not good. It was time to get out. Now.

She looked again at the bank down which she had fallen and finally abandoned all thoughts of it as a means of exit. In the other direction it was only a matter of a hundred yards or so to where her car was parked but it felt as if she were about to embark on a journey into dangerous, uncharted territory.

There was a young ash tree beside her. She grabbed one of its branches and swung down violently until it gave with a crack. She tore the thin shoots from it and snapped off the slender tip, turning what was left into a sturdy stick. Then she began to make her way towards the perimeter wall.

The brambles were thick and they tried hard to hold her back, plucking at her tough jeans as she waded into them. With the stick she beat the ground in front of her, testing it for unexpected holes or sudden dips.

It took her ten minutes to cover the short distance. She was tired and sweating when she noticed that the light was a little better and then she saw that that was because she was at the edge of the wood and the wall was just a little way ahead. Relieved, she discarded the stick and stopped for a second to catch her breath.

She could hear civilisation again, the sound of cars on the road just beyond. She would be out of here in a few moments.

And then she heard a noise.

It came from behind her. In spite of the wind she heard it, a sharp, loud crack like a branch snapping, and as she turned towards the sound it registered in her brain that a small animal couldn't do that.

She stood and stared into the increasing gloom behind her. It was hard to see. Nothing moved. Nothing, but . . .

There!

A shape. A figure. Disappearing behind a tree. Had she seen it or had she not?

194

She would not wait to find out.

Her heart was in her throat. She turned away and pushed forward through the clinging brambles, wishing she could run, knowing that was impossible. The thorns attacked her hands but fear prevented her feeling it.

The wall seemed to be receding rather than getting nearer.

If there was someone behind he would be able to reach her quickly, grab her, pull her back into the trees. No one would see what happened to her. No one would hear her cries beneath the sound of the wind.

She thought she heard something again but this time she did not turn to look. She had to keep going.

And suddenly she had reached the wall, her fingers touching its cold, safe stone. With one heave she pulled herself over, feeling the road reassuringly firm beneath her feet.

She stepped away from the wall, towards her car, looked back into the blackness of the trees but she saw nothing. She didn't want to see anything. She fumbled in her pocket for the keys, then got in, reversed recklessly out of the cul-de-sac and drove away.

She found herself on a narrow, curving road that she did not know, driving at a speed that was downright crazy. She lurched into a laneway and jammed on the brakes, then sat waiting for her breathing to slow down and her reason to return.

She had panicked, that was all. She had been frightened by the fall and in the dark embrace of the forest, the place where her nightmare had begun, her fears had taken hold.

She had gone there to exorcise ghosts and she had found them all around her.

She sat for a while. Her back was painful. The angry scratches on her hands throbbed. After ten minutes she started the engine again, turned the car and went back, heading for home.

She drove beneath a sky that was the density of molten lead. Rain began, the first heavy drops slapping onto the windscreen. She put her sidelights on. As she drove past the woods, she did not look.

It was twenty minutes since she had clambered safely over the wall.

In that time, had she stayed and not driven off, she would have seen a figure emerge from the trees, not far from where she had entered, then walk down the road towards the hospital where a blue Fiat waited in the car park.

On the Lisburn Road, she stopped at a pharmacy and bought antiseptic lotion and Bandaid. For a doctor, she did not keep much in the medicine cupboard.

She handed over the money and saw the woman behind the counter looking at her hands. There was a scratch on her neck, too, she had discovered from a glance in the rear-view mirror, and mud on her jeans and shirt.

'Slight accident,' she explained. 'Nothing serious.'

At home she ran a bath and took off her clothes in front of her bedroom mirror, twisting so that she could see her back. The cut was more of a nasty graze and it had not bled much.

It stung like hell, as did her hands, when she slid into the hot tub. She put a little lavender oil into the water and its strong, sweet aroma seemed to soothe her as she lay there, feeling a heaviness being taken out of her body. She stayed in the bath for twenty minutes, safe again and calm, then got out, dried herself gingerly, and put the antiseptic cream on her cuts as well as a plaster over the abrasion on her back to stop it being irritated by her clothing.

She was hungry. She hadn't eaten all day.

A quick inspection of the cupboards told her she would have to go shopping tomorrow. She put some pasta shells into boiling water and opened a tin of tuna, then rang Elizabeth. She needed to talk to somebody, thinking that there were few options. Even Elizabeth would not be around much beyond the end of the year.

She had no friends and no opportunity to make any. She needed a job. Anything. A place where she could meet people.

Elizabeth wasn't in. There was just the answering machine. She left a message and the time and said she would call again tomorrow.

She settled down to watch television for a while but soon she was yawning. The day had drained her.

She was in bed and asleep at eleven when the phone rang. She sat up abruptly and grabbed it, feeling her body aching, the cut on her back stiff and painful.

'Hello,' she said and heard her own drowsy voice.

There was no other sound.

'Hello,' she said again, more forcefully, alert now and listening to the silence. It lasted for a few eerie seconds and then there was a click.

She dialled 1471 straight away but it was the same as before. Number withheld.

She sat up in bed, staring into the darkness of her room. Outside she could hear the wind. It did its best to rattle the secure double-glazed windows which her father had installed. Down the street somewhere, a gate was open, clanging backward and forward against iron garden railings.

The phone rang again and seemed shockingly shrill.

'Hello. Who is this?' she demanded.

'It's me. You called me,' Elizabeth said, taken aback. 'What's the matter?'

'Oh, Elizabeth,' she said with relief. 'I'm sorry.'

'What's going on?'

And then Meg told her about her day.

When she got to the anonymous phone call, Elizabeth said, 'Well, *now* will you call the police? Or do you want me to do it for you?'

Meg thought of Florence Gilmour's card under the magnet on the fridge.

'No,' she said. 'I'll do it. I'll do it tomorrow.'

'You promise?'

'Yes. I promise.'

She lay awake for a while after Elizabeth had rung off. She picked up a book and tried to read but her mind kept wandering towards the woods and she found herself reading the same page over and over again. After half an hour she turned the light off and lay down. Sometime about midnight she dropped off.

In her dreams, the gate down the street was still banging.

And then she was awake because it wasn't a dream at all.

The noise was not down the street. It was nearer than that and she realised it was coming from the rear of the house. It sounded like her own gate, the big wooden one that led out on to the back lane. But it had been bolted. She had checked it this morning before she went to Antrim and she had not been out there since.

She got out of bed in the dark, put on her robe and went to the landing window to look. It was her gate all right. She could see it swinging open.

There was something else.

She stepped back from the window, into the shadows. It looked as if someone was standing there. In her back garden. Just there – where the little seat was.

She strained her eyes but could not see clearly. Her glasses were on her bedside table. She hurried back for them but when she returned to the window and looked again the garden was empty.

She saw nothing now, just the wisteria and honeysuckle on the fence being whipped viciously by the wind.

There was no one. Maybe there never had been. She cursed her imagination.

197

The gate banged intermittently for the rest of the night and she lay awake listening to it, a torture that she was powerless to stop. It was simply a matter of going out there and bolting it again but she could not bring herself to do so, imagination or not.

Not until first light, when the wind had gone, did she venture out, trying to tell herself that she mustn't have fastened it properly in the first place.

Twenty-four

The following evening, she came out of the big supermarket half a mile from where she lived and within a few minutes wished she had brought the car instead of deciding to walk.

The first problem was two heavy bags of groceries. She had not planned on buying so much but as she went up and down the aisles she remembered there was such a lot she did not have in the house.

Then there was the weather. She turned into the Lisburn Road, heading for home. Behind her, out in the country, was the last of the day's sunlight but ahead, towards the city, the sky was glowering, almost black. A rainstorm was not far off.

On top of all that, she had the feeling she was being watched.

On the way to the supermarket, a car had passed, a black Mercedes. She thought for a second that it had slowed down but when she had glanced its way, it had speeded up and driven on before she had glimpsed the driver or thought of getting its number.

She looked up and down the road but she did not see it now. Yet she still felt as if there were eyes on her. It was a sensation on her skin, like electricity, and she could not shake it.

She wished she had been able to reach Florence Gilmour.

She had tried her this morning only to be told that she was on leave. Then she had rung the policewoman's mobile number and got a recorded voice that told her the thing was switched off.

She had not wanted to talk to anyone else. Maybe that was a mistake.

She walked quickly, feeling unprotected, weighed down with the shopping. Carrying the bags made her feel as if her hands were tied. People hurried past, anxious to get indoors before the storm arrived, paying no attention to a woman alone.

Thunder rumbled. A collision in the sky. The first raindrops hit the dry pavement and spread like ink on a blotter.

She wondered if she should stand in somewhere, maybe nip into one of the coffee shops or a pub and wait for it to blow over,

199

but this rain could last for hours. Home was just a couple of streets away.

There were more drops. The blots were joining, forming bigger shapes. And suddenly it was a deluge.

She had no coat, just a cotton jacket over a t-shirt and jeans. She began to hurry faster. She half ran, her trainers slapping the wet street, the shopping bags giving her an awkward, ungainly rhythm. Within moments she was soaked, her hair plastered to her head and rain dripping from her nose and chin. It formed a film on the lenses of her glasses and made it impossible to see properly.

But she consoled herself with the fact that she was nearly there. Only two streets to go. She would be home in a minute, out of these things, warm and dry.

Cars swished past and she had to dodge and weave as waves of water arced on to the footpath.

Ahead of her a car pulled up.

She could see its brake lights, a distorted red glow through her wet glasses. She couldn't be certain but it looked like a black Mercedes. And it had stopped at the end of her street.

Someone got out. A man. She could not see him clearly, just that he was in a dark coat with a hood pulled up. He began to walk quickly towards her.

She was at a corner. She made a decision and turned down it suddenly then hurried along, away from him. After a few yards she looked back. He was still behind her. This was not her imagination.

She started to walk faster, wishing she did not have the damned shopping. She cut into an alleyway between two streets, looked back again and knew what she would see. He had come into the alley with her.

There was only one thing to do. She dropped the shopping and began to run. The bags fell open. Tins spilled out, a bottle cracked. Oranges, liberated, bounced along the ground and rolled ahead of her.

Out of the alley, she turned left into another street, ran to the bottom of it and headed right. Fear drove her on but now she saw that what she was doing might be a mistake because she was taking herself further away from the main thoroughfare and from her own home.

These streets were empty. There was just the rain and the thunder and a sky that was biblically overcast.

He was still behind her, gaining all the time, and she was beginning to tire.

She heard his voice call something. But she did not stop.

She ran past a car body shop that was closed and shuttered,

then a terrace of little houses with lace curtains. There were lights in a front room, a geranium in the window, an elderly woman looking out. She thought of hammering on the door for help but he would have reached her first.

And then the night erupted.

It did so in an enormous, deep-throated roar that almost stopped her in her tracks.

'*Ooooooooooh!*'

The sound soared in the air over the rooftops and as she heard it her heart soared with it because she realised what it was. She was in a street that was on the other side of the railway track from Windsor Park football ground.

There was a match. There were people. Thousands of them. Just a short distance away.

The singing began. '*Stand uupp – for the Ulstermen! Stand uupp – for the Ulstermen!*' Some part of her brain noted that the tune was the old Village People anthem, *Go West*.

It changed to a chant. '*Northern Ire-land!*' With it was a rhythmic hand-clapping and she felt it spurring her on.

She reached a set of steep steps that she figured would lead to the railway bridge. Once across, she would be safe, alone no longer. Whoever was behind, he would not try to attack her in front of a crowd.

She ran. Up and up. Her legs were weakening but she had to keep going. The open sides and top of the bridge were covered with a network of safety netting but it did not keep the rain out. It lashed at her as she ran across, her feet pounding the wooden floor.

At the end of the bridge was a wall decorated with a confusion of spray-paint graffiti. She recognised some of it – UVF, LVF, the initials of the old terrorist gangs – and it did not make her feel any safer.

There were steps leading left or right. She chose left. Her foot kicked a beer can and it clattered down the steps in front of her.

'*You sad bastard! You sad bastard!*'

The roar of the crowd enveloped her and there before her was the ground.

Towering above the pitch, floodlight pylons trained their steady glare as she tried to work out where she was. She was at the side. Fifty yards away, across a tarmac no-man's land, was the west stand, grey brick walls that were as high and solid as those of a prison. Water streamed down them.

And then she saw something else. Just in front of where she stood there was high metal fencing, topped with razor wire, and iron gates that were shut. There was not a soul in sight.

201

Her heart sank. Here, in this open space, she was as vulnerable as she had been in the woods. There was no one to see her, no one to hear, no one to help. They were all inside those forbidding walls, hordes of them under the shelter of the grandstands, watching two football teams battling in the rain.

She reached the bottom of the steps, exhausted and beaten. Fear held her as she turned to face her pursuer.

Someone scored.

The cheer was instant, deafening. There were horns and sirens. Heavy feet stamping on the floor of the stands.

He stepped towards her.

The hood fell back from his head and her heart shuddered when she saw who it was.

'Meg.'

She saw her name on his lips but with the noise of the crowd she could not hear it.

He took another step forward and as he did, someone appeared on the steps behind him.

She gasped and stepped back.

He turned as Dan Cochrane leaped at him.

The two of them hit the tarmac hard but Cochrane got up quickly and pulled the other man to his feet. He held him by the lapels of his coat and punched him hard in the stomach. The man doubled up with a grunt and Cochrane swung his right fist back to hit him in the face.

'Don't!' Meg shouted. 'Don't hit him again! It's all right. I know him.'

She pushed Cochrane out of the way as Noel Kennedy got up, gasping for breath and staggering. He reached forward and leaned on the wall before lowering himself down on to a step. He put his hand behind his neck and when he took it away again, there was blood.

He coughed hard and painfully. 'Jesus, I'm bleeding.' He looked up at Cochrane. 'That crazy bastard might have killed me.'

Cochrane stepped towards him but Meg waved him back. She bent over Kennedy and looked at the injury. He had hit his head and there was a cut but the blood was mixed with the rain and she figured that it looked worse than it was.

'Let me see,' she said. 'Do you know who you are?'

He nodded but did not say.

'Who? Who are you?' she insisted.

'Noel. Noel Kennedy.'

'Who's Noel Kennedy?' Cochrane asked.

'You keep out of this for a minute?' Meg said without turning round. 'And who am I?'

202

'Meg.' Kennedy said. 'You're Meg.'

The response satisfied her. She crouched in front of him and put her hand under his chin, lifting his face to her. Then she pulled back one of his eyelids gently. She did not have a light to shine to see how the pupils would respond but they seemed normal. There was no bruising around the eyes that might indicate a fracture at the base of the skull. That was good. She checked next for bruising behind the ear that might mean a leakage of blood – 'Battle's sign', as it was known. She found nothing, although she knew something like that might take longer to develop.

'Have you got a handkerchief?' she asked.

'Yes.' He fumbled in his pocket and gave it to her. It was white, a perfectly folded square, unused.

'Hold that behind your head,' she said. 'As far as I can see, you'll have a nasty bump and a cut but nothing more serious.'

She straightened up and stood back, then looked at each of the men in turn. 'What the hell were you doing? Have you been following me around? Watching me?'

The questions were for both of them but Kennedy had one of his own. He stared at Cochrane. 'Who the hell is he?'

Cochrane turned towards Meg. 'I was driving around, looking for somewhere to park, when I saw you running down the street with this guy coming behind you. By the time I got rid of the van, you'd disappeared. Then I saw the railway bridge and tried it. It was the only place you could have gone. He looked as if he was going to attack you. I had to do something.'

'But what are you doing here?' Meg asked.

'I was in Belfast collecting an order. Yours was part of it. I'd had something to eat in town and I decided to come by and drop the stuff off if you were home. It's lucky I did.'

She looked at him, wondering. It seemed a fortunate coincidence. For a stand-in shopkeeper he was being very attentive and she felt certain there was more to this than customer relations. But she was glad of his presence, whatever the reason.

She looked at Kennedy. 'This is Dan. He's a friend,' she found herself saying. 'Which you are not. Why were you chasing me?'

'Meg, I'm sorry,' he said. 'I didn't know what to do. I had to talk to you after the last time but I didn't know what to say. I rang you a couple of times but I just froze. I couldn't speak.'

'You rang me?' She glared. 'Those phone calls? That was you?'

'I'm sorry. I didn't mean to frighten you. It was the wrong thing to do but I couldn't stop myself. I had to hear your voice.'

'And that was you I saw in my garden last night, too, I

suppose. And the woods, out where the accident happened – were you there, by any chance? Did you follow me there, too?'

He looked confused. 'I don't know what you mean. I wasn't in your garden. Why would I do that? I haven't seen you since you came to my office and I haven't been anywhere near you until tonight. After I made that call last night, I decided I had to come and talk to you, to explain how I felt. I love you, Meg. I've never stopped.'

'Oh don't give me that.' She turned her face from him, not wanting to hear.

Behind the walls of the ground there was a cheer, then a groan and howls of protest.

'I drove here and saw you leaving your house,' Kennedy said. 'I followed you to the supermarket and then decided to wait for you to come back. I drove around a bit, watching you – God it sounds terrible but I didn't know what I was going to say or do – and then it rained and I stopped for you and you saw me and started to run and I . . .' He looked at Cochrane staring at him through the rain. He was wearing a waterproof jacket that was wet and glistening. His fists were clenched by his side and in the shadows cast by the floodlights there were dark hollows in his cheeks.

Meg looked at Kennedy and knew she should report this. But he looked pathetic sitting there, a beaten man in every way, so instead she told him, 'Why don't you get the hell out of here and leave me alone. And if I get any more funny phone calls or see you anywhere near my house, I'm calling the police.'

He picked himself up gingerly. 'Meg, I'm sorry. Can't we talk about this?'

'Just get out of here in case I change my mind.'

He looked at her for a second and she was not sure whether it was rain on his face or tears, then he stood and hurried back up the steps. At the top he turned the corner and was gone.

'You're soaked,' Cochrane said. 'You'll get pneumonia.'

She smiled at him. 'Thank you,' she said, 'for what you did. I don't think he was going to hurt me but thank you anyway.'

'Do you . . .' He hesitated. 'Do you want to tell me about him?'

Behind them in the stadium, voices were baying for blood. She looked towards where the other drama of the night was being played out.

'He's a long story,' she said, 'that's what he is.'

When they got back to the other side of the railway bridge, Kennedy had vanished without trace.

Cochrane's van was on a double yellow line at a corner,

untroubled by the likelihood of a parking ticket in such weather. They got in and he drove back towards Truesdale Street, retracing Meg's steps.

First they found where she had dumped her shopping, then salvaged what they could of it. The tins and bottles she had bought were fine, an exception being a jar of beetroot which had smashed and stained the wet ground purple. They even managed to locate some of the runaway oranges. What was beyond redemption, they left in someone's wheelie bin.

When they got to the house, he carried a cardboard box from the back of the van. 'Your order,' he explained.

She found him a towel for his hair and he hung his jacket on a peg behind the kitchen door. The rain dripped from it on to the tiled floor and when he had finished with the towel, he put it down to soak up the drops.

She looked at him. He was in a baggy sweater, jeans and old trainers which were wringing. His hair was dishevelled and all of a sudden she wanted to reach out and tidy it into shape with her fingers.

It was cold in the room. 'I think I'll turn the heat on,' she told him. 'Why don't you take your shoes off and stick them on top of a radiator. It won't take long warming up.'

'That would be good,' he said, and sat to undo the laces.

'We could probably do with a drink but I'm afraid I don't have anything alcoholic.'

'There's coffee,' he said. 'I know that.' They had rescued a jar of decaffeinated.

'Then you could make us some while I go and change. I'll only be a moment.'

She showed him where the cups were kept, then ran upstairs, got another towel from the bathroom and peeled off her sodden things. Even her underwear was wet.

She dried herself vigorously and felt her skin glowing as she padded around the bedroom, getting fresh clothes. She could hear him moving around in the kitchen below, opening cupboards. She shivered and it was not from the cold but from a kind of excitement that came with the realisation that he was here, in her house, and she was naked, just a short distance from him.

She dressed in a shirt and a warm jumper and pulled on a pair of sweatpants. She could smell the coffee as she ran back downstairs in bare feet.

'Milk?' He had got some from the fridge.

'Thanks. No sugar.'

They sat at the kitchen table. He sipped his coffee silently. She knew he wanted to ask her more but he did not do so.

'I think I owe you some sort of an explanation,' she said at last. 'I said it was a long story. It is.'

Without making a conscious decision to do it, she told him everything: the accident, the murder, her coma, the amnesia, her discovery of the affair with Kennedy. Everything.

It felt like a kind of release, laying it all out like that, her life and what had happened to it. He listened silently. He was the first person to whom she had had to explain who she was and she found it peculiar that he did not know already. She had assumed everyone knew but perhaps she was not the big sideshow attraction she thought she was. People had their own problems, their own lives to lead. Headlines came and went. Other nine-day wonders had replaced her by now.

She was curious, though. 'You haven't heard about the case?'

'I'm not sure. Maybe. I don't know. I don't read papers much or watch TV a lot.' He finished his coffee.

Meg considered something. 'You know, this business tonight, maybe I really should report it.' She looked at him for an opinion.

He shrugged. 'It's up to you but if you ask me I don't think much will come of it if you do. No crime has been committed as such, has it, and you don't think he was going to harm you. You said that yourself. He's had a pretty bad night, I'd say. He'll go off and lick his wounds and I doubt if you'll be hearing from him again.' He put his hand to his chest. 'But that's just my opinion.' He smiled. 'Who knows – what if you report it and the police go to see him and he has me done for assault?'

She thought. 'Maybe you're right.'

'But will you talk about this to anyone else?'

She shook her head. 'My friend Elizabeth, that's all. She knows about him. She was the woman with me in your shop that day.' She looked at him to see if he remembered and he nodded. 'But that's it. I certainly won't mention it to my parents. That would mean having to tell them about me and him. They'd be upset about that. *An affair with a married man.* They've had enough anxiety.' She smiled at him. 'So here I am pouring my heart out to a complete stranger.'

He looked at her from under shy brows. 'You don't believe that.'

'What?'

'You don't feel that I'm a stranger.'

'No,' she said and met his eyes. 'No, I don't suppose I do.' And she knew then that he had turned up tonight simply because he had wanted to see her.

In the silent seconds that followed it seemed that something almost tangible passed between them. Then he pushed back his chair and stood up. 'I'd better go,' he said quietly.

She knew it would not be the last she would see of him. Without speaking a word, they had agreed that.

He tested his shoes. 'They're still damp but they'll do.' When he had put them on, he said, 'You'll be all right?'

She nodded. 'I'll be fine.'

He got his coat. 'I'll call you. To make sure.'

'That would be nice.'

She opened the front door. It was still raining heavily. The water ran in rivulets along the slope of the street and it poured down the drainpipes at the side of the house, gurgling into the gratings.

'You've got a bit of a journey,' she said.

'I'll manage. I'm used to it.'

She held out a hand to him. She did not know what else to do. 'Thank you. For being there.'

He took her hand and held it for a long moment. It was the first time they had touched. His grasp was strong and warm and comforting.

'I don't know anything about you,' she said.

'That's for another day,' he said. 'I'll call.'

And then he was off, running, splashing down the street towards the van, his coat pulled up over his head.

She was in the shower the next morning when the phone rang.

She wrapped herself in a towel and ran to it, thinking it might be him. It was a man's voice but not one she knew. He was an American.

'Am I speaking to Dr Meg Winter?'

'Yes?'

As she heard the word *Doctor*, she remembered with sudden satisfaction how instinctively she had reacted last night to Kennedy's injury. But in a flash, too, she saw Cochrane hitting him, a punishment as much as an act of protection, and she wondered for an instant how badly he would have hurt him if she had not stopped it.

'This is Vectra Pharmaceuticals,' the man said. 'I've been asked to give you a call. You were looking for an address.'

Twenty-five

Cochrane did ring shortly afterwards and he rang three times more over the next week.

On each occasion, she found herself being soothed by the sound of his quiet voice, even though their conversations did not add up to much. Talking to him set her at ease and she did not feel vulnerable any more. Instead, she felt protected, as if he were watching over her.

During that time, she put Elizabeth in the picture but she said nothing of any of this to her parents.

Her father took her for lunch.

They drove out a country road near Hillsborough to a pub which described itself as a 'casual gourmet diner'. The place had recently been refurbished in rustic style. She had something called a symphony of seafood, which was a kind of stew. Her father had seared salmon and stir-fried vegetables and a glass of white wine which came in its own miniature bottle. Meg stuck to her usual mineral water.

'What would you say if I told you I was thinking of retiring?'

'I'd say it was about time. You deserve it. You've had a hard couple of years – thanks partly to me, of course.'

He began to protest. 'I don't mean—'

She waved him silent. 'It's true, though, Dad. It's taken an awful lot out of you. Bound to have. But if you retired, what would you do? You've always been so busy.'

'I'm not sure,' he said. 'Dabble in a wee bit of property, maybe, to keep myself active.'

She pictured her own house and remembered her mother's implication that its renovation had not been entirely philanthropic. She whisked the thought away.

'I've bought a place on the west coast of Scotland,' he said. 'I like it there.'

'I know,' she said. He went to Scotland to stay with friends almost every Christmas.

Christmas. She wondered what she would do and she thought of Dan suddenly, alone in Ardglass. Or did he have someone?

The fact was she just didn't know.

'I might go and live there,' her father said.

'What's brought all this on?' It was not just idle musing. He had never indulged in that. Everything he did was carefully thought out and had a purpose.

He looked around to make sure he would not be overheard then lowered his voice. 'I think he's going to sell Malone Group.'

'Who?'

'Sir Brian. Sir Brian Malone.'

'Oh, right.'

She had no real interest in business matters. It did not mean a lot to her: buy-outs and takeovers and flotations and all that sort of thing. It had consumed her father all his life but it had just been a sort of background noise in hers. Yet she was acutely aware of how much she had benefited from his interests and the wealth it had made for him.

'He doesn't need the company,' he said. 'It's small beer to him. There are a couple of possible bidders and if he sells, the value of the shares will rocket and then maybe that would be the time to take the money and run.'

'And Seasons Construction?'

'It's not mine any more anyway. Time somebody younger was looking after things there.'

'I need a job,' she said. All she had told her parents was that for the time being she had shelved thoughts of resuming medicine.

'If it's money,' he said, 'you need never have to worry about that.'

'It's not the money, it's people. I need to be around people.'

'You need to get yourself a man,' he said.

She thought of Dan and wondered if she should say she had met someone but she hesitated. If she spoke about it, it would make it into more than it was.

'Who would have me?' she said. 'In my condition.'

He smiled. 'If I went to live in Scotland would you come and visit me?'

'Absolutely not,' she said. 'I'd be glad to see the back of you.' Then she gave him a big grin and leaned across the table to kiss him on the cheek.

She sent her mother a birthday card. She picked it in a greetings shop near the City Hall, avoiding anything that had a religious message or was too humorous.

Mother was out, too; those cards were covered in flowers and sentimental verse which she imagined being dreamed up by a

209

team of bored hacks in a dingy office somewhere.

The card she selected in the end was dainty and relatively simple: a golden cake with candles on a plain background and the words *Happy Birthday* underneath. As she posted it, she realised to her shame that she had forgotten exactly how old her mother was. Fifty-nine, was it? Not sixty, surely?

On the day itself, she thought she would drop in and surprise her.

She drove to Carryduff with the present from the pottery, wrapped now in red and gold paper with a satin sheen. There were cars in the street outside. She saw Pastor Drew's BMW among them. She paused for a second then she opened the kitchen door and walked in.

'Anybody home?' she called.

A kettle was coming to the boil and a woman she did not know was standing at the work surface taking a Sainsbury's birthday cake out of a box and putting it on a large plate. She was in her fifties, stoutly built, dressed in a skirt and jumper that were expensive but plain. She stared at Meg.

'I'm looking for my mother,' Meg said. She could hear other voices now, coming from the living room beyond, one of them male, with a familiar resonance.

'Yes, indeed,' the woman said. 'Gloria,' she called. 'Your daughter's here.'

Meg put the parcel down on the kitchen table and walked past her gaze, feeling it trained on her like the sights of a gun. She pushed open the living-room door. There were other women in the room, clones of the one in the kitchen. Her mother and Pastor Drew got to their feet. The dog leaped from the settee and threw itself at her.

'Margaret,' her mother said. She looked flustered.

Everyone stopped talking and stared at Meg. She stooped and patted the dog, then she glanced up at her mother. 'You didn't think I wouldn't come to see you on your birthday, now, did you?'

'It's very good to meet you again,' Drew told her.

She smiled with civility but did not return the sentiment.

'I'm afraid we caught your mother unawares,' he explained. 'And under false pretences. We have a Bible Week coming up and I persuaded Gloria to allow us to have a meeting of the organising committee here.'

'Somehow they knew it was my birthday,' her mother added.

'And I walked in on the surprise,' Meg said and she could see that her mother was having trouble with that. She had intruded

210

into a world of which she was not a part.

She looked at the other women. Their beatific smiles were like a forcefield, a threat rather than a welcome.

Any one of them could have written the letters.

But in her mother's eyes that would not be the problem.

She was the problem.

She had not come to heel when bidden. Instead, she had spurned Drew and the church, embarrassing her mother in the process, then she had gone on television and said those things. There would have been no anonymous letters if she had done so.

'You'll stay for a cup of tea?' her mother asked, not wanting her to.

'No, I can't,' Meg lied and saw the relief in Gloria's eyes. 'I've got to be somewhere. I just popped out with a present for you. I've left it in the kitchen.'

'That's kind,' her mother said but made no effort to go and see what it was.

'You can open it later.' She turned towards the door. 'Nice to meet you all.' Her mother had not attempted to introduce her to any of them.

There was a chorus of goodbyes. 'God bless you,' Drew proclaimed.

'I'll see you out,' Gloria said and they walked into the hall.

'I'm sorry if I disturbed you,' Meg said at the front door. She felt hurt and unwanted. From nowhere, a vision of her empty childhood came to her. There was a garden. She was alone, in a party frock, and little shoes with white frilly socks.

'It's not that,' Gloria tried. 'I just wasn't expecting ... you came at a bad time.'

There was something in Meg's throat. She gave her mother a quick hug. 'Happy birthday, Mum,' she said.

She managed to get round the corner and out of sight before she had to stop the car to blow her nose and dry her eyes.

211

Twenty-six

Ten days after the incident with Kennedy she drove into County Down to meet Dan Cochrane.

It was a Sunday morning. October had arrived, bringing slate grey days that were colder. Hedgerows sparkled with diamond drops left over from the night's rain.

She had thought he would never ask.

'Sunday,' he had said on the phone. 'Are you doing anything?'

'Not a lot, no.'

'Do you like walking?'

'Yes, but I don't do enough of it.'

'Do you know where Castle Ward is?'

She did.

'Then I'll meet you at eleven thirty in the bottom car park, at the cornmill. You'll see the signs directing you if you don't know how to locate it. Don't wear anything you don't mind getting dirty. Have you got walking boots?'

'Yes,' she had said. She had, somewhere. 'And then what?'

'Then we'll go for a walk and afterwards we'll have a nice lunch.'

Castle Ward was a National Trust property just a couple of miles along the coastal shore from the village of Strangford.

She was not a Trust member so she paid the attendant at the gate lodge, then went on into the grounds, driving past heavy rhododendron bushes and fields of grazing sheep that were abundant with wool.

In a few moments, across the meadows on her right, she saw the house that gave the place its name. Built in the eighteenth century, it was an architectural oddity. The original owner and his wife had been unable to agree on an overall style so that one side, the one she saw now, was classical in construction, while the other, facing out over Strangford Lough, was gothic.

As instructed, she followed the signs to the cornmill and turned towards the car park. He was sitting on a tree stump, waiting, and she felt her heart beating harder when she saw him.

She got out. 'Hi,' she said.

'Hi,' he answered and they stood for a moment smiling nervously at each other.

She could not see his van. 'Where's your limo?'

'I left it in Strangford and walked here.'

She looked puzzled.

'Well, I thought we'd walk into Strangford and I didn't think you'd want to walk all the way back again after lunch.'

She aimed a forefinger at him. 'Good thinking,' she said.

She got her boots out of the car and put them on. She had bought a pair of thick socks and she tucked her jeans in, then pulled a waterproof over her head.

'Very good,' he said. 'You look the part.'

She peered at him. He was wearing a chunky sweater, a pair of rainproof trousers and sturdy leather boots that were muddy already.

'No coat?'

'It won't rain. Not until tonight. I checked the forecast.'

'Very trusting of you,' she said. 'So, come on then. Lead the way.'

They headed out of the car park and down towards the shore. There was almost no wind at all and the tide was out a little way. Black-headed gulls bobbed on the surface of the water and the smell of seaweed was pungent in the air.

He cut through a crumbling stone gateway and into the woods. They followed a broad path with heavy tyre tracks embedded deeply in soft mud, passing trees which had fallen and been cut neatly into piles of logs. She could smell the damp sawdust.

She thought immediately of her last venture into a forest.

This was different.

They did not talk much; she did not feel the need. Instead she listened to a stillness broken only by the soft sound of their feet on the earth, the sweet melody of a robin in the bushes, and the call of a curlew out over the water.

It reminded her of walks when she was young – what, thirteen? Fourteen?

There had been a boy the same age. She couldn't recall his name. She remembered how his eyes would scout ahead, seeking out a suitable tree, and then when he reached the spot he would pull her in behind it and she would pretend to be surprised.

She remembered awkward kisses. Cold lips on cold lips. Each of them trying to hide the fact that they had runny noses, which meant holding your breath for impossibly long periods until you broke apart, gulping for air and searching for a handker-chief.

And she remembered the tingling feeling of icy, furtive fingers making their persistent way past protective barriers of clothing.

She realised with a start that she was imagining Dan's hands, that she was thinking of his touch on her skin.

She saw that he was looking at her with a little frown. 'You OK?'

'Me? I'm fine,' she said, hoping he would think that the redness in her cheeks was the result of the fresh morning air.

They met two young people coming the other way, a boy and girl of about seventeen with an energetic golden retriever, its legs encased in black mud. A younger boy, about twelve and chubby, lagged several yards behind them.

The girl turned. 'Run, Forrest, run!' she called back to him.

The youngsters laughed, Cochrane, too, as they passed.

'What's so funny?' Meg asked.

'*Forrest Gump*,' he said.

'What's forest gump?'

He glanced at her for a second and realised. 'Of course – you wouldn't know. It's a film. It was a big hit when you were—'

'In a coma,' she finished for him. 'Don't be embarrassed. This sort of thing happens all the time.'

After half an hour, they reached Strangford.

They entered the village all of a sudden. They came down a sloping stony pathway called the Squeeze Cut and when they turned the corner, there it was. The harbour was below them and on the far side of the shore she could see the town of Portaferry. A gentle sun had cut through the clouds, bathing the buildings along its seafront. Windows flashed like signals in morse code.

She felt warm. Thirsty, too. And hungry. 'So where are we having lunch?'

'I'll show you. We're nearly there.'

They walked on, past substantial stone houses of well-kept privacy, until they reached The Square. A row of cars was lined up, waiting for the ferry which would take it on the short journey to the far side.

'This is it,' Cochrane said and opened the door to the Cuan pub and restaurant.

They stepped into the hallway and wiped their muddy feet. In the heat, her glasses steamed up straight away. She took them

214

off and rubbed them with a tissue.

Although it was early, there was already the sound of activity in the bar and the smell of food.

'Yes sir?' a waiter said, stepping forward to welcome them.

'We're going to have lunch,' Cochrane said. He looked down at his boots and then at Meg's. 'In the public bar will be fine.'

'Certainly,' the waiter said and led them there, handing them two menus on the way.

In the hearth there was a fire and the heavy smell of peat.

'Can we sit at the window?' Meg said. 'I'm roasted.'

She took off her waterproof top and her sweater. She had a polo shirt underneath. She felt his eyes on her for a moment but it did not trouble her.

'That's better,' she said. 'Now, what's good today?'

They both went for the home-made Irish stew. It was hearty and full of flavour and they devoured it with hardly a word. Cochrane had a pint of Guinness to go along with it; Meg had a Coke and then a coffee.

'That was great,' she said. 'So was the walk. Brilliant idea and thank you very much for thinking of it.'

'I thought you might enjoy it. Get you out into the good country air.'

'I don't think I've ever done that stretch before. Funnily enough, this part of the coast was never a family haunt. We always went further along. Ardglass direction – where you are. My grandmother had a house there.' She folded her arms and gave him a meaningful stare. 'And now it's your turn.'

'What do you mean?' He looked wary.

'That night at my house. I said I didn't know anything about you. You said we'd leave that for another day. Well, here it is. Another day.'

'So it is.' He smiled. 'What do you want to know?' He sipped his drink then licked the cream from his lip.

'Anything. All I know is that your name's Dan Cochrane and that you're looking after that pottery for somebody. That's hardly a lifetime's vocation.'

'No,' he said, 'I suppose it's not. OK – I'm twenty-nine and I've got a degree in psychology from Queen's University but for reasons I don't want to bore you with I haven't got a job at the moment and I'm doing this as a favour. How's that?'

'It not much but it's a start. Is there a Mrs Cochrane?'

She had assumed not but she had a sudden worried feeling and wondered what she would do if the answer was yes.

'No,' he said and she relaxed again.

'Was there ever?'

215

'No. Well, yes. My mother.'

'I didn't mean that. But your mother—'

'She's dead. My father, too.'

'I'm sorry.'

'That's OK.'

Two priests came in and were greeted like regulars. They wore golf sweaters over black clerical shirts and dog collars and they took seats at the fire with pints of lager. One of them opened a small tin of tobacco and went through the elaborate ritual of lighting a pipe while the other folded a copy of the *Sunday Telegraph* into a compact square at the crossword page.

'Psychology,' she said. 'Now there's a subject I've been in contact with of late. Did you ever practise?'

'For a time, yes. I was with one of the education boards.'

'What did you do?'

'Oh, children's assessment. Kids with learning difficulties and psychological problems, often stemming from dreadful home circumstances. But I had to give it up. A family situation of my own.'

He did not elaborate and she could see that he did not want to.

'Any brothers and sisters?' she asked.

'No.'

He looked away from her, towards the window, and she wondered if she had touched something she wasn't supposed to. The glass in the window was frosted, impenetrable. Like you, she thought, looking at his dark, brooding expression. She felt the mystery in it drawing her closer to him but she sensed that she was wandering where she was not wanted. Trespassing.

'I could probably qualify as a psychologist myself,' she said.

He turned to her. 'Your memory – has anything at all come back to you?'

She shook her head.

'But since you've been out of hospital, have you felt, well, as if you were on the verge of remembering at all?'

'I always feel on the verge. But it doesn't lead anywhere.'

'How does the amnesia seem to you, when you think about it? How do you picture it?'

She considered the question, then she said, 'It's . . . it's like a heavy black blanket. I know I can almost get out from under it, that *everything* is out there, just beyond, but I can't manage to shake the thing off. I reach out from underneath but I can't touch anything, I can't feel anything. I stretch out my hand but the blanket falls more firmly over me. It's suffocating. It chokes me.'

'Well, that at least is pretty vivid,' he said.

She told him about going to Vectra and meeting Alice Harte. 'Then last week I got a call from them and an address for Paul Everett's parents. I've made a couple of stabs at writing a letter but it just ended up in the bin. It's so hard to know what to say to them.'

'Just tell it straight. Tell them how you feel.'

'The consultant who was helping me—'

'What was his name?'

'Dr Paddy Sands. Do you know him?'

'I know of him. He's rather eminent in this whole field of traumatic disorder. Sorry. You were saying?'

'Well, yes, just that. He's of the view that something may have happened earlier that night, that perhaps the accident – the murder – was the culmination of some deep psychological trauma and that in spite of my physical recovery, this psychogenic amnesia has remained.' She put her hand to her heart. 'Even though I feel as if I desperately want to remember, my inner self won't allow me.'

'There are various types of memory,' Cochrane said.

'I know. They explained it all to me. The semantic memory, the procedural memory and the episodic memory. That's where my trouble is. That last one.'

'That seems about right,' he said.

'Some people subscribe to the theory that we keep all of our experiences in the brain forever, filed away. They're in the dark in there somewhere, just waiting for a light to be shone on them. Do you agree with that?'

'Engrams,' Cochrane said.

'What?'

'Engrams. Memory traces. They're called "engrams". They're fragments of past episodes and experiences, stored away in our minds where they stay until for some reason our memory decides to retrieve them. But we don't keep them all. That would be ludicrous. Everyone forgets things. It's perfectly natural, just like the way you clear out a drawer from time to time, keep some of the stuff that's in it and junk the rest. People worry too much about forgetting. They see the onset of Alzheimer's every time something slips their mind but that isn't the case at all. The brain only remembers what it needs, what's important. We'd go insane if we remembered everything that ever happened to us in our lives. Our heads would be full of chaos.'

He swished his glass around to revive the remains of the drink in it. 'The memory is a uniquely powerful thing. It's not just a record of something that happened. When we remember

217

something we also recall how we felt about it at the time – pain, joy, whatever – and we experience that emotion all over again. I would say Dr Sands is right. You're like a battle victim, a war casualty, overloaded with some bad experience. Those particular engrams are still there,' he tapped her gently on the forehead with his finger, 'but your mind has hidden them away because it can't cope. It just needs the right key to open the lock.'

'But how do I do that?'

'You might not. You might never remember at all. Not if your subconscious mind doesn't want you to. But sometimes memories force their way to the surface by themselves. That will have happened to you at some time in your life. It happens to everyone. You hear a sound that evokes something. Or maybe it's a smell. Something that's significant to you and means absolutely nothing to anyone else.'

He pulled at his sweater. 'With me, for example, it's the smell of wet wool. Every time that smell comes to me, I get a crystal clear picture of my mother standing in our kitchen, ironing on autumn afternoons. I can even see the leaves in the lane outside. I've just come home from school and I've thrown my schoolbag onto a corner of the settee and I'm getting something to eat out of the fridge. I feel warm and content and secure. The thing is, I can conjure up that memory any time I like but without the smell, that unexpected, accidental trigger, the recollection isn't anything like as sharp, nor do I re-experience the feelings I had at the time. Am I making sense?'

'Totally,' she said.

She had followed every word, watching his lips, fascinated by the concept and the eager way he explained it. For a second, too, she had glimpsed the world of his childhood and she wondered what else he had to tell but was reluctant to share.

'I had an experience something like that the other day,' she told him. 'I was leaving my mother's house. There was no *trigger* as such, just a feeling of sadness and loneliness that was depressingly familiar to me. I had a sudden sight of myself as a child. Later I remembered what it was. It was my birthday and I had done something my mother didn't like, I've forgotten what. She was going to let me have a few friends in for tea and then she phoned all their mothers and cancelled it. I was on my own.'

'What you've been trying to do,' he said, 'visiting the scene of the crash, the Clarendon Dock, that sort of thing – it's the right way to go about it. You're putting yourself in situations where you might remember. But you must be careful not to put too much strain on yourself.'

'In what way?'

'You're getting frustrated because it doesn't appear to be leading anywhere. Like I said, maybe it never will. And in that case, you'll just have to live with it, adjust to the fact that part of you isn't there any more. It's . . .' he searched for an image, '. . . it's just as real a loss as if you had a limb amputated. After a while you've got to get used to that and face up to the reality that it won't grow back again.'

'Delightful thought,' she said.

'On the other hand, sometimes the re-creation of certain circumstances, a kid of reproduction of the context, can trigger recall. What you felt at your mother's house was a bit like that. I remember reading once in a book on memory about a man who suddenly woke up one day and found that he couldn't remember anything at all about himself. Nothing. He was taken to hospital and they found that he'd had a kind of stroke which had damaged the left thalmus.'

'Which is what exactly?'

'It's a sort of control centre in the brain, where all the switches are, if I could describe it like that. Just about all our sensory input is routed through it. Anyway, nothing could be done for him. For a year, his memory was virtually a blank sheet of paper. And then one day he had to go to hospital. He had heart problems and he needed to have a pacemaker fitted. But when he was being wheeled towards the theatre, he started feeling a bit scared and he remembered feeling exactly the same way in identical circumstances twenty five years before when he'd had to go into hospital to undergo an operation for a hernia. Suddenly, he began to remember other aspects of that particular day: what the weather was like, what he'd been doing beforehand, how he'd got to the hospital and so on, and within minutes his head was swimming. A whole ocean of memories. His entire life came flooding back to him.'

The thought excited her for a second but then the feeling subsided.

'That's great for him,' she said, 'but I've got no great desire to drive a car into a tree and bang my head in order to get the same result.'

He looked at her, pondering something. 'Listen, here's an idea. Would you like to do a little test?'

'What sort of a test?'

'Nothing elaborate. Just some cues. I throw words at you to see what memories spring up.'

'Like word association?'

'Not quite. Not like *branch – tree* or anything like that. If I say the word "tree", I want you to think about a tree from your past.

What do you say? Do you want to try it?'

'OK,' she said with a little hesitation. She gave a nervous laugh. 'What am I getting myself into here?'

'Nothing. It's simple. Right then. *Tree*. We might as well start with that.'

'Tree – OK. The house where we used to live. Before my parents split up. There was a yew tree in the garden at the back, right in the centre of the lawn. Its bark was all scratches where my father kept banging the lawnmower into it.'

'Good, you've got the hang of it. *Car*.'

'A Volkswagen Beetle. My father bought it for me when I passed my driving test. I painted it a kind of pink, I remember.' She laughed. 'It must have looked disgusting. But I loved that car.'

'OK – *hospital*.'

'Getting my tonsils out when I was about twelve. They told me I'd feel sick afterwards but I didn't realise how much. It was dreadful. God, enough of this. It makes me feel ill just thinking about it.'

'Just one more. *House*.'

She thought for a second. 'My grandmother's house near Ardglass. It was full of places to explore and interesting things she didn't mind me touching or playing with. I could be alone there but I never felt lonely. She's gone now. So's the house, more's the pity. There's a horrible hotel there instead, which my father built.'

He said nothing for a few moments. He had been taking notes on the back of the bill which the waiter had left and he seemed to be concentrating on what he had written.

'Interesting,' he said.

'What is?'

'Well, it wasn't a very thorough test, not by a long way, but look at your responses. Every one of them's from your child-hood or that part of your past. There's not a single recent recollection. Not even when I said "hospital". Everything that comes to your mind is from a long time ago. Now, I wonder what we could do to bring you a little nearer to the present?'

Twenty-seven

Dear Mr and Mrs Everett

I hope this letter does not upset or distress you, although I fear it may do so. I am sorry if that is the case but it is a letter which I simply had to write.

My name is Meg Winter. I am the woman who was in the car with your son on the night he was murdered four years ago.

As you may or may not know, I was seriously injured in the crash and although I recovered from my physical injuries, I was left in a coma.

It is my good fortune to have now recovered from that also, although it has left me with what is known as psychogenic amnesia. In short, I can remember nothing about that night, nor can I remember anything at all about your son. I have been shown photographs of him but I am afraid I have no recollection of him whatsoever and no knowledge of what I was doing with him that night.

I am writing to you now because, since regaining consciousness, and in spite of this huge gap in my memory, I have been consumed with strong feelings that somehow I played a part, however unwittingly, in what happened to him.

The grief and sadness which you have both suffered has troubled me greatly. The fact that he was with a complete stranger that night and that no one has yet managed to solve the mystery of his death must be a dreadful burden for you.

The very least I can do is to attempt to remain a stranger no more and to tell you how sorry I am for everything that happened. Nothing I can say will change those events, I realise that, but I felt it was important to try to make contact with you, so I approached Vectra Pharmaceuticals who very kindly provided me with your address.

Reading this back, I fear that it is not as coherent as I would wish, nor does it really express my sympathy strongly enough, but I want you to know that it is meant very sincerely. I hope you understand.

Since getting out of hospital just a few months ago, I have become more and more determined to get my memory back. Your son was the last human being with whom I had contact before his death and my injury. I know little about him – just his job, where he came from, but nothing of any great detail. It does not tell me what sort of a person he was and I would really like to know more.

I do not know how you will react to this letter. I hope you will do so with kindness and if you can bring yourself to reply to me, I would appreciate the gesture.

May I extend to you my condolences and my good wishes.

Yours sincerely

Meg Winter

She sat in the deli with the *Independent* review section and a mocha. She was getting the hang of this coffee business.

The deli had changed hands recently, although it did not make much difference except that now there was bratwurst in the chill cabinet. The new owner was German, called Werner, a scrawny man in his late forties, maybe even beyond, with a thick mop of hair that was early George Harrison.

She drank her coffee but her attention had drifted away from the paper.

She thought of Dan. It was still all a bit tentative, frustrating. Neither of them seemed ready to take the big step.

Maybe he didn't want her. Or maybe he was just afraid it would go wrong.

They had been to the cinema a couple of times and a concert, the Corrs at the Waterfront Hall. One night he had come round with a pizza and a video. It was *Forrest Gump*, starring Tom Hanks.

Now she got the joke.

She finished up and paid. Werner walked past and stuck something on the big front window. When Meg went outside she glanced to see what it was. In thick red marker it said: 'PART-TIME STAFF REQUIRED. APPLY INSIDE.' She stood looking at it for a few moments and then she went back in.

★ ★ ★

There was a little office at the rear of the kitchen. When Werner asked her whether she was working anywhere at the moment, she levelled with him.

He listened while she explained, his blue eyes giving her a cool examination from under the edge of the Beatle thatch.

'When could you start?' he said.

'Any time. Today. Tomorrow.'

He thought. 'Your national insurance would have to be sorted out.'

She could see that he was not certain about her but that he was tempted. She was presentable and she wasn't stupid. Plus he needed someone in a hurry.

'All right,' he said, 'I'll try you out. See how you do. Come in tomorrow. One of the other girls will show you the ropes.'

'Great,' she said, 'great.' She shook his hand, which he was not expecting, then she said: 'There's just one other thing. I'd appreciate it if you didn't tell any of the staff about my – my background. At least not straight away. I'd rather do that myself.'

He shrugged. 'Sure. Fine with me.'

The hours were eight to four, three days a week, except Sunday when it was eight to two. The money wasn't much, two-fifty an hour, but the money wasn't the point. She found herself getting up in the mornings and looking forward to going to work, glad to have something to do at last.

Apart from Werner she was the oldest person working there. Her first shifts she spent with two girls, Ruth and Bronagh, who were both twenty-two and were still hunting for a proper job a year after leaving university. They were curious about her but they did not know who she was and she did not enlighten them. Not yet.

'What did you do before?' Ruth asked. She was tiny with large breasts crammed into a white t-shirt and Meg watched how men's eyes followed her round the room.

'I used to work in the old Central Hospital before they closed it. Then I was away for a while.'

'Were you a nurse?' Bronagh wondered. She had long hair, tousled, and it reminded Meg of her own before she cut it.

'No,' Meg said and turned away to wipe a table. That would be enough for now.

Dan called in after the first couple of days and drove her home when her shift was over. They sat in the van while she told him all about it, how much she was enjoying having something to do. She would have been happy if he had come in

223

and stayed for a while but he didn't suggest it and she was afraid to offer.

They told her Sunday mornings were the busiest and they were right.

Her first one exhausted her. People came with their families. They queued for tables and then ate bagels with smoked salmon and scrambled eggs or else bacon with waffles and syrup. Newspapers were strewn everywhere. By two, when her shift ended, she wanted to go home and lie down.

She was getting ready to leave when Ruth came to her. 'Bronagh and me were wondering. Are you doing anything on Wednesday night?'

Meg pretended to leaf through her mental diary. Then she said: 'No, I'm not. Why?'

'Have you ever been to the Fly?'

She shook her head. 'No, what is it?'

'It's a pub in Lower Crescent. They have salsa nights sometimes. Great music and everything. Drink at cheap prices.'

Bronagh joined them. 'We thought we might go, the three of us,' she said, then smiled. 'It'll be a late night but we're all off the next day.'

Meg looked at them as they waited for her answer. They would have been talking about her, wondering. They knew she lived on her own. They thought she was lonely. And maybe they were right.

'That sounds great,' she said and they both grinned.

She found herself girlishly thrilled by the idea of having somewhere to go and the task of finding something to wear.

She felt comfortable and not too ostentatious with a black jacket and trousers, like a man's dinner suit, that she tried on in Oasis. She bought a plain white shirt to go with it and strappy black shoes with heels.

Bronagh and Ruth picked her up in a taxi that hooted at her front door.

Ruth was bursting out of a scarlet dress with thin straps. Meg found it hard to keep her eyes off the mountainous bosom. Bronagh was in trousers and a see-through blouse, under which her bra was an elaborate pattern with flowers blossoming at the nipples.

Flaming torches mounted on the walls lit up the Fly's front door. A couple of grinning bouncers in cerise shirts greeted them like long-lost friends but that was because of Ruth, Meg reckoned, bouncing ahead of them into the bar.

Inside, the decor was purple and orange with huge silk lampshades shaped like witches' hats. There was an open spiral staircase leading to two other floors above and trompe-l'oeil cobwebs had been painted up the walls. People were dancing, drinking, trying to make themselves heard above the music. The DJ stood under coloured spot lamps in a loose silk shirt with a pattern of Bacardi bottles on it. Above a bass and piano riff and a battery of congas and timbales, a sparkling trumpet solo split the air.

Meg felt as if they had just arrived in Cuba.

Ruth caught her by the arm and hauled her over to a table where there was a group of young men, slick-haired, expensive shirts, their teeth dazzling in the coloured light. She tried to introduce them but Meg didn't get any of their names. They probably didn't get hers either. She raised a hand and mouthed 'Hi.'

One of them moved over for her to sit down. He was about twenty-three.

Bronagh had vanished but now she was back, carrying three bulbous, stemmed glasses full of a cloudy liquid and crushed ice. She set one in front of Meg.

'What's this?' There were little straws in it.

'It's a margarita.'

'Oh, no, really – I don't—'

'Try it,' Bronagh said. 'Just a sip.'

She did. It didn't seem too heavy on the tequila.

Maybe just the one.

She had three over the next couple of hours. Then she drew the line and went on to mineral water, to everyone else's disapproval. But she had begun to feel a dangerously relaxed inner glow and the boy beside her had made her laugh once or twice. He wasn't bad looking.

He asked her to dance.

Out on the floor, he pranced in front of her, eyes closed, his face fixed in an intense expression. Meg felt suddenly that he looked ridiculous and in that moment she wanted to be somewhere else. With someone else. Not this silly boy.

She excused herself and went to the ladies' room. When she came out he was dancing with Bronagh. Ruth was kissing one of the other boys, whose hands didn't know where to go next.

She went outside and found a taxi. She was back home within minutes.

It was twelve fifteen. She dialled Dan's number. His voice was drowsy when he answered.

'Were you asleep? Did I wake you?' she said.

'Meg?'

'Just thought I'd ring and say goodnight.'

'What . . . what time is it?'

'Quarter past twelve. I've been out partying with some of the girls from work. Salsa night down at the Fly. I came home early. Too old for that sort of thing.' She was giggling.

He paused. 'Have you been drinking?'

'As a matter of fact I have. Margaritas. Very nice.'

'How many?'

'Well, I probably shouldn't drive. Have you had anything to drink tonight?'

'No. Not a drop.'

There was a little silence. 'Well then, you could drive, couldn't you?'

She was naked under her cotton robe when she opened the door to him at one thirty. There were no words.

They kissed with a desperate hunger. His hands explored her, his coat rough on her skin, the buttons cold against her nipples.

She unzipped him and from the pocket of her robe she took a condom which she had bought from the machine in the ladies' room at the Fly.

He groaned and she had a feeling they would not even make it to the stairs.

Twenty-eight

It was December. The radio beside the bed came on at seven a.m. as usual and she heard someone talking about Christmas being only three weeks away. She reached over and switched it off.

'Christmas,' she groaned.

Beside her, Dan Cochrane stirred. 'Christmas,' he agreed, his voice husky.

He sighed, then slipped out of bed and she spread herself into the warm space left by his body. She did not have to go to work today but he had to get to Ardglass to open the shop.

She was drowsy, her limbs heavy. Somewhere in the wee hours they had made love again, blindly, silently in the dark, and she smiled to herself at the thought.

She watched him fumbling with his clothes. She looked at his strong shoulders, the silky dark hair on his chest, the thin track of it that ran from his navel to the thicket below, where his penis was timid now.

'I haven't heard you mention it,' he said.

'What?'

'Christmas.'

'I don't want to think about it,' she said but she thought about it nevertheless.

Christmas was a time when cracks in family relationships were laid bare. It had always been a bleak period for her. This year there would be lunch with her mother and she did not know what else. Her father would be in Scotland.

'Have you any plans?' she said.

She looked at him, wondering. Since that first night after the Fly, their relationship had developed but into what, she was not at all certain. It was sketchy still. Shutters came down when she asked too much.

She did know more about him but she had had to winkle it out. What she had discovered had gone a long way to explaining the inner gloom she sometimes saw. His father and his sister had been killed in an IRA explosion when he was young, leaving his mother to run the family farm single-handed. He had given up his job to help her but the farm had had to be sold to pay off debts. His life appeared to have gone into a kind of neutral after that. And now his mother was dead too.

But learning this from him did not erase the feeling that he was somehow managing to keep her at arm's length, in spite of their physical intimacy.

When they were together at night it was always here, in Truesdale Street. She had never been to the flat above the pottery and he had never suggested going there. Was that where he would spend his Christmas?

He shrugged. 'I don't know. I might go away for a few days.'

'What about the pottery?'

'I'll close on Christmas Day and Boxing Day anyway. I've got someone in to help at the moment. They could stay on if I wanted a bit of time to myself.'

'So where would you go?'

'Don't know. I haven't really thought about it.'

'You could come here,' she suggested. 'Christmas night. I could go to my mother's, get that out of the way, and then come back in the afternoon. It would be nice. The two of us. Don't you think?'

He was straightening a sock. He gave her a look. 'Have you told anyone about – about you and me?' His question didn't answer hers.

'Elizabeth,' she said, 'no one else. Why? Do you want me to keep you a secret?'

He said nothing. He sat on the edge of the bed to put the sock on and then unravelled the other one.

She sat forward and put her hand on his shoulder. 'You look worried. Is there a problem?'

He finished and stood up. 'No, there's no problem. It's just that I don't like the idea of being seen as – as a kind of specimen. Your first – well, you know what I mean.'

He looked away. She sat up straight and pulled the duvet across her breasts. She was wide awake now.

There was a second or two of silence and then she said, 'Dan, why don't we have a party?'

'What?'

'Why don't we have a party? You could invite your friends. You never talk about any of them, I know, but I assume you have some?'

He looked at her with an anxious frown. 'What are you getting at? I'm not big on parties.'

'No, I didn't think so. I didn't think you'd warm to that

suggestion somehow. Which brings me to my next question. How come we never meet anyone? How come we hardly ever go anywhere where we might be seen together – the sort of thing normal couples do? Think about it – the cinema once, a concert once. In among a crowd. Apart from that we hang out here, eating pizza and fucking. Do you find me embarrassing, is that it? The crazy coma woman with the amnesia. Is that what you don't want to have to explain to anyone? Could it be that you think of *me* as the specimen, Mr Psychologist?'

As he stood gawping at her, she got out of bed abruptly, grabbed her cotton robe from behind the door and slipped into it. She did not want to be naked in front of him. Not just at this moment.

She hurried down the stairs. She didn't need this. She put water on for coffee.

He walked into the kitchen. 'Meg, it's not like that. I didn't mean—'

'Don't bother trying to explain. I don't want to hear.' She opened the fridge. There was no milk. 'Damn,' she said.

He looked at the empty shelf in the fridge door. 'I'll go and get some. We'll talk about this when I get back.'

She thought that right now she would prefer it if he did not come back at all. But she did not say it. She did not say anything.

He looked uncomfortable. 'I'll take your keys.'

They were on the kitchen table. It was the usual arrangement when he had to nip out to the van or to one of the shops. It saved her having to let him back in all the time.

He went to the door. 'There's a letter here for you,' he called before he went out.

She sat with her indignation for a couple of minutes and as it subsided she thought of what she had said to him and began to wonder that maybe she had blown up like that not because of what he thought of her but because of what she thought of herself. Wasn't it a fact that at the root of it all was her own desperate insecurity?

He had said something about a letter. She went to the hall and picked it up from the floor.

The first thing she noticed were the stamps – a commemoration of the centenary of the Klondyke gold rush.

She stared.

Her name and address were printed on the front in small, sloping handwriting. There was an air mail sticker.

She turned the envelope over and saw the sender's name.
Everett.

229

Below that was an apartment number in a house on Eastern Promenade, Portland, Maine, USA – the address to which she had written.

She looked at the thing for a few seconds in disbelief, then she needed to sit down.

It was weeks, months, as a matter of fact, October, since she had sent the letter. She had given up watching for a reply. She took a deep breath, opened the envelope and began to read.

Dear Meg

Thank you for writing. We're very sorry to take so long to reply but it's been a question of finding the right words. We hope you'll understand.

We feel a great loss. It's a feeling that's never very far below the surface and it welled right up again when we got your letter. But once we got over that, we got to thinking about you. We had no idea what happened to you after you were injured and we were relieved to find out. Whatever happened that night when our son was murdered, we're so pleased that you survived because that's what Paul would have wanted.

The words seemed to jump out of the page. She read that last sentence again, feeling her skin go cold under the thin robe.

Some weeks before it happened, he called us on the phone, something he didn't do as regularly as we would have liked although we used to get to see him from time to time when he came back to the Vectra headquarters in New Hampshire. He seemed very happy. He told us his job was going great and that he'd met a wonderful, young woman, a doctor, working in ER at one of the hospitals over there.

Then about a couple of days before he died we got a letter from him. Now that was a rare thing. Letter-writing wasn't ever something Paul had much time for. He told us your name was Meg Winter and that he was thinking of getting married. We were really very excited.

Unfortunately, we never got to talk to him again. His mother wrote him but before she had mailed the letter he was dead.

The thing is, Meg – this thing of you having amnesia, not being able to remember anything about him – it's all so tragic. From talking to Paul, from that letter of his, we got

230

the feeling that you were very close. You had to be if marriage was being discussed.

Then there's the business of the drugs. You can't imagine how badly that hit us, too. It's hard for us to picture him being mixed up in something like that. It just doesn't match up with the Paul we knew. Somehow we feel they must have got that wrong.

We hope this letter finds you well and that you are making good progress. Life can't be easy for you.

We would like you to know that we don't blame you for anything that happened. Perhaps we did feel angry at first and maybe, inside, we took out some of that anger on you, the woman who had come into his life. I suppose we needed somebody to blame. But we don't feel like that any more.

Please write again. We would like that very much. We've got a lot to discuss and we should get to know each other better. Maybe we can even meet some day.

Yours sincerely

Laurence and Marcie Everett

She did not know how long she had been sitting there, reading the letter over and over again, when Cochrane came back.

He put a carton of milk down. 'I took a walk,' he said. 'I thought you might need a little space before we talk.'

She looked up towards him, her eyes distant, her face like chalk.

'What is it?' he said. 'What's wrong?'

She held the letter out to him and pulled the robe tighter round her thin frame.

He took it from her and read in silence.

'Jesus,' he said when he had gone over it a second time. 'This is incredible. But it's a bit of a breakthrough at last, isn't it?'

'Breakthrough?'

'Yes, of course it is. This means that even though you can't remember, you must have known him after all.'

She stared at him. 'What are you talking about? Must have known him. Damn it, I didn't know him. How many times do I have to say it? Don't you believe me?'

'Meg, listen, it's not a question of that. I believe that you don't remember. Of course I do.' He waved the letter towards her. 'But this tells you more, doesn't it? Meg, think about it. You forgot Noel Kennedy. You could have forgotten Paul Everett too.'

231

'Just go,' she said quietly, getting up and turning her back on him.

'Look – wait – we have to talk.'

'I don't want to talk about anything with you.'

There was a pause. Then he spoke again, quietly. 'I understand. Of course. This is difficult. You'll need time by yourself to take this in. I'll just—'

She faced him. 'Just go!'

They stared at each other and she saw that he had retreated somewhere, away from confrontation. He gave a little nod of assent, then he turned quickly and walked out.

The sound of the front door closing shook her and for a second she wanted to run after him and tell him to come back. But she just stood there until she heard his van starting up and driving away.

She looked at the letter lying on the table. She shouldn't have been like that to him. But what he had said . . . what the letter said . . . she couldn't grasp any of it. She was trembling. She went upstairs and dressed but she still felt cold.

She had to think. *Think.* She whispered the word through clenched teeth. She read the letter again. It was in a strong, precise hand, the style articulate but simple. She read the grief and the coming-to-terms in it but she could not, just could not, accept what it told her.

She went round the house, searching through her things, some of which were in boxes she had brought from her mother's.

Searching for what?

Something that told her the letter was right? She would find nothing to tell her it was wrong.

She unearthed the bloodstained shoulder-bag again.

Where had she bought that? She couldn't remember. What if *he* had bought it? His face came to her, smiling in the photograph.

She had dumped Kennedy. What if she had dumped him for Everett? What if Dan was right and she had forgotten both of them?

No, damn it, no. She did not know him.

'I didn't know him,' she said aloud, slamming the door of a wardrobe in an empty, echoing bedroom.

Wait – what had it said? She grabbed the letter again and read:

A couple of days before he died we got a letter from him.

She ran downstairs, found paper and a pen and then she sat for a few moments, forcing herself to become calm, to think straight.

He had written to his parents. If only there was some way of seeing that letter.

She had nothing to lose by asking.

Twenty-nine

'There has to be some sort of a mistake,' her father said when she rang and told him.

'I never mentioned Paul Everett to you?' she asked for the umpteenth time since she had first heard the name.

'No,' he said but she could detect unease in his voice and she knew this had unsettled him.

She told her mother next.

'That's all very strange, isn't it,' Gloria said in an odd, suspicious tone. 'What are you going to do?'

'I'm writing back to them.'

'Do you think that's wise?'

'I don't know whether it is or not but it's what I have to do.'

Elizabeth rang and asked her to dinner at the flat the next night. Vincent had just come home again. He would be in Ireland until after Christmas and in the New Year they were moving to a house they had rented in London.

'He's dying to meet you,' Elizabeth said. 'And bring your young man, of course, what's-his-name.'

'Dan,' Meg said.

'Yes. Bring Dan.'

'Actually, I might not. We had a bit of a disagreement.'

'Oh yes?'

Meg told her about the letter and said they had fallen out over it. She did not mention the conversation which had started the ball rolling. 'He's right,' she said. 'I do need a bit of time to myself to think about this.'

'Careful you don't let him drift away,' Elizabeth said. 'Unless you want him to.'

No, she thought when she had hung up. She did not really want that at all.

It was cold the following evening with heavy skies, the sort that always threatened snow in this corner of the world but never seemed to deliver.

She got to Elizabeth's flat at seven thirty. She rang the bell and Vincent O'Malley came to the door. He was in a short-sleeved shirt, a man used to a hotter climate. He had lost weight since the wedding pictures and he had less hair.

'Meg,' he smiled and held out his hand. She took it, then he leaned forward and kissed her on the cheek. 'At last.' He stood back from the door. 'Come in, come in. Let me take your coat.'

The dining table was set with gleaming cutlery and sparkling wine glasses. The flat was country-cottage quaint, a little fussy for Meg's taste. There were dried flowers in stone jars and a lot of tie-backs and stencilling. Chairs and settees sat demurely under long skirts.

Something rich was being cooked. Elizabeth came out of the kitchen, her face glistening. She wore a tight black skirt and a low-cut red top with sequins. She hugged Meg and as they air-kissed, Meg caught a hint of gin and what was possibly Chanel. Both duty-free, at a guess.

The three of them stood and looked at each other and Meg knew instantly that something was not quite right.

'Well, we can't stand here all night. Get us a drink,' Elizabeth said to her husband. 'My glass is in the kitchen. You can top me up.' She went to get it.

'Of course,' O'Malley said. The drinks were on a table over by the window. Outside, cars sped silently along the Stranmillis embankment, slowing occasionally to cross the King's Bridge, braking in a blur of red light. The reflection of a row of street lamps was like a chain of gold coins floating on the surface of the river.

'What can I get you?'

'Just something soft,' she said. 'Mineral water, if you have it.' Since the Fly she had resumed her teetotal ways.

'She's become awfully boring and doesn't drink,' Elizabeth said, coming back with her empty glass. A thick slice of lemon lay at the bottom of it. 'Same again, please.' She thrust the glass at her husband.

O'Malley lifted a bottle of Gordon's and said nothing but in his silence Meg heard a lot.

'Where's Catriona?' Meg said.

'Down for the night, I hope,' O'Malley told her. 'I've just read her a story.'

'Can I go and kiss her goodnight?'

'Of course,' he said and smiled.

The little girl had not graduated to a bed yet. She was in a high-sided cot with a Teletubbies frieze. Meg peered over the edge. She was on her side, eyes closed, the corner of a blanket soggy in her mouth.

Meg tip-toed out of the room again. When she got back to the living room she knew there had been words of some kind. It was in the air and on their faces.

'Too late,' she said, whispering. 'She's asleep. I didn't want to risk waking her.'

'I've got things to do in the kitchen,' Elizabeth said. 'Why don't you two get to know each other a bit? I won't be long.'

Meg and O'Malley looked at each other blankly when she had gone. 'Where should we start?' Meg said.

They sat with their drinks. O'Malley's was a glass of white wine.

'The . . . the ordeal you've been through,' he said. She saw that he would have been wondering how to broach the subject. 'I . . . I'm at a loss for words. It's just . . . just remarkable.'

'It's been nice to have Elizabeth around,' she said. 'I shall miss her. And I'm glad you two . . . well, that things are better.'

His face clouded. 'I don't know that they are. The thing is – our move to London. It's only going to be for six months. I'm going to have to go back to Malaysia for a while after that. I plucked up the courage to break the news to her just before you came.' He shook his head. 'Not exactly brilliant timing. I'm sorry you've landed in the middle of it.'

'Ouch,' Meg said. 'You don't need that, either of you. These big companies, they just push people around. I don't know how you stick it.'

'I might not, for much longer. I can't get Elizabeth to understand. You see, when I go back to Malaysia it's to finish a big financial project. Once that's complete, it'll be something quite substantial for me. A real feather in the cap. Other companies will want to employ me and I'll be able to choose who I go to. I just can't convince her that it's for the best, that in the end it will help our future. Meg, do you think you could talk to her?'

The request, blurted out, took her by surprise. Elizabeth came back with the starter, salmon pâté and asparagus tips, before she had a chance to answer. Not that she was sure what she was going to say.

'Right, table please.'

They ate quietly, apart from sounds of appreciation from Meg and O'Malley and some small talk about Christmas. He explained that they would be going to Dublin for a few days to stay with his relatives. His house there was for sale.

As Elizabeth finished off a glass of Sauvignon Blanc, he reached for the empty plates.

'Leave those,' she told him.

'I'll just take them to the kitchen.'

'No, you sit there. I can manage by myself.' She gave a bitter little laugh. 'I'm kind of used to it by now, don't you think?' She took the plates from his hands and left the room with them.

'You're sure you won't have a glass of wine?' O'Malley said to Meg.

'Positive. Look, Vincent, this really isn't something I can get involved in. You've got to sort it out yourselves.'

'She listens to you.'

'Not always. If she mentions it, I'll discuss it with her. But I won't raise the subject.'

Elizabeth brought in the main course, a beef casserole that had been kept too hot and had congealed. Meg found it heavy going but did her best. The hostess had a couple of glasses of Cabernet to wash it down.

'So this letter, then,' Elizabeth said, pouring herself some more. 'Tell us all about it.'

It was almost a relief to do so. Tension was hanging over the table like a fog.

When she had finished the story, Meg found O'Malley studying her.

Elizabeth saw him. She laughed. 'He doesn't know what to make of you, do you, Vincent?'

His face reddened. 'Sorry, I'm being rude. I just find this fascinating, that's all.'

Elizabeth looked at Meg. 'Are you going to tell the police?'

'I've been thinking about that but I'm not sure. I don't know that it takes the murder case any further. What would I say to them that didn't make me look stupid? At any rate, I'm certainly not going to say anything until I know more.'

'So you've written back,' O'Malley said. 'What did you say?'

'I thanked them for writing to me. I told them the letter had been something of a shock and I asked them if they'd let me see the letter he wrote.'

'Do you think they will?'

'I don't know. It's worth a try. Until I see it I won't actually be able to believe it.'

'I haven't done a pudding,' Elizabeth announced. 'There's cheese if you want some.'

'Not for me,' Meg said.

'Or me,' O'Malley echoed. 'But why don't I make some coffee.'

When he had left the room, Meg groaned. 'God, Elizabeth, it's so confusing. I'm beginning to doubt myself. You still believe me, don't you?'

'About what?'

'That I didn't know Paul Everett.'

Elizabeth shrugged. 'Why not? I believe everything you tell me.'

Meg tensed. 'Meaning?'

'Meaning six months. Six fucking months and then he's off to Malaysia again. How do I make a marriage out of that?'

Meg waited for the rest of it.

'You were the one who persuaded me to give it another go. And now I'm being left high and dry again. I should have just ended it when I had the chance. Not listened to you.'

'I didn't persuade you to do anything,' Meg said. 'I told you that you should sort your problems out face to face, not run away from them. I still think that was the right advice. The final decision – to go back to Vincent – that was yours. And if you want to know, I think it was the right one, too. He's a good man. I've only met him tonight for the first time but I think I can see what sort of person he is. He doesn't like this situation any more than you do.'

'How do you know?'

'We kind of discussed it.'

'Oh you did, did you? When my back was turned?'

'He told me how he felt and I believe him. Why don't you give him a chance?'

'Whose side are you on, anyway?'

'I'm not on anybody's side. Or rather, I'm on both your sides. I just don't want you to do something stupid. And filling yourself full of drink doesn't help either.'

O'Malley came back with a tray of coffee. 'Here we are,' he said cheerily.

Elizabeth ignored him. She glared at Meg. 'Well, fuck you. Don't talk to me like that. Don't give me a fucking lecture.'

'I'm not. I'm just trying to be honest with you.'

'What on earth's going on?' O'Malley said, frozen with the tray in his hands.

Meg stood up, trying to stay cool. 'Look, I'm sorry, this is getting a bit out of hand. I think – I think maybe I'd better go before we say something we'll regret.'

'Regret,' Elizabeth scoffed. 'What are you worrying about? Sure, if you say something you regret you can develop amnesia and just forget about it. That's always a good way out for you, isn't it?'

'Christ, Elizabeth,' O'Malley said, 'what do you think you're doing?'

'Fuck off. You keep out of this,' Elizabeth said and walked across to where the gin bottle stood. O'Malley put the tray down and followed her. They began arguing.

238

Meg walked from the room and found her coat, then O'Malley appeared in the hall. 'Meg, I'm sorry. Don't go like this. She didn't mean it. She's upset and unsettled about things. She's had a bit too much to drink.'

'Let her go,' Elizabeth's voice called. 'Better still – why don't you go with her. I don't need either of you.'

O'Malley looked helpless. 'I'm sorry,' he said again.

'So am I,' Meg said.

And as she closed the door of the flat behind her, she thought that she was not angry at the things Elizabeth had said, just tired of it all.

Thirty

There were apologies, of course. Both O'Malley and Elizabeth rang the next day. Flowers were sent, a big arrangement of lilies that she put without much delicacy into a tall vase in the window. When she had finished, she sat and stared at them, feeling emotionally numb and enveloped in their powerful scent.

The postman brought a Christmas card from the nurses at the Musgrave.

She had been safe there, among friends. That afternoon she went to see them but first she stopped at a gift shop along the road and bought a few things to distribute among the staff; scented candles, little packets of pot pourri, lavender drawer fresheners.

She did not attempt to see Liam Maginnis. She made straight for her old ward, feeling a welcoming warmth as she walked down the remembered corridors.

Freda Doran, the ward manager, was overjoyed to see her. 'You look wonderful. Your hair and everything.' She hugged her like a prodigal daughter.

'I feel really guilty that I haven't been back before now,' Meg said.

'Not at all,' Freda insisted. 'You're better keeping away, getting on with your life. That's what's important. It's not that we haven't been thinking about you, you know. We all saw you on TV. You must be doing really well.'

'I'm managing,' Meg said. 'It will take time.'

The comforting smells and sounds of the place wrapped themselves around her like a soft blanket. She had been protected here, free from harm and other people's woes. If Freda had asked her to stay the night, in her old bed, she would have said yes.

Other nurses appeared, happy to see her. They had tea, cakes were produced from somewhere and she left late in the afternoon, when it was just on the verge of being slightly peculiar that she had stayed so long.

As she drove home, she wished she could talk to Dan about it. She missed his quiet, strong presence in her life. What had happened between them had been her fault, not his.

Later in the evening, she called him.

'Dan – it's me, Meg,' she said when he answered.

There was a pause. 'Hi. How are you?' He sounded strange and she wondered if there was someone with him.

'I'm fine,' she said. 'No, that's not true. I'm not fine. I feel bad about the other day. The things I said. I was very stupid. I rang to say I'm sorry.'

'That's OK.'

'Do you forgive me?'

'Don't be silly.'

'I thought you might have called me.'

'I thought you should have some time.' He paused. 'Both of us.'

There was a distance in his voice that she didn't like. 'I know,' she said, 'but it was my fault. I sort of threw you out. You weren't to blame. The letter from the Everetts – it was all a bit much for me.'

'I understand.'

There was a silence.

'So, can we talk about this some time?' she asked. 'Can I see you?'

He said nothing and she thought briefly that something had happened to the line.

'Dan, are you still there?'

'Yes, I am,' he said. 'Look, Meg, I've been doing some thinking, too.'

Her heart began a gliding descent.

'I . . . I think,' he went on, 'I think perhaps we shouldn't see each other for a while. Maybe a bit of a break is a good idea.'

She swallowed. 'What are you saying?'

'You've got this Everett business to sort out and I've got things on my mind, too. There are decisions I have to make. I've got to get myself back on track somehow. You were right – this isn't exactly a lifetime's vocation. And maybe, you and me, we ought to think about what it is we want out of all this.'

Anxious thoughts careered through her mind. He was hiding something. He had talked mysteriously of going away at Christmas. Was there someone else somewhere? Was that it?

'Are you dumping me?' she asked all of a sudden. She felt wounded and it was making her angry. She had called him up, cap in hand, apologising, and this was the result.

241

'No, I'm not dumping you. I just need to be by myself for a bit.'

She felt desperate. She wanted to tell him not to do that, that she needed him. Instead, she gathered her pride tightly around her and said: 'That's crap. It's the sort of thing people come out with when they're too cowardly to tell the truth. You're dumping me.'

'No, I'm not. I *am* telling you the truth. You don't understand.'

'Oh, I understand all right,' she said just before she put the phone down.

Thirty-one

The week before Christmas brought a bizarre spell of warmth and sunshine that was like spring.

In the lane, snow is glistening . . .

In the lane, snow was not glistening. In the lane, or at least in Truesdale Street, cats were sleeping on sunny windowsills and people were drinking beer on their patios. Someone in a house further down the street even had a barbecue one evening. Meg could smell the greasy smoke as it drifted in through her open window with their laughter.

On television, there were reports of early snowdrops and lambs. Scientists were trotted out to talk about the state of the ozone layer and how much time we had now before the world came to an end.

Walking in a winter wonderland.

Hers was the only house in the street without decorations and a tree glowing in the front window. She had not sent anyone a card yet and she did not feel like it. The few she had received lay in a little pile on the kitchen table.

It was a charade and she did not want to be part of it. She wandered among the city centre crowds, feeling as if she were watching it all from a distance.

Have yourself a merry little Christmas . . .

Everyone had let her down in the end. What was the point of it all, of being restored to a life that was empty and hopeless? Alone and depressed, she did not think about the future any more. Or the past. Nothing mattered.

Then, on 20 December, she got another letter from the Everetts and everything changed again.

The letter came in a large brown envelope which also contained a second envelope, smaller, with her name on it.

Dear Meg

It was good to get your letter. It gave us a lot to think about.
I'll get right to the point. You asked us if we'd send you a

243

copy of Paul's last letter to us. I'm afraid that won't be possible. As I'm sure you understand, that little letter is a very significant thing for me and my wife to have. To say it has sentimental value is an understatement. My wife keeps it in a box in her closet along with some of Paul's other papers and she just won't let it out of the house, not even for me to take it away and photocopy it. Apart from that, I have to say that I felt a bit strange about it myself, the idea of making a copy of something that's so personal to us.

Maybe this doesn't make a whole lot of sense to you but bereavement and emotion are powerful forces and it just didn't feel right to us. Nevertheless, we started thinking more about you. The thing is, we have no objection at all to your seeing the letter. As a matter of fact, we'd like you to see it. We'd like to see you, too, like we mentioned before. That's why we've taken a bit of a liberty. In the enclosed envelope you'll find something that I hope you'll be able to accept. If you can't, well then there's no harm done.

In the envelope, there's an open ticket for a return flight with Aer Lingus from Belfast to Boston. I made some inquiries from a travel agent friend of mine and I discovered that there's a flight to the US every Thursday. This ticket is valid until the end of January which isn't the busiest time on that route. If you decide to come, all you have to do is contact your local Aer Lingus office and get yourself a firm reservation. And if you don't want to come, then just send the ticket back to me and I'll get a refund.

Portland's only about an hour and a half's drive from Boston on the I-95. We really do hope you'll accept this invitation. My wife and I aren't getting any younger. I've got problems with arthritis and we're just about to move out of this apartment and go to a smaller place, right after Christmas. But you can still write back to this address and it will get to us. Or you can call.

What do you say, Meg? It would be the best present we could have.

Best wishes and a Happy Christmas,

Laurence Everett

She looked at the top of the page. This time they had left a phone number.

She opened the second envelope and took out a flimsy airline ticket written in ballpoint. It weighed hardly anything but she felt that it represented an awful lot.

Laurence and Marcie Everett wanted to talk to her every bit as much as she wanted to talk to them. She wondered what they looked like, how old they were. He had arthritis. Maybe he was quite elderly, seventies, eighties? It was impossible to tell from the writing.

They had made a big decision, a big effort. They had taken an enormous, adventurous step. She looked at the ticket. She had made the first contact with them and this was the outcome. It was nothing like she had expected – but then what *had* she expected when she had written blindly to them those months ago?

Should she go?

No matter what Laurence Everett said, she knew that if she turned them down they would feel hurt and snubbed. Nevertheless, the thought of flying across the Atlantic, into the unknown, to meet two complete strangers whose son had been murdered, filled her with doubt.

But seeing them, meeting them face to face, was the only hope she had left of getting anywhere near the truth.

She had to think about it. Still, she should not leave it too long. They would be anxious to know. She imagined them listening for the phone, watching for a letter, waiting for her to decide.

Thirty-two

The door of the Ulster Bank in Downpatrick opened and Harry Glover, the assistant manager, came out into a throng of shoppers who were laden with parcels and serious intent. Pretty soon, he acknowledged, he would have to fall into step with them. Christmas was getting dangerously close and he had not yet bought his wife a present.

It was lunchtime and he was going to Ardglass. He got into his car, then headed for the road out of town. He drove slowly; there was no other choice. The place was jammed, the shops were packed and he cursed the fact that there were so many traffic lights in such a small place.

He was going to Ardglass because the bank had a small sub-office there. Normally, it opened only one day a week, just as a gesture, since Downpatrick was near enough for everyone to do their banking business in the main branch, but Christmas was not normal and in the two weeks leading up to it the Ardglass office was open full time.

He had delegated two young cashiers to work there and he had decided on a whim to drop in and see how they were getting on, then have a quiet lunch in one of the local pubs.

He smiled as he drove, mocking himself. *A morale-boosting visit, Harry. Is that what this is?* A drive was what it was. A chance to take the air.

When he reached Ardglass he headed towards the harbour, parked and got out. The weather had changed for the worse. The warmer temperatures of a few days ago seemed like an illusion, some kind of a cruel joke. Now the sky was a turbulent grey and from the sea there came a forceful, stinging wind that could work its way up into a gale if it felt like it.

He shuddered, pulled up the collar of his coat, then dug his hands into the pockets, delving for warmth. He looked around at the empty harbour and the gloomy, quiet streets, wondering if there was any point in opening the branch next year.

He halted his gaze when it fell on the Harbour Pottery.

246

Banking business left his mind and the face of his wife came to him instead.

Peter Quinn's place. He had forgotten about it. It had all the sort of stuff she liked. Nice glasses, Celtic jewellery, and the pottery, of course. He could get a present there. That would be ideal.

He walked towards the old stone building, thinking how grim it looked in spite of the colourful shop sign above the entrance. He tried the handle on the front door but it would not turn. Then he noticed the 'closed' sign in the window. He frowned and tried to peer through the glass. It was dark inside, the only light coming from the little strips illuminating the display shelves. The van, with *Harbour Pottery* inscribed on its flanks, was parked outside. He stepped back and looked up at the top windows of the building, where he knew there was a flat, but there was no indication of the presence of an occupant.

He turned round and headed along the road to the bank.

As he walked, he thought about Quinn and the day he had come into his office to sort everything out before he went off to Japan. Peter was a sensible guy. Glover had known him for a few years and they had even played golf together a couple of times at the club at Ardglass where they were both members, but privately, before that fellow Cochrane had arrived for the meeting, he had asked him if he was sure of what he was doing. There was all that business with the fire at the hotel and Cochrane's subsequent jail sentence. The case had got a lot of column inches in the local papers.

Well, it had to be said, hadn't it? And at least he had been able to talk to Peter from a position of objectivity since his bank, the Ulster, had not been involved in any way with the Cochrane family's declining circumstances.

But Peter had insisted. It was his business after all, his decision, and that was that.

He pushed open the door of the sub-office. There were no customers and only one cashier. The other one would be at lunch.

The barren scene made his mind up for him. No Christmas opening next year.

'Surprise,' he said.

Geraldine Moore was twenty and came from Dublin. She had thick brown hair tied back and gold-framed glasses which she put on to see who this was.

'Oh,' she said, 'what's this? Trying to catch me working?'

She did not take herself or anyone else too seriously but she had the personality to carry it off without appearing insubordinate.

'And I haven't managed to, have I?' Glover fired back. 'Just thought I'd drop by. How's it been?'

'Slow. A few lodgements. Some cheques cashed. Hardly worthwhile. I was thinking we could go in for tumbleweed manufacturing.'

He looked at her, puzzled.

'You know,' she said. 'Like in a western. The deserted town.'

'Oh, right.'

'Forget it,' she said. 'It doesn't work when you have to explain.'

'Maybe it's the way you tell them. Listen, before I forget, you don't happen to know anything about the Harbour Pottery, do you? I'm friendly with the guy who owns it only he's in Japan at the moment. It's just that I was thinking of buying my wife something but it appears to be closed. Then again, maybe it's shut for lunch.'

'Oh, that place is never open,' Geraldine said. 'At least it never seems to be. I've never seen anybody around it since I've been here.'

'Really?'

She nodded. 'And funnily enough, I heard a couple of customers mention it yesterday. They said it seemed to be closed more often than it was open these days.'

He thought about it a little later on his way back to Downpatrick, wondering what, if anything, he would do. Was there some kind of a problem? And where was that guy Cochrane?

When he got into his office he sat down behind the desk, coat still on, and called up the pottery customer account on his computer. The details unfolded across the screen. His practised eye swept over the figures but found nothing particularly unusual. Everything was a bit static, maybe; not a lot coming in.

Remembering something, he hung his coat up and went out to the main banking room, at the back of which files were stored in shelves that covered one wall. He searched under 'Q' until he came up with *Quinn, Peter, Harbour Pottery*. Into the file he had slipped a sheet of paper with the details, which Quinn had left him, of where he would be in Japan.

'In case of emergencies,' Quinn had said, 'but of course there won't be any.'

There was an address in Kyoto, as well as telephone and fax numbers and an e-mail address.

He didn't want to worry him. It wasn't really the bank's business, or his, either.

He thought for a second or two and then decided. He closed the file again and went back to his own office.

An e-mail wouldn't do any harm. Just to make sure.

Thirty-three

In a display of solidarity not seen since her days in hospital, Meg's parents descended on her once she told them about the Everetts' latest letter and the airline ticket.

They arrived in separate cars, the Golf and the Range Rover, but stood together on the doorstep with uniformly worried looks.

'Is this a deputation?' she asked.

They did not find it funny. 'Sorry,' she said. 'Just a joke. You'd better come in.'

She made tea while her father studied the letters and the ticket with a forensic frown. 'You're seriously telling me you're going to go and see these people?'

'I'm seriously thinking about it, yes,' she said as she poured for them.

'This is crazy,' he protested. 'What if you land yourself in trouble? What if they want to harm you?'

'Harm me? Don't be ridiculous, Dad. What do you think – that they're serial killers or something?'

'How do you know they're not?'

She laughed. 'Come on. They're Paul Everett's mother and father, two grieving parents. You've read the letters. What do you think?'

'But you don't know anything about them,' her mother told her.

'That's the whole point, isn't it? I want to find out more. No, what am I talking about – *more*. I want to find out *anything* – anything I can.'

'But what do you think it will achieve?' her father asked her. He left his tea untouched.

'I'm not entirely sure. But you're not the one who has to live with this every day, this awful emptiness. Fair enough, OK, I grant you that this mightn't make any difference but I've got to go, I have to meet them. Surely you understand?'

'Well, I don't think you should,' Gloria said and turned away from her as if it was her last word on the subject. She folded her arms and stood staring out into Truesdale Street. 'I don't know what you're up to these days. Working as a waitress. Now this. You must be mad.'

'That's always a possibility,' Meg said with a dark glance at her mother's back. She sipped her tea, trying to swallow her annoyance with it, and suddenly a memory came to her.

Each time that happened she felt uplifted. It signalled a new achievement, even when the memory was an unhappy one, as this one was now.

She had had a pen-pal once, when she was about fourteen, a girl from near Lake Como in northern Italy, to whom she had been writing for at least a year. The girl had invited her to come and stay one summer but Meg's mother had refused to let her go: 'They're foreigners. You don't know what sort of people they are.'

Meg had never written back. She had not been able to bring herself to say that she couldn't come. The girl's letters stopped.

Meg wondered what had become of her. Sixteen years ago.

'You'd just go and see them and then come back?' Her father's voice returned her to the present. He was looking for assurance.

'A couple of days, that's all.' Determination was needed. 'Look, Dad, I don't want to be rude but I'm not asking your permission. I thought I'd fill you both in on what's going on. I knew you'd be interested – concerned, too, I understand that. If I decide to go it'll be my decision but I didn't want to set off on this without letting you know.'

'You're in my prayers every night,' Gloria said, turning from the window. 'Why do you insist on worrying us like this?'

Emotional blackmail. Her mother had always been expert in its use.

'What do you want me to do, sit here and wither away? If I just sat here all day, never did anything, you wouldn't have to worry, would you?'

'Wait a minute,' Sam said. 'Let's calm down.'

'This man you're seeing,' Gloria said. 'Has he anything to do with this?'

'No, of course not. And I'm not seeing him now anyway.'

'Oh?' Her mother raised an eyebrow and the curiosity in her eyes had a cruel glint.

Instantly Meg regretted that she had given her an opening. 'And I don't want to discuss it either.'

Her father gave a resigned sigh and dropped the ticket onto the kitchen table. 'I don't suppose there's a lot we can do to stop you.'

251

'I don't want you to try to stop me,' Meg said. 'I want you to understand how I feel. I want you to support me.'

'Support you? Of course we support you. What do you think we've been doing?'

He said it irritably, as if she was being stupid, and the words blew on the spark of anger which her mother had already succeeded in igniting.

'I'm not sure any more,' Meg said. 'You think that because you've done all this to the house and left me with a bit of money in the bank that you're supporting me and, to that extent, of course you are and I'm very grateful. But where's the emotional support, Dad? The sort that I give *you* when you need it? You see, the thing is, you confuse support with having some sort of control over me. That's not support. Oh you might not mean it, but that's the way it is.' She gestured to the room. 'This house. Look at me. I'm a prisoner here. A prisoner of your generosity. I'm even driving around in a car which you've provided. I've lost my independence as well as my memory. Sometimes I think I'm losing my mind.'

'Now hold on a minute,' her father said. 'I've tried to do my best for you.'

'Don't be so ungrateful,' Gloria chided. 'You have a lot to be thankful for. Thankful to the Lord.'

Meg turned her way. 'And you, Mum. So you pray for me every night, do you? Well, I don't know why you bother. Let's be honest – as far as you're concerned, I'm an embarrassment and an inconvenience.'

'Don't talk to your mother like that.'

'But it's true. While I was in a coma, she could play the part of the bereaved parent, robbed of her only child, even though I wasn't actually dead. Not technically.'

'Look, that's enough,' her father said.

'No, Dad, I'm going to finish this.' For a second she was aware of how Elizabeth had described the *old* Meg, a woman who spoke her mind, regardless of the consequences.

She faced her mother. 'And then, when I regained consciousness, I wouldn't play the game. You tried to bamboozle me with your pastor friend but I wasn't having any of it. I had the strength to resist, thank God – if you don't mind me using the expression. I would have been a terrific little trophy for you, Mum, wouldn't I? Another ornament for your church friends to come and admire.'

'Stop it,' her father snapped. 'How dare you talk like that? Have you any idea of the disgrace you brought us?'

The words were sudden and unexpected and sharply painful.

252

She knew her mother felt this way. But not her father.

'Yes, disgrace,' he said when he saw that he had shocked her. 'Since home truths are on the agenda, maybe you should hear a few yourself. Have you any idea what it was like for your mother and me? All those stories in the papers and on TV. A murdered man up to here in booze and cocaine. And you, drunk, in the middle of it. We were devastated, of course we were, that you'd been hurt so badly and then when you didn't regain consciousness, God it was terrible. But you've no idea what the rest of it was like. The whispers when I came into a room. The fake smiles. The business deals that suddenly weren't there any more because nobody wanted to get involved with me, not when my daughter was tied up with some kind of drugs scandal. *Who knows, maybe her father's mixed up in it, too* – that's the way their minds worked. And if Malone Group hadn't come along when they did, with a most generous offer, well, it's anybody's guess what might have happened.'

He paused and took a deep breath and seemed to rein in his anger.

'Yes, we felt ashamed. I'm sorry I had to say it like that but I can't take it back. Maybe we shouldn't have felt like we did but that's the truth of it. We were at a low ebb, Meg.' He looked at Gloria. 'Whatever you may think of your mother's religious beliefs, at least she had that to sustain her. It was more than I had.'

Her mother had a handkerchief out. 'Why are you like this?' Her voice quivered. She stared at Meg as if she did not know her and then blew her nose loudly.

'Try not to get upset, Gloria,' Sam said.

Meg looked at them. Her mother's tears. Her father's hurt. It was like watching a performance. But she was unmoved by it this time and did not feel its emotional pull.

Her father shot her a glance as her mother continued to sob. 'None of this was necessary,' he said.

'No, probably not,' she said. 'But it's done now, isn't it?'

'Sweetheart, you know we're just thinking of you.' His tone was softer.

'Of course.' She gave him a smile without any warmth in it.

At about eleven a.m. the following day she was at work, taking dishes into the kitchen to be washed. The mid-morning coffee rush was always frantic for half an hour or so.

When she went back on to the floor, she saw that more customers had come in. A man and a woman had taken a seat at the window. The woman was black-haired, fifty, bleak-faced. The man had his back to her.

Bronagh was serving someone else so Meg walked over to them.

'Now,' she said, 'can I take your order?'

She looked into the face of Liam Maginnis.

He blinked, startled, then pushed back his chair loudly and stood up. At the sound, Bronagh looked over.

'Good Lord,' he said, then gave a nervous laugh. 'What a surprise. I didn't expect to see you here.' He smiled. 'How are you?'

She smiled back. 'I'm fine,' she said. 'Fine.'

'And what . . . are you working here?'

'Part-time. It gives me something to do.'

The dark-haired woman was staring, her eyes narrow. Bronagh was listening. Maginnis looked as if he did not know what to say. 'Great,' he said, then recovered himself. 'Oh, I'm sorry – Meg – Meg Winter, this is my wife Denise.'

'Pleased to meet you,' the woman said, although she did not look it. Her eyes flickered towards her husband for a second, demanding more.

'Meg was a patient of mine,' he explained. 'You remember. She'd been in a coma.'

The woman's eyes widened. 'Oh yes. The woman in a coma. Of course.' She gave Meg a more comprehensive appraisal. 'But I thought you were a doctor. Why on earth are you working in here, doing this sort of thing?'

'I'm joining in with the world. You meet all sorts of people here.'

They stared at each other in mutual dislike. Meg wondered how Maginnis had ever landed himself with someone like this.

'Well, you look very well, if I may say so,' Maginnis said, sitting again, not noticing the look the two women had exchanged. 'It's wonderful to see you. I heard that you'd been back to see the staff. That was very nice of you. But you should have called on me.'

'I didn't want to bother you. I thought you'd be too busy.'

'Never too busy to see you,' he said.

His wife gave him a sharp glance. 'Look, Liam, if we don't order something soon, I'm going to have to go.'

'Of course, dear. What would you like?'

Two days later, two men came in.

Bronagh served them, her face white. One of them had a big square bag that he put on the floor beside his table.

Meg was certain they were watching her. Then, as she passed, one of them said: 'Excuse me, are you Miss Winter?'

She said yes before she realised.

The second man had taken a camera out of the bag and he suddenly started taking pictures of her as she stood there.

'We're from the *Sunday World*,' the first one said. 'I wonder if we could have a word with you.'

'I don't think so,' she said and headed for the kitchen. There was a back door.

She passed Bronagh and gave her a look that could kill. She should have seen this coming.

'I'm sorry,' Bronagh said, 'I mentioned something about you to a friend the other night. I didn't think—'

'Forget it,' Meg said.

Werner came out of his little office.

'You better dig out your 'help-wanted' sign,' Meg said, untying her apron and handing it to him. 'I quit.'

They got a good enough picture to put it on their front page that Sunday.

With it there were a lot of quotes from her, all a work of imagination. There were remarks from Bronagh and Werner, too, but she had no way of knowing whether they were any more real.

She felt betrayed and under surveillance. She even found herself glancing over her shoulder from time to time. She thought of Dan and wondered what he was doing.

But she thought of the Everetts as well. America, and the welcome of strangers, was becoming more inviting by the minute.

Thirty-four

Christmas at her mother's was a frosty affair, each of them enduring a penance they could not discuss.

They exchanged gifts. Meg had bought Gloria a jumper from Marks and Spencer. Her mother gave her a cheque for fifty pounds. 'I didn't know what to buy you.'

For lunch they had turkey fillets, since a whole bird, however small, would have been a preposterous idea. They sat at opposite ends of the dining table, as if avoiding each other, and just before three Meg went home.

In the evening, when she thought the time difference would not matter too much, she steadied her nerve and dialled the number that Laurence Everett had written down. She waited, listening to the soft purr of an American telephone. After several rings there was a click and she heard a man's voice. 'Hi,' he said, 'we can't take your call right now but if you leave your name and number after the tone we'll get back to you.' There were three short bleeps and then a longer one.

They were out. Spending Christmas somewhere else. She hung up.

That was stupid. She rang again. This time, after the long tone, she took a deep breath and spoke.

'Hello, Mr Everett.' And as she said it, she thought she should have worked out a kind of script beforehand. 'This is Meg Winter calling you. It's seven o'clock in the evening here in Belfast. Christmas Day. Merry Christmas to you – I suppose I should say that, shouldn't I? Look, I should have got in contact before now. I just wanted to call and thank you for sending me the ticket and I wanted to let you know that I'm going to take you up on it. I'll not waste time now in case your tape runs out. I'll fix everything up the day after tomorrow and then I'll write to you to let you have the flight details and where I'll be staying. But in the meantime, you can call me here if you like.' She gave her number and paused. 'I'm really looking forward to seeing you. Bit nervous as well. I should say that, too.'

When she had finished, she sat there, excitement fluttering in her heart. She had done it.

At around the same time two nights after that, she got a call.

'Is that Meg?'

Her heart leaped. She knew who it was before he told her.

'Yes – Mr Everett?'

'Laurence. Larry,' he said. 'Call me Larry.'

'Larry,' she echoed.

'Sorry we weren't around when you called.' His voice was not an old man's. His reference to arthritis had thrown her a bit but she reminded herself now, thinking of the son's age, that he could be in his fifties. She would have to wait and see.

'That's all right,' she said.

'We're delighted you've decided to come and see us. It's great news but, look, I feel bad about not offering to put you up.'

'No, it's fine, honestly. I've got something fixed up.'

'You have?'

'Yes. I've booked the flights and everything and a couple of nights at the Holiday Inn By The Bay.'

'Oh, I see. The Holiday Inn. Well, if that's OK—'

'Of course, it is. You've been more than generous.'

'The thing is – this new apartment. There's just the one bedroom. There's a couch in the living room. I didn't think—'

'Don't worry about it.'

'I should have said.'

'It's not a problem.' She wanted to be there now, face to face with these people, reading that letter from their son, asking them questions. But at the same time she wondered if she would be able to handle the answers when the time came. 'It's good to talk to you at last.'

'You, too,' he said. 'So, tell me, when are you planning to get here?'

Three weeks later, she was sitting at her kitchen table, ticking off the items on the list she had made.

Passport, credit card, driving licence, cash, traveller's cheques. She had all those. Ticket – yes, she had that, too.

Outside it was evening. She was going tomorrow. She could hardly believe it.

And on the day she came back it would be her birthday. She thought of everything that had happened since her last one.

She had made all her arrangements with a travel agent just along the Lisburn Road. She had hired a car, too; a compact, whatever that was. The agent reckoned it was cheaper to rent

257

one at this end and it saved a lot of time. All she had to do was produce her voucher when she got to the Dollar rental place at Logan Airport.

Boston. She would not get to see a whole lot of it. Not this trip. Some other time, perhaps.

She tried to slide the list under the big magnet on the fridge where she kept all the scraps of paper that she did not want to lose but as she did so the whole thing collapsed. Notes, receipts fluttered to the floor like leaves. There were phone numbers, addresses. Elizabeth's number was there, so was Florence Gilmour's calling card. She picked them all up and as she stuck them back carefully she thought for a second of calling Gilmour and putting her in the picture.

No, it would wait until she had returned.

There *was* something she had to do, however. Something unfinished that had been niggling at her, and she could not go tomorrow without putting it to rest. She grabbed her car keys and her coat and went out.

Ten minutes later she was pulling into the visitors' parking bay outside Elizabeth's flat. There was a 'For Sale' sign now.

Elizabeth opened the door, looking tired. She gave Meg a weary smile.

'Life's too short,' Meg said. 'Can I come in?'

They talked and drank tea and massaged their emotional bruises. Meg got the impression that Elizabeth was on the wagon but she did not broach the subject.

Vincent was installed in London and Elizabeth would be moving to join him in a week. Everywhere there were things in boxes.

At eleven, Meg looked at her watch. 'It's late. I'd better go. It'll be a long day tomorrow.'

At the door she remembered something. She took a slip of paper from her pocket and handed it to Elizabeth. 'I'm at the Holiday Inn By The Bay in Portland. This is the number, just in case you need me for anything. My parents have it as well.' She had shoved a letter in the post to each of them this afternoon. Short and factual. No fond farewells.

'I'll be busy with this lot,' Elizabeth said, looking round the hallway where there were more boxes. 'You'll be back before I know it.'

'And then you'll be off yourself,' Meg said.

'Something like that.'

'Take care.' They squeezed each other fiercely.

'You, too,' Elizabeth said.

'I just want everything to be all right for you, you know,' Meg told her and as she said it she thought she sounded just like her father.

At about the same time Meg was leaving Elizabeth, Dan Cochrane emerged from a pub in the village of Killough, just along the curving shoreline beyond Ardglass. The Guinness he had drunk alone tonight had tasted bitter, like his thoughts.

Behind the steamed-up windows of the bar he had just left there was the sound of laughter and clinking glasses. He stood for several minutes in the cool air, looking at the moonlight on the water, then he walked across the road to the edge. The tide was in and it licked gently at the stony shore.

There was a decision to be made.

He turned and went to where he had parked, then drove the few miles back to Ardglass. When he got to the pottery he let himself in and went straight upstairs. In the bedroom that was his, the bed was unmade, as always. Clothes lay where he had dropped them. The room was stale and he opened the window to a sharp breeze that chilled him instantly.

He closed the window after a few moments, then began to tidy up. He picked up a pair of jeans, opened the wardrobe and put them on a hanger. He stood, thinking about something, and then he reached up on tiptoe and took a box file from the top.

Setting it down on the floor, he opened it and began to examine its contents.

There were photographs, photocopied documents, newspaper cuttings. He spread the whole lot out before him but it was the photographs which occupied his attention most. He looked thoughtfully at each one, then laid them out carefully in rows, like a game of solitaire.

After a couple of minutes, he pushed himself to his feet, his legs stiff and cramped from crouching on the hard floor, and looked at his watch. It was after midnight. Too late for him to phone now. He would call in the morning, after another night which he knew would be without sleep.

Thirty-five

She had checked the weather forecast.

Maine in January was always cold and to make matters worse, there were reports now of ice storms, rain freezing on top of snow, winds blowing down trees and power lines. But that was inland. Portland was on the coast. She had her fingers crossed.

She had crammed what she needed into a big sports bag which she hoped would qualify as cabin luggage and she was going to carry a warm-lined moleskin jacket she had bought a few days ago in Gap. She had thermal underwear, too, and gloves, as well as a woollen ski hat, which, she reminded herself now, she had forgotten to put into the bag.

She looked at the clock. Eight a.m. Time she was out of there. Her flight left at eleven and she was supposed to check in hours before that.

She hurried up to her bedroom and found the hat. Downstairs again she shoved it into her bag and after a last swift look round she headed for the door.

As she opened it, the telephone started. For a second she thought of letting the thing ring but then she dropped the bag and her coat and grabbed it.

'Hello?'

There was no response. Her heart seemed to miss a beat. She saw Noel Kennedy's face.

'Hello, who is this?' she said.

'Meg?'

Her heart thumped. 'Dan?'

'Yes. Look, Meg, I need to talk to you.'

She could hear trouble in his voice. 'What is it? Has something happened?'

'No. I just need to talk to you. There's something I have to tell you.'

She groaned. This could not be happening at a worse time. 'Dan, look, I can't talk now.'

'Meg, please. There are things you need to know.'

'About what?'

'Not on the phone. I have to see you.'

She wanted to see him, too, but it was impossible. 'Oh Dan, this is awful. If you'd called a moment later you wouldn't have got me at all. I'm on my way to the airport. I'm flying to Boston.'

'Boston?'

'Yes. I'm going to see the Everetts. Look, I haven't the time to talk about this – any of it. Whatever you have to say, it'll have to wait until I come home. I'll only be away for a couple of days. Dan, I'm sorry but I have to hang up.'

'Meg, no, don't. Wait. Just listen to me.'

'No, Dan, I can't. Don't do this to me. We'll talk later. When I get back.'

She rang off and it was as if she had cut him loose. She grabbed her things and ran out the door, feeling terrible and wishing she had told him she was glad he had called.

Maybe she would ring him from Portland. That would be good.

She threw the bag into the back seat of her car and pulled out quickly from the kerb without checking her mirror. There was a screech of brakes. A horn blared.

A red mail van was inches from her front wing. She had not seen it at all. The postman driving it glowered at her. It was her usual man, the bald one. She gave him an apologetic wave, mouthed 'sorry', and drove on.

Just after eleven, as the Aer Lingus Airbus with Meg on board turned onto the main runway at Belfast International Airport and increased speed for take-off, Dan Cochrane drove into Truesdale Street.

He was not in the van today.

This time he had brought his own little blue Fiat.

He found a parking space a few doors down from number thirty and got out. As he walked back up the street he looked around discreetly but there was no one to observe him. Meg's front gate squeaked as he opened it. He took a couple of keys from his pocket and checked that he had the right one. 'Keys cut in five minutes', said the sign in the window of the hardware shop just along the road, and they had been as good as their word. He had got this particular one cut the day he had gone for the milk, the day the letter from the Everetts had arrived.

He stepped into the hall and closed the door behind him, thinking about what he was looking for and where he might find it.

The postman had been, obviously after she had left, because there were letters still on the floor. He picked them up. One looked like a bank statement, another was a bill or a circular of some kind.

But it was the third letter that got his attention.

It was bulky and it bore the logo of Granada Television. They had made that programme she had appeared on. He felt it in his fingers for a second or two, debating, then he slid his thumb under the flap and opened it.

There was another letter inside and a note on Granada headed paper.

Dear Dr Winter

This came recently. The sender asked us if we would pass it on to you. Seeing who it is from, we thought you might want to see it.

Hope everything is OK with you.

Best wishes

Sally

Cochrane looked at the sealed envelope. *Meg Winter*, it said. *To be forwarded*. He turned it over and read the sender's name and address on the back.

He blinked in disbelief. This couldn't be right.

Then he tore it open.

There was just one sheet of lined paper and what it contained was written in an unsteady hand. He read the letter swiftly and when he had finished, there was a cold sheen of sweat on his brow.

He shoved the letter into his pocket and began his search.

He tried Meg's bedroom first, going through drawers and the things in her wardrobe. Handbags, a dusty briefcase. He stopped in his tracks when he found a shoulder-bag with stains on it that looked like blood.

He went back downstairs again and straight away he found everything he wanted in the kitchen, where he should have started in the first place. It was all under the magnet on the door of the fridge.

He sat and spread the notes on the table, setting the phone beside him. He had calls to make. Urgent, desperate calls.

He looked at his watch and tried to work out what time it was in New England.

Just after six a.m. he reckoned. Early. But he couldn't leave it any later. Every moment counted.

Thirty-six

In 1974, the Portland police had moved out of the old head-quarters on Federal Street so that the place could be levelled to the ground.

Where the building once stood, there was now a parking lot that served the Cumberland County courthouse. Since then the police had operated from an angular, modern building of brick and glass that stood on the corner of Middle and Franklin Streets.

In the Bureau of Investigations office on the fourth floor a tousled man in a v-neck sweater that was a little tight over his gut sat alone at a window, watching the day begin and his night shift finish.

The waters of Casco Bay looked like steel. It was six twenty a.m. and orange-pink streaks were beginning to grow stronger in the sky. The colours made the dawn look warm but he knew that was a lie. The temperature would not rise above freezing today and tonight, once more, it would drop way, way down.

And there was the rain.

It was his last night duty for a couple of weeks and in a few minutes he would be out of here, heading away from the city towards the dormitory community of Gorham.

There had been more rain in the night, freezing as it fell, coating power lines and the branches of trees with layers of ice that made them too heavy to hold themselves up. He wondered if there was any power at home but there was no one who could tell him.

He had lived in the house alone since his wife left. It was a year now but the hurt was deep.

The weather was keeping everyone indoors, even those who might have had mischief in mind. There had not been much of that for him to deal with during the night and certainly nothing that the uniforms had not been able to handle. Thank God he hadn't had to go out.

But he was wondering about the phone call he had taken a few minutes ago.

263

He had just finished putting it into the computer log. A strange one.

He swivelled round towards his desk. There were little plastic name plates on each of them. His said, 'Detective Roy Flynn'.

As he looked at the notes he had scribbled down when the call came in, the door at the end of the room opened.

'Jeez, it's a cold one out there.'

Bob Reglinski's fleshy face with its bushy moustache peered out from under layers of wool. In his gloved hands he carried two containers of java from On The Go, the coffee shop next door.

He handed one to Flynn who inhaled the aroma deeply. 'Ah, great. Thanks, Bob.'

'Anything?' Reglinski said, squeezing his bulky backside into his own chair and putting his feet on the desk. His heavy boots were wet. They smeared some of the paperwork lying there but he did not seem to notice or, if he did, he did not care.

Flynn made a face. 'Nah,' he said and stood up. He tore the page of notes from the pad and stuck it in his pocket, then went to the rack in the alcove for his coat. 'I got a call a little while ago. Kinda weird. I might do a quick check on something on my way home.'

Reglinski wasn't that interested. 'You back on tonight?'

'Nope. I got a couple of rest days and then I'm on earlies. Catch you later.'

The police parking lot was a skating rink that he crossed with tiny, careful steps. The rain that had fallen on his car during the night had become a shell and stilettoes hung from the wing mirrors. He chipped at the ice with a plastic scraper, watching it crack and slide away and fall to the ground like sheets of thin, pebbled glass. It took him ten minutes to clear it all, stopping every now and then to drink some of his coffee.

The big gritting trucks had been spraying all night to give the surface of the streets some grip. But as he drove, he bounced his way over lumps of ice which had been welded to the ground by the pounding of the traffic and were now as hard and immovable as stone.

In a few minutes he was pulling up outside a big hotel. He got out and the glass doors parted to let him into the building. He wiped his feet on a thick mat that had been put down on the edge of the lobby carpet in an attempt to keep it clean, then he walked towards the reception desk, glancing at a sign on an easel. It said: 'The Holiday Inn By The Bay Welcomes The Roundtable Center Conference'.

Behind the desk, a pale young woman with sleep on her mind

watched him coming. The tag clipped to her jacket told him her name was Naomi Waitt and that she was an assistant manager.

'Just finishing?' he said as he reached her.

'Just starting.'

He winced and let her have a sympathetic smile, then he took his police shield from his inside pocket. She looked at it and gave him a nod that said she already knew, the way people always did.

'Yes, Detective,' she said. 'What can I do for you?'

'Not entirely sure. Just something I'm checking. Can you tell me if you have anyone called Meg Winter registered with you?'

She turned to her computer. 'Winter,' she muttered, flicking through the details. 'Winter, Winter. Yes, here we are – oh, no, we don't. At least not yet.'

'What do you mean?'

'I mean we don't have her yet. She's due to book in some time later today.' She frowned. 'Is there a problem?'

He made a face. 'No, no, I don't think so. It was just in relation to something – a call I got. Look, it's probably nothing. Don't mention anything to her, if you don't mind.'

'That's OK – as long as you're sure there's nothing wrong?'

'No, no. Thanks for your help.' He backed away, holding his palms up in surrender. 'It was just a routine check, that's all.'

As he reached the main door, two young men in bellhop uniforms were carrying the easel and the sign away. They read the question on his face.

'Cancelled,' one of them said. 'The ice storms strike again.'

At Shannon, there was a short stop.

The plane from Belfast was actually going on to New York which meant Meg had to change for her flight to Boston. Everyone got off. They had to anyway. Shannon was also an outpost of US Immigration and when she reached Boston she would be glad of the time that saved her.

With each minute, her anticipation grew. But Dan was on her mind now, too. His had been a peculiar phone call. It would be hours before she could ring him. She thought of trying him from Shannon but she was worried that there wasn't enough time so she didn't risk it.

The long journey made her impatient.

Over the Atlantic she ate the flight meal, watched a movie and failed to get any sleep. They made landfall over Canada, turning south, and she looked out of the window at a view which gave her a taste of what was to come. As far as her eye could see, there was whiteness, broken only by dark patches of forest and grey veins that were roads and rivers. She saw vast frozen lakes with snow thick on the ice, enormous ploughed fields that had been transformed into patterns like fingerprint negatives.

And then they were coming in over Cape Cod and Martha's Vineyard and suddenly Boston's tall buildings were shining in the sun and they were landing on a runway at the edge of the water.

The plane took an eternity to come to a halt. When the doors opened, only the first class passengers were off before she was.

She strode down the ramp into the terminal building, following the car rental signs, seeking out the Dollar desk, where an attendant checked her voucher and then directed her to a coach waiting in a parking bay outside.

She put her coat on before walking out of the terminal and into fresh air.

The incredible cold took her breath away.

It gripped her nose and seized her ears and made her eyes water. She was wearing jeans but it ignored the thick denim and it clasped icily at her knees. She put her bag down, fumbling in it hurriedly for her gloves, then put them on and pulled the zipper of her coat up as far as it would go.

The door of the coach swung open with a hiss and the driver reached out and took her bag for her. He was wearing a coat with quilted panels and a leather cap with furry flaps down over his ears. He saw her shocked, frozen expression, her red, pinched cheeks, and laughed.

'Heh, heh. Cold enough for you, Miss?'

'Unbelievable,' she said, taking a seat near the heating vents. They were blasting like a furnace.

'Where you from?'

'I just got off a plane from Ireland.'

'Ireland, huh. Does it get cold over there?'

'Not like this.'

Still chuckling, he looked out the window, scanning the terminal exits. 'OK,' he said, 'guess you must be the only one. You getting the VIP treatment today.'

He swung away from the kerb and into the airport traffic, following a baffling array of signs and slip roads. In a couple of minutes, she saw Hertz, Avis and Budget. Then Dollar. The driver stopped, got off first and took her bag down for her.

'There you go, Miss. You have a nice day.'

'Eh – you, too,' she said awkwardly.

She queued at the desk, then handed in the voucher and signed something. The woman who dealt with her was called

266

Dolores. She handed her a set of keys with the car number on a tag. 'Your car's in bay number nineteen. It's a dark blue Plymouth.'

'I'm driving to Portland,' Meg said. 'I haven't a clue how to get there. Somebody told me I needed the I-95.'

Dolores nodded and took a leaflet and a street map from her desk. 'The I-95 north. Don't go south or you'll end up in Florida. This will tell you everything you want to know. How to get out of this terminal for a start. You don't want to find yourself driving in circles around here for the next couple of days.'

Meg looked at the leaflet and then she looked at the map. It was a street map of Portland. 'This is terrific. How much do I owe you for this?'

'On the house,' Dolores said. 'All part of the service.'

The car was an automatic, which she was not used to, and after five minutes she had not gone anywhere. An attendant, menacing in a hooded parka, watched for a while then he walked over and yanked the door open, startling her.

'It's OK, miss,' he said. 'Just use your right foot. That's all you need.'

He closed the door and she reversed out of the space successfully.

'There you go. You got it,' he called after her, waving.

She waved back briefly, then concentrated on trying to get into the traffic.

Once she was away from the airport and heading in the right direction, she began to relax, adjusting her seat so that she was more comfortable. She gave a sigh of relief and then smiled excitedly to herself.

Made it.

She was in America, snow all around her, driving a strange car on a strange highway to a strange town to meet two people she did not know and she felt good about it. No, she felt terrific. She had been in the country for only about an hour and she felt more at home than she had for a long time.

In a land of strangers she did not feel like one.

It was mid-afternoon. She turned on the radio and found a talk station where they were interviewing people in the street about some scandal or other involving the President. There was always one of those.

'They're hounding people,' a man protested. 'It's never been the same since Watergate. And that was another thing that was blown out of all proportion.'

She found a country station instead and listened to it for a while. The roadside advertising signs fascinated her. They were

267

for pizza, beer, cars, furniture stores. She passed a thirty foot-high fake cactus with the name of a steak and rib restaurant emblazoned on it.

Flashing dot matrix signs thanked emergency crews for helping out during the ice storms. On the radio, a weather forecaster warned that more was on the way.

Behind her, the sun was beginning its descent. As she looked in her rear-view mirror along the miles she had driven, she could see its dazzling brightness turn gradually to pink and mauve smears. She turned her sidelights on.

The road took her out of Massachusets and into New Hampshire. She searched for change at a toll plaza while the attendant waited, but she had the money ready the next time, when she crossed into Maine.

It was dark and starting to snow when she reached Portland.

It was like no snow she had ever seen: dry, fine powder, deceptively gentle in its fall. She tried to follow the street map but it was difficult to do while driving. She pulled into a petrol station on Congress Street. A woman in a coat and gloves stood behind the counter, watching an ice hockey game on TV.

Meg explained where she was trying to get to. The woman took off a glove and drew a wavy line on the street map with a pencil. 'It's a one-way system. Just follow this and you can't go wrong.'

The directions were simple but nevertheless she managed to make a couple of wrong turns before she found what she wanted: Spring Street.

The Holiday Inn sign that lit up the building ahead of her was like a warm embrace.

She checked her watch. Nine p.m. Two a.m. at home. Sixteen hours since she had left Truesdale Street. She felt tired and hungry and in need of a hot bath and she decided to call Dan tomorrow.

Thirty-seven

Hollow-eyed, Peter Quinn stood at ten thirty the following morning beside one of the luggage carousels at Belfast International Airport.

He had just got off a shuttle from London but the labels and stickers on the two big, bulging suitcases that he saw coming along the conveyor belt towards him showed that he had travelled from the other side of the world.

He grabbed the cases with strong hands and hauled them with ease onto a trolley. Then he looked around for a telephone and dialled Harry Glover at the bank.

'Harry, it's Peter Quinn.'

'Peter – where are you?'

'I'm at the airport. About to make some taxi driver's day by getting him to take me to Ardglass.'

'It's not so bad. You'll be there in about an hour.'

'It's not the journey, it's the cost and I don't think they take Japanese yen. Listen, is there any chance you could meet me when I get there?'

'Of course. I think I can get away for half an hour. And I need to talk to you anyway about your friend Cochrane. There's some news.'

'He's turned up?'

'Just the opposite. I wasn't here yesterday – I spent the day at another branch – but I've now discovered he's withdrawn three thousand pounds from the account and that he's changed a lot of it into US dollars.'

'Dollars? Jesus Christ, what's he playing at?' Quinn said. 'Look, I'll go and get a cab. I'll see you at the pottery in about an hour.'

The taxi rank was in a lay-by beside the exit to the terminal building and he found a driver keen enough to take him.

'But go the quickest way,' he said. 'I'm in a bit of a hurry.'

They avoided Belfast and took a route that went down into Lisburn, across to Ballynahinch and then towards Downpatrick.

Quinn stared out at countryside that was a colourless wash behind a mist of drizzle.

The day he received Harry Glover's unexpected e-mail in Kyoto, he had tried to call Cochrane but there had been no reply, just the answering machine with his own voice on it, which had sounded weird. He had left a message, asking Cochrane if everything was all right, although he didn't say exactly why he was calling. Twenty-four hours later he had phoned again. This time Cochrane was there, sounding fine, assuring him that there were no problems and when Quinn told him about Harry Glover's e-mail he said there must have been some mistake. He sometimes had to pop out for things and close up for a little while, that was all.

But Quinn had called several times since then, at times when the shop should definitely have been open, and had received no reply at all, not even the machine. So he had e-mailed Harry Glover and told him he was coming home a little sooner than planned.

And now this. Money being taken out of the account and turned into a bundle of US dollars.

When the taxi got to Ardglass it was raining properly. Gulls circling above a trawler making its way into harbour screamed like fans round a cornered pop star. He got out of the taxi, breathing in the familiar smells of fish and diesel oil that told him he was home, and hurried through the wet to the pottery.

The van was outside, which raised his hopes, but not for long. The place was obviously shut and Cochrane's own little car was not there.

He unlocked the door and the driver helped him carry his cases in. The fare was forty pounds and he did not have enough cash but he was relieved when he found twenty pounds in the till. Only there was not much else in it, he noticed.

'Not enough for a tip, I'm afraid,' he said. The driver muttered his disappointment and left.

When the cab had gone, Quinn put the lights on and looked around.

'Dan?' he called, although he knew there was no point.

The place was dusty and smelled damp. There was a pile of letters behind the counter and when he picked them up he saw that they were bills mostly, many of them unopened.

'God damn,' he said to himself, going through them. Some were final demands. There was even an overdue VAT bill. Had none of these been paid?

He called out again. 'Dan? Are you here?' But it was more in anger than in hope.

He headed upstairs to the flat and found Cochrane's room in a state, clothes scattered everywhere, drawers pulled open, as if the place had been ransacked.

He began to look for anything that might make sense of it all. What the hell had been going on here? He stood in the centre of the room and gazed around.

A box file was sitting on a chair.

It was the sort kept downstairs for invoices and receipts but what was it doing here in the middle of this mess?

He pulled the covers up on the bed, sat on the edge and opened the file. As he started to go through its contents he felt first a growing unease and then a sense of dread. Slowly and carefully, he took everything out and spread it on the bed.

'Jesus,' he whispered, 'what the hell's he up to?'

There were newspaper clippings and copies of documents relating to Seasons Construction and Malone Group PLC. Then there were cuttings about the hotel fire and Cochrane's jail sentence. There was a magazine profile of Sam Winter, copies of annual company reports.

'God, I thought he had let all this go,' he said.

And then he saw what else was there.

The headlines hit him first.

'RIDDLE OF MURDER CASE COMA WOMAN'
'BACK FROM THE DEAD!'
'COMA GIRL SPEAKS OUT ON TV'

He heard a car door slam, then Harry Glover's voice. 'Peter?'

'I'm up here,' he called without looking away from what he was reading. He could not take his eyes off any of it. There was just about everything that had ever been written about Meg Winter, the daughter of the man Cochrane blamed for the destruction of the farm and the death of his mother.

Christ, it was all still there in his mind.

He found the photographs last, at the bottom. They were all pictures of the same young woman, slim with short hair and glasses, taken at different times and in different locations. All apparently without her knowledge.

She was in a blue suit coming out of a building and getting into a car, she was standing in front of what looked like an old farmhouse, she was walking along a street in the rain carrying shopping, she was in a wood somewhere, she was at the front door of a small terraced house.

Glover came into the room. 'Christ, what's all this?'

'I'm afraid to think,' Quinn said. He stood and started

271

searching the room. Drawers did not yield anything and so he tried the wardrobe. At the bottom he found a camera bag. Inside it there was a Canon SLR and a clutch of lenses, several of them for long shots.

He pushed past Glover and lifted the phone beside the bed.

'What are you doing?' Glover said.

'Calling the police.'

Her body clock was confused so it woke her at four a.m. She got up for a glass of water and put the TV on for a while, then she dropped off again at seven and slept like a log until she woke with a start at nine, blinking and dry-mouthed, not knowing where the hell she was.

And then she remembered.

She had to let them know she was here. She dug the Everetts' letters out of her bag, then dialled their number. But there was no one home, just the answering machine. She had their new address, a place on Elmwood, which Larry Everett had told her was out on Stevens Avenue, but she had no idea where that was and she did not want to just turn up at the door without a bit of notice. They had agreed when last they spoke that she should have the morning to herself to recover from the flight and get her bearings and that she would see them in the afternoon.

She left a message on the machine, giving them her room number and saying that she had arrived safely.

It would be about two p.m. in Ireland so she tried Cochrane but he was not there, which she thought was odd. The machine wasn't even switched on. She let the phone ring for several minutes before she gave up and went to the shower.

While she dressed she turned on the TV again. Channel WGME13 had the latest on the ice storm; more low temperatures and freezing rain on the way. They were giving details of events cancelled this weekend. There would be no St Andrews Society Burns supper, no youth basketball games, no Saturday workshops at the Portland School of Ballet. The list went on.

By ten, no one had called and she felt restless sitting around waiting for the phone to ring, so she decided to go out for breakfast and see the city.

She wrapped up warmly: hat, gloves, scarf and coat. She had brought a small shoulder-bag that she slung securely across her body. In it were essentials like her money and her credit card and she had the two letters from the Everetts in there, too. There was no way she would have left them at home. They were almost the first thing she had packed away. She felt as if they were a kind of accreditation for her.

272

She did not take the car but headed into the morning on foot. The day was dazzling and she was thankful that her glasses were the sort that darkened when brightness hit them.

She had never been in a place so frozen. Great mounds of snow lay piled up all along the edges of the streets and scrawny, leafless trees coated with ice sparkled as if they were made of sugar. People struggled slowly by, trying to walk on pavements that were like layers of slippery rock. She followed their example by staying close to the sides of buildings, grateful when she came to a patch that had been dug away by a shop owner, and reluctant to go beyond it.

Using her street map, she headed for the district known as the old port. Portland, she concluded quite quickly, was not a very big city; it was about the size of Derry back home. Nor was that the only resemblance to Northern Ireland, she realised. Maine had a Bangor and a Belfast too.

Soon she found herself on a street of brightly painted shop fronts and colourful awnings. There were bookshops and jewellery stores and shops selling arts and crafts that reminded her a bit of the pottery.

Java Joe's was a coffee shop where everyone looked like a student. They wore outsize sweaters and combat pants with voluminous side pockets and they all seemed to know each other with the result that she felt like an intruder. Bare wooden floors absorbed the wetness from booted feet and the high walls were papered with posters. Old Beatles songs were being played and a thin young man with a black t-shirt and a goatee beard stood behind the counter, singing along.

'Coffee?' Meg said, interrupting his version of *Things We Said Today*.

'Help yourself.' He pointed to a platoon of flasks lined up on a shelf, all of them labelled with an individual blend. She went for an organic Colombian.

'That everything?' he said.

She spotted bagels on a plate under a transparent cover. 'I'll take one of those.'

'Cinnamon and raisin?'

'That'll be fine.'

'You want me to heat it up for you?'

'Yes, please.'

'You want butter or cream cheese with that?'

All these damn decisions. 'I'll have cream cheese,' she said and paid him.

'You go right ahead,' he said. 'I'll bring this over to you when it's ready.'

273

She took her coffee to a table where someone had left a copy of the *Boston Globe*. There was a picture of the President on the front page and headlines about whatever trouble he had got himself mixed up in.

The waiter brought her bagel. 'There you go. You all set?'

'Thanks,' she said.

Used plates and other debris littered the next table and he started to clear it on to a tray.

'You got power?' He said it like *powah*, his Maine accent almost English.

'I'm sorry?'

'Have you got power? At home. Power?'

'Oh, I see. No, I don't live around here. I'm staying in a hotel.'

'Then you're OK. What are you – on vacation or something?'

'Kind of. I'm from Ireland. I'm just here for a few days.'

'Ireland, huh? Is that so? I'm third generation Irish myself. Name of O'Brien. My family came from County Mayo originally.' He looked at her as if all this should mean something.

She nodded. 'O'Brien's a very Irish name. Lots of O'Briens. Although, to be honest, I don't think I actually know anyone called O'Brien myself. And come to think of it, I'm not sure I've ever been to Mayo either. Maybe when I was a kid.'

His looked showed his amazement. Someone from Ireland had to know the O'Briens from County Mayo.

'But then Ireland's a bigger place than you'd think,' she said. 'Anyway I'm from the northern part.'

'You mean like Belfast? Where all the trouble is?'

'Not any more. Touch wood.' She tapped the table. She had placed her street map on it and it gave her a thought. 'Listen, I'm hoping to visit some people who live in Portland.'

'Oh, you got friends here?'

'Sort of. They're the parents of . . . of someone I was connected with. You don't happen to know a place called Elmwood, do you? I'm told it's off Stevens Avenue but I can't find it on this map.'

He looked at it. 'Stevens Av. That's way out.' He waved a hand towards the street. 'Stevens Av.,' he said again, thinking, then shook his head. 'Nope. The only thing I know out that direction is the cemetery.'

She stayed in the coffee shop for half an hour and when she left, she spent some time exploring the streets, finding that she had this part of the city almost to herself.

There was hardly anyone around. A lot of restaurants and shops were closed and it was as if the place were hibernating.

274

Maine was a summer state where the car number plates bore the legend 'Vacationland'. Winter was something to be endured.

She was back at the hotel at around one and found that her bed had been made up but that the air conditioning had been set too high. The room was chilly. As she went over to adjust the setting, she saw a red light blinking on her phone.

It was her voice mail. She had two messages.

While she had been asleep, a detective from Downpatrick CID and two uniformed officers had arrived at the pottery. The appearance of police cars all of a sudden was causing a stir in Ardglass. People watched from behind their curtains. Along the harbour, even the trawlermen took an interest.

The CID man was Detective Inspector Donal Murray. 'What do you think?' Quinn asked when he and Harry Glover had filled him in.

Murray held one of the photographs of Meg Winter in his hand and studied it. 'Well, there's no evidence that a crime has been committed here,' he looked up at the two men, 'not unless we turn up evidence of embezzlement or theft and that will take a while. But this . . .' he tapped the picture, '. . . this causes me a lot of concern. It looks like he's been stalking this woman. So we'd better find out where she is first.'

He turned to one of the uniformed officers. 'Parcel all this stuff up and we'll take it into Downpatrick.' He looked at Quinn and Glover. 'I'd like you both to come, too, to get all this down on paper and try to locate your friend Cochrane.'

As the policemen piled the material into the box file, a cutting escaped their grasp and fell to the floor. Murray lifted it. It was about the unsolved murder of Paul Everett four years ago. 'And I'll need to talk to whoever's still working on this case,' he said.

Things moved quickly after that.

At shortly after two o'clock that afternoon, Detective Sergeant Hugh Nixon and Detective Inspector Florence Gilmour were shown into a waiting room beside the executive offices on the top floor of the Malone Group building in Belfast.

Nixon was sweating under a heavy coat and he was out of breath, even though they had taken the lift. He whistled softly as he looked out of the window on to the bustling city. 'Some view, eh?'

Gilmour wasn't interested in it. She paced the room, a folder under her arm.

The door opened and a trim woman in a smart suit came in. She was in her fifties with short hair and cautious eyes. 'I'm Brenda Brennan, PA to the chief executive. I understand you're looking for Mr Winter?'

'That's right,' Nixon said. 'We need to talk to him about his daughter.'

BB's eyes widened. 'Has something happened to her?'

'Not that we know of,' Gilmour said, 'but we need to know where she is.'

'Mr Winter's in an important board meeting. It's just started. It's being chaired by Sir Brian Malone on a video circuit from New York. Perhaps this is something that can wait?'

'No,' Gilmour said, 'no, I don't think it is.'

BB saw the determined look in her eyes and acknowledged it with a slight smile. 'Then I'd better get him out of there, hadn't I?'

In thirty seconds she was back with an anxious Sam Winter. 'What is it?' he said. 'What's wrong? Has something happened to Meg?'

'Let's all sit down, shall we?' Gilmour said. 'Nothing's happened to your daughter that we're aware of but we need to know where she is.'

'She's in America,' Winter said, looking at them as if he expected them to be aware of that. 'She went yesterday. Look, what's this all about?'

Gilmour and Nixon tried not to look at each other. Now they knew why Cochrane had needed dollars.

'Why is she in America?' Gilmour asked.

Winter told them.

'Damn it,' Nixon said, 'she should have told us about this development.'

Gilmour fired a quick look at him and he sat back. 'Let's leave that for the moment,' she said. 'We'd better explain to Mr Winter what's been going on.'

As she did, she took from her folder some of the photographs which had been found in the flat.

'Oh my God,' Winter said when he looked at them.

'What time did Meg go yesterday?' Gilmour wondered. 'What were her movements?' He told her.

'Do you know where she's staying?'

'At a Holiday Inn – "the Holiday Inn By The Bay", I think it's called. She left me the number.'

'Do you have it?'

He shook his head. 'Not here. It's at home.'

BB had stayed at the back of the room, listening in silence.

276

Now she came forward and picked up the phone. 'I'll get it from inquiries for you. It would be a good idea if her father spoke to her, don't you think?'

'Yes,' Gilmour said. 'If she's at that hotel, she should check out of it as soon as possible. Cochrane may know that's where she's staying. Tell her to find another hotel and then call you with the number. But, Mr Winter . . .' she sat forward towards him and tried a smile, '. . . all this is just a precaution. We may be jumping to entirely the wrong conclusion here, you understand. Cochrane may not be anywhere near her at all. But it's best to be on the safe side.'

He nodded but she saw that she had not convinced him.

BB finished the call and handed her a yellow sticky with the hotel number on it.

'Let's ring her now,' Gilmour said.

'Do you have another phone?' Nixon asked.

'Of course,' BB said. 'My office next door.'

Sam Winter took the number and started punching it in. While he did, Nixon guided Gilmour to one side. 'Boss, I don't think we should waste time trying to go through Interpol with this. I'm going to try the Portland police direct, see if they'll help, and get them to keep a look out for these two. I'll warn them that Cochrane might try to harm the girl. I can get our people to fax them his record as well. What do you think?'

'Go ahead,' she agreed.

He left the room with BB. Gilmour waited for Winter to get through to the hotel.

'Christ,' he said eventually, 'she's not there. There's just a voice mail.'

'But she's checked in OK?'

'Yes.'

'Then leave a message on her phone. Get her to call you.'

When he had done so, he said, 'My meeting. I'd better tell Sir Brian what's going on.'

He strode down the corridor towards the boardroom, opening the door abruptly and startling the others sitting around the long table. One of them had been explaining something about exponential growth and profit margins but Winter's sudden entrance interrupted him.

At the end of the table there was a wide screen that showed Sir Brian Malone behind a desk, writing on a pad. The video link made his movements jerky, like individual frames in a film. On the top left-hand corner of the screen there was a shot of the table and the people round it, which was what Malone would see in New York when he looked at his own monitor. He raised his glance and as he spoke his voice from the speakers had an eerie echo as it travelled across space and time.

'You've stopped talking. Have you become bored with what you were saying? Because I certainly was.'

'Sir Brian,' Winter butted in from the back of the room.

'Who's that?' Malone said. 'I can't see you.'

Winter took his seat and his image appeared on the screen with the others. 'It's Sam Winter,' he said. 'Look, I'm sorry about this but I'm going to have to ask you to adjourn this meeting for a few minutes. There's something I need to say to you privately.'

'Can't you speak in front of your fellow board members?'

'No, it's personal. Something for your ears only.'

'Then I'd better hear what it is. Give us five minutes, please.'

The rest lifted their papers and filed out, giving Winter dark, suspicious looks, wondering what he was up to, but no one asked him.

When they had gone, Winter told Malone what had happened.

'That's dreadful, Sam,' Malone said. 'Your lovely daughter. If there's anything you need, any help at all, a plane, anything, you only have to call me. You know that, don't you?'

'Yes. That's very reassuring.'

'Now go and do whatever you have to do and let's hope everything turns out for the best.' Winter got up from his seat. 'And send that other lot back in again.'

Thirty-eight

The first voice mail message was from Larry Everett.

'Hi Meg,' he said. 'I'm really sorry. Seems I'm never around when you call. How do I manage to do that? It's just that Marcie had a medical appointment and wanted me to go with her. But we're back now and all's well. Listen, I'm so glad you've got here. We can't wait to see you. But I've got to tell you what I've arranged. Now, I don't do much driving these days, not in the winter anyhow, on account of this arthritis of mine, but my brother Tom lives nearby. If you don't mind, he'll swing by the hotel at about three-thirty and bring you to see us. I could give you directions but this place is kind of tricky to find so I thought it would be a better plan if Tom just picked you up. Give me a call if that doesn't suit you. Talk to you later.'

She frowned. She was quite prepared to try to find their home by herself. She had a car. But if he had worked all this out, taken a bit of trouble to organise it, then maybe she would just go along with what he suggested.

The voice mail light was still flashing, reminding her that she had not picked up the second message. She accessed it and was taken aback to hear the voice of her father.

'Meg,' he said, 'call me as soon as you get this. It's urgent. Please – as soon as you get this. I'm at the Malone Group office in Belfast.' He gave her a direct line number.

Something had happened. That was the only reason he would make a call like that. She always worried about him but what if it was her mother? Her fingers trembled as she dialled.

A woman answered. 'Brenda Brennan.'

'This is Meg Winter,' Meg said. 'I'm looking for my father. He told me to ring here.'

'Oh, Meg, at last.' BB put the receiver down and called out. 'Sam! It's your daughter!'

He sounded breathless when he picked up the phone. 'Meg?'

'Yes, Dad. What is it? What's happened? Is Mum all right?'

'Your mother? Of course, she is. Look, where are you? Are *you* all right?'

'Well, yes. Why shouldn't I be? And what are you talking about – where am I? I'm in my hotel room in Portland. I just got your message.'

'I want you to get out of there straight away.'

'You want me to do what?' She gave a nervous laugh. 'What is all this? Don't be ridiculous. I'm not going—'

'Just listen to me,' he said with a firmness that silenced her and then he told her everything that had happened.

As she listened, the phone seemed to burn into her ear, his voice and the unbelievable things he was saying lighting fires of pain and confusion somewhere behind her eyes where Dan Cochrane's face kept coming into view.

She felt weak. Her father was asking her something but she had not heard him.

'Meg, are you there?'

'I just can't believe it,' she said, almost whispering it to herself. There was a numbness now and she found it hard to concentrate. 'I thought I knew him.'

'What? What are you talking about – you thought you knew him? Who do you know?'

'Dan,' she said. 'Dan Cochrane. You remember I was seeing someone? Well, that's who it was. I've been seeing Dan Cochrane.'

Sam whispered, 'Wait – say that again.'

Then she explained.

As she did, telling him how they had met and got to know each other, although she decided to avoid any reference to Noel Kennedy, she found that odd things which she had chosen to ignore were starting to make sense.

'God, tell me this isn't happening,' her father groaned. 'Look, does he know where you are? Did you tell him where you're staying?'

'No . . . no, I didn't. He called me at home just as I was about to leave for the airport and I told him I was flying to Boston. I hadn't time to talk. I tried to call him from here but I wasn't able to reach him.'

'No, you wouldn't have. At least that's something. But Meg, you've got to get out of that hotel, no matter what. Did you tell anyone else you would be staying there?'

'Elizabeth. I told her. I gave her the address and phone number. The same as I gave you.'

'Does Cochrane know Elizabeth?'

'Not really. He knows who she is, though. I was with her the day I met him.'

'What's her number?'

'It's – ah – it's . . .' It had gone from her memory. She felt a sudden ripple of fright. God, what was happening to her? 'Wait. I'll get my diary.'

She read him the number, then he said, 'I'm going to call and see if he's tried to contact her. And the police will need to hear all this too. In the meantime get your things packed. I'll call you back in a couple of minutes. Now hurry.'

But when he had gone, she did not feel able to do anything. Instead, she sat on the edge of the bed, piecing her thoughts together and finding how easily everything managed to fit.

There was the business of the credit card which she had apparently dropped that first day she had been in the pottery. Thinking about it now, she was certain she had put it back in her bag. But there had been all the excitement with Catriona and the broomstick. That would have created a very handy diversion for him so that he could have taken the card without being noticed. By that stage she had signed the slip for the goods and – Christ, even more helpful – she had given him her name and address and telephone number.

The card had provided the excuse to call on her, to see where she lived, to begin the process of getting to know her better. But why? What was his plan?

She thought of Noel Kennedy. He had admitted making the anonymous phone calls but he had denied hanging around in her back garden and had seemed totally surprised when she threw that at him. She had told herself that she had imagined that one. But what if she hadn't? What if she had really seen someone?

Dan.

Photographs had been found in the pottery. On the phone her father had tried to describe them to her. But without even seeing them she thought she understood.

Like that day when she had gone back to the woods. She had thought there was someone else there, someone behind her, and she had fled in panic. She had told herself she had imagined seeing a figure hiding amidst the trees but she had, damn it, she had. Dan had been there, taking pictures of her.

He had been everywhere, following, watching.

The night of the confrontation with Kennedy . . .

She shook her head at her stupidity. Well now, that had been a happy coincidence, hadn't it – how he had managed to be in the right place at the right time, with the handy excuse that he had just been dropping by with the present for her mother. She thought she had seen through him – that his real reason for being there was his interest in her.

How true that was. But not the way she had imagined it.

Once more she thought of how hard he had hit Kennedy and again she wondered what he would have done if she had not stopped it. There was a violent streak in him and she had seen it.

She shivered suddenly even though the room was warm now. God, she had confided in this man, trusted him, slept with him.

And yet it didn't altogether make sense. She had felt secure when they were together. She had felt watched over, and not in any sinister way. She wasn't that easily taken in, was she?

But the evidence was there now. Those photographs. She imagined how he must have stalked her and the thought of it made her feel violated.

After all was said and done, what did she know about him? He had revealed little about himself and she had no way of knowing whether anything he had ever told her was really true. And in the telling, he had left out one important part of his story: the fact that he was the man who had tried to burn her father's hotel down and had gone to jail for it.

Why had he phoned her yesterday? What had he wanted to say that was so important? He had sounded concerned. Or was this just another act, another stunt designed to unhinge her. Well, he was making a damned good job of that.

The phone rang.

She leaped up from the bed and stepped back, staring at it, not wanting to answer in case he was the caller.

But she had to pick it up.

'Meg?' It was a woman's voice. 'It's Florence Gilmour. Do you remember me?'

'Yes,' Meg said, dazed.

'Meg? Are you all right?' Gilmour spoke up, as if she were trying to make herself heard.

'Yes, I think so.'

'There's no one there with you?'

'No.'

'OK, that's good. Now, there's a couple of things I have to tell you. Are you listening?'

'Yes.'

'All right. First, we spoke to your friend Elizabeth and she tells us that Dan Cochrane phoned her yesterday, sometime after eleven a.m. She says he was very anxious to get hold of you, said it was very important, but he didn't know where you were staying. So she told him.'

Meg swallowed hard but said nothing.

'Still there?' Gilmour asked.

'Yes.'

'Now, we've also discovered that he took a flight from Belfast to Heathrow yesterday and then he bought a British Airways ticket from London to Boston. The thing is, he could be in Portland at any time now. So we want you to get out of that hotel immediately, like your father said, but listen – don't check out. Do you hear me? Don't check out. We want Cochrane to think you're still there. We've been in touch with the police in Portland and we hope they'll take it from here. Now you need to get a move on. Find somewhere cheap and cheerful and call your father at his number when you get there. And Meg . . .'

'Yes?'

'When you do – stay inside. Don't go out of doors. We'll keep in touch. Have you got all that?'

'Yes.'

'OK,' Gilmour said. 'So good luck.'

When they had ended the conversation, Meg thought for a moment. How was she going to find somewhere else to stay? She didn't know any other hotels, cheap and cheerful or otherwise, and she couldn't very well ask the staff in the lobby or they would wonder what was going on.

And what about the Everetts? Someone was supposed to pick her up here at three thirty. That was only half an hour away.

She lifted the phone and dialled their number, frowning when she found she had got the answering machine again. Damn.

She left a message. 'Hi, it's Meg calling. Listen, there's a problem. I'm not going to be at the hotel when – what's-his-name – Tom – comes by for me. I can't explain right now. I'm just going to make my own way to you. Don't worry. I'll find you OK.'

She hung up, grabbed some things from the drawer and her washbag from the bathroom and threw them into her bag. The rest could stay until this was over.

A dark Dodge sedan sitting across from the hotel started its engine as she pulled out into Spring Street, her map folded on her lap, feeling decidedly less confident about finding the Everetts than she had indicated on the phone.

Twenty-three Elmwood. That was the address she was looking for.

She had worked out that if she took a left just along here, it would take her onto Congress Street and eventually out of town. She could see Stevens Avenue on the map. Like Congress, it was a long artery that seemed to go on forever, eventually disappearing off the page.

She reached a complex intersection where the lights did not allow her to go straight on so she did what most of the traffic in front did, turning left, which, she realised when she found herself in South Portland, was a mistake. But in a few minutes she managed to find a way of doubling back to the intersection again. This time she took a right and after a couple of mistakes and another quick circuit to correct them she realised with satisfaction that the road she was on was called Stevens Avenue.

'So far so good,' she muttered to herself.

She drove for a couple of miles, peering right and left, but she did not see anything called 'Elmwood'. She passed the imposing grey stone building that was Deering High School and then she saw a huge sign that told her she was passing Evergreen Cemetery.

She turned right into a residential avenue, just in case this Elmwood place might be somewhere along it. She passed gardens that were buried under snow. Green winter wreaths with red ribbons were vivid on the front doors of tall white houses.

It was all very nice but there was no Elmwood.

She looked at her watch and wondered if the Everetts had picked up their messages. It would be too bad if Tom, the brother, was at the hotel, not knowing why she wasn't there.

She picked up speed but she drove aimlessly, turning corners at random, and eventually she saw signs directing her to the Portland International Jetport where, she could see from the map, she did not want to be.

She found signs pointing back towards the city so she followed them and twenty minutes later she was approaching the cemetery again, this time from the other direction. It had a big, open gateway. She pulled in through it. She would park for a moment, examine the map properly and try to get her bearings.

She got out and looked around her. A notice told her that entry to the site after sunset constituted a criminal offence. Not all of the trees were evergreen, she observed. Some were bare and bleak with branches spread like bony fingers. The cemetery stretched as far as she could see and the tops of some of the gravestones were barely visible above the surface of the perfect, crystal snow. But many others stood tall, in sombre dignity. There were huge carved crosses and granite obelisks, Christ figures with outstretched arms and, in places set apart, separated from the common herd in death as they had been in life, the bones of the rich rested in pillared family tombs surrounded by manicured fir trees.

She saw that the route to all of the graves was via a network of narrow roads with little green signs on thin poles telling you

284

where you were. She looked at the sign beside her. She was standing at the edge of somewhere called Eastern Avenue.

The cemetery office appeared to be open. Lights were on inside. Someone in there might know where this Elmwood was.

She pushed open the door and walked into heat that was almost suffocating. There was a big counter with neat piles of leaflets about funerals and the facilities the cemetery had to offer. A chart of the place, like a street map, took up a large portion of one wall.

A small man with heavy glasses sat at a desk behind a computer terminal. He got up with a smile when he saw her.

'Can I help you?'

'I hope so.' She put her folded map down on the counter. 'I'm trying to locate people who live in a place called Elmwood. I'm told it's off Stevens Avenue but I can't find it. You don't happen to know where it is?'

He scratched his head. 'Well now, Stevens Av. is pretty big, a lot of residential property around here, new houses all the time, but I've been working here for twenty years and I've never heard of any Elmwood. You sure you've got the right name?'

'I'm certain. Is it possible that it *is* a new development of some kind? The people I'm looking for have moved there recently. To an apartment.'

He made a face. 'An apartment building – could be, but it's a new one on me. The only Elmwood I've ever heard of is the one we have here.' He gave a little laugh.

Her heart stumbled. 'I'm sorry,' she said. 'What did you say?'

'Well, there's an Elmwood here, in the cemetery.' He leaned over the counter towards the wallchart. 'There you go.' He tapped the spot with his finger. 'But I don't suppose that's the one you want, is it?' He laughed again. 'Nobody *lives* there.'

She took her glasses off and looked to where he was pointing. Along each line that was a cemetery road, a name had been printed. There was Redwood Avenue, Maple, Sunset, Hickory, Fuchsia, most of them, she guessed, named after the trees and the shrubs which adorned these resting places.

She saw Woodlawn Avenue, Highfield.

Elmwood.

She stared at the word. Then she asked, 'Are the graves numbered? Do you have a record of who's buried where?'

'Well, naturally we do,' he said, as if she had a cheek to question his efficiency. 'We've got a two hundred and thirty-nine acre site here. It would be kind of stupid not to.'

She turned and gave him the best smile she could manage.

'Of course. I wasn't thinking. But would it be possible to check something?'

He was wondering what she was up to. It was on his face. But he said, 'If I can.'

'Elmwood. Could you find out who owns plot number twenty-three?'

'That's easy,' he said, walking back over to his computer and sitting down. 'Have that one for you in a second.' He tapped and clicked a couple of times. 'Here we go. Number twenty-three. That plot's owned by a family by the name of Everett.'

Meg had been leaning on the counter but now she gripped the edge of it, afraid that she would fall. There was no strength in her legs.

He walked back to her. 'Miss, are you all right?'

Her mouth was dry and she did not feel that she could open it to answer him. He was staring. She forced herself to speak. 'May . . . may I take one of these?' Photocopies of the cemetery layout sat on the counter.

'Sure. That's what they're for. But are you sure you're OK? You look a little pale.'

'The heat. It's just the heat in here, that's all.'

'Yeah, well, believe me, when you're in and out of here all day like I am, you sure need it.'

She grabbed a leaflet and muttered her thanks, then went back outside where icy winter was waiting. She walked towards her car, her feet slipping a little.

'You want to be careful on that ice,' he called. He had come out of the building after her and was watching. 'And if you're going to drive round the cemetery, stick to the avenues that have been treated. Some of the others are very dangerous.'

She gave him a little wave, then started the car and drove forward at a slow, cautious pace, holding the cemetery map against the steering wheel. In her mirror, she saw that he was still there and she knew that he would be curious about the behaviour of this strange woman.

But that was not important. What was important was that she had to see. She had to see for herself what was there.

Her wheels slid a couple of times and she slowed to let the car regain its grip. Across the frozen grave-fields a funeral was taking place, a silent, distant scene, hearse and mourners stark and black against the unblemished whiteness. She drove along Eastern Avenue, then on to Sunset, left into Mulberry and in a few minutes she saw it.

Elmwood was a far corner of the cemetery, lonely and dead. Almost engulfed by the snow, headstones were simple slabs in sober shades. Like a windbreak behind them, rows of tall larch and beech trees stood naked in the cold, stripped of the leaves that would one day provide shade from the summer sun.

She stopped the car and got out. She stood for a few moments and then began to walk along, trying to read the names from the roadside, finding that some were obscured completely. She stepped forward on to the snow, her feet sinking into its deep softness, but she was nearer now and she could see better.

Twomey. Croce. Croy. Thibodeau. Hinckley. Sabatino.

Everett.

The name was etched into a mottled green marble that was the colour of seaweed. It was all she could see, just that one word. She crouched in front of the headstone and she scraped the snow away with her gloved hand to reveal what was underneath.

There were two names.

Paul Everett's was the first.

She stood up and stepped back. He was in there, buried in the hard ground. She was near him again, near this man she did not remember.

She read the date of his birth, she read the date of his death. And then she read the second name.

Marcia Everett.

She wondered if the pounding of her heart would cause it to burst.

There were dates below. Marcia Everett had been born twenty eight years before her son.

And she had died a year after him.

Marcie Everett – whom she was expecting to see this afternoon. In her home at a place called Elmwood.

There was a stillness in the cemetery that she could feel on her skin. Not a bird sang. Traffic was a distant whisper. Somewhere far away there was the long wail of a train and the faint clink of the rolling stock along the rails.

She stood motionless, her brain reverberating with questions that had no answers. She thought of her father's warnings about coming here, warnings that she had dismissed. What was going on in Larry Everett's mind? And Dan – surely it wasn't possible that he was somehow part of this too?

The afternoon light was dimming, a faint hint of pink beginning to bleed into the sky. She felt alone. But when she looked around she saw that she was not.

A dark Dodge had parked some distance behind her car and she realised that she had not heard it drive up. A few yards along a man in a brown wool coat and a muffler over his mouth was arranging flowers on a grave.

She gave a sigh of relief. The presence of this stranger ensured her safety. No one would be mad enough to try to harm her in front of him.

Harm her? Was that really what was happening here? She took her glasses off and tried to rub away the pain that was looming in her head.

Yet no one knew she was here in the cemetery. No one knew she had discovered the grave. Whatever Larry Everett had dreamed up, this would not have been part of it.

She had to tell someone but who? She could call her father or Florence Gilmour although they seemed very far away, too far away to be of help. But there was the Portland police. Hadn't Gilmour said she had contacted them?

That was the answer. She turned and began plodding back through the snow towards her car.

The man in the dark coat had finished tending the grave and was walking in the same direction. She looked at him and their eyes met and it occurred to her that she did not know what Larry Everett looked like. God, she did not know if he even existed.

The muffler slipped from the man's face. There was something about him.

She tried to shake her memory awake.

She was a fool. She was alone in a secluded part of the cemetery with this stranger coming towards her. She stepped back, away from him.

He spoke. 'Miss, is anything the matter?'

He had stopped and she saw that he was between her and her car. She did not answer him but as she looked at his face something flashed in her mind.

There was a fire blazing in a hearth. Music. People laughing. *She had seen him before.*

How or when or where she did not know but the certain knowledge of it stabbed at her and with the knowledge came the sickening presence of danger.

She turned away from him and tried to run but the pathway was like polished glass and her feet almost went from under her. Somehow she kept her balance and managed to get on to the snow again but it was deep and heavy and it held on to her, clinging to her legs and weighing her down.

He was behind her.

It was hopeless. It was like trying to run through deep water. She stepped on something uneven and lost her balance. A pain shot through her ankle and she cried out as she fell. Bright lights sparked behind her eyes and then he had thrown himself on top of her heavily, straddling her, pushing her down.

She wriggled under his weight and his bulk and tried to burrow herself forward. The snow was wet in her eyes and it was cold in her mouth.

He began wrapping the muffler round her throat.

'No!' she managed to cry, hearing her voice coming back to her in an echo from the trees. She twisted to escape his grip but he was heavy and she was losing strength.

She called out again. 'Help! Somebod—' Then he forced her face into the snow and she felt her glasses snap at the bridge.

'Hey! What the hell do you think you're doing?'

The shout startled the man and as he turned his head towards the voice, his grip eased a fraction, just long enough for her to take advantage. She raised herself on one knee and launched herself forward like a sprinter. His fingers grasped at her foot but she was free.

'You there! Stay away from that woman! I'm calling the cops!'

She was on her feet, but barely, staggering on towards her car, every stumbling step a torture because of the pain in her ankle. She could not see clearly – her glasses were in pieces in the snow somewhere – but she saw a man get out of a pick-up truck and she knew it was the caretaker.

He moved towards her attacker. 'Now listen here, mister—'

The man tried to push him out of the way but the caretaker wasn't going to make this easy. He was stocky and strong and he struggled. He grabbed the bigger man's coat and held on to it, pulling him off balance so that he lost his footing and fell sideways. The man threw out his right arm to stop himself hitting the ground hard and did not feel something fall from his pocket into the snow. He pushed himself to his feet, then swung towards the caretaker and hit him hard in the side of the face with a gloved fist, knocking him backwards.

Their confrontation took just a few seconds but it gave her time to get into her car and she rejoiced that she had left the keys in it. She started the ignition and gunned the accelerator, the engine whining as the wheels spun on the ice.

His hand was on the door handle, pulling at it, but then the car shot forward in a violent thrust of speed.

She had no idea where she was or where she was going. All she knew was that she had to get out of there and find a way to the exit somehow but she had to do it without her glasses and with the light of day fading.

Her face and hair were soaked from the snow and she was trembling. But that was fear and shock, not the cold. She drove

289

madly, skidding from side to side on the winding, frozen avenues. Huge statues and memorial monuments loomed into her blurred vision like figures on a ghost train, and she spun the wheel to try to escape them. She took one turn, then another, sliding and screeching as she jammed her foot to the floor to power the engine.

The place was a maze and she had no idea how to get out of it. She glanced in her mirror. His car was right behind.

And then something started happening to her.

As if a circuit had tripped in her brain, images began to pass across the eye of her memory. They were like slides in a viewfinder, focussed and vivid, staying for a split second then moving on.

First she saw a road. Then blinding headlights in the darkness. She saw herself in the passenger seat of a car being driven much too fast. She heard her own voice crying out, wordless sounds of anguish. She felt a shudder that jarred every bone in her body and then she heard an engine roaring as if in pain. She felt herself being plunged down, down into emptiness.

The vision vanished and she gasped.

There was something ahead. She was almost on top of it.

It seemed to be standing in the road in front of her. A huge figure with its arms open wide. There were bright colours. She turned hard but the wheels locked and the car spun sideways.

It slammed violently into the stone embrace of the Virgin Mary.

Her robes were coloured sky blue and she had a cloak that was a terracotta red. She stood on top of a narrow pedestal in the centre of a small raised roundabout, gazing benignly on all who passed her by.

Meg's head hit the steering wheel.

The force of the crash rocked the figure but she stayed on her feet, seeming to stare down on to the car crushed into her base and the woman now bleeding and unconscious in the driving seat.

The Dodge skidded to a halt and the man leaped out. He wrenched open the passenger door and stared at Meg for a second. Then he reached in and tried to grab her bag. But it was wrapped around her and he could not free it. He ripped the catch open and began searching for something.

The little truck roared up. The caretaker called to him. 'The police are on their way. I called them on my cell phone. You won't get far, buddy!'

A hundred yards away, along another avenue, a hearse and a procession of shiny black cars had slowed to see what was happening. Some people were starting to walk forward.

The man jumped back into his car and with the caretaker still shouting after him he raced in the direction of the exit.

It was only two hundred yards away. She had almost made it.

Thirty-nine

The control room at Portland police headquarters was kept locked from the inside.

No one was exactly sure why; someone said it was a precaution against anyone trying to take it over during a civil disturbance, which no one could quite envisage ever happening, but those who worked in the room liked to keep it secure nevertheless.

Half a dozen officers sat around radio consoles, taking calls from the cruisers which patrolled the city.

One had driven over to Evergreen Cemetery after a nine-one-one for police and paramedics and now he was reporting in. The control room logged it as both a ten-fifty-five, which was a car accident, and a PI, which meant a personal injury, then they passed it up to the Crimes Against Persons Unit on the fourth floor where Detective Scott Gleason took it.

Gleason was in his twenties, a recent recruit to the squad. He frowned as he listened to the control room. He took notes, then he called to his partner, Detective Roy Flynn.

'Hey, Roy, I think maybe we could take a look at this one. Woman attacked by some guy in the Evergreen Cemetery. He chased her round the damn place in a car until she crashed into a statue. They've taken her to the Maine Medical Centre.'

Flynn was grumpy and out of sorts. This was supposed to be a rest day after his stretch of overnights but they had called him in to do a middle shift, four to midnight, since somebody had gone down sick.

He looked at Gleason's notes, remembering that he had once been fresh and eager just like that, then he hauled himself out of the chair and went to the rack in the corner for his coat. 'OK,' he said, 'but you're driving.'

By the time they got to the cemetery, other police had arrived and had sealed off the area, including a grave site down one of the other avenues where the caretaker said the attack had taken place. The wrecked car, a Plymouth, lay against a statue of the Virgin Mary. Flynn looked up at her cool, impassive face. She had seen everything but she would not make much of a witness.

The caretaker was standing beside his pick-up truck with a uniformed officer who filled them in. Gleason and Flynn introduced themselves.

'Mack Perry,' the little man said. 'I'm in charge of this place.'

'Pretty big job,' Flynn said.

'Two hundred and thirty-nine acres,' Perry said for the second time today. 'You bet it's a big job.'

'So why don't you tell us what you saw?' Gleason said. He wore a wool-lined leather flying jacket and he stamped his feet in the cold.

'I just told it all to this guy.' Perry jerked a thumb in the direction of the uniformed officer.

'I know,' Flynn acknowledged, 'but we'd like to hear it for ourselves.'

'OK,' he said. 'This woman comes into the office a while ago and says she's looking for a place called Elmwood, that some friends of hers have moved there. I tell her I never heard of any place of that name, except the Elmwood here in the cemetery. I showed it to her on the map.'

'Map?' Flynn asked.

'Big map of the whole site. It's on the wall in the office. I have copies, too. I gave her one.'

'Then what?' Gleason asked.

'Well, then she went kind of quiet, asked me to look up the files and see who was buried in grave number twenty-three. So I did and I told her it was owned by a family called Everett. Right then I thought she was going to faint. I asked her if she was OK but she said it was the heat in the office – I keep it up kind of high, I like it that way – and then she left. I went out and watched where she went – she had acted very strange, you know – so then I got my coat and decided to follow but before that the phone rang and I had to deal with something first. By the time I got down to Elmwood, she was laying in the snow, struggling with this guy who had driven up there in a Dodge. I shouted at him and she managed to get away. I tried to grab hold of him but he knocked me down and then he went after her.'

'That was pretty noble of you,' Flynn commented, 'but a little reckless, Mr Perry, if you don't mind my saying so. The guy might have had a gun.'

'The prick,' Perry said. 'I don't like men hurting women. I just wanted to stop him. I got into my truck and followed. They went flying round here like it was a racetrack and the next thing she slams into this statue here.'

293

'What about her attacker? Did you see where he went?' Gleason queried.

'He got out and pulled the door of her car open. Appeared to me like he was looking for something. Then he drove off out of the cemetery and I didn't see after that.'

With his gloved hands, Flynn opened the door of the car. A sports bag lay on the back seat. He unzipped it and looked inside. There were clothes, a wash bag. Another officer came and spoke to Gleason who walked over to a patrol car and picked up the radio handset.

Flynn turned back towards the caretaker. 'Registration?'

Perry shook his head and looked sheepish. 'I should have got that, shouldn't I? But in the excitement, you know—'

Flynn squeezed his shoulder. 'Don't worry, Mr Perry, we'll find him. And anyway it looks like you saved this girl's life.'

Gleason came back. 'Hope so. Just getting a report on her condition. She seems to have hit her head hard and they're trying to find out how serious her injuries are. I've asked one of the patrolmen who went with her to stay there just in case.'

'Good thinking. Any idea who she is?'

'Yep. The car's a rental. It was picked up at Logan yesterday by a woman called Meg Winter. UK driving licence and an address in Ireland. Says on the form that she's staying at the Holiday Inn By The Bay.'

'What was that? What was her name again?'

'Meg Winter.'

'Christ!' Flynn said.

'What is it?'

'Shit. I got a weird call the other night from somebody who said he was ringing from Ireland. Said there was this woman called Winter staying at the Holiday Inn and she was in all sorts of danger. I thought it was some nut but I stopped by the Holiday Inn on my way home just in case. She had a reservation there OK but she hadn't checked in at that stage. I forgot about it after that.'

Another officer interrupted. 'Detective, we found these.'

He held out two plastic bags. Flynn took them from his hand and saw that one contained a pair of glasses that had been broken, snapped in two pieces right at the bridge. In the other bag there was a small black Nokia mobile phone.

'What's all this?' Flynn said.

'We found them over at the grave where the struggle happened.'

Flynn turned to Gleason. 'Let's go see.'

They got into their car and drove there. They parked and got out, careful not to get in the way of one of the crime scene boys who was moving around gingerly, using snow print wax to take casts of the clearer footprints.

Flynn looked at the dark gravestone. The daylight was going so he shone a torch. Flecks in the green marble glittered in its beam.

'Paul Everett,' he read. 'Marcia Everett. *Everett?* That name rings a bell.' He clapped his hands. 'Christ, I should have remembered when the caretaker said it. Damn, that was another name the guy mentioned on the phone. Something about fake letters and the murder of a guy called Everett.' He looked at the gravestone again. 'Jesus, Scott, let's get back to the office and try to find out what the hell we're into here.'

As they pulled into the early evening traffic on Stevens Avenue, Gleason radioed to say they were on their way in.

'Police in Belfast have been in contact with us about this woman who's in the hospital,' the voice at the other end told him.

'Belfast?' Gleason said. 'What the hell's it got to do with them?'

'That's where she's from,' Flynn said.

'Belfast?'

'Belfast, Ireland, dummy. Not Belfast, Maine.'

By the time they got back to Middle Street there were faxes for them to look at, photocopies of the criminal record of one Daniel Cochrane who had got two years for trying to burn down a hotel that had been built by the injured woman's father. According to the police in that other Belfast, the one across the Atlantic, it looked as if he had been stalking her.

'Maybe caught up with her, too,' Gleason said, studying the sheets.

'Hold on a minute,' Flynn said. 'There's something funny here.' He went to his computer terminal. 'Cochrane. Yeah – that's it. Cochrane. That was the name of the guy who phoned me.' He looked at Gleason and frowned. 'Now why in hell would somebody tell us about this woman, warn us about her safety and then attack her himself?'

Gleason threw up his hands. 'What can I say? He's Irish.'

Flynn snorted. 'Yeah. Aren't we all?'

He looked at his watch. It would be night in Ireland but he was going to have to try to call the contact numbers the Belfast police had left. In turn, they were going to have to tell this woman's relatives what had happened to her.

He rang and got someone called Detective Inspector Florence Gilmour and as he spoke to her he wondered idly what she looked like. He was on the phone for twenty minutes. When he had finished, he knew a lot more than before.

He sat back for a few moments, thinking.

Gleason said: 'Maybe we should go over to the Holiday Inn. There might be something in her room.'

Flynn nodded, then got up for their coats. 'You're right. And on the way, I'll fill you in on all of this.'

Assistant Manager Naomi Waitt was on duty.

She recognised Flynn but she frowned as she saw him and Gleason come in. There was a sense of purpose in their demeanour.

'Looking for your friend?' she said. 'I could try her room.' She checked the computer screen for the number.

'She's not in her room,' Flynn told her with certainty.

She glanced from Flynn to Gleason. 'I don't like the look of this.'

'You think we could have a peep inside the room?' Gleason asked.

She tensed. 'Now just a minute. Maybe you'd like to tell me what the problem is and how you know she's not here.'

'Because she's in the hospital,' Flynn said. 'Somebody tried to kill her.'

Naomi didn't bat an eyelid. 'I thought you told me there'd be no trouble,' she said, handing him a swipe card from a drawer.

'Not for you or the hotel,' he said. 'Tell me – has anyone been asking for her?'

'Just you, but I guess that doesn't count.'

They took the elevator to Meg's floor and let themselves in. The room was undisturbed, freshly made up.

Gleason opened drawers. 'Some clothes,' he said. 'That's all.'

'Where was she going with the bag?'

'Nothing much in here,' Gleason said from the bathroom. 'What about phone calls? Let's talk to that assistant manager again and see if she's made any.'

The telephone rang, as if on cue.

They looked at each other for a second, then Flynn picked it up but he did not say anything.

Naomi Waitt spoke to him. She was whispering. 'Hello, hello . . . are you there?'

'Yeah, we're here. What is it?'

'There's a man down here. He's asking what room Meg Winter's in.'

296

Forty

She began to regain consciousness in the ambulance, sensing its speed and hearing the scream of the siren.

She felt as if she were chained up but she understood why; American emergency procedures would be no different from British. They would have strapped her on to a spinal board and into a cervical collar with head restraints to keep her immobile, a precaution in case there was spinal cord injury which was a frequent consequence of road traffic accidents and, basically, that's what the crash in the cemetery was.

As soon as they got to her, they would have carried out their primary survey, following the universal ABCD system: A for 'airway', B for 'breathing', C for 'circulation', with control of any external haemorrhage, which instinct and pain told her she had. Last of all there was D for 'disability'. She wiggled her fingers and her toes and felt sure that she was not paralysed.

But she knew she must look a mess. The left side of her face ached and her mouth seemed twice its normal size. She moved her tongue around delicately, tasting the rusty tang of blood, and she wondered if she still had all her teeth. She was also having difficulty opening her left eye properly. The tissue round it felt heavy and hooded.

The ambulance stopped and she felt herself being placed on a gurney by the paramedics. They wheeled her in through big doors with the word 'EMERGENCY' lit over them. She saw the ceiling moving above her and the blurred faces of the medical staff peering down, asking her if she knew her name and where she was. She groaned groggy answers and then they told her not to try to talk any more.

She could hear someone say that you never knew with head injuries. She wanted to tell them they should look for any sign of a depressed fracture or any damage to the base of the skull, that they should ask the paramedics if they had found any blood or cerebrospinal fluid leaking from her ears. They would know, as she did, that the fact that she was conscious again was a good sign but not definitive; sometimes people suffering from intracranial bleeding, like a subdural haemorrhage, regained consciousness for a time, then lost it again. When that happened there was trouble.

With an awareness that was fragile, she listened to them and watched them work. They put sutures in her lip and above her eye but a local anaesthetic had made her face numb and she could not feel what they were doing. She would feel it later, that was for sure, when the anaesthetic wore off.

Finally they undressed her, releasing her from her wet, blood-ied clothes, and put her into a gown, then they left her in a bed in a curtained area from where she would be taken for further, more detailed examination.

'We're going to keep you here,' a nurse told her, 'just to make sure everything's OK. We've got you down for a CAT scan but don't worry about it. Your face has taken a beating and you'll look like you've gone ten rounds with Tyson for a while but there's nothing broken and we don't think there's anything more serious to worry about. It's just a precaution. So try to rest.'

The nurse pulled the curtain across and smiled at the patrol-man who had taken a seat just outside the cubicle. Thirty seconds later, when all hell broke loose, she and the patrolman and everyone else in the ER had forgotten about her.

Somewhere out in the sticks, a huge branch impossibly laden with ice had cracked off a tree and fallen across a school bus. The driver had lost control of the vehicle and it had tumbled off the road and into a storm drain. One child was dead; most of the rest were on their way in with injuries ranging from minor to very serious.

Then there was the truck driven by a seventy-year-old man who had fallen asleep at the wheel and rammed his vehicle at high speed into a tollbooth out on the turnpike, demolishing the structure and injuring himself and the toll attendant badly. They were on their way in, too.

Here and now, though, there was the fire: three children, all under eight, rescued with their mother from a house at Munjoy Hill which had gone up like matchwood. They had severe burns, the youngest child in particular.

The doors of the ER burst open and the first of what threat-ened to be an endless stream of casualties came in, to be met by trauma teams on full alert, their numbers augmented by staff from elsewhere in the hospital. Even the patrolman joined in to help with the fetching and carrying.

From her cubicle Meg listened to the familiar soundtrack of an emergency. She heard the clamour of voices, instructions being shouted and information being passed in tones that were terse and urgent, the messages precise. She heard the sound of equipment being moved in a hurry, the dull thud of feet running, the squeak of rubber soles on rubber floors. And there were the unique smells of the ER: cleanliness and sterility mingling with harsher odours, like the damp cloying smokiness she could sense now, coming in from the world outside. And from there, too, came the sounds of pain: the crying of children, the wailing of a grieving woman.

The curtain had left a little gap and she tried to lever herself up on one elbow to see what was going on, but without her glasses all she got was the impression of moving shapes. She lay down again. Her lips felt the size of cushions. Her ankle was very painful too, but she wasn't going to tell anyone about that, not just yet. They had more urgent tasks to attend to.

She felt a weariness weighing heavily on her and she told herself that was the shock taking hold. She needed rest; the nurse was right. And she needed to think about what had happened.

Someone had tried to kill her in that cemetery. She lay back on the pillow and closed her eyes.

In her mind, the doorway to her memory was opening and light was flooding in . . .

She had walked into her house that afternoon all those years ago, realising that she did not remember a single thing about the journey home. All she had seen while driving was her own rage and Noel Kennedy's face.

Well, it was done now, wasn't it?

'You bastard,' she said out loud and she didn't give a toss whether the neighbours heard her or not.

She poured herself a large vodka and tonic and paced round the tiny kitchen with the glass in her hand. She took the drink in gulps and finished it quickly.

'Not the appropriate remedy for stress, Dr Winter,' she said, looking at the empty glass. But she ignored herself and poured another, then she went and ran a bath. While the water thundered in, she sprinkled some aromatic oil over the surface, undressed and pinned her hair up.

The combination of the drink and the hot bath did not relax her; instead she felt supercharged and her heart was racing. Tomorrow she would think about what she had done and, perhaps more important, about what she was going to do now, but tonight she would go out somewhere. She felt the need to –

if not celebrate exactly – at least mark this occasion, whatever it was.

Half an hour later, she sat in her robe in the kitchen with the TV on, doing her nails. Carefully and evenly, she stroked each one with the soft varnish brush. The task calmed her and she started to think about what had happened.

She saw Kennedy's office. Her resignation letter. But she didn't want to think about any of that.

She got up abruptly and poured herself another drink. It was important to maintain the buzz. If she were to let it die, that would be a disaster. It would mean thoughts of regret, self-recrimination, more anger and the feeling that Kennedy was right. Maybe she *was* too impetuous.

Look where it's got you.

She brushed the thought away, blew on her nails and drank some more.

The local news programme had an item about an event at the Clarendon Dock, some kind of blues night. There were shots of a marquee where the bar would be and on a stage with the word Guinness emblazoned all over it, a band was rehearsing.

The reporter was a young woman who stood with her back to Belfast Lough, the wind blowing her hair into her eyes.

'From seven o'clock tonight there'll be bands from all over Ireland at what promises to be a great night for blues fans young and old. There'll also be a special mystery guest and word has it that it will be none other than Belfast's own Van Morrison.'

Clarendon Dock was part of an area earmarked for upmarket redevelopment, peace and tranquillity permitting. Meg had never been there; that whole corner of the city was a mystery to her. But why not go tonight? It would be somewhere to have some fun and get lost in the crowd.

A spot of company would be good, though. She picked up the phone and dialled a number. 'Elizabeth? Hi, it's Meg. How are you?'

'Well now, here's a surprise. Where the hell have you been for the past six months?'

'It hasn't been that long.'

'It has, you know. I thought you'd forgotten about me.'

'No – how could I do that? I just didn't get around to phoning, that's all.'

'I tried you a couple of times,' Elizabeth told her, 'but then I just gave up on you.'

'Oh, Elizabeth, I'm sorry. Do you still love me?' she implored in a poor-little-me voice, then giggled.

'What are you on about? Have you been on the sauce?'

'Just a bit. To deaden what has been a dreadful day. Listen, I really would like to go out somewhere tonight and wipe away all memory of it, thank you very much. Want to come with me?'

'That depends. What had you in mind?'

'There was a thing on the news just now. That Clarendon Dock place – have you ever been?'

'Is it down at the docks?'

'Well, it would be, wouldn't it?'

'Heard of it,' Elizabeth said, 'but I've never been there.'

'Well then, do you fancy going tonight? There's some big blues thing on – not that it's my kind of music exactly – but it might be fun. Van the man and all. And ... and, well, there's things I have to tell you.'

'Such as?'

'Mmm ... I'll save it until later. It would take too long.'

'Juicy?'

'Yeah, well – depends on your point of view.'

Temptation plus a lifetime of friendship did the trick. They arranged to meet at Clarendon Dock at nine thirty.

Meg left her house at eight, after vodka number four, and walked along the Lisburn Road to the Chelsea wine bar. The evening was warm. She was wearing a jacket over a short dress with a low neckline and as she walked into the bar the bow-tied bouncers at the front door eyed her with a mixture of appreciation and curiosity. A woman going into a pub alone was a rare enough thing in this city.

Once inside, no one noticed her much. The place was crowded with people who were either out early or who had not yet gone home from work. She ordered a glass of wine and sat with it and the *Belfast Telegraph* thinking, *why the hell not*. If a man could do this, come into a pub and have a quiet drink, then why couldn't she? She was a professional woman with a responsible job ... except, she reminded herself, now she didn't have one. Sinking feelings began to return. She left and got a taxi to the Clarendon Dock.

The cab driver dropped her at the end of Pilot Street. 'This is as far as I can go, love. They have it all blocked off down there with them hamburger vans and everything.'

She got out. Somebody was singing about his 'Sweet Home Chicago', the thud of the bass line bouncing off stone walls.

'Will I be able to get a taxi back?' she said, counting out change from her handbag.

'It's kinda hard,' he told her. 'But sometimes the people who run these things organise a free bus back into the city and everybody gets taxis from there.'

'That'll do me,' she said and gave him a decent tip with the fare.

'Thanks very much, love.' He grinned at her and ground the gears into reverse. 'Enjoy yourself now. Don't do anything I wouldn't.'

There was a gate into the dock and an entrance fee of six pounds. Hamburgers were sizzling on a grill in the open air and she could smell fried onions, too. She was starved. She bought a burger with lots of mustard and walked on in.

One way or another, there were a couple of hundred people scattered round the site, sitting on steps, lined up three or four deep at the bar in the marquee or just standing in front of the stage listening to the music. Most were drinking Guinness out of plastic pint tumblers.

She looked at the band. There was a grizzled, grey-bearded bass player with a pony tail and a kind of fez. Beside him, the lead guitarist's face seemed pained with the effort of hauling strings of notes out of an instrument reluctant to give them up.

After the first couple of bites, the burger turned rapidly from an object of desire into a greasy mess. She dropped the remains into a litter bin and headed for the bar where she ordered a half-pint of Guinness. When in Rome and all that.

By ten o'clock, she had had a second one and at last she had to admit she was feeling a bit drunk. She was not noticeably out of her head, she was sure of that, and not loaded enough to stop. Not just yet.

She was also getting tired of looking round for Elizabeth who had still not appeared and now, damn it, it was starting to rain. She had seen that there was a bar over on her right: Pat's Bar, it was called. She pushed her way across the courtyard towards it, thinking that she should get there quickly before everyone else had the same idea.

The pub was small and dark and crammed full of people. A couple of women were standing outside the ladies' so she fell in behind them. As she waited, her gaze roamed over the walls. Faded theatre bills were mounted alongside signed black and white pictures of actors long since forgotten.

When she came out of the lavatory, she heard a woman's laugh. It was a hearty, natural laugh and she looked instinctively for its owner, thinking that if Elizabeth turned up it would not occur to her to come in here. At a table in a corner a dark-haired woman in black trousers and black jacket was sitting beside a young man in a smart office suit. A mobile phone lay on the table with their drinks and they looked as if they had come straight from work.

Meg went to the bar and got another half-pint, watching them out of idle curiosity. Another man joined them. Meg thought they might be lawyers. Doctors, maybe. The world was full of them. Even out-of-work doctors.

She could hear their conversation. 'So – did you find out?' the first man was asking.

'Yeah – he won't be appearing,' the newcomer said.

'He's not? Ah, that's crap. What's the problem?'

'Some contractual hassle, apparently. He's doing a concert in Botanic Gardens in a couple of weeks and the deal is that he can't appear anywhere in the vicinity within a certain time limit either side. Bit of a bummer that, isn't it?'

'Too bloody right,' the first man said. 'Shit, that's the only reason I came.' He downed his drink, then stood. 'Right then, I'm off.'

'Me too,' the second one said. 'What about you?' They looked at the woman. 'You coming?'

She shook her head. 'Not just yet. I'll finish my drink.' She had a tall glass with something icy. She lifted the mobile and gave a little smile. 'I'm waiting for a call anyway.'

'Oh, very secretive,' one of the men said and grinned. 'OK, then, we'll see you tomorrow.'

They kissed her on the cheek and left. As they opened the door Meg could see that it was pouring outside.

The blues burst in. *I went down to the crossroads. Got down on my knees.'*

She had been standing for a long time and she was tired of it. There was only one place where she could sit. She took her drink over to the table.

'Excuse me, do you mind if I sit here?'

The woman gave her a quick once-over and a smile that looked slightly amused. 'Help yourself.'

'Thanks. Hope I'm not disturbing you.'

'Not at all.'

They sat for a couple of minutes, sipping their drinks, not speaking, alone in their separate worlds. The room was buzzing in Meg's head. She could feel the woman watching her.

'On your own then?'

'Sorry?'

'Out on your own?' the woman said.

Meg made a face. 'Sort of. I was supposed to meet a friend but she didn't show and I'm not going out into that rain to look for her.' She gestured at the vacant seats. 'I see your friends have abandoned you.'

303

The woman smiled. 'A couple of colleagues. Friends from work. We really only came because we heard Van Morrison would be on. Apparently it's a false alarm.' She twisted her glass which was empty now. She gave Meg a quizzical look. 'Listen, I'm going to the bar to get myself a drink. Will you join me in something?'

Meg looked at her, trying to read the offer. Was she coming on to her? If she was, she would not get very far. She should say no. But she hesitated instead.

It was only a drink; that was all. She could look after herself.

'Sure, why not. But I think I've had it with the Guinness. A vodka and tonic would be nice.'

Forty-one

Flynn and Gleason came down in the elevator and walked out into the lobby.

The man was standing at the desk, looking through leaflets about guided trails in the Maine woods and ferries to Nova Scotia while the receptionist made a pretence of trying to get through to the room.

He had not seen them yet so they were able to get a good look. He was in his late twenties or thereabouts, wearing jeans and a waterproof jacket that would not do much to keep out the cold. Flynn remembered that the caretaker had said the man in the cemetery had worn a brown wool coat.

Naomi Waitt was at the end of the desk and when she saw them she gave an almost imperceptible nod in his direction. They spread out. Flynn approached from the right, Gleason on the left.

'Excuse me, sir,' Flynn said.

The man looked round.

Flynn reached into his pocket and held out his shield. 'Police officer. Could we have a word with you?'

The stranger spotted Gleason now. He began to look alarmed.

'You were asking about Meg Winter,' Flynn said.

'Yes.' The man stared at them. 'Oh God, has something happened to her?'

'And you are?'

'My name's Dan Cochrane. Look, has anything happened to Meg?'

'Where're you from, Mr Cochrane?' Flynn asked.

'Ireland – Northern Ireland.'

'Could I possibly see some ID?'

Cochrane put his hand to his pocket. The two policemen stiffened. Gleason's right hand moved nearer his belt holster.

'Slowly, if you don't mind,' Flynn said.

Cochrane took his passport out and handed it to him.

'What's your connection with Miss Winter?' Gleason said, while Flynn studied it.

'I'm a friend. I came here to warn her that she's in danger. The night before last I called the police to tell them.'

'Excuse me, gentlemen,' Naomi Waitt said. 'Is it possible you could have this conversation somewhere else? Somewhere a little more discreet, maybe?' She pointed over her shoulder. 'There's an office back here if you want.'

Flynn paused. Other people in the lobby were looking. 'Maybe you could come with us to headquarters, Mr Cochrane.'

Cochrane did not respond directly. Instead he said: 'Do you know where Meg is?'

'Yes, we do.'

'I'm not going anywhere until I know where she is.'

Flynn looked at him. 'She's in the hospital.'

'Hospital? What happened? Is she all right?'

'Somebody attacked her out at the Evergreen Cemetery.'

'Where? A cemetery? I don't understand.'

'And neither do we. But maybe you could help us in that regard,' Flynn said.

He grasped Cochrane's arm but felt resistance.

'Are you arresting me?' Cochrane said. 'Do you think it was me? Damn it, I didn't attack her – I was the one who tried to tell you people something was going to happen. Look, is she all right?'

'As far as we know,' Flynn said, 'but if you come downtown with us maybe we can sort all this out.'

He relaxed his grip. Cochrane nodded. 'OK,' he said.

They put him in an interview room and a uniformed officer sat with him for a few minutes while Gleason got a cruiser to bring Mack Perry in and Flynn got an identity parade organised.

Then they went back to him. Flynn asked if he would like anything.

'Water. I could use a drink of water.'

Gleason got some from the cooler, then they sat down across the little table from him.

'OK, Mr Cochrane,' Flynn said. 'The first thing to tell you is that the Irish police have been in touch with us. Somebody found pictures of this woman Winter in your apartment, pictures apparently taken under kind of strange circumstances, like they were surveillance photos or something. They've sent us a copy of your criminal record, too. We know you did a jail term for the fire at the hotel built by Miss Winter's father's construction company – so they've made a bit of a connection there, you understand. I'm sure you can see it. Like – she flies to the US, you follow her—'

'Which seems to be a habit of yours,' Gleason butted in.

'—and then, hey presto, some guy attacks her in the cemetery. Now us . . .' he gestured to Gleason and himself, '. . . we can't make head nor tail of any of this so I figure that the best thing is for you to explain it from your point of view. Know what I mean? Tell me how you feel about that.'

Cochrane looked from one to the other. 'It might take a while.'

'Don't worry about it,' Gleason told him. 'We've got all night.'

That, Flynn reflected ruefully, was probably true.

Cochrane sighed. 'Jesus, where do I start?' Then he plunged straight in. 'Her father, you see, Sam Winter, he was involved with the bank that took my mother's farm because she couldn't pay her debts. Then the bank sold the land to another company he was connected to and he built the hotel. My mother became ill and died. I blamed Winter for everything: ruining my mother's life, killing her. The night of her funeral I got drunk and tried to set fire to the place.'

Flynn nodded. Apart from what was on record, Detective Inspector Gilmour had given him other parts of the story.

Cochrane went on. 'I saw Meg being interviewed on television talking about what had happened to her: the coma she'd been in for four years, the accident, the murder of this man Paul Everett.' He looked at them as if they might not understand and therefore he should explain. 'I spoke to someone on the phone the other night and tried to tell him all of this.'

'As a matter of fact, you spoke to me,' Flynn said.

'Then you know what I'm talking about.'

'I think so,' Flynn told him. Florence Gilmour had gone over that part with him, too, and there had been a lot of stuff about letters and airline tickets.

'When I got out of prison, I was working in my friend Peter Quinn's place, his pottery. Meg and her friend came in. I didn't recognise her at first: her hair was shorter than before, when she'd been on television. But then she ordered something, a present for her mother, and gave me her name and address. The name was on her credit card, too. I knew who she was then.'

He looked at them, confusion in his eyes. 'I . . . I don't know what went through my mind at that moment. I was still feeling very bitter, so much hatred about the past and the fact that because I had a prison record my life was ruined now, too. Meg seemed to . . . to be just handed to me, like some kind of opportunity. In a flash I saw this as some way I could get back at Sam Winter. Exactly how – well, I had no idea – but I thought that if I got to know her, then maybe there was a way of finding out something about him, something I could use for my own purposes. I wanted justice, you see. And there was Meg herself, of course, his beloved daughter. He would be vulnerable where she was concerned.' He shook his head. 'God, I must have been crazy.'

Flynn stared at him and for a few seconds his mind strayed to the problems in his own painful life.

He saw the face of his wife and the face of the man she had gone to live with in Philadelphia. He thought of how much he had hated that man when he had taken her from him and how he had begun to dream up ways of getting to him, to exact some sort of punishment for what he had done.

At one point, when his grief and anger could plunge no further, he had even thought of killing him.

But then he had come to his senses.

He looked at Cochrane and saw in his pale face the despair he himself had once felt. *Crazy*, Cochrane had said. Maybe. But maybe it was not the craziness of a psychotic killer or a homicidal maniac; more the anger that came from a desperate loneliness, from a life and a future destroyed.

'There was a bit of a commotion in the shop,' Cochrane went on. 'Her friend's child nearly broke something. When she wasn't looking I took her credit card, then I turned up at her house the next day, saying she'd dropped it. I wanted to see where she lived, what her home circumstances were like. After that I decided to follow her and I took pictures. I used my own car, not the pottery van, so she wouldn't notice. I thought that if I shadowed her I would see what sort of a person she was, maybe find some weakness, something I could use.'

He sipped his water and finished it. 'Could I have some more?'

Gleason obliged.

'I followed her to the place where Paul Everett had worked and then I followed her to where the accident happened. When she got there she fell down a bank in the woods. She might have been hurt but I saw that she was OK. I really wanted to help her but I couldn't. How could I have explained what I was doing there? So instead I just watched, taking pictures. Christ, how creepy is that?'

Neither Flynn nor Gleason commented. They waited for the rest.

'But then the more I saw of her after that, the more my attitude changed. I could see how lonely she was, how vulnerable. She didn't seem to have any friends; she was always doing things on her own. And being a bit solitary myself, I began to

308

have an idea of how she must feel and how strange and unwelcoming the world must look to her.'

He paused. They said nothing, letting him take his time, but as Flynn looked at him he knew that whatever Cochrane's motives had been then, harming Meg Winter wasn't on his agenda now. He and Gleason were listening to a difficult love affair here, not a murder plot.

'I was watching her the night she ran away from that guy Noel Kennedy,' Cochrane continued.

Gleason held up a hand as if stopping the traffic. 'Now, wait a second. Noel Kennedy? Who's this?'

'Meg once had an affair with him. He's the medical director of Belfast Central Hospital. It turns out he'd been calling her on the phone, then hanging up. He followed her one night when she'd been shopping. She ran away from him. I saw what was going on and stepped in to help.'

Gleason was scribbling on a pad. 'Noel Kennedy. Central Hospital. Better ask our friends in Ireland to see where he was this afternoon.'

Cochrane looked at them in disbelief. 'It couldn't have been him.'

'How can you be sure?' Flynn asked.

Cochrane had no answer.

'So that night,' Flynn said, 'what happened?'

'After that, well, everything changed. After that, all I could do was think about her. I wasn't concerned about her father any more, or of getting back at him – any of the obsessions of the past. I'd seen her threatened, or so I thought, and I wanted to protect her, to . . . to love her.'

Flynn saw Cochrane's surprise at what he had just said. 'Did you tell her that – that you loved her?'

Maybe if he'd told his wife that. Maybe if—

'No,' Cochrane said. 'Tonight – that's the first time I've said that.'

Gleason broke the mood. 'So then did you – did you, like, get it on with her?'

Cochrane tensed. 'Our relationship developed, yes.' He turned to Flynn as a more sympathetic listener. 'But I knew there were risks, that there was a possibility she might find out who I was. If her father heard my name, well, it would all be over then. I didn't want it to end like that so I decided to call a halt before that happened. We'd argued. That gave me the chance to back off. I knew she'd be upset but it was nothing to what she'd feel if she discovered who I really was and what I'd done.'

309

'So when did this happen? When are we talking about?' Flynn queried.

'Just before Christmas. But damn it, I missed her. So a few nights ago I decided to tough it out and tell her the truth. I told myself that maybe she'd forgive me, that it was worth a try. At any rate, I couldn't live with this thing any longer. So on Thursday morning I called her. That was when I discovered she was on her way to Boston. She was in a hurry and hadn't time to talk. I called the airport to check on flight times and drove straight there in the hope that I might be able to catch her but by the time I arrived she'd already checked in and gone to the international departure lounge. It was no good.'

'So then you flew to Boston yourself?' Gleason asked.

'I drove back to Belfast first and went to her house. I had a key. I wanted to see if I could find out where to reach her when she got to Portland because I knew this was where she was going. And that was when I found this. It must have been delivered after she'd gone.'

He put his hand in his pocket and handed a letter to them.

'The TV company forwarded it to her. It's from Laurence Everett – the real one.'

Flynn unfolded the flimsy paper. The date was at the top and an address in New Hampshire. He read aloud:

'Dear Meg Winter

I saw you on TV this morning talking about my son. You disgusting bitch. What gives you the right to go on there and rake it all up again? My son and my wife are dead because of you. Paul's murder ruined her health and there you are on TV, whining about losing your memory. Why were you spared when he was not? Why did someone kill him and not you? I know what kind of person you are. You're lying, lying to the world. You're a doctor and doctors can get hold of drugs. What did you do to him? If he hadn't got mixed up with you he wouldn't be dead. I will go to my grave believing that. God won't forgive you for what you've done. You'll rot in hell.

Yours sincerely

Laurence Everett'

Sincerely, Flynn thought, was an interesting touch. He asked, 'How do we know this is the real deal?'

310

'Because I rang him. I got international inquiries to find his number – his address is on the letter – and I spoke to him. It was early in the morning in New Hampshire and I woke him. He wasn't too happy about it but from the conversation I had, oh, he's Laurence Everett all right.'

'His wife's buried with her son in Evergreen Cemetery,' Flynn said.

'I know. He told me. I don't quite understand how he managed to see Meg on TV, though. It was an interview on British television so how would he get it here?'

Flynn looked at Gleason. 'We should check the local affiliates, see how come they were running this item. The date's on the letter.'

'Look, I've been straight with you,' Cochrane said. 'What happened in that cemetery?'

Flynn explained and he included in his brief narrative Mack Perry's account of his conversation with Meg.

A uniformed officer came in. 'We're ready for you now.'

'Ready for what?' Cochrane asked.

'We want you to take part in a line-up,' Flynn said.

'What – you still think I did it?'

'What I think doesn't matter,' Flynn said as they led him into another room. 'It's evidence that we go on here.'

There were four other men, approximately Cochrane's height and build. Gleason made him stand second from the right, then they went into an ante-room with a darkened window. Flynn stood beside it with Mack Perry and began to explain the procedure.

Perry interrupted. 'You know, I did this once before. There were some kids vandalising the cemetery. I had to pick them out.'

'Then you know the score. So when I pull up this blind I want you to tell me if you see the man who attacked the woman today.'

Perry looked. 'Nah,' he said almost immediately.

'Now take your time about this.'

'I don't need to. The guy's not there. He was older than these people. Mid-forties, I'd say.'

They went back to the interview room. Cochrane was brought in. 'Well?'

'OK,' Flynn said, 'you'll be glad to hear that we don't consider you a suspect.'

Cochrane sighed. 'That's a relief.'

'But we do need all the help you can give us on this.'

'Meg got letters,' he said. 'Letters that were supposed to be

311

from the Everetts. I saw one of them. It said Paul had been writing to his parents about her before the accident. Then she got a plane ticket. Someone wanted her here so they could kill her. I bet the guy who attacked her today is the guy who killed Paul Everett four years ago. As long as Meg was in a coma, he was OK, but as soon as she recovered she became a risk.'

'But why lure her over here?' Gleason said. 'Why not kill her in Ireland?'

The three of them thought about that, then Cochrane said: 'Maybe because this is where he lives. Listen, she would have brought the letters with her, wouldn't she? She didn't leave them at home – I looked. Did you find them among her belongings?'

Gleason groaned.

'What's the problem?' Cochrane asked.

'The guy in the cemetery,' Flynn explained. 'The caretaker said that when the car crashed he opened the door and seemed to be looking for something. Her things are in a bag in the evidence locker. We'd better check but I would lay odds we won't find them.'

Gleason left the room on what they knew was a pointless errand and in a few minutes he was back to confirm the fact. 'I'll try the hospital,' he said. 'We need to find out if we can talk to her yet. You never know, maybe there's something in her pockets.'

'There's another thing,' Cochrane said. 'You see, those letters didn't just arrive out of the blue. They were a reply to a letter Meg sent in the first place. She wrote to Everett's parents because she wanted to find out more about their son.'

Flynn sat up. 'Then how did she get an address?'

Before Cochrane could answer, they were interrupted by Gleason on the phone. 'Now, wait just a minute, say that again – she's got a visitor?'

'Jesus,' Flynn said. 'Where's that cop we sent?'

He hit the door running.

Forty-two

She was in a half-world between sleep and wakefulness, between the past and the present.

She could feel the pain in her face now and her ankle was agony.

She tried to see. There was just a pinpoint glimmer of light through the swollen flesh over her left eye. The vision in her right fought to compensate.

Perfume. She could smell perfume.

There was a shape. Someone standing beside the bed, holding something.

'My ankle,' she mumbled. 'It's very painful. I think I've sprained it.'

She squinted up at the figure, wondering if it was a nurse or a doctor.

Sitting there in Pat's Bar, it had been like turning on a tap.

Amid the noise and laughter of the crowded pub, Meg sat with this woman, a complete stranger, and poured her heart out. Kennedy, the job, the lot. She didn't know whether the woman was interested or not but she certainly seemed to be. She was a good listener and Meg wanted to talk.

It was the drink, of course, otherwise she wouldn't have dreamed of gabbling on like this. Somewhere in her mind, where what was left of her good sense lingered, she knew that tomorrow's hangover would bring embarrassment when she remembered.

'You've had a bad day,' the woman said when she had finished.

'The worst,' Meg agreed.

'It'll work out all right. You'll get another job. There are lots of hospitals.'

'Northern Ireland's a small place. Word gets around.'

'You don't have to stay here. You're young. With your skills, you could go anywhere in the world.'

As Meg pondered on the thought, the mobile phone rang.

'It might be for me,' she scoffed and drank some of her vodka. 'Some big emergency down at the hospital and they can't do without me. Ha! I don't think.'

The woman smiled at her and lifted the phone. She put her hand over one ear to keep out the din.

Somebody was telling her something. 'Oh really? Really . . . fantastic,' she said. 'Fabulous news.' There was a pause. 'Well, let's see – I can be there in half an hour. Who's with you?' She listened. 'Sounds good. Oh, and wait a minute . . .' She glanced at Meg and smiled, then she said into the phone, 'That gives me an idea.'

She turned away and Meg could not make out the rest of what she was saying.

'I'd better go,' Meg said, pushing back her chair. 'I'm in your way. Thanks for the drink. Sorry about laying all my worries on you.'

The woman put the phone in her bag, then reached out and touched Meg's arm. 'No, wait, don't go like that. That would never do at all. Listen, my dear Dr Winter, you need a bit of cheering up so here's an idea. That was a close friend of mine on the phone. He's got a few friends in at his place. He's had a bit of good news, something to celebrate. It's a rather private, very select little party, better than this bedlam. I think you'd enjoy it. So what do you say?'

Meg looked at her. 'But I wouldn't know anyone.'

'So what? Maybe that's a good thing.'

Meg thought, although not for long. She did not want to go home just yet. Home, where she would be alone.

'We'll never get a taxi,' she said.

'I've got a car.'

It was parked a couple of hundred yards away and they ran to it in the rain with their jackets over their heads, shrieking now and then as they stepped in a puddle. As the woman started the engine Meg realised she did not seem to be drunk.

'Are you OK to drive?' she ventured.

'Fine. I was coasting back there. Just a couple of spritzers. I'll make up for it in a minute. There'll be champagne.' She flashed a smile. 'And who knows what else.'

They drove through the wet streets with the wipers on fast speed, by-passing the city centre and heading south, onto the Malone Road then out into the countryside past Barnett's Park. They crossed a set of traffic lights and the woman clicked on her left indicator, turning into what looked to Meg like a Protestant housing estate. Bunting was strung from lamp-posts, kerbstones were red, white and blue, and flags

314

with the red hand of Ulster hung limp and damp from darkened windows.

'Wait a minute,' Meg said. 'This is weird. Where are we going?'

The woman gave a little laugh. 'Don't panic. It'll be all right in a minute.'

They drove past better housing now and came to what seemed to be a dead end. But then Meg saw an entrance on the right and a sign saying 'IN'. The car turned towards it, rumbling over rough stones, and the headlights lit up a wooden sign in front of some low buildings.

'Ardnavalley Scout Activity Centre,' she read aloud. 'Come on, what is this? Where the hell are you taking me?'

'No, wait. Just hang on. You'll see.'

They drove up to a set of low wrought iron gates, beside which stood an intercom. The woman lowered her window and pressed the button.

A man replied, his voice tinny from the speaker. 'Yo!'

'Hi, it's me,' the woman said. 'We're here.'

There was a buzz and a click and the gates swung open slowly. They drove in, along a winding avenue lined on the left by a row of tall trees and on the right by a high wooden fence which separated the property from the grounds outside. There were big shrubs and rhododendron bushes and at the head of a long, sloping lawn stood a huge white country house with lights from hidden lamps playing up on it.

A big, broad flag, sodden and miserable in the rain, drooped from a pole set into the wall and as the wind took it for a second Meg saw that it was the stars and stripes of the United States of America.

'Jesus,' she said. 'Where are we?'

The woman laughed again. 'Welcome to the good old US of A. Or at least to a teeny weeny bit of it.'

'What is this place?'

They drove round to the back of the house. Meg saw two cars: a big Mercedes and a small red sports car, an MGB, with a soft top.

'This is the home of the American Consul,' the woman said, turning the engine off. 'He's the friend I was telling you about. Come on.'

She got out and Meg followed her to a solid wooden door almost tucked away and strangely tiny for such a big house. It opened as they approached and a man stood silhouetted in the light from inside. He was in shirtsleeves with his tie loosened.

'Hi. You got here.'

315

Meg heard the American accent. The woman threw her arms round him and they kissed, full on the lips.

'This is Meg,' the woman said. 'We met tonight. She's had a bad day and she's in need of a bit of TLC. I told you I might bring her along.'

'Great,' the man said. 'I'm Matt Ross.' He shook Meg's hand. 'Come on in.'

They stepped into the hall and she got a better look at him, seeing a man in his early forties, not tall, but solid and fit, with dark eyes and hair and a beard that was not much more than stubble. She cast a quick glance around. On one wood-panelled wall there was the American seal, on another a portrait of the President and framed letters from previous holders of that office to previous consuls in Belfast. From a room somewhere beyond, Bruce Springsteen was being played loudly.

'Matt's the Consul,' the woman explained.

Ross held his hands up in surrender and smiled. 'Off duty right now. Just relaxing with a few friends after an eventful and historic night. Come in and meet them. We'll get you girls a drink.'

Meg felt damp and bedraggled and she knew her hair would be a mess. 'Can I use your bathroom first?'

'Sure.' He pointed up the stairs and told her where it was. 'Join us when you're ready. Just follow the noise.'

In the bathroom, Meg looked at herself in the mirror and asked her bleary reflection what the hell she was doing here. It was like she had stepped into another world. But then again, she reasoned, as she fixed her make-up and brushed her hair, it was different, wasn't it, a bit of fun, which was what she'd wanted, and what was the harm?

She walked back downstairs, then paused and smoothed her hands down her skirt. Through a partly open door, voices and laughter mingled with the music. She pushed the door open and walked in.

'It's – ah – Meg, right?' Ross said when he saw her enter.

'Yes.'

'We're drinking champagne. OK with you?'

'Terrific,' she said as he handed her a fluted crystal glass that twinkled with a drink she did not need.

It was a big, comfortable sitting room. In an open fireplace, logs flickered. Ross and the woman, Meg could see, were an item. The kiss at the door had said as much and the way they draped themselves around each other now confirmed it.

There were two other men in the room. 'This is Paul,' Ross said, gesturing to a tall young man reclining on a settee with his

316

shoes off, wriggling his toes to music which was not Springsteen any longer but had become an old Steely Dan track.

He smiled up at her from under an untidy quiff. 'Hi. How're
you doing?' He was an American, too.

'And this is Chris.'

Over by the fire, a lean man in his mid-thirties looked at her
from under hooded brows. He was smugly handsome and
expensively dressed and instinctively she did not like him. He
came over to her. 'Pleased to meet you,' he said. She heard an
Ulster accent and saw a smile that was a leer.

She glanced round and caught the woman looking on with
amused curiosity.

Through the alcoholic fog it dawned on her.

She had allowed herself to be picked up; that was it.

'Why don't we go and sit down?' the man called Chris said,
indicating a settee. 'You can tell me all about yourself.'

'No, I'm fine here just for the moment, thanks.'

She would have been seen as an unattached woman, a bit
drunk, looking for uncomplicated fun, a few more drinks. Sex
would not have been out of the question either.

They were looking at her.

Sex with all of them, maybe. Who could tell what kind of a
party this was.

She was the right sort of social band, too, not just any old slut.
That would have been attractive.

'You're a doctor, I hear,' Chris said.

She watched his eyes drift down towards her neckline and the
upper swell of her breasts.

'Yes, I am.'

'Interesting. Do you kind of *specialise* in anything?' he asked,
raising an eyebrow, and she knew he wasn't talking about
medicine.

She said, 'Venereal diseases – syphilis, gonorrhoea – that sort
of thing. I get to meet all kinds of pricks and assholes.'

She sipped her drink, enjoying the taste and his startled
expression. The man on the settee began to laugh. 'Beautiful,' he
said, 'just beautiful. Your move, Chris.'

There was a champagne bottle on the coffee table beside the
settee, resting on an orderly pile of American periodicals: the
New Yorker, *Forbes* magazine, *Political Science Quarterly*. Meg
refilled her glass and waved the bottle. 'Want some?'

'Yeah, why not,' the man called Paul said and straightened
up.

She fell, more than sat, beside him.

The fire was hot, the champagne potent. Chris watched from

317

a distance, looking morose and unsteady. Ross and the other woman had lost interest for the moment. Glasses in hand, they were dancing to *Do It Again*, keeping their bodies apart, except for occasional, tantalising collisions.

'She . . .' she pointed. 'What's-her-face . . . she said this was a celebration.'

'Yeah, it is. Nobody tell you? Matt here's been made a big offer. He's going to be the right-hand man to the next President of the United States.'

'Really? And who's that?'

'His brother. Senator Aiden Ross.'

Meg shrugged. 'Never heard of him.'

Paul laughed. 'Oh you will. Believe me, you will.'

'Well, then,' Meg said, 'here's to the both of them.' They clinked their glasses and drank.

Across the room, Chris folded himself into a chair, sulking.

'You want to watch him,' Paul said. 'He usually gets what he wants. He doesn't like it when he doesn't.'

'Fuck him.'

'Yeah, well, I think that's kinda what he had in mind.'

She giggled and put an arm round his shoulders. 'I like you. You're nice.'

He turned to her with a smile. 'I should tell you I'm also gay.'

'Then maybe that's why you're nice. No big macho come-on. No big swinging dick stuff.'

'And who's to say?' He pretended to be indignant and they laughed again.

After that they talked for a bit and he explained who they all were. They were in various kinds of business, apart from Ross, the consul. He used to be in the CIA apparently and she thought that was interesting but she was becoming too drunk to take much of it in and she was finding it hard to finish her thoughts and her sentences.

She slumped deeper into the settee, put her head back and closed her eyes. The music thumped behind her. Steely Dan were singing about drinking whisky and dying behind the wheel.

'Paul?'

She opened her eyes and looked up. Ross was standing at the door. Chris and the woman were nowhere to be seen.

'Sure. Be right there.' Paul looked at her. 'Back in a minute.' He winked. 'A little something to attend to.'

For just a second she wondered what was going on, then she sloped sideways and fell asleep almost instantly.

★ ★ ★

318

She woke because the music had stopped.

As she tried to blink her eyes into focus, she did not know whether she had been asleep for moments or hours.

She felt cold, in spite of the fire. It was still crackling so perhaps she had not been out for long. A headache was beginning to rumble like far off thunder and her mouth tasted really bad. She wanted to go home.

She was alone in the room. She had to find a phone, order a taxi.

Her bag. What had she done with it? The bathroom – that's right. She must have left it there.

She stood up, light-headed and a bit queasy, and staggered to the door, bumping against a table and knocking a glass over. It fell, spilling champagne on to the thick carpet, but she left it where it was – *who cares* – and went out into the hall. The bathroom was upstairs somewhere; she remembered that.

As she put her hand on the banisters she heard voices coming from another room. She should tell them what she was doing, that she was going home.

She opened the door and found herself in a dining room heavy with old furniture. The dark polished table was long and narrow and she saw the three of them sitting at the end of it, huddled over something. As her vision and her brain groped towards understanding, she realised it was a mirror and that Paul was arranging white lines of powder on its surface with the aid of a Swiss army knife.

They stared at her, caught as if she had shone a bright light on them.

For a moment they looked uncertain what to do, knowing that she had seen and that she recognised what she had seen.

Then Paul smiled and said: 'Come in. Join the club. Want to try some?'

She shook her head. To her surprise she found that she was shocked.

'Suit yourself,' he said. 'You don't know what you're missing.' Then he bent his head to one of the lines and vacuumed it up through a candy-striped drinking straw. He gave a final, almost defiant snort, and pinched his nostrils to seal the cocaine in.

'Need to find a phone,' she mumbled.

She backed out of the room and hurried upstairs to get her bag but she could not remember which door was the bathroom and she tried two doors before she found the right one.

She felt afraid. What if the police came? Forget the phone. She would walk and find a taxi somewhere along the road.

The bag was over on the floor beside the washbasin. She bent down to pick it up.

When she turned, Chris was standing at the door.

She started. 'You made me jump.'

'What are you doing?'

'Going home. Have to get a taxi.' She walked to the door but he stood in her way.

'Come back downstairs. You should try it. It's just a bit of fun. No harm in it.'

She looked at him. His face was flushed and his eyes were bright, darting. The pupils were pinpoints and she thought he looked a little crazy.

'I don't do drugs,' she said and tried to push past.

He grabbed her arm and held her back. He smiled. 'Then maybe you want to do something else.'

'I don't think so.' She tried to get free.

'Oh no? Is that a fact?' He had both hands on her now, gripping her forearms.

'Let go.'

He pulled her to him and tried to kiss her but she turned her head away. His lips were hot and slippery on her neck.

'Let me go!'

'Think you're too good for me, is that it?' he murmured into her ear, nibbling at the lobe. His teeth gnawed at her painfully. 'You came here for some fun so you're going to have some. Both of us. A little fun.'

'You bastard!' she said. 'Get away from me.'

She tried to struggle out of his grip but the more she did so, the more his strength seemed to increase. She felt herself being bent backwards towards the floor. His mouth was still on her neck and he was muttering under his hot breath.

'You like to pretend, don't you. But you want me to fuck you. That's what you want, isn't it? You want me to fuck you.'

He was too powerful. She was on the floor with his weight on her. He shoved a hand down the front of her dress, clasping her breast, squeezing the nipple painfully. Then she gasped as she felt a hand between her legs.

He pushed his fingers up into her. The shock of it jolted her body but it stung her into action.

She lifted her head and bit him hard on the side of the neck.

He bellowed with pain, then sat back and felt where she had sunk her teeth in.

He saw blood on his fingers.

'You fucking bitch,' he said and slapped her hard across the face.

320

Then, holding her down with one hand, he unzipped himself with the other and took his penis out.

She could see it. Hard and threatening, red, as if with rage.

She tried to push herself back, away from him, but there was nowhere to go.

'What the fuck are you doing?'

Almost before she realised who it was, Paul was reaching forward, pulling Chris off her, dragging him away by the shirt collar. Chris coughed and choked as it tightened at his neck.

Meg scrambled to her feet. The two men stood there, Chris with his trousers open and his penis out.

'Jesus Christ. You sick bastard,' Paul said.

'It's a game, that's all. She's a cock-teaser. Let me go.'

He lunged towards her again.

Paul swung him round and punched him in the pit of the stomach. Chris grunted as the breath went out of him. Then he stumbled backwards off balance and as he fell to the floor he hit his head a glancing blow on the side of the bath.

He groaned for a moment and then began to pick himself up.

Paul grabbed Meg's handbag and threw it to her. 'Come on. We're getting out of here.' He looked at Chris. 'Fucking animal.'

As they ran down the stairs, they met Ross and the woman coming up.

'What's going on?' Ross said.

'It's that asshole. He needs to be locked up. He tried to rape her, for chrissake.'

Ross held his hands up as if to block their way. 'Now, hold on a minute. Let's try to sort this out. I'm sure we can—'

Chris appeared behind them at the top of the stairs. He had zipped himself up but he was still dishevelled and there was fear in his eyes now.

Paul pushed past Ross. 'Fuck him. And fuck you, too, if you think I'm going to stick around while that prick tries to make excuses.'

He grabbed Meg's hand and pulled her after him. They stumbled down the stairs and out through the front door.

The MGB was his. He helped her into the passenger seat, then got in himself. The engine sprang to life and they sped off down the drive. At the gates he pressed a buzzer that opened them.

When they reached the main road, he turned left, not right towards the city. He drove fast but erratically, wavering towards the verge or else to the centre of the road. A couple of times Meg felt sure they were going to crash.

'Where . . . where are we going?' she said, clutching herself.

She was shivering with cold and shock and her teeth were chattering.

'I'm taking you to my place. There's a spare bed.'

She did not argue. She could not think clearly. The day, the night – it was all madness. The world sped past, black and bewildering.

He careered along wet roads that were empty at this hour but within a few minutes they were no longer alone.

Headlights appeared in his rear-view mirror, flashing at him, dazzling . . .

Forty-three

Her hair had been dark four years ago and long, not the short ash blonde creation it was now, but the earrings were the same little silver things she had worn the day Meg went to Vectra Pharmaceuticals to see her.

She held a folded hospital blanket in her hand.

'Just like before,' Alice Harte whispered. 'I'm the one who has to finish it.'

She placed the blanket over Meg's face and began to press down. The movement stabbed into the pain, enraging it, and Meg almost fainted.

But she was not going to die easily. Not now that she knew.

Her arms were imprisoned below the bedcovers and she could not move them. Even though it hurt cruelly, she twisted from side to side, fighting to break free of Alice's grip.

She fought for breath. The hand over her mouth was strong. The blanket was across her eyes, blinding her. There was no air in her lungs and as she tried to inhale, the effort filled her nostrils with fibres and sucked the blanket into her mouth.

Then suddenly men were shouting and at the same moment she felt the pressure ease. She got a hand free and pulled the blanket away, gulping air desperately.

There were figures behind Alice Harte, hospital security guards, pulling her back, away from the bed. A police patrolman trained his gun on her. Someone asked Meg if she was all right but she was too exhausted and in too much pain to say. She coughed, trying to rid her throat of flecks of wool.

She lay there gasping, wanting to tell them who the woman was, to tell them everything she had remembered, but there was no one who would understand.

In the visitors' car park across the street from the hospital, Matt Ross sat at the wheel of his rented Dodge, looking out at the descending evening gloom, waiting for Alice to come back.

Ambulances were arriving all the time and so were the police. A patrol car had shrieked up to the door a few minutes ago.

Now another car, unmarked, came roaring past him with its siren whooping.

He scratched his chin, a nervous habit left over from the days when he had the beard. She should have been out of there by now. It had been a crazy idea. A last, desperate throw of the dice. But they had been given no choice.

He got out of the car and walked in the shadows to where he could observe the ER entrance. The police cars sat there with their roof lights flashing in silence.

Then he saw her. And in that moment he knew for certain it was finished.

She was walking out of the hospital between two men. One of them was in a heavy overcoat, the other wore a thick flying jacket. Her hands were cuffed in front of her but just the same they held her securely by the arms.

He did not know if she had accomplished what she had set out to do, whether she had killed Meg Winter before they caught her.

It did not matter. It was over.

In reality, it was over the moment he dropped his mobile phone in the cemetery where the police would undoubtedly have found it. No, that wasn't true. It was over long before that. It was over that night in Belfast four years ago, for God's sake. They had been fools, deceiving themselves into thinking that everything would be all right, that no one would know. But they had been living on borrowed time.

The last he saw of Alice Harte was the frozen set of her face as they put her into the caged back seat of the patrol car and drove away with noisy haste.

He listened to the sound fading as he stood in the bitter cold of the New England night and the knowledge of his own certain doom.

He looked at his watch.

They were expecting him in Boston. He would be there in under two hours. He walked back to where he had left the car.

It was time to put a stop to all this.

One hundred miles south, the busy night-time streets around Harvard Square were gritty and grimy where the snow and the ice had started to thaw. People wore heavy shoes and comfortable boots and they stamped their feet before they went into the bustling bars and restaurants.

But Senator Aiden Ross's mind was not on any of this as his car made its way towards the Harvard Faculty Club. Instead, his eyes were on the pages of script he held in one hand while with the other his pen took out a word here, added another there, or scribbled something in the margins.

In a car in front were two secret service agents who had been assigned to the task of protecting him once his candidacy had become so public and so prominent. A third agent drove this car, a discreet black limo, in the back of which Ross sat with Phyllis Halpin, Stan Rybeck and Rybeck's laptop.

The first of the Primaries, New Hampshire, was only weeks away.

Tomorrow he would make what he hoped would be a landmark speech. It would be delivered at the JFK Library out at Columbia Point, a place with obvious echoes and chosen because of it, and in the speech he would highlight his own Irish connections.

Rybeck was on the second draft and it was that which Ross was studying, talking to its author about the things he liked and the things he didn't, that perhaps needed another spin. His instructions had been clear. 'It's got to embrace the great strengths which Kennedy possessed but it's got to say that I'm different: different from Kennedy, different from the current President, better than both of them, and it's got to underline the campaign theme of decency and American values.'

There was more to it, of course. There were significant hints and pointers about the economy, about taxation, about government investment in the infrastructure of the nation. They had brainstormed for hours: him and Halpin and Rybeck and the growing team of advisers he had built around him. Tomorrow he would be nailing his colours to the mast, outlining the framework of policies that, once elected, he would have to deliver.

He handed Rybeck the document and put his pen back in his pocket. 'It's great, Stan. It'll be even better when you and Phyllis go back to the hotel and work on it some more.'

'Yeah, right, thanks,' Rybeck muttered morosely and opened the laptop.

Ross sat back, smiling. He had no real worries about the speech or how it was going to be received. He was going to be the next President.

And his dinner meeting tonight would seal it.

He looked at Halpin. She was staring out the window with her chin in her hands.

'Cheer up, Phyllis.'

'What does he want?' she said.

'Who?' he asked, although he knew.

'Malone. What does he want?'

325

'He wants to endorse me as his favoured candidate. And you know what that means – the weight of his newspapers and his TV companies – we've discussed it. You know that.'

'But what does he want in return? Has Matt managed to find that out?'

His brother had come to him several weeks ago to say that Sir Brian Malone wanted to have a meeting. This was it tonight: a quiet dinner in a private room in the Faculty Club. Matt would join them later. Malone had requested that he do so although Aiden was not entirely sure why and Matt had not been able to enlighten him.

'And what the hell is Matt up to anyhow? Where is he?' Phyllis said.

'Up in Portland, in answer to your second question. And in answer to your first – I try not to ask.'

She gave him a look. She had become increasingly uneasy about Matt's secretive activities and the free hand which his brother gave him.

'Nixon didn't ask either,' she said.

'Come on, Phyllis, Matt's not like that. There are no burglaries here. I trust him and he knows what he's doing – nothing illegal, just . . .' he made a see-saw gesture with his hands, '. . . delicate. Anyway, look at the polls. Look what they're writing about our opposition and what they're writing about me. We can thank Matt for that.'

'In part,' she conceded. 'But mostly it's because people believe in you. You're the right man for this country. We don't need this other horseshit, Aiden. You've got everything it takes to do the job. You'll provide real, firm, honest leadership at a time when the nation is crying out for it.'

Ross looked at Rybeck whose face was lit by a ghostly glow from the computer screen. 'Are you getting all this, Stan?' he smiled. 'It's terrific stuff.'

Rybeck grunted and kept typing.

'Be careful of Malone,' Halpin said. 'He's after something.'

'Relax,' Ross said. 'I can handle him.'

The two cars pulled up outside the Faculty Club, an elegant two-storey brick building with a row of dormer windows along its roof. Ross got out with the two agents from the first car. 'You take this car back to the hotel,' he said to Phyllis and Rybeck. 'When we're all through, I can come back with the boys here.' He gave Halpin a grin. 'And don't worry.'

The car drove off, back to Boston and the Copley Plaza Hotel, and the three men strode up the little pathway to the front door where coach lamps shone warmly in the cold night air.

Inside, the lobby was arranged as a big open sitting room with rugs on a polished wooden floor that creaked under their feet. The room was lit dimly by table lamps, two of which stood on a grand piano at one of the rear windows. There was a studded green leather settee and occasional chairs of varying antiquity. American landscapes and portraits of long-gone alumni adorned the green papered walls.

The duty manager was waiting. 'Senator Ross. Delighted to have you here. Everything's ready upstairs.' He indicated the curving staircase that led up to the next floor. 'Your *friend*,' he emphasised the word so that Ross would see how discreet he was, 'hasn't arrived yet, but would you like to come up and wait for him?'

While he spoke, the agents took a quick look round. There were rooms on either side of the hall. In one, the main dining room, a handful of people enjoyed a leisurely meal and did not notice their presence. In the reading room, an elderly man sat at the fire with the Wall Street Journal.

The duty manager led them up the stairs and along to a private dining room. A table had been set for two and there were soft chairs around a fireplace. Drinks had been arranged on a trolley and a waiter stood ready to serve. He smiled as they came in.

'This will be fine, gentlemen,' Ross said, turning to the two agents. 'I think you can leave me to it.'

'We'll wait in the hall,' one said.

'Would you care for something to eat?' the manager wondered.

'Thanks. We've eaten,' the agent said.

'But some coffee would be good,' his partner suggested.

The three of them left. The waiter turned to Ross. 'Drink, sir?'

'Yes, why not. I think I'd like a gin and tonic.'

He had barely tasted it when the door opened.

Sir Brian Malone walked in and the coldness of the night seemed to cling to him. He wore a camel hair coat which he took off and handed to the waiter without a word, then he shook Ross's hand.

'Glad you could come,' he said.

'I was intrigued by the invitation.'

'Whisky, please,' Malone said to the waiter before being asked.

The two men stood for a few seconds, weighing each other up. Then Malone smiled and said: 'Why don't we do this sitting down?'

They sat in the soft chairs with their drinks and made amiable small talk about the weather, the Superbowl and their respective

327

journeys to Boston. Then Malone told the waiter: 'I think you could leave us now and tell them we're ready to eat.'

When the door closed, Ross said. 'OK, why don't you cut to the chase and tell me why we're both here?'

'All right,' Malone smiled. 'You've probably guessed anyway. It's quite straightforward. We'd like to back you for the Presidency.'

It was what Ross had expected him to say but he hid his delight. Instead, he nodded sagely, as if evaluating the offer, and thought for a second about Phyllis Halpin's gloomy concerns.

He said, 'That's an exciting prospect and one which I'd be foolish not to welcome but I'd like to hear more from you on what your thinking is.'

Malone gestured as if it were obvious. 'It's because you're the only game in town. Anyone with any sense knows that. Oh, I know some people are still hitching their horse to Todd Vernon's ancient wagon but that's a big mistake.'

'So what's the deal? There has to be a deal.'

Malone smiled. 'What I have in mind is more a kind of partnership, one where there's a lot of mutual benefit.'

Before Ross could respond, the door opened and two waitresses came in pushing a trolley.

'Wonderful,' Malone said. 'Let's talk over dinner.'

They sat down to mushroom risotto followed by lamb and then a freshly baked pecan pie. As they ate, oiling their palates with a hefty Shiraz, Malone told him why he was a prospect worthy of support. He went over his career, his achievements, the unique qualities he could bring to the job, and at the end Ross felt impossibly puffed up with the food and the flattery.

The staff took the plates away and left them on their own again.

'So what do you think?' Malone said.

'Without wishing to sound ungracious, I'm waiting for the strings. You said something about a partnership. What does that mean?'

'Not ungracious at all. But "strings"?' He weighed the word '. . . suggestions, perhaps. Nothing you should find impossible or unpalatable.'

'Try me.'

'All right, then, I will. You've obviously been thinking about what happens after this is all over, when you're elected – what sort of a team you'll have around you – in the Cabinet and in the Administration in general.'

'Of course.'

'There are some names I'd like you to consider.'

'There are what?'

Ross glared but Malone didn't seem to notice. He took a small sheet of paper from his pocket. 'It's not a very long list. You'll see that they're capable people who would perform very useful functions, particularly in the Treasury and the Department of Commerce and in your foreign policy team.'

Ross stared in shock and disbelief that the man would attempt anything as blatant as this. He had expected something more subtle. But this – this was outrageous.

In spite of himself he looked at the names.

He knew them all. Some were Senators like he was, another was a former state governor, two were with distinguished law firms. They were people he could appoint to influential, middle-ranking positions without it raising an eyebrow.

But the thought was sickening.

'God, you've got a nerve,' he said. 'So you own these people?'

Malone made a face. 'We have connections, yes.'

'And if I appointed them, you'd own me, too. They'd be your own little network, right at the heart of the administration. You'd know everything – foreign policy, economic decisions here at home. Jesus Christ, I'd be virtually handing executive power over to you. You'd be able to manipulate the markets, world investment, even influence the decisions we took.' He laughed. 'Damn it, Malone, do you take me for an idiot? Did you seriously think I'd go along with something like this? You're fucking crazy.'

He threw his napkin down and stood up.

Malone sat, unruffled. 'Well, before you storm out of here with your integrity intact, I'd like to tell you a story.'

'I don't want to hear it. I've had enough of this.' He headed for the door.

'Oh, I think you do. It's about my son. And your brother. And a dead man called Paul Everett.'

Ross turned and saw that Malone had taken a small tape recorder out of his pocket. 'Better still, we'll let my son tell the story himself.'

He placed the recorder on the table and switched it on.

Forty-four

Flynn and Gleason looked at the woman called Alice Harte. 'You're allowed a phone call,' Flynn said. 'You might want to contact a lawyer.'

She sobbed and dried her eyes. She had been crying ever since they brought her back to headquarters. 'Not yet,' she said. 'I just want to talk to someone about this. All of it.'

'Who was the man in the cemetery?' Gleason asked.

'He forced me to go to the hospital. He threatened me that if—'

There was a knock on the door. Another detective peeped in. 'Roy, can I have a word?'

'Jesus, can't it wait?'

'No.'

Flynn stepped outside. 'What is it?'

'You're not going to believe this. That phone we found in the cemetery – we traced it. Its bills are paid out of an account run by Senator Aiden Ross's election campaign.'

Flynn stared at him. 'I think maybe it's about time I talked to the Chief.'

They moved Meg to a private room where a uniformed officer sat outside.

Cochrane wanted to see her. Flynn agreed so a car took him over to the hospital.

She listened as he told her everything he had told the police. She watched his lips as he spoke. She felt separated from him, wondering what kind of mind lay in the depths behind his eyes, thinking how much she did not know him and never would.

She felt weary and beaten and incredibly sad.

She had regained her memory but she was depressed and burdened by it, not elated.

She knew why the man in the cemetery was familiar. He had had a beard the first time, that night she was taken to his house.

Alice Harte, too, had changed so much in appearance. Meg had gone to the woman's office and not realised a thing.

330

She thought of the man called Chris, who had tried to rape her. Where was he in all of this?

Paul Everett had protected her and had died because of it.

They had tried to kill her, those people she had met on that awful, sordid, murderous mistake of a night that she wished she could not remember at all.

A nurse gave her something to make her sleep.

Cochrane was still by her bedside when she woke an hour later. With him was a man who introduced himself as Detective Roy Flynn.

'My memory,' she struggled to say through stiff and painful lips. 'I know what happened that night. The man in the cemetery. He was there. He had a beard before. He was the US Consul in Belfast.'

'Ross. Matt Ross,' Flynn said. 'He's the brother of Senator Aiden Ross, the Presidential candidate. Damn, it's warm in here.' He took off the overcoat and laid it over the back of a chair.

She nodded. 'Ross. That's right. Yes. I remember.'

It seemed strange to be saying that.

'This woman Alice Harte,' Flynn said, 'she's been giving us her version of events, starting with what happened to you four years ago. She says she met you in some bar when you were drunk and she took you back to Ross's house for a party. She and Ross were having a thing at the time. She'd met him through this guy Everett who was actually her boss at the pharmaceuticals company. She says they were friends as well as colleagues. Also there was another friend, a guy called Chris Malone. They liked to do coke every now and then.'

He loosened his tie. 'That night the three men had been at a dinner where a speech was being given by Ross's brother, the Senator. The Senator told Ross he was going to run for President and offered him a job.'

He took a pad out of his pocket and checked the notes he had written a short time before.

'She says the party was just a spur-of-the-moment thing. Matt Ross called her and happened to mention that Malone was looking for female company. She was with you at the time and thought you might fit the bill. Everett was gay, apparently. He was just their friendly neighbourhood occasional cocaine provider. Anyhow, when you got there you wouldn't play ball with this Malone so he tried to rape you. At which point Everett smacks him and takes you away in his car. How does that tally so far?'

She nodded. 'It's what I remember. I found them doing cocaine

331

in the dining room when I was looking for a phone.' She frowned. 'Then this other man came upstairs after me when I went to the bathroom. All I remember was that he was called Chris. I didn't know his name was Malone. But that name . . . a company called Malone Group bought my father's building firm.'

'I'm coming to that,' Flynn said. 'According to Alice, Malone and Matt Ross followed you and Everett, leaving her at the house. She's very careful to emphasise that, that she had nothing to do with what happened later, so I probably don't believe her. She says they went after you to talk to you, to try to get the whole thing hushed up. They figured that if any of it got out it would ruin them. It would have put paid to the Senator's election campaign before it got off the ground – a brother mixed up in drugs, using the safety of the US Consul's house to do it, an attempted rape. Quite a scandal. But it got worse when the car crashed. She says Everett survived but there was a struggle and Ross bashed his head in with a flashlight, or so they told her afterwards. In the end, you were in a coma, Everett was dead, and nobody was going to be talking about anything. Or so they hoped. Anyway for the time being, things didn't turn out so bad. Ross went to work for his brother, Alice got Everett's job and life went on. Except for Chris Malone who cracked up not long after you regained consciousness.'

'He killed himself,' Cochrane said suddenly, as it came to him.

'He killed himself,' Flynn agreed.

'I remember that now,' Cochrane said. 'It was big news.'

Flynn looked at Meg. 'He went to pieces after you came out of the coma, according to Alice. Guilt, the fear of being discovered – it all got to him so he strung himself up in his backyard.'

Meg stared at them. She felt strange. 'So now . . . now two people are dead because of me. That's what this means.'

'Hold on a minute,' Cochrane said. 'Let's get this into some kind of perspective. You almost died in that crash and four years later they're still trying to kill you. Don't forget that. You can't hold yourself responsible. You're the victim here.'

Flynn said, 'The way Alice explains it, remorse and guilt were the real reason Chris Malone bought your father's company and paid a price above the odds. You were in an expensive private hospital. Making sure your father had plenty of money and could afford it was his way of compensating, of making amends.'

'Thoughtful of him,' Cochrane said in a voice that was sour.

Meg did not know what to feel any more. Anger, guilt, regret, they were like tides, each drawing her out in its current then washing her ashore again.

Flynn told her, 'It seems that before he hung himself he made a tape but Alice says he lied in it and implicated her, saying she did the actual killing, which, of course, she totally denies.'

'Where's the tape now?' Meg said.

'He left it for his father, Sir Brian Malone. I'm sure you're well aware who he is. Her friend Ross think's he's planning to use it to gain some sort of influence over the Senator.' He paused and looked at Meg. 'As for you, well, you scared the hell out of them. As long as you couldn't remember, everything was fine but if you regained your memory, then the game was up. Alice says that when you came to see her looking for the Everetts' address, she realised it was only a matter of time. What Ross did was take out a short lease on an apartment here on the Eastern Prom so that you'd have somewhere to write to. He paid for it out of some kind of phony bank account. Alice herself picked up the letters on visits to her company headquarters in New Hampshire and Ross wrote the replies.'

'They must have been mad,' Cochrane said.

'If you mean desperate and scared shitless, then I figure they were,' Flynn said.

Meg tried to sit up but it hurt. Cochrane helped her with the pillows. 'But I spoke to someone,' she said. 'And there was an answering machine.'

'He was able to pick up the messages via his mobile,' the detective explained. 'That's what he used when he called you, I guess. If Alice is to be believed, it was Ross who concocted this whole scheme, at Sir Brian Malone's insistence, once you started asking about Everett's family. Ross went to Everett's funeral four years ago and he remembered that the grave was in a very secluded part of the cemetery, well off the beaten track. She says he came up with the idea of killing you there. The plan was to slit your wrists, which would make it look like you'd committed suicide. You'd have either bled or frozen to death before anyone found you. The general conclusion would be that there was some sort of connection between you and Everett which you'd either not admitted or had just discovered and that you killed yourself out of grief or despair because your mind was unhinged. But not for the first time, things didn't go right for them. Ross was waiting at the hotel to pick you up, pretending to be Everett's brother, gambling that you wouldn't recognise him, when he saw you coming out. He followed you to the cemetery and when you saw Everett's grave he knew he had to kill you there and then.'

'But there were letters,' Cochrane said. 'A plane ticket. How would they explain that?'

'You brought the letters with you, didn't you?' Flynn asked. Meg nodded.

'You write these people, you go see them, you're going to bring their letters, wouldn't you say? You're not going to leave them at home. You'll keep them with you as a kind of proof, like a passport. Even if you didn't, well then, sure, OK, it wouldn't be as neat and tidy, but by the time they were discovered, in your home or wherever, you'd be dead and the secrets of four years ago would all be buried again.'

'But I saw one of the letters,' Cochrane said.

'I showed them to my parents, too,' Meg added.

'But where are they now? Taken from your bag by Ross. And if the letters can't be found, who's to say you didn't just write them yourself as part of some elaborate suicide plot conjured up by your poor sick mind?'

He smiled softly at her to make sure she knew he did not mean it. 'Like the ticket,' he said.

'What about the ticket?' Meg asked him.

'Alice bought it at the Aer Lingus office in Belfast. Paid cash but they issued a receipt to her in the name of Meg Winter, which is what she was calling herself that day.' He sat back.

Cochrane wondered, 'If someone as powerful as Sir Brian Malone is involved, why didn't he just hire a hit man? You hear of people being able to do this kind of thing.'

'It had to be Ross,' Flynn said. 'He had to be personally involved. It would ensure that the future President was in Malone's pocket, just in case there was any doubt. That much I can figure out for myself.'

'But Ross could have refused.'

'With a tape likely to go into circulation implicating him in the first murder? No, I don't think so.'

His mobile phone rang and he answered it.

'How do you spell that?' He wrote something on his notepad, then he said: 'Thanks, that was quick work. I'm much obliged.'

He rang off. 'That was the medical examiner's office. We found some stuff in a bottle in Alice Harte's purse. There was a syringe with it, too. Turns out it's a kind of . . .' he looked at what he had written, '. . . benzodiazepine anxiolytic, if I've got that right, a sedative, a tranquilliser, which, no doubt, Alice hadn't any trouble getting her hands on. It's stuff that's used for treating anxiety and insomnia but she had enough in the bottle to cure insomnia forever. No doubt that was how they were going to subdue you so that they could finish the job without your putting up much of a fight.' He gave a little smile and shook his head. 'No, I don't think our friend Alice is quite the innocent party in all this that she'd like us to think.'

'Ross,' Meg said. 'Where is he now?'

Forty-five

The Chief called the Mayor because he was not going to go it alone on this one and the Mayor called the Governor because he knew the Governor was a friend of Aiden Ross.

As a result, they lost valuable time. They all spun around in a panic for a while before the Chief said he had better get in touch with the FBI. The woman Harte had said where Matt Ross was headed. It meant you had a fleeing suspect crossing through a couple of states, not to mention the possibility of a foreign national multi-millionaire tycoon involved in some kind of conspiracy involving a Senator running for President.

Christ, they had better get this one right.

By then, Matt Ross was in Massachusetts, watching for the off-ramp signs on the interstate that would direct him to Cambridge and Boston, his mind roaming over everything that had happened and the things that might have been.

That night four years ago, when Aiden had asked him to come on board, he had felt his future opening up before him in a way that he would not have dreamed possible.

He had begun to feel trapped in a backwater in Belfast. Oh, it had been interesting enough for a time; he had kept the State Department well briefed on the Ulster situation and he had even acted as a go-between on a couple of occasions so that the British Government and the IRA could establish contact with each other. But he had begun to wonder where the next posting would be and none of the prospects attracted him.

He had friends in Belfast, of course. There was Paul, good-humoured and always amusing, and there was the cocaine he provided every now and then.

He had indulged on and off since his Harvard days. They did it in complete privacy and safety. The house was out of bounds to the local police, even if they had suspected anything, which was unlikely, and they did it only when none of the other consul staff were likely to be around. It was one of the advantages of living alone.

That night Aiden had set off for Dublin straight after dinner, driven by a couple of consulate people, and so the coast had been clear.

They were all to blame. Himself included.

He thought of Chris Malone, a bit of an asshole at times, especially when he had too much to drink or he was doing too much coke, but he had never seen him like he was that night. The damn fool.

And there was Alice. Their affair had been uncomplicated, governed by mutual sexual gratification rather than any real affection.

And then in the woods he had seen what she was capable of doing.

Chris had fucked them that night. And when he had killed himself he had fucked them again, leaving that goddamned tape which had let his father into the picture.

He was entering Cambridge.

It had been stupid to let Alice bring the other woman in the first place.

And then the fucking car had crashed.

In his mind he saw it again, as he had seen it every day for the past four years – the girl mangled against the dashboard, Paul and Chris struggling and then Alice with the flashlight, battering the life out of him.

He shuddered. The truth was, he could have stopped her but he had not done so. Instead he had stood aside and let her do it.

And now – had she killed again?

They had had to get rid of Meg Winter. There was no choice – Alice had made that point more than once – and then along came Malone breathing down their necks, insisting they get it done. The tape had let him get his hooks into Aiden.

But not for long.

He reached Harvard Square. It was raining. Alone in the car, he shook his head. 'No,' he said. 'Time to call a halt.'

When he got to the Faculty Club, he saw the dark familiar shape of the Secret Service car. He parked beside it, took something from the glove compartment, then got out.

The two agents were in the entrance hall. They looked up when he entered, then smiled at him. They had coffee and magazines. They pointed up the stairs and told him which room.

'See if you can find out how long they're going to be, Mr Ross,' one of them asked.

Ross smiled. A little sadly, the agent would remember later.

'Not long,' he said, then walked up the stairs.

Outside the room, he paused for a second, then opened the door.

The two men were sitting at the table, the tape recorder between them, silent now, and he could see from his brother's ashen face that its message had been delivered with cruel clarity.

Malone had his back to the door but he turned with a smug smile. 'Mission accomplished?'

Ross did not answer. He put his hand in his pocket and took out two letters which had been addressed to Dr Meg Winter of 30, Truesdale Street, Belfast, Northern Ireland. He threw them on the table.

Malone lifted them and nodded with satisfaction. 'And the rest of the matter?'

Ross was suddenly very tired. 'There's no point,' he sighed.

He put his right hand into his coat pocket, took out a small Walther TPH, and as Sir Brian Malone sat waiting for an answer that would never come, Ross shot him twice in the head.

Malone's body tumbled out of the chair to the floor and his blood splashed on the tablecloth and the walls.

Aiden Ross pushed himself to his feet and began to back away in horror.

His brother turned, pointing the gun at him for a second. 'I'm sorry, Aiden. Sorry for everything.'

Feet were thundering up the stairs. As the two Secret Service men came through the door, shouting at him to drop the weapon, he jammed its barrel hard into the roof of his mouth and pulled the trigger.

Forty-six

She let her father in and closed the door again hurriedly before the photographers got a shot.

There were only two of them this morning. Interest was waning at last.

Sam Winter looked closely at her face. Six weeks after her return from America, the bruising was now just the faintest of shadows but every time they met she saw him examine her.

'I can't stay long,' he said. 'I'm on my way to a meeting. The break-up of Malone Group. I just wanted to show you this.'

He held out a cheque. It was for ten thousand pounds and made out to Peter Quinn of the Harbour Pottery.

'It's to pay off what your friend Cochrane owes. Maybe it'll make up a bit for any lost revenue as a result of his erratic opening hours. I've spoken to Quinn about it and he's happy enough. He says he wants to let the matter rest but I thought he could do with the money. None of this was his fault, was it?'

'No,' Meg said, 'That's good of you, Dad.'

'Maybe that's the last we'll hear of Cochrane, too,' he said but it was more of a question than a statement and she did not know the answer.

Since the events in Portland and the killings at Harvard, she and Dan had been carried along on a tidal wave of worldwide publicity that had allowed her to avoid dealing with her inner feelings.

It was time she did.

He had done things that she found hard to accept. Following her, taking those photographs, weaseling his way into her life. Yet in the end he had come after her in order to save it.

'Maybe,' she said. 'I don't know.'

'By the way. I've written him a letter.'

'A letter to Dan?'

'Yes. That business of his mother's farm. I want him to know that that was nothing to do with me. I want him to be clear about that. It was Christopher Malone who had connections at the bank, not me. When he told me the land was available at a knock-down price I was happy to buy. I had no idea of the story that lay behind it. Cochrane victimised us both for nothing.'

They sat in uncomfortable silence for a moment. Then he said, 'Your mother—'

'I'm going to see her this afternoon.'

'Good. She's lost weight. It's the stress, I know, but she won't see a doctor and she won't take any advice, not even from her beloved Pastor Drew. She might listen to you.'

'I don't see why. She never has before.'

'Please, Meg, don't start.'

'Don't worry, Dad. I'll do my best.'

She showed him out a few minutes later. The photographers would have preferred a picture of her but they snapped him anyway. She saw him scowl and mutter something at them as he got into the Range Rover and drove off.

She turned back to the room.

There were cards everywhere, some of them saying *get well soon*. Flowers, too. Elizabeth had been one of the first to send a card although she had also come back from London to see her in person, armed with a huge bouquet. She looked at the other greetings. Among them was one from Liam Maginnis at the Musgrave Park, one from the nursing staff and one from Teresa Caffrey at Knockvale House.

She had never been back there. That was shameful. She would have to visit them soon, to see the place where they had cared for her for so long, to thank them for everything they had done.

There was even a card from Florence Gilmour. She had called with Sergeant Nixon because they still had an unfinished murder case to sort out. Meg had made a formal statement about what she remembered from that night.

She picked up another card. There was a drawing of a spray of flowers on the front and the message: *Hope everything goes well for you now.*

She looked inside. It was signed – *Noel*. She put it down again.

Every day when she woke up she found it hard to believe everything that had happened, how it all led back to her.

Senator Aiden Ross had withdrawn his candidacy as President of the United States. He could not have done otherwise. The race for the White House was now wide open again and President Vernon was looking more confident every day. And that – all of that – was because of her.

She checked herself and thought of what Dan had said in the hospital. He was right.

It's not because of you – it's because of them. They killed Paul Everett – you didn't. And if Dan hadn't come in here and found

340

that letter, they'd have killed you too.

The phone started but she let it ring unanswered.

She had the machine on permanently because the newspapers had got her number somehow. They were calling her from all over the world. She had thought of escaping, disappearing somewhere for a few weeks, but in the end she had felt it was best to tough it out here, in her own familiar surroundings.

'Hi, Meg,' a voice said, 'it's Roy Flynn calling you from Portland. I just thought I'd bring you up to date but maybe you're not home right now.'

She grabbed the phone. 'Roy?'

'Oh, hi. Is that the real you or another bit of the message?'

'It's the real me.' She smiled down the phone at him. 'Good to hear from you. What's the latest?'

'The latest,' he said with a sigh, 'is that it looks like they're going to charge Alice Harte with attempted murder.'

'And about time too.'

'Although I have to tell you that if she pleads guilty to a lesser charge, the DA might be happy to go along with that.'

'A lesser charge? Like what?'

'Like assault, maybe.'

'But she tried to kill me.'

'I know,' he said and she heard the apology in his voice, 'but they're practical people. They won't want the hassle and the expense of a long trial, bringing you and Dan Cochrane back here again. I figure that if she cops a plea, her lawyer'll make a deal.'

'And what will that add up to?'

'With good behaviour she'll do a couple of years, maybe as little as eighteen months.'

'Eighteen months? But what about Paul Everett? What about her being extradited to face murder charges here?'

'Well, I don't know how the law works over there in Ireland but I reckon the most they can charge her with is being an accessory and withholding information. She says she wasn't there when the murder took place and even though the Malone tape says she did it, there's no way that can be used as evidence. Apart from her, you're the only person left alive who was there that night and you didn't see what happened.'

She was stunned. 'But you believe she did it?'

'Me? You bet I do. But what I believe doesn't make any difference. I think Chris Malone was telling the truth on that tape. I think Alice Harte did the actual killing. We all know she was capable of it.'

Meg suddenly remembered the blanket across her face. She

could taste it and smell it with total clarity, as if it was happening now. She felt the fear again.

What was the word Dan had used?

Engram.

'So what's likely to happen now?' she said.

'Well, after her stretch here, there'll be a trial in Belfast and another sentence maybe. If she pleads guilty, then with the fact that she'll already have done time here in the States, she'll get maybe five years, tops.'

'So, you're telling me that in five, six years from now, she could be out?'

'That's the way it looks, yes. I'm sorry, Meg.'

'It's not your fault.'

'I know you want to see justice done but I'm afraid this is the best you're going to get.'

'It doesn't seem right,' she said. 'After all this.'

She met him in the car park at Castle Ward, where they had met before. The choice was hers, somewhere safe from prying eyes and camera lenses.

He was waiting for her and as soon as she saw him she knew it could never be the same.

It was a sunny morning, cold. They sat on a bench and talked, looking out at the lough where dozens of migrant brent geese bobbed like a fleet at anchor, their soft cries echoing across the still water.

'I love you, Meg,' he told her and she saw that he did. He had never said that to her before but it was too late now.

He asked her to forgive him.

'Forgive you,' she said. 'Yes, I forgive you, if that's what you want. But I can never forget. It would always be between us, Dan. There would always be suspicion, mistrust. Eventually it would eat away at anything we had.' She looked at him. 'It's time to move on.'

She walked back towards her car alone. Just then the geese rose, responding to some secret alarm signal that only they recognised. She turned at the sound and saw them wheel and bank in the air with absolute precision, then head further inland along the shore.

He was standing at the edge of the water watching them.

For a brief time, before she had known the truth, it had been good.

All that was gone now. But at least she could remember. At least she could do that.